Praise for Roddy Doyle

"Doyle's Jimmy Rabbitte reappears, dealing with cancer, mortality, and love. . . . I was undone by the emotional clarity of the writing itself, and by the calm, but never static, way Doyle has of presenting a scene."
—*The New York Times Book Review*

"Quintessential Doyle . . . both laugh-out-loud funny and disarmingly moving . . . [It] contains some of the snappiest, wittiest, most believable, and exhilarating dialogue in fiction. . . . To make a story about middle-aged men battling cancer a largely effervescent lark without a trace of sentimentality is a notable achievement." —*The Boston Globe*

"The feat of *The Guts* is Doyle's ability to create in Jimmy a character who hangs together even while so many of his certainties have collapsed. And to get a few good jokes in as well." —*The Washington Post*

"*The Guts* has plenty of soul. . . . Despite all the poverty and adversity and illness Doyle depicts here, he's written a novel filled with so much joyful love and life and song that it might—picture this—it might even have made Samuel Beckett smile." —Alan Cheuse, npr.org

"Roddy Doyle is a great master of dialogue, which is his narrative medium—the main way he tells. And it's impossible for anyone, I would think, not to laugh out loud at the wit and shock of it. . . . If [*The Guts*] has a unifying theme, it is the awareness of death, and the fresh perspectives on life thrown by its advancing shadow."
—*The New York Review of Books*

"Doyle's collected works are a superlative study of family, aging, and the dignity of the working class—and his latest novel is a worthy addition. . . . The novel revisits an area Doyle explored previously in *The Van*: what it means to be a man at middle age." —*The Atlantic*

"A hilarious, compelling, and ultimately joyous look at a man facing possible mortality with courage and the support of a wide circle of family and friends." —*The Seattle Times*

"Fans of Doyle's first three novels will find plenty to enjoy as they reimmerse themselves not only in the lives of the Rabbittes but also in the vibrant language of Doyle's Dublin, which is impossible not to hear echoing in your head for days afterward." —*The Philadelphia Inquirer*

"Doyle hits the mark perfectly with this long-awaited sequel: it is rich, fun stuff for those familiar with the earlier novel. . . . Also a fine introduction to these characters for first time readers."

—*St. Louis Post-Dispatch*

"[A] hilarious and tender sequel to *The Commitments* . . . Doyle's witty and lively ninth novel captures much of the fun of *The Commitments*, even as the Commitments themselves struggle with a notably more sobering world around them." —*Publishers Weekly*

"It's rare to read about a man's midlife crisis . . . and burst out laughing. Yet acclaimed Irish author Doyle pulls it off. . . . There are plenty of poignant moments among the laughs, too. . . . This work is too good to miss." —*Library Journal*

"Doyle expertly evokes the generational confusion over new technologies, the sentimentality of children growing up way too fast, and the sobering fear and anxiety of living with a potentially fatal disease—all of this without being overly morbid or maudlin." —*Booklist*

"The novel is probably the most contemplative that Doyle has written—as a meditation on the importance of family, it is at times unbearably moving. . . . The characters are all so warm and funny and irritable, so brimming with rude life, that this novel about illness and death never manages to become morbid. . . . Reading *The Guts* is like catching up with old friends." —*The Sunday Times* (London)

"Remarkable, relevant, and, surprisingly, for a book that's ostensibly about cancer, joyful . . . *The Guts* is a book about a dogged search for meaning in the overwhelming face of mortality—but funnier than that sounds. And softer, too." —*The Times* (London)

"Fantastic . . . In many ways, *The Guts* is about a man facing up to whether the best of his life—and possibly all of his life—is past. . . . The book embraces the comedy of life as well as the tragedy, as is Doyle's wont." —*The Sunday Independent* (London)

PENGUIN BOOKS

THE GUTS

Roddy Doyle is an internationally bestselling writer. His first three novels—*The Commitments, The Snapper,* and 1991 Booker Prize finalist *The Van*—are available both singly and in one volume as *The Barrytown Trilogy,* published by Penguin. He is also the author of the novels *Paddy Clarke Ha Ha Ha* (1993 Booker Prize winner); *The Woman Who Walked Into Doors*; *A Star Called Henry*; *Oh, Play That Thing*; *Paula Spencer,* and *The Dead Republic*; two collections of stories, *The Deportees* and *Bullfighting*; and a nonfiction book about his parents, *Rory & Ita*. Doyle has also written for the stage and the screen: the plays *Brownbread, War, Guess Who's Coming for the Dinner, The Woman Who Walked Into Doors,* and *The Playboy of the Western World* (as cowriter); the film adaptations of *The Commitments* (as cowriter), *The Snapper,* and *The Van*; *When Brendan Met Trudy* (an original screenplay); the four-part television series *Family* for the BBC; and the television play *Hell for Leather*. Roddy Doyle has also written the children's books *The Giggler Treatment, Rover Saves Christmas, The Meanwhile Adventures, Her Mother's Face,* and *Brilliant*; the young adult novels *Wilderness* and *A Greyhound of a Girl*; and contributed to a variety of publications including *The New Yorker* and *McSweeney's,* the anthology *Speaking with the Angel* (edited by Nick Hornby), the serial novel *Yeats Is Dead!* (edited by Joseph O'Connor), and the young adult serial novel *Click*. He lives in Dublin.

Roddy Doyle

The Guts

PENGUIN BOOKS

PENGUIN BOOKS
Published by the Penguin Group
Penguin Group (USA) LLC
375 Hudson Street
New York, New York 10014

USA | Canada | UK | Ireland | Australia | New Zealand | India | South Africa | China
penguin.com
A Penguin Random House Company

First published in Great Britain by Jonathan Cape,
The Random House Group Limited, 2013
First published in the United States of America by Viking Penguin,
a member of Penguin Group (USA) LLC, 2014
Published in Penguin Books 2015

Copyright © 2013 by Roddy Doyle

THE LIBRARY OF CONGRESS HAS CATALOGED THE HARDCOVER EDITION AS FOLLOWS:
Doyle, Roddy, 1958–
The guts / Roddy Doyle.
pages cm
ISBN 978-0-670-01643-3 (hc.)
ISBN 978-0-14-312609-6 (pbk.)
1. Middle age—Fiction. 2. Cancer—Patients—Fiction. 3. Music fans—Fiction.
4. Families—Fiction. 5. Friendship—Fiction. I. Title.
PR6054.O95G88 2014
823'.914—dc23
2013036812

Printed in the United States of America
1 3 5 7 9 10 8 6 4 2

For Belinda

My thanks to Keith Cullen, Peter O'Connor, John Walsh, Dan Franklin, Deirdre Molina and John Sutton.

—D'yeh do the Facebook thing?

—Wha' d'yeh mean?

They were in the pub, in their corner. It wasn't unusual any more, having a pint with his father. In the early evening, before he went home after work. He'd phone, or his da would phone. It wasn't an organised, regular thing.

It had started the day his da got his first mobile. His first call was to Jimmy.

—How's it goin'?

—Da?

—Yeah, me.

—How are yeh?

—Not too bad. I'm after gettin' one o' the mobiles.

—Great.

—I'm usin' it now, like.

—Congratulations.

—Will we go for a pint? To celebrate.

—Grand. Good. Yeah.

Jimmy's da had still been working when he got the phone. But he'd retired a while back.

—There's fuck-all work, he'd told everyone when he'd made the announcement on Stephen's Day, when Jimmy had dragged the kids to his parents' house to collect the presents and kiss their granny.—So I might as well just stop an' call it retirement.

Jimmy's own job was safe – he thought.

—Well, said his da now in the pub.—Facebook. Yeh know it, yeah?

—I do, yeah, said Jimmy.

—What d'you make of it?

—I don't know.

1

—Yeh don't know?

—No, said Jimmy.—Not really.

—But you've kids.

—I know tha', said Jimmy.—I've four of them.

—Is it the four you have? said his da.—I thought it was three.

—No, said Jimmy.—It's been four for a good while. Ten years, like.

This was what Jimmy liked. It was why he phoned his da every couple of weeks. His da was messing, pretending he didn't know how many grandchildren he had. It was the way he'd always been. A pain in the hole at times but, today, exactly what Jimmy wanted.

—It's Darren has the three, is it? said his da.

His name was Jimmy as well.

—No, said Jimmy, the son.—Darren has two. Far as I know.

Darren was one of Jimmy's brothers.

—Ah now, yeh see but, said Jimmy Sr.—I knew there was somethin'.

He put his pint down.

—She's pregnant.

Fuck, thought Jimmy. Fuck fuck fuck it.

—Is she? he said.—That's brilliant.

—Yeah, said Jimmy Sr.—Darren phoned your mother this mornin' to tell her. She's three months gone.

—Ma is?

—Fuck off. Melanie.

Melanie was Darren's wife – although they'd never got married. His fuckin' *life* partner. They'd been trying for another baby for years. There'd been so many miscarriages, it had become a rule between Jimmy and his da: no more jokes about Melanie's miscarriages. Their other two kids —

—The two that managed to hang on in there.

They'd broken the rule once or twice.

The other two kids were twelve and ten.

—She's well on her way so, Jimmy said now.

—Yeah, said his da.—Fingers crossed.

He sniffed the top of his pint.

—I don't think I could cope with another miscarriage, he said.

He drank.

—Anyway, he said.—Facebook.

—Yeah.

—What is it? Exactly.

2

—I don't know much about it, said Jimmy.

His da had a laptop at home. He knew how to google. He'd booked flights online. He'd backed a few horses, although he preferred the walk to the bookie's. He'd bought a second-hand book online, about Dublin during the War of Independence. He'd nearly bought an apartment in Turkey but that had been a bit of an accident. He'd thought he was clicking to see inside the place – a tour – but he'd stopped when the laptop asked him for his credit card details. He knew he'd gone wrong or it was a scam. But the point was, his da knew his way around the internet. So Jimmy didn't know why he was pretending to be completely thick.

—Why d'yeh want to know? he asked.

—Ah, for fuck sake, said his da.—Every time I ask a fuckin' question.

—What's wrong with yeh?

—I ask a fuckin' question and some cunt says why d'yeh want to know.

—You're askin' the wrong cunts, said Jimmy.

—Must be.

—Wha' questions?

—Wha'?

—What questions have yeh been askin'?

—Well, said his da.—I asked a fella in Woodie's where the duck-tape was. An', granted, he didn't say why d'yeh want to know. He said, wha' d'yeh want it for. I told him I wanted to fuckin' buy it.

—He just wanted to help.

—That's not the fuckin' point. There was a time when he'd have just said, over there or I haven't a clue. He wouldn't have asked me why I wanted it. That's the problem. Somehow or other he's become an expert on duck-tape. The shops are full of experts. The country's full of fuckin' experts. Tha' haven't a fuckin' clue.

—Facebook.

—Yeah.

—It's a social network.

—What's tha'?

—How come every time I say somethin' some cunt asks me a question?

—Tou-fuckin'-shay, said Jimmy Sr.

—Listen, said Jimmy.—Your phone there. Your mobile.

—Yeah.

—Your contacts. Your friends an' their numbers. Your kids. All the numbers yeh'd want. Facebook's a bit like tha', except with pictures.

—So it's just a list o' people's numbers an' emails?

—No, said Jimmy.—There's more to it than tha'. But that's the start. The foundation of it, I suppose. Friends. You're going for a pint, d'yeh phone the lads to see if they're goin'?

—No point, said Jimmy Sr.—I know the answer.

—Just go with me on this one, Da, said Jimmy.—I'm tryin' to educate yeh.

—Go on.

—You're goin' for a pint, like. An' you want to know if your buddy, Bertie, will be there. D'yeh phone him?

—No, said Jimmy Sr.—Not anny more.

—Yeh text him, yeah?

—Yeah.

—An' he texts back.

—He never fuckin' stops.

His mobile buzzed and crawled an eighth of an inch across the table.

—There's the cunt now.

He picked up the phone and stared at it. He took his reading glasses out of his shirt pocket, put them on and stared at it again.

—Your mother, he said.—She wants milk.

He put the phone down and took off his glasses.

—She used to be able to walk to the shops herself, he said. —She was very good at it.

—He texts yeh back, said Jimmy.—Yeah, or somethin'. An' you text him. Grand.

—That's righ', said Jimmy Sr.—Tha' sounds like a day in my life.

—Well, that's social networkin', said Jimmy.—More or less. It's like a club but yeh have your own room, for the people yeh want to meet. Except there's no room an' yeh meet no one. Unless yeh want to.

—A club.

—That's the best way to see it.

—Grand.

—Why?

—Why wha'?

Jimmy watched his da look across to the bar, squint, wait, and lift his hand, one finger up.

4

—Did he see me?

—Think so.

Jimmy Sr was having another pint. He knew Jimmy wasn't.

—Why did yeh ask abou' Facebook?

—Somethin' Bertie told me, said Jimmy Sr.—Somethin' he heard.

—It's illegal if it's Bertie.

—No, said Jimmy Sr.—It's not. It's fuckin' immoral but.

—You'll have to tell me now.

—I'm goin' to tell yeh. I've every intention of tellin' yeh. Is he workin' on my pint over there?

Jimmy pretended to look across at the bar and the barman he didn't know behind it.

—He is, yeah, he told his da.

—Grand.

—Are yeh goin' blind?

—No. But – no. It's like everythin' else.

Jimmy knew what his da meant and it was a good place to give him his own news. But he couldn't do it. He wasn't ready.

—Bertie, he said.

—Fuckin' Bertie, said his da.—He told me his youngest fella, Gary I think it is. He's about the same age as your Marvin.

—Seventeen.

—Abou' tha', yeah. A year or two older. A little fucker, by all accounts. Annyway, he told Bertie and Bertie told me that he – Gary, like – gets off with older women on Facebook.

—I heard abou' that alrigh'.

—Did yeh?

—I did, yeah.

—Wha' sort of a fuckin' club is tha'?

—A good one, said Jimmy.—If it's what you're into. They're called cougars.

—What are?

—The older women tha' prey on the younger men.

—Jesus, said Jimmy Sr.—Veronica watches tha' one.

—Wha'?

—*Cougar Town*. On the telly. And that's what it's about, is it? I thought it was like *Born Free* or somethin'.

—What's *Born Free*?

—A film, said Jimmy Sr.—Before you were born. One o' those nature things. Africa, lions, a load of shite. Andy Williams sang the song. Where's tha' cunt with my pint?

He was squinting across at the bar again.

—Does he know he's supposed to be bringin' it down? Jimmy asked.

—He should.

—Stay there.

Jimmy went up to the bar, paid for the pint, waited for his change, and brought the pint back to his father.

—Good man.

He waited till Jimmy was sitting again.

—So, he said.—This *Cougar Town* thing is abou' oul' ones chasin' after young lads?

—I think so, said Jimmy.—I've never seen it.

He was lying. He loved it. Courteney Cox still gave him the horn.

—Yeh don't think Ma's up to anythin' like tha', do yeh? he asked.

—This conversation isn't goin' the way I wanted it to, said Jimmy Sr.—No, I don't. She'd tell me.

—Would she?

—No.

—You're safe enough, I'd say, said Jimmy.

—She's seventy-one, for fuck sake.

—That's not old.

—Ah, it is. The cougars, they're late 30s, early 40s.

—You've seen it.

—No, I haven't – fuck off. Just the pictures in the paper. Annyway. This Facebook thing. It's the young lads, Gary an' tha', who're chasin' the older birds.

—The older birds are chasin' them as well. That's what I meant by social networkin'. Are yeh thinkin' of givin' it a go yourself?

—No, I'm not.

He smiled.

—But —

—Because, if you are, said Jimmy.—I have to tell yeh. Most o' the women older than you are actually dead.

—Well, at least I wouldn't have to talk to them. An' just so yeh know.

He sat up, moved his pint an inch.

—What I said earlier. Abou' goin' blind an' tha'. Everythin' deterioratin' when yeh get older.

He waited, made sure Jimmy was paying proper attention.

—Go on, said Jimmy.

—I still wake up with a hard one, said his father.

—Do yeh? said Jimmy.

Don't blush, he told himself. Don't blush.

—Every mornin', said Jimmy Sr.—Includin' Sundays.

—That's great. Well done.

—Fuck off.

Jimmy Sr picked up his pint, took a swig, put it back down.

—I know, he said.—You're my son an' all. So it's a strange thing to be tellin' yeh an' it isn't even dark outside. I wouldn't have told yeh twenty years ago. I wouldn't've dreamt of it. But what're yeh now? You're wha'? Forty-seven?

—Bang on.

—Well then, I thought I'd let yeh know, said Jimmy Sr.—I noticed yeh grunted there when you were sittin' down. An' there's a lot more of your forehead on view than there used to be. Happens to us all. It's desperate. Men are hit particularly bad. So, but. It isn't all bad, is what I'm tryin' to say. Father to son, like.

—D'you know wha', Father?

—Wha'?

—That's the first time you've ever spoken to me like tha'. Father to son.

—Is tha' right?

—Yeah.

—No.

—Fuckin' yeah.

—You're not annoyed, are yeh?

—No, I'm not.

—Grand.

—But tell us, said Jimmy.—Wha' do yeh do with your hard one?

—You're missin' the point, son. That's a different conversation. An' I don't think it's one we'll ever be havin'.

—Grand, said Jimmy.

They said nothing for a bit.

—How come Bertie has such a young son? Jimmy asked.

—Ah Jaysis, said Jimmy Sr.—He rode his missis. It's no great mystery.

—Still though, said Jimmy.—He's quite old to be havin' a teenager for a son.

He watched his father shrug. One of the shoulders was slower coming back down than the other and he seemed to be in a bit of pain as the second shoulder settled.

—Bertie'd be a bit younger than me, said Jimmy Sr.

—Not that much, said Jimmy.—One of his kids, the mad one. Jason. He was a year behind me in school. He must be forty-five or six now.

—He must be, said Jimmy Sr.

—Where is he these days?

—Over there, said Jimmy Sr.

—The fat guy in the Arsenal jersey?

—That's him, said Jimmy Sr.—He's let himself go since he came off the heroin. Still lives at home.

—Hate tha'.

—Don't be talkin'. It's not natural. The state of him. Bertie says he has an Arsenal duvet cover an' all.

—They're not a bad team.

—They're overrated. Ah, it's sad. He did time, yeh know.

—Portlaoise.

—That's righ'. Gun but no bullets. Still, he had the gun. Walks into a credit union with it. So, fuck'm. He deserved what he got. But annyway.

He picked up his pint. There was about half of it left.

—Hang on, said Jimmy.

He went up to the bar to order another pint for his da. He wanted to stand, just for a bit. He was restless, angry. Not really angry – nervous.

He looked at Bertie's Jason. He didn't look like a man to be scared of, a man who'd done time for armed robbery. He was sitting beside two other guys – now they looked a bit frightening – but he wasn't really with them. They were much younger than Jason, harder, firmer, shouting quietly at each other.

—Fuckin' did.

—Fuckin' didn't, fuck off, m'n.

He waited for the pint and paid for it. He took the change.

—Thanks.

And he went back down to his da.

—There yeh go.

—Good man, said Jimmy Sr.

He put the empty glass on the table to his left, and put the new one on top of his beer mat.

—So. Young Jason.

—Yeah.

—He gets out. But the family's gone.

—Where?

—No, not gone anywhere. Just not his any more. She doesn't want annythin' to do with him. A lovely bird, by the way. You'd never guess it, looking at George fuckin' Clooney over there in his Arsenal gear. Fuckin' lovely.

—Kids?

—Two. I think. They don't want to know him either. She did a great job while he was away. I'm not bein' sarcastic. She did a great fuckin' job. Bertie'll tell yeh himself.

—Yeh fancy her.

—I do, yeah, said Jimmy Sr.—Absolutely. I walk past her house every day. I sit on her wall.

Jimmy laughed.

—She's gorgeous, said his father.—An' she has the two kids, boy an' a girl, one of them in Trinity College doin' law for fuck sake, and the other one in London, workin' in a bank that actually lends money. An' that makes her even more gorgeous.

He picked up his pint and knocked back about half it.

—So Bertie an' his missis are lumped with poor Jason.

—Jesus.

—Yeah, said Jimmy's da.—It's rough.

They looked across at Jason.

—It's not the fact tha' he's there in the house, said Jimmy's da.—That's not too bad. There's only him an' the young lad, the Facebook fella. The rest are gone, so there's plenty o' room. It's not that. It's more the fact of him. Remindin' them. He's a fuckin' disaster. A fat middle-aged teenager.

—That's harsh.

—I'm quotin' his father. An' I see what he means.

—Every family has its fuck-ups, said Jimmy.

—I know, said his da.—I know tha'. I'm not bein' judgmental. Well, I am. But I know.

Leslie was the name hanging, swaying, right in front of them. They both knew it; they both saw it. Les was Jimmy's other brother. He'd walked out of the house after a row with his mother, twenty-two years before.

—I know, said Jimmy's da.

He sighed.

—Yeh do your best, he said.—We all do. Bertie as well. But

fuck. I'm sure they love him. They probably love him. They try to. But it's his lifestyle.

They were laughing again.

—The boom bypassed him.

—It fuckin' did. An' judgin' by the head on him over there, he's missin' the recession as well. I'd say just sayin' recession would take a lot out o' poor Jason.

—What's he on? Jimmy asked.—He's on somethin'.

—Fuck knows, said Jimmy Sr.

He took a slug from his pint. He put the glass back on its mat.

—She goes into his room, Bertie's mott. An' she comes out cryin'.

—Why doesn't she just stay out?

—That's what I said, said Jimmy Sr.—An' Bertie says she can't help it. She feels guilty. She's a woman, yeh know yourself. How's your own woman?

—She's grand. How's Ma?

—Grand. Are yeh havin' another?

—No, said Jimmy.—I'm drivin'.

—Fair enough.

—I have cancer.

—Good man.

—I'm bein' serious, Da.

—I know.

Jimmy was shaking. He hadn't noticed while he was working himself up to tell his father. But he knew it now. He pressed his hands down on his thighs, made his arms stiff. He wondered if his eyes were bloodshot, because they felt like they had to be.

—Jesus, son.

—Yeah.

—Wha' kind?

—Bowel.

—Bad.

—Could be worse.

—Could it?

—So they say, said Jimmy.

—They?

—The doctors an' tha'. The specialists. The team.

—The team?

—Yep.

—What colour are their jerseys?

10

Jimmy couldn't think of an answer.

—It's terrible, said his da.

—Yep.

—When did yeh find ou'?

—A few days ago, said Jimmy.—Monday.

—God.

Jimmy relaxed his arms. The madness was gone; they seemed to be his again. His father was fidgeting, like he'd found something sharp he'd been sitting on. Then Jimmy knew what he was doing. He was trying to get nearer to Jimmy without actually moving. Without making a show. He leaned across the table and put his hand on Jimmy's arm. He kept it there.

—It's not natural, he said.

—Cancer? said Jimmy.—I think it is. It's —

—Stop bein' so fuckin' reasonable. It isn't natural for a father – a parent, like – to hear tha' kind of news from his child.

—Well, I had to tell yeh.

—Sorry, Jimmy. Sorry. I'm makin' a mess of it.

He took his hand off Jimmy's arm, and put it back.

—What I mean is, it should be the other way round. D'you know wha' I mean?

—I do, yeah.

Jimmy Sr took his hand away and sat back into his chair.

—How did Aoife take it?

—Wha'?

—Aoife. How was she when yeh told her?

—I didn't tell her, said Jimmy.

—Wha'?

—I can't.

—You have to.

—I know.

—Fuck the drivin'. Have a pint.

—No.

Jimmy wiped his eyes, although he wasn't crying.

—I'm afraid to eat or drink annythin', he said.—I kind of expect it to be agony.

—Is it?

—No. Not at all.

—How did yeh find out?

—Blood, said Jimmy.—I was bleedin'.

—God —

—Nothin' spectacular. Just, yeh know —

Jimmy watched his father wipe his eyes. He *was* crying.

—Sorry.

—You're alrigh'.

—Who else have yeh told?

—No one, said Jimmy.

—I'm the first?

—I thought I'd tell you. Get it done, the first time. Then it'd be easier. I'll be able to tell Aoife.

—I'm flattered.

—Sorry.

—You're grand, said Jimmy Sr.—I *am* flattered. Weird, wha'.

—I was goin' to tell Ma but somethin' made me swerve towards you instead.

—It'll kill her.

—You always say tha'.

—Fuck off.

—It's true, yeh do. Even tha' time when I said the Beatles weren't as good as the Stones.

—But look it, your mother loves the Beatles.

—She couldn't give a shite about the Beatles.

—You're right, said Jimmy Sr.—Truth be fuckin' told, it was the Bee Gees tha' made your mother giddy. The early stuff, yeh know.

—Could be worse.

—It fuckin' could. So.

Jimmy watched his father brush his thighs with his open hands.

—Wha' now?

—Chemo, said Jimmy.

—Fuck.

—Yep.

—What is it? Exactly?

—I'm not sure yet, said Jimmy.—I started googlin' but I stopped.

—Frightenin', said his da.

—Yeah, said Jimmy.—But borin' as well.

—Borin'?

—Yeah.

—How is it fuckin' borin'? Jesus, son, yeh don't have to pretend.

—I'm not.

—Cancer's borin'?

—No, said Jimmy.—Just readin' about it.

He realised – he knew the feeling: he was enjoying himself. A weight – one of them, a big one – had been lifted. He definitely felt lighter.

—Even if you have it? said his da.

—Especially if you have it, said Jimmy.

Literally lighter. And light headed. He was tempted. He could leave the car in the car park, have a few pints, walk home or get a taxi and risk the smashed windscreen or wing mirror.

—So anyway, said his da.—Wha' happened?

—Okay, said Jimmy.—I went to the specialist cunt an' he gave me the good news. It's early days, so they should be able to deal with it. Surgery an' —

—Surgery?

—Yeah, said Jimmy.—Did I not mention surgery?

—No, yeh didn't.

—Well, yeah, said Jimmy.—An operation. They're takin' it out.

—Your bowels?

—Most of them – it. About 80 per cent.

—For fuck sake.

—But the chemo thing, said Jimmy.—He tells me I'll be havin' chemo. An' other things I don't remember. I listened. But —

—Too much to take in.

—That's it, said Jimmy.—But anyway. He mentions chemo. An' he shakes my hand an' brings me to meet the team. An' it's all grand. They're great – no messin'. Very reassurin'. Although that's shite, because it hadn't sunk in. It's fuckin' weird – I was kind of delighted. Grateful, like. But anyway, I'm in good hands. So.

He really was enjoying himself.

—I went back to work, he said.

—That's a bit strange but, is it? said his da.—A bit of a fuckin' under-reaction or somethin'.

—I don't think so, said Jimmy.—I know what yeh mean. But no. I was numb, Da. I hadn't a clue. So I went back. I was hungry on the way back. Starvin'.

—Did yeh drive?

—I did, yeah. No one told me not to. But I was grand. I got back to work. Bought a sandwich an' a packet of Tayto –

—Maybe your last.

—Fuck off.

—D'yeh want a pack now?

—No, said Jimmy.—No, yeah. I'd love one. Thanks.

His father groaned as he stood. Jimmy watched him straightening as he walked across to the bar, hitching up his jeans with a finger in the loop where the belt went at the back. He watched him wave across at Bertie's Jason, watched him pat some guy at the bar's shoulder – Jimmy didn't know the guy. He watched his da order a pint and two bags of crisps, watched him head over to the jacks, watched the guy at the bar opening one of the Tayto bags.

He'd go soon. Home. He'd talk to Aoife – he'd tell her. It wouldn't be too bad.

It would be fuckin' terrible.

He felt fine, though. He was grand. He watched his da coming back from the jacks. He was slower – was he? Of course he was. The man was seventy-four or something. He watched him pay for his pint and the crisps. He watched him push the open bag at the guy at the bar. He heard them laugh. He saw the barman shove a fresh bag across the counter. He saw his da take it.

He lobbed one of the bags at Jimmy as he sat down and parked his new pint. The arse and the glass landed at the exact same time.

—What're yeh grinnin' at? said his da.

—Nothin'.

—Yeah, maybe. Where were we?

—Me bein' bored, I think, said Jimmy.

—That's right. Fuck sake. Go on.

—So, like, I bought a sandwich an' the Tayto —

—It's all comin' back.

Jimmy opened the bag he had now and took out a good big one.

—An' I sat at me desk, he said,—an' I googled chemotherapy. An' I clicked on the first link, the Wikipedia one, an' I read. It was somethin' like this, listen. Chemotherapy is the treatment of a disease with chemicals by killing micro-organisms or cancerous cells, an' so on. An' I just thought, I can't read this shite.

—I'm with yeh.

—It wasn't that I couldn't take it in. I didn't want to take it in. It was borin'.

—Ignorance is bliss, maybe.

—Maybe that too as well, yeah. But I'll tell yeh. There was a picture – on the Wikipedia page, like. A woman gettin' her chemo.

14

She had the scarf, yeh know – the baldness. Sittin' back in a big chair.

—Was she good lookin'?

—Park tha' for a minute. She was wearin' big mittens, on her hands, like, and these wine cooler yokes, padded tubes. On her feet. To reduce the harm to her nails.

—An' was tha' borin'?

—No, said Jimmy.—No. Tha' frightened the shite out o' me.

—Yeh don't want to damage your nails.

—Fuck off, Da. It's not – it's. If it can damage fingernails, what'll it do to the rest of me?

—Toenails are even harder.

—I know, said Jimmy.—I could cut meat with mine.

—Me too, said Jimmy Sr.—I broke the fuckin' nail scissors tryin' to cut them. How're the crisps goin' down, by the way?

—Grand, said Jimmy.—Why?

—Well, said Jimmy Sr.—Wha' yeh said earlier. You said yeh were afraid to eat annythin'.

—Oh, yeah. Yeah. No. I'm grand.

—I thought crisps might be a no, said Jimmy Sr.—They look like they'd rip the hole off yeh. Just the look o' them, yeh know.

—Here, said Jimmy.—D'you want the rest of them?

He held out the bag.

—No, you're grand, said his da.

—I need water, said Jimmy.—The salt.

He stood up and went across to the bar. He'd go home in a few minutes. The barman was looking at the golf on the telly over the door to the toilets. Jimmy waited. He counted the tellys. There were seven of them. All on, sound down. Golf, news, golf, singing, rugby league, ads and golf. The barman looked away.

—When you're ready.

—Yeah?

He looked foreign, Polish or Latvian or that part of the world. But he wasn't foreign.

—Could yeh give us a glass of water, please?

The barman sighed and turned away.

That proved it, Jimmy decided. The cunt was a Dub.

The barman came back with a pint glass of water. Jimmy took it.

—Thanks.

Nothing from the barman. The ignorant prick.

He went back to his da.

—I'll have to go in a minute, he said.

—Yeah, said Jimmy Sr.

—I'll tell Aoife – tonigh'.

—Won't be easy.

—No.

—Fuckin' hell, son.

—I know.

—D'you want me to tell your mother?

—No, said Jimmy.—No. Thanks. I'll tell her myself. Tomorrow – probably. There's the kids too – fuck.

—How'll yeh manage tha'?

—I haven't a clue, said Jimmy.—There's probably a book. Or a website. How to tell your kids you have cancer. Fun with cancer dot fuckin' com.

He smiled.

—I'm gone, he said.

He took the car key from his pocket.

—Seeyeh.

His father stood up too.

—I'll come with yeh.

—To the house?

—No, said Jimmy Sr.—The car park just. I'll see yeh to your vehicle.

—I thought you were here for the nigh'.

—No, said Jimmy Sr.—No. I think those days are gone.

—You're a new man.

—I'm an old fuckin' man, said Jimmy Sr.—I can't have a few pints annymore without havin' to get up to go to the jacks three or four times a night. So I have my pints earlier an' I call it a day, earlier, if tha' makes sense. An', fuck it, I'm happy enough.

—What about the lads?

—The lads, said Jimmy Sr.—The lads are kind of a distant memory. But that's a different story. Not for tonigh'. Come on. We'll get you home.

They walked to the exit. Jimmy let his da lead the way. His da waved at someone in a corner – the pub had more corners than New York – but Jimmy couldn't make out who it was. The place was fuller than it had been. It was still quiet enough but most of the tables were occupied. It felt foreign, in a way. He didn't know who was who, or what was going on. He didn't go to places like this any more. Not that he couldn't catch up. There wouldn't be much training needed, or upskilling, to get back in the swing. Not the drinking – the reading, the knowing. The guy beside the cigarette machine was definitely waiting for someone. The way he was standing; he half expected to get thrown out. And Jimmy half recognised him. He'd gone to school with his brother – or his father. And the woman sitting on her own with her vodka parked exactly in the centre of her table, like it might be someone else's.

Jimmy knew her.

—Imelda?

She looked at him.

—Jimmy Rabbitte! For fuck sake!

She laughed and stood and opened her arms and he marched in there between them and felt her hands slide across his back. He was late with his own hands, getting them to move. She kissed his cheek, about half an inch from his lips. Then she stepped back, nearly into the table behind her. She laughed again.

—Let's see yeh.

She smiled at him.

—You're lookin' well, Jimmy.

—So are you, he said.

—Ah well.

She *was* looking well. She might have been a bit pissed – Jimmy wasn't sure – and a few kilos heavier, but Imelda Quirk would never not look well.

His da was at the door.

—Yeh righ'? he shouted.

—Just a minute, Jimmy shouted back.

—Yeh goin' somewhere? said Imelda.

—Yeah, said Jimmy.—Yeah. *Home to my wife, to tell her I have cancer.* 'Fraid so.

—Typical Jimmy, said Imelda.—Always runnin'.

He didn't know what to say – he hadn't a clue.

—Get out your phone, she said.

—Wha'?

He could feel his da looking at him. But he looked across to the door and his da wasn't there.

—Your phone, Jimmy, said Imelda.—Not your mickey.

He laughed. He wasn't blushing, and that made him ridiculously happy. He took his mobile from his pocket.

—Ready? she said.

—You're givin' me your number.

—You're still a fuckin' genius.

He laughed again. She recited the number, quickly.

—Get tha'?

—No bother, he said.

He saved the number.

—Phone me, she said.—When you want to.

—Will do, he said.—Great seein' yeh. It must be twenty years.

—Don't fuckin' start, she said – she smiled.—I was still in primary school twenty years ago. Is that understood?

—Loud an' clear, said Jimmy.—I'm gone. I'll phone yeh.

He probably wouldn't. He had cancer, kids, a wife he loved.

—Grand, she said.

She was sitting down again. There'd be no kiss goodbye, no hug.

—Tomorrow maybe, he said as he left.

—It's up to you, Jimmy.

His da was leaning against Jimmy's car and the alarm was going. He'd heard it inside when he was talking to Imelda. Now though, it was loud – and his. He pointed the key and clicked. It stopped.

—Did yeh fuckin' jump on it?

—No, said his da.—It went off the minute I fuckin' looked at it. I was only walkin' over.

—Anyway, said Jimmy.—I'm gone.

—Grand, said his da.

—To face the music.

—It must feel like tha', does it?

—A bit, said Jimmy.—But look it. Thanks.

—You're grand, said Jimmy Sr.

He rubbed his hand across his mouth.

—It hasn't sunk in, he said.

—I know.

—I'll say nothin' at home.

—No. Thanks.

—Well —

Jimmy's da put his hand out, high. He touched Jimmy's neck.

—Fuckin' hell, son.

—I know.

—Go on.

—I'm goin'.

—Phone me, said Jimmy Sr.—Any time, righ'?

—Yeah, said Jimmy.—Thanks.

He opened his door.

—D'you want a lift?

—No. You're grand. I'll walk.

—Righ'. Good luck.

Jimmy got into the car. It was warm. There'd been heat in the sun, although it was getting dark now. He waited till his da was walking away before he shut the car door.

He filled the dishwasher. He took a white wash out to the line and hung the clothes in the dark. He kept an eye on the kitchen window while he did it, to see if Aoife was alone in there. She wasn't. He watched her, angry and gorgeous, giving out shite to Mahalia. He came back in – she was gone. He made tea. He didn't drink it. He emptied the dishwasher. She came in, followed by Brian, then Mahalia.

He tapped Brian on the shoulder.

—Come here. You as well, May.

He brought them in to the telly. He pointed at it.

—That's a television.

Brian laughed.

—Now, said Jimmy.—You sit in front of it. That's right, good man. Perfect.

He held up the remote.

—Have yeh seen one of these before?

—Yep, said Brian.

—Good man again, said Jimmy. – You can watch it for half an hour, okay?

—I already had my half-hour, said Brian.

—You're too honest, Smoke, said Jimmy.—I told yeh. Be a bit sneaky.

—Sneaky.

—That's right, said Jimmy.—Have you had your telly today yet, Smokey?

—No!

—Have you not? Well, here yeh go.

Jimmy lobbed the remote at him, and Smokey – that was Brian – caught it.

—I don't want to watch telly, said Mahalia.

Jimmy kept forgetting she was thirteen – although she looked it.

He'd never get used to it. His oldest child, Marvin, was a seventeen-year-old man. The youngest, Brian, was too big to be picked up.

—Just do me a favour, May, said Jimmy.—Stay here for a bit. I need to talk to your mother.

—Begging forgiveness, are we? said Mahalia.

—Somethin' like that, he said.

—Good luck with that, she said.

—Is that eye shadow you're wearin'?

—Did you just ask me to do you a favour, Dad?

—I did, yeah.

—The eye shadow is my business then, said Mahalia.

—You don't need it, yeh know.

—That's not an argument.

—I love you.

—So you should.

He left them there. Brian wouldn't budge and Mahalia loved being involved in the messy, stupid world of the adults, even if involvement meant staying out of the kitchen for half an hour.

But Aoife was gone. There was a kid with his head in the fridge and he wasn't one of Jimmy's.

—Who are you?

The kid stood up and, fair play to him, he blushed.

—I'm hungry, he said.

—Good man, Hungry, said Jimmy.—But what're you doin' pullin' the door off my fridge?

The kid looked confused, his red got redder. Jimmy felt like a bollix.

—Jimmer said you wouldn't mind. Or Missis – your wife, like. Are you Mister Rabbitte?

—Yeah.

—Jimmer said she – Missis Rabbitte, like – wouldn't mind if I, like, got something to eat.

Jimmer was young Jimmy, another of Jimmy's sons.

The kid's face had gone past red; he was turning black in front of Jimmy. He was holding a chicken leg.

—Will I put it back?

He was an old-fashioned young fella.

—Did you eat any of it? said Jimmy.

—Kind of, said the kid.

He looked at the leg.

—Yeah.

20

—You'd better eat the rest of it so, said Jimmy.

—Thanks.

—Where's Jimmy?

—Your son, like?

—Yeah.

—Upstairs.

—Grand.

—We're doin' a project, said the kid.

—What's your name?

—Garth.

—What?

—Garth.

—And what's the project about, Garth?

—Supertramp.

—Wha'?

—The group, like.

—You mean, the group tha' were shite back in the '70s twenty years before you were born and are probably even shiter now?

—No way are they shite, said Garth.

—Who listens to them?

—I do, said Garth.

Jimmy liked Garth, and he liked the feeling that he liked him.

—And tell us, Garth? he said.—Are you some kind of a born-again Christian, tryin' to convert my son to Supertramp?

—No way, said Garth.—He converted me.

—He what?

—He says the CD's yours.

—It isn't.

—He says it is, said Garth.—It's old looking and the price on the sticker is in old punts, like, not euros.

Aoife walked in.

—Tell Garth here, said Jimmy.

Garth was turning black again and he was trying to put the chicken leg into his pocket.

—Tell him what?

—That I hate Supertramp, said Jimmy.

—You don't, said Aoife.

—I do!

—Don't listen to him, Garth, said Aoife.—He loves them. Or he used to.

She walked across the kitchen. Garth was trying to get away

21

from her. He looked like he was going to climb up into the sink.

—Go on then, Jimmy said to Aoife—Name one Supertramp song.

She hadn't a clue – she never had.

—'Dreamer', said Aoife.—'The Logical Song', 'Breakfast in America', 'Take the Long Way Home', 'It's Raining Again'. I think that's the order they're in on the Greatest Hits collection you used to play all the time. Is your dad a music fascist too, Garth?

—Don't know.

Jimmy gave up. There was no point in trying to talk to Aoife now – not about Supertramp; fuck Supertramp – about the cancer.

He went in and sat with Brian for a while. He sent Brian up to bed, then sent Garth home, and the others went to bed. It was running taps and the toilet flushing for about an hour, and quiet shouts, and a loud thump that must have been Marvin giving young Jimmy a dig or young Jimmy giving Marvin a dig. He hadn't seen either of them all night but the house was full of them. And he could hear Mahalia singing. He sat in the dark and listened to the life above him.

I'll miss this.

He hadn't felt it coming and he got rid of it quickly.

Sentimental shite.

Now he lay on the bed with Aoife. She was crying onto his chest.

And he liked it.

—I bet Supertramp have a song about cancer, he said.

—Fuck off you.

—I never liked them.

She lifted her head.

—You did.

—Okay.

She put her head back down.

—You're such a baby.

—It's why you love me.

He heard her gulping back her tears, trying to stop.

—Sorry, he said.

She said nothing.

—I had to tell you.

—I knew, she said.

—Knew?

22

—Yes.

She patted his stomach.

—How? said Jimmy.—Did someone phone you? They'd no right —

—No.

They spoke softly. The bedroom door was open, a bit. In case Brian woke.

—I just knew, said Aoife.—You weren't yourself.

—So I had cancer?

—Something was wrong. It was in your face.

—I should've told you.

—Yes.

—I was goin' to.

—Why didn't you?

—I was goin' to tell you that I was goin' for the test, said Jimmy.—Then I decided – I suppose – to wait till after. If it was clean —

She hit him. He hadn't – he could never have expected this. It was like she'd driven her fist right through him.

—Jeee-zuss!

He got his hand to her shoulder and shoved her away, almost over the side of the bed.

—Shit —

He reached out to grab her. But she wasn't falling. They were both breathless and scared. Her hair was shorter these days but it was still hanging over her eyes.

The silence was loud and colossal.

A mobile phone buzzed.

—Fuck – !

They'd both jumped – the shock.

—Yours, said Aoife.

She exhaled, and breath lifted her fringe.

—It doesn't matter, said Jimmy.

—Go on, she said.

—It doesn't matter, I said. It's only a fuckin' text.

—It's your dad, she said.—He's the only one who texts you this late.

There was no hostility in what she said.

He found the phone and she was right. It was from his da.
Wayne fuckin Rooney!!

—Is anything wrong? Aoife asked.

—No, said Jimmy.—Not really. It's grand. I'm sorry.

—Me too.

She was on her knees, on the side of the bed. Jimmy leaned across and she let him hug her. Her face was wet. He kissed it. He didn't cry, and that seemed good.

—I'd better answer him, he said.

He knew she was looking at him, looking for difference or slowness – or bloodstains. He picked up the phone. He wrote, or whatever it was called – texted. *Complete cunt.* He sent it back to his da. He put the phone on the floor, and lay back.

—I know I should have told you, he said.

—It's okay.

—I thought it would go away. Fuckin' stupid. Once I did the right thing an' made the appointment.

—I understand.

—It was stupid.

—So are lots of things.

—I suppose. Anyway. I didn't want to worry you. That's the truth. Then I found out.

He stopped for a while. He was grand.

—And I was stunned, he said.—Fuckin'—. When I went back to work after. And I eventually had to talk – this fuckin' twit wonderin' where an order was supposed to go. When I opened my mouth there was no jaw. I couldn't feel it. Like I'd been at the fuckin' dentist. As if goin' to the – here we go – oncologist. Impressed?

—Good lad.

—As if goin' to the fuckin' oncologist hadn't been enough, I had to drop in on the dentist on the way back. But your man didn't notice.

—Is he really a twit?

—No. No, he's grand. He's young.

—Oh, that.

—Yeah. So anyway. I came home. And I was goin' to tell you. That was the plan. I even stopped off at SuperValu an' bought a bottle of wine. Remember?

—Yes.

—I had it all mapped out. The two of us in the kitchen. Some fuckin' hope.

—Brian had a match.

—That's right.

—I drank the wine while you were gone.

—That's right.

—Well, I opened it.

—You drank it.

—Okay. Not all of it.

—Grand.

—Anyway. I wasn't pissed.

—You were all over me, said Jimmy.—Later, like.

He looked at her.

—You rode a man with cancer.

—Jesus.

—And I couldn't tell you after that.

—I wouldn't have believed you.

—That's music to my fuckin' ears.

Now he cried. He couldn't help it. Actually, he wanted to. He felt no better and he felt no worse but it seemed natural, something she'd have wanted to see. Reassurance. And then he couldn't stop for a while.

—Can I not just text everyone?

—No, said Aoife.—It wouldn't be right.

—But last night you said —

She'd said this after she'd made him come in about three seconds.

—You said I was to think about nice things, said Jimmy.

It was Saturday morning. The kids – he hadn't told them yet; Jesus – were either out or still in bed. Brian was on a sleepover and the mother of his pal, Ryan, was bringing them both to the football. The father was in England, working. Jimmy would go and watch the second half and bring them back here. But now Jimmy and Aoife were alone.

—I said that? said Aoife.

—Look on the bright side, you said. That kind o' shite. And now I've to —

He picked up the sheet of paper, the list.

—I've to go from door to door. From Barrytown —

He was going there today, later, to tell his mother. He looked at some of the names.

—to Castlepollard.

His sister, Linda, lived there. It was in Meath or Westmeath, miles away.

—I've to tell —

He looked at the list again. He pretended to count.

—fifteen or sixteen people that I have cancer. And I've to do it in a rush so no one feels upset because I told him or her before I told him or fuckin' her.

She was smiling and he loved it.

—I've to travel the length and breadth of fuckin' Ireland and tell them all. And this is goin' to cheer me up?

—I'll come with you, she said.

—No.

—I want to.

—No, he said.—I'm not doin' it. It's mad.

—How then?

—Don't know, he said.

She took the list.

—I'll phone Sharon and Linda and Tracy, she said.

They were Jimmy's sisters.

—It makes sense, he said.—Is it okay?

—Yeah, she said.—No, you're right. But you didn't put my side on the list.

—I wasn't finished, he lied.

—We'll have to go to my parents'.

—Okay.

—I'll phone the others.

She added names to the list, the brother Jimmy thought was a wanker, the sister who was mad and getting madder.

—Sound, he said.—I'll phone – let's see. Darren. She's pregnant, by the way.

—I know.

—Who told you?

—She did.

—Melanie?

—Yeah. I met her.

—I thought you didn't like her.

—What's that got to do with anything? Jesus, Jimmy, grow up.

—I hope to, he said.

—Haha. Anyway, I do like her. She just annoys me.

—Grand.

—Sometimes.

—Okay.

It wasn't too bad. If he'd been asked what it was like, that was

26

what he'd have said. He had his mother coming up, and the kids. Telling them was going to be dreadful. And his boss – he'd have to tell her. Although she wasn't really his boss. But anyway, other than that, it really wasn't too bad. He had no dates yet; he wasn't counting down the days. He was in limbo for a while, and it was okay.

Mahalia was going to look after Brian and his pal, Ryan. Her first big professional job. Five euro for the hour, or however long it took.

—Will we go to my parents after? said Aoife.

—Ah Christ.

—It makes sense.

—Okay.

—We can go for a coffee on the way.

—Fuckin' wonderful.

She smiled.

Mahalia wasn't having it.

Five euro for most of the day, nearly? No way, like.

—Ah look —

—I have a life, like.

—I know, said Jimmy.—Ten euro.

He watched her face. A tenner was a fortune. The excitement, the little grin – it was lovely.

—Fifteen, she said.

He'd bargained her down to twelve, and now they – himself and Aoife – were on their way to Barrytown.

He was driving.

—Can you manage? she'd asked when they were walking out to the car.

—I remember where my parents live, he'd said.—I grew up there.

—I mean, I thought you might be a bit anxious.

—I'm grand.

—And I don't want to die on the way, she'd said.

—Fuck off now.

He drove onto the roundabout and indicated left – the turn-off for Barrytown. He decided to avoid the shopping centre. It was Saturday afternoon. Although it was never busy. It had started to look like a monument to a different era a couple of years after it had been built, when Jimmy was still a kid. When his Uncle Eddie from Australia had seen it the first time, he'd thought it was the local jail, all the barbed wire on the roof. It wouldn't be busy now but Jimmy didn't particularly want to see it.

—When's best to tell the kids?

—Before *The X Factor*, said Aoife.

They laughed.

—Seriously but, said Jimmy.

—Tonight, said Aoife.—We can make sure they'll all be there.

—Chinese, said Jimmy.—Special occasion. I want to tell the boys first though. Marv and Jimmy.

—Yes.

—I'm right, yeah?

—Yeah.

He drove past his old school, then left, onto the green.

—No one here.

—It's lovely, said Aoife.

—No kids any more. All grown up and gone.

They sat outside his parents' house, holding their door handles.

—When are you going to tell your friends? said Aoife.

He thought about this.

—I don't have any.

—Ah, you do.

—Ah, I don't.

—You do.

—I don't know, he said.—I haven't really thought about it. And that probably proves I'm right. I don't really have any.

—You do.

—Okay.

Maybe he was imagining it. But maybe there was some sort of a scent off him; the cancer was doing it. His wife wanted to ride him. He was sure of it. It was a biological thing, his body sending out the message; he had to reproduce before he died. There was sex in the air, in the car – definitely. He'd start the car, before anyone in the house noticed. He'd drive them up to Howth summit, or down to Dollymount. It was a miserable day; there'd be no one there. They'd do it like two kids half their age. Or to a hotel, one of the ones called the Airport this or Airport that. The one beside Darndale was nearest. A room for the afternoon. And he wouldn't remind her about his vasectomy.

—We'd better go in and tell my mother I'm dyin', he said.

*   *   *

28

—How did she take it? Darren asked him.

—Not too bad, said Jimmy.

It was true. His mother – *their* mother – hadn't torn her hair out. She'd cried. They'd all cried. He'd told her he'd be fine. The success rate – he was beginning to like the language – the success rate was encouraging. She already knew her chemo and her radiation. Her brother, Jimmy's Uncle Paddy, had been through it and survived.

The surgery, though, was news. He realised it as he told his mother: he hadn't told Aoife. He'd told his father but he'd forgotten Aoife. She went pale as he spoke. He thought she was going to faint. He really had forgotten. He couldn't believe it, but it was true.

—They'll take out 80 per cent of your fuckin' bowels? said his da.

—Just stop it, said his mother.

—Wha'?

—The language, she said.—For once. Just stop it.

—Righ', said his da.—Sorry.

—They said it won't make any difference, Jimmy told them.— I'll be able to eat everythin' as normal.

—With what's left.

—Yeah.

Aoife still looked wrong.

—The 20 per cent, said Jimmy's da.

—Fair play, said Jimmy.—You were always good at the subtraction.

It wasn't working. His laughter in the face of bad luck. There was no one smiling.

—Look, he said.—It's not life and death. That particular part. The operation's nearly just routine. It's part of the journey through my treatment.

He picked one of the buns on the table, to prove he was still able to eat. It was a low point – the low point. He'd fucked up. He hadn't told Aoife.

—I forgot, he said, to only her.

She nodded, once.

—Weird, he said.

She nodded.

—It was grand, he said now to his brother, Darren.

He was sitting on the stairs in Aoife's parents' house. He didn't know where Darren was. He could hear voices in the background.

—Where are yeh?

—Liffey Valley.

—Hate tha'.

—Give me cancer any day, said Darren.

—I'm a lucky man.

It was Jimmy who'd phoned Darren. He'd forgotten to tell Aoife – he really had; he kept testing himself – and now he felt the urge to tell everyone, to get it out there as quickly as possible, so everyone who needed to know would hear about it properly.

—Yeh shoppin'?

—Kind of, said Darren.

—With Melanie.

—Yeah.

—How's she doin'?

—Grand. Great.

—Congratulations there, by the way.

—Thanks, yeah. I was goin' to phone you.

—I know. You're grand. Da told me.

Darren and himself weren't close, but that meant nothing. They were brothers. Jimmy decided: he was going to find Leslie.

—So yeah, said Darren.—Everything's grand. She's had to give up the kick-boxin' and the crack cocaine. Other than that, it's business as usual.

—Great, said Jimmy.—We should meet up for a pint.

They wouldn't.

—Yeah, said Darren.—When?

The air was full of the unexpected. Jimmy reminded himself: he had cancer. He was telling the people who mattered and they were responding.

—Don't know, said Jimmy.

—When suits you?

—Wednesday? said Jimmy.

—Okay, said Darren.—After work?

—No, said Jimmy.—Before.

—That'd be good, said Darren.

Jimmy didn't actually know if Darren drank, if he was a drinker the way their father was a drinker. He doubted it. Or if he was a wine drinker, a bottle or two at home with Melanie – although she wouldn't be drinking now. She'd be guzzling the infusions, some blend of rhubarb and nettle that guaranteed the kid would be a fuckin' genius.

—What's that? he said.—I lost yeh there.

—About six, said Darren.—I'll come in straight after.

—Straight after what?

—Work.

—Oh grand, said Jimmy.—You still have a job so.

—I have, yeah, said Darren.—I've hidden it.

—Good man.

Darren was a lecturer, out in Maynooth.

—You? said Darren.

—I'm grand, I think, said Jimmy.

—Nostalgia's always big in a recession.

—Fuck off, said Jimmy.

—Am I right, though?

—You might be, yeah. I'll tell you all about it when we meet. And you can stick it in one of your fuckin' lectures.

—Where?

—In the middle. I don't care.

—Where'll we meet?

—I don't mind.

—Where's good near you?

—Don't know really, said Jimmy.—I'll ask some of the younger ones in work. Then we can go somewhere different.

—That makes sense, said Darren.—And look.

—What? said Jimmy.

—I'm sorry – yeh know?

—You're grand, said Jimmy.—Thanks. I'll let you get back to your shoppin'.

—Duvet covers, said Darren.

—Brilliant.

—I'll photograph them for yeh, send you the jpeg.

—Lovely, said Jimmy.

—Wednesday so.

—Yeah, great, said Jimmy.—I'll text you the pub.

He stayed on the stairs for a while. He could hear the rest of them in the front room. Talking low, just a bit above whispering. He thought he heard a sniffle. Aoife, maybe, or maybe her mother.

He'd stay put for another minute.

* * *

He followed the boys into the bedroom and closed the door.

—Listen, lads, he said.—I've a bit of news.

Jesus.

The three of them stood in a huddle between the radiator and the bed. The boys were taller than Jimmy now. He felt like the kid.

—Don't worry about this, he said.—It'll be fine.

He looked from face to face.

—I've got bowel cancer.

They stared at him. They were waiting for the punchline but they knew there wouldn't be one. Jimmy was the world's biggest bollocks. What he'd just done was illegal – or it fuckin' should have been.

The boys were still waiting to be rescued.

—So, said Jimmy.—So. I wanted to tell yis—. Jesus, lads, I'm sorry about this.

—It's cool, said young Jimmy.

And that saved Jimmy; he could go on.

—It'll be grand, he told them.—It'll be a bit – I don't know – inconvenient. For a while just.

—It's cancer, said Marvin.

—Yeah.

—That's not inconvenient, Dad.

—Yeah, said Jimmy.—Yeah. Come here.

He put an arm around each boy's shoulders. He had to reach up to do it. He felt himself going, falling over, but they held him.

—I'll be grand, he said.

They were stiff there, angry, frightened. Jimmy was talking right into the side of Marvin's head.

—It's not the worst of them, he said.—The cancers, like. And we've found it early enough.

—What's that mean?

—It's confined, said Jimmy.—It hasn't spread, you know.

He could feel the boys trying to control their breath, trying not to push away.

—It can be beaten, he said.

—How? said Marvin.

He was the stiffest, the angrier one.

—Well, said Jimmy.—Chemo and surgery.

—What's chemo? young Jimmy asked.

—Chemotherapy.

—I know. What is it?

—Chemicals, said Jimmy.—I suppose that's the simplest way to – I don't know.

They were still clinging to one another. He wanted to sit down.

—They nuke the bad cells – the chemicals, you know. Basically.

—Sounds good, said young Jimmy.

—I'm lookin' forward to it, said Jimmy.—It'll be like goin' mad in a head shop.

The boys tried to laugh.

—I'm really sorry about this, said Jimmy.

He let go of them. They seemed to expand, to rise above him. He wanted them back. But he sat on the bed. They stood there in front of him. They were awkward, polite, lovely. And separate – they stood like young men who didn't really know each other. They waited for permission to go.

—I'll be grand, said Jimmy.

Marvin nodded. Young Jimmy was going to cry.

—It'll just be—. Keep an eye out for your mam.

—For fuck sake, said Marvin.

Jimmy laughed, delighted. He held his hands up.

—Sorry, he said.—Yis hungry?

They were starving. They were always fuckin' starving.

—Sort of, said young Jimmy.

—Me too, said Jimmy.—But I'll be tellin' May and Brian about it – the news, yeh know. Downstairs. But I wanted to tell you first. I thought you could handle it.

—Man to man, said Marvin.

He was an angry kid.

—There's no good way, Marv.

—S'pose.

—Boys, said Jimmy.—I love you.

—Love you too, young Jimmy whispered.

—Yeah, Marvin whispered.

Jimmy got up off the bed and hugged them again. They let go a bit, properly. They cried a bit. The snot flowed.

—Check your shoulders, lads.

They were back down and dry-eyed in time for the arrival of the Chinese. They all sat around the table. It was a bit of a squash – it had been since the older pair had taken off and become the world's tallest Rabbittes, or Egan-Rabbittes. Aoife glanced at Jimmy. He shook his head; he'd wait till they'd finished eating.

33

Young Jimmy looked pale, although he was still ploughing into the Chicken Cantonese Style.

—What're you havin', May? he asked.

Mahalia had come home two days before, a vegetarian.

—Leave her alone, said Aoife.

—I was only askin', said Jimmy.—I'm curious.

—It's okay, said Mahalia.—Chicken with lemon sauce but I'm taking the bits of chicken out.

—I'll have them.

—Me! Brian shouted – he often had to.—She said me. Didn't you?

—Yeah, said Mahalia.

Another problem. Brian was a bit heavy. They had a fat kid on their hands. It kept Aoife awake. But Jimmy knew she wouldn't object tonight. Fill them all with sugar and monosodium glutamate; sedate the fuckers. That was the plan.

—I don't know what to eat yet, said Mahalia.—So before you tell me there's, like, bits of chicken in the sauce, I know, like.

—I wasn't goin' to say anythin', said Jimmy.—I respect your decision.

—Okay.

—And so do the chickens.

—Has anyone noticed, said Mahalia,—that we've one of the funniest dads in, like, the whole country?

—Yep.

—Yep.

Brian looked at Jimmy and smiled, just to let him know that he wasn't being treacherous, before he went —

—Yep.

—Poor Jimmy, said Aoife.

—Poor me.

—Can we've ice cream?

—There's animal fats in ice cream, said Marvin.

—Fuck off.

—Mahalia!

—Sorry.

—Hang on, said Jimmy.—Hang on.

He waited.

—Forks down. Brian. Good lad.

He waited a bit longer. He smiled at Aoife, at young Jimmy and Marvin.

34

—I've somethin' to tell yis.

—What?

—I'm gettin' there.

Mahalia had bawled. She'd thrown herself at him before he'd
got to *cancer*. But it had worked out fine. It was easier to work
his way backwards, to explain why he wouldn't be dying. She'd
believed him – he thought she had. They'd have to see – because
he'd been crying too as he spoke, as he'd stroked her head the
way he'd always done, as she'd cried through his jumper and shirt.
Aoife had cried. Young Jimmy had cried. Marvin had allowed
himself to cry – he'd stood up first and walked halfway to the
hall.

Brian hadn't.

He sat watching everything. He didn't blink. He held his fork,
waiting for the okay to get on with his dinner.

—Alright, Smoke?

—Yeah.

—Good man.

Maybe he'd just believed Jimmy. He was still young enough;
the older boys had been the same. They'd believed everything he'd
told them. The word – cancer – meant nothing to him. Fried rice
did, though.

—It's a phase, he said later, in the bed.—He'll be grand.

He didn't believe it. And he didn't believe it when Aoife seemed
to be agreeing with him.

—Yeah.

—You agree.

—Yeah.

—You don't.

—No, I do.

—Well, I fuckin' don't.

—Oh, fuck off, Jimmy. I'm just trying to put it off.

—Put what off?

—Everything. I'm tired.

—So am I.

—I know.

—Strange, though.

—Brian?

—No, said Jimmy.—Yeah, but no. I mean, the day.

—What about it?

—It was nice, said Jimmy.—I enjoyed it.

—Me too.

—Spent the whole day tellin' people I love that I've cancer, and I enjoyed myself.

Her head was on his chest again.

—You still tired? he asked.

—Oh God.

He couldn't get out of the car. He couldn't move.

It wasn't sudden – the feeling. It had been there since he'd woken up.

It was getting worse.

It wasn't depression. Although he didn't know.

It wasn't black.

It didn't have a colour – or weight.

He'd never understood static electricity, how or why it happened, why one door handle was a shock and another, the same design, wasn't; why Mahalia's hair had stood up straight whenever he'd pulled off that green jumper she'd had when she was a little thing. He didn't think he'd ever been interested in why it happened. It just did.

This was the same as static. It was how he'd have started to describe it.

The car park was small. There was space for eight cars. Noeleen's car wasn't there yet.

He hadn't told her. He would, today.

Tomorrow.

He was in no fit state to tell her today.

He'd touch something, the wrong thing, and he'd die. That was how he'd start, if he was trying to explain it. But, actually, he didn't have to touch anything. That was what paralysed him. Earlier, in bed, he woke up thinking he'd died. He was waking into his last thought. If he woke up properly, he'd be gone; he'd never even have existed.

It would go away. He just had to wait.

Terror. That was it.

He'd be grand. The dread would be gone – it was going; he knew it was nothing. He'd just wait another minute.

He'd be angry then. He had the routine. He'd get rid of that too. He'd slam a door, fire off an email – reply to some fuckin' eejit and have to apologise later.

36

Fuck it.

Fuck it.

He had the radio on. He could hear the news; he could separate the words. Gaddafi was dead – that was the biggie. He'd remember that. Sitting rigid in his car, in the car park behind work, and hearing that Gaddafi had been killed – how wasn't clear; a grenade, a bullet or a bayonet – maybe all three. Where the fuck would you buy a bayonet these days?

He'd go in in a minute. Face the day. Try to sell a few records. He might even tell Noeleen. Get it over with.

He'd see.

Probably not.

He'd watch the news later, at home. He'd make Brian watch with him, and Mahalia. A big day. The death of a dictator. Maybe not, though – Brian would want another Chinese, to celebrate.

Poor oul' Muammar. Jimmy wouldn't be selling him any Irish punk or post-punk hits of the '70s and '80s. A lost opportunity. Gaddafi could have died plugged into his iPod, listening to the Halfbreds or the Irregulars.

There was a thought.

Jimmy would go in now and stick it up on the homepage: Gaddafi died listening to Irish punk. Get a few laughs, shift a few units.

In a minute.

The parcel was on the table in the kitchen.

Waiting for him.

It was propped there, against the ketchup. Facing the door, so he'd see it. Brown cardboard, from Amazon.

—Nice one.

Aoife was at the counter, chopping something. He picked up the package.

—What is it?

—A puppy, said Aoife.

He pulled back the flap.

—Gift wrapped. For fuck sake.

He read the message. *I love you. XXX*

—Loveyoutoo, he muttered.

She smiled. He was imitating the boys. And he was Jimmy again, not the jittery lump she'd seen leaving the house earlier. He pulled off the ribbon and tore at the blue wrapping paper.

He looked at the yellow cover, and laughed.

—Brilliant. *Chemotherapy & Radiation for Dummies*. Fuckin' brilliant.

—You like it?

—Love it.

He laughed again.

—Fuckin' great.

He was delighted.

And so was she.

—You haven't read it before, no?

—No.

He held her with one arm and held the book over her head. He read the blurb at the top of the cover.

—Understand cancer treatment options, get a handle on the side effects, and feel better.

He lowered the book.

—Fuckin' hell. I feel better already.

He kissed her.

—Thanks.

—You're welcome.

He flicked quickly through the book – lots of lists and pictures.

—It'll be very useful, he said.—Very instructive.

—It was supposed to be a joke.

—I know, he said.—And it is. A good one as well. Because, especially. Let's face it. You're not great at the jokes.

—I am! Am I not?

He laughed.

—Gotcha.

—Oh Jesus.

It was Mahalia. She'd stopped at the door.

—Is it, like, safe to come in?

—Why wouldn't it be? said Jimmy.

—The flirting, said Mahalia.—It's disgusting. At your age, like.

—Feck off, you.

She passed him on her way to the fridge.

—Don't eat anything, May, said Aoife.—Dinner'll be in a minute.

—You should be happy I'm not, like, anorexic, said Mahalia.

—We are, said Jimmy.—Very happy. Although now, the way things are goin' in this country, some anorexic kids wouldn't be such a bad idea.

38

—Ah, Jimmy! He's joking, May.

—No, I'm not, said Jimmy.—D'you know what a recession is, May?

—Yeah, actually, said Mahalia.—I do. A period of —

She lifted her hands and did the quotation marks thing with her index fingers.

—temporary —

She dropped her hands.

—economic decline during which trade and industrial activity are, like, reduced.

They stared at her as she shut the door of the fridge.

—That's brilliant, said Jimmy.—Where'd yeh learn that?

—School, said Mahalia.—Hello!

—Can you say it in Irish?

—The sound of silent laughter, said Mahalia, as she went past him, out.

—Where did she come from?

—My side, definitely.

Jimmy found a good picture in the book. He read the caption.

—A healthy, protein-rich breakfast starts the day off right.

—Can't argue with that.

—Looks like an omelette, said Jimmy.—The picture's a bit grainy. Tomatoes, mushrooms.

She said nothing.

He read a heading – the book was full of them.

—Embracing carbohydrates and fats.

—Jesus, said Aoife.—It never occurred to me that you'd read the fucking thing.

Jimmy slapped the book shut.

—Fair enough, he said.

—It's a horrible word, though, isn't it?

—Wig?

—Cancer.

Jimmy had brought the book up to the bed.

—So loaded, said Aoife.

—Yeah, said Jimmy.—Anyway, look it. I won't be goin' for a wig.

—God.

—It'd just be stupid.

—No, said Aoife.—I agree. It's just the thought. Your hair —

—Hardly me best feature, said Jimmy.—Let's keep it real, love.

She loved what he'd said but it couldn't stop the tears. He joined her; he couldn't help it. It had become the nightly event – nearly every night. They often chatted as they cried, as if they were just chopping onions.

—Will the kids accept me without hair? Jimmy asked.

—I don't – why wouldn't they?

—Well, said Jimmy.—Like – they've grown up with it.

—It's a bit thinner, said Aoife.—Sorry.

—I know, said Jimmy.—It's still there but. And it started – we call it receding in the trade. Another fuckin' recession.

She smiled.

—There's a little patch at the back.

—Fuck off now.

—It's sweet.

She put her hand on the back of his head.

—There.

—Thanks for that, said Jimmy.—Anyway —

—Shave it off, said Aoife.

—Good idea. Brilliant. Now?

—Your head's a lovely shape.

—I know. Now?

—Yes, said Aoife.—Tomorrow.

—Fuck that. I'm doin' it now.

He got out of the bed.

—They can see me bald and healthy.

—Can it not wait till – ?

—No.

He was gone. She heard him stomping quietly into the bathroom. She heard the water. She heard something drop. The water went off. She heard nothing – then the water again. She thought about going after him. She wanted to watch him do it. She wanted to help – she wanted to stop him. She heard what she guessed was Jimmy soaping his head. She heard – she thought she heard a scrape, his razor.

—Fuck!

She heard his feet. He was back.

—It's too long.

He was holding a towel, one of the good white ones, to the side of his head.

40

—What did you do?

He climbed into the bed. With no groans at all. She could tell: he was excited, worked up.

—I cut the side o' me fuckin' head, he told her.

He was grinning and grimacing.

—I'm a fuckin' eejit, he said.

—Take it out of the way there.

She held the hand that was holding the towel and made him lift it away from his head, behind his ear.

—Why did you start there? she asked.

—Don't know, said Jimmy.—I didn't want to start at the front. The top, like. In case I made a balls of it.

—You did.

—I know, he said.—But it's hidden. You'd want to be lookin'.

—I am.

—Is it bad?

—Look.

She took the towel from him and flapped it open. She pointed at the speck.

—There.

—It felt worse.

—I'm sure.

—You sounded like Mahalia there. Like.

—You'll be fine, she said.

—I'll get it cut short tomorrow, he said.—A three blade or somethin'.

She hadn't a clue what that meant. There'd never been short hair in the house. The boys had disappeared behind their hair years ago. They came out to eat.

—Then I'll finish the job at home, said Jimmy.

—Fine.

She didn't ask him why he wouldn't just let the barber shave his head, and avoid the blood and drama. The book, the decision to go bald – she hadn't seen him so lively and happy in weeks.

—How's the poor heddy-weddy?

—Fuck off.

The snow was a shock.

—It's fuckin' November.

He heard himself sometimes; he was turning into his da. He

could even feel it in his back, in the way he was standing. But it didn't stop him.

—*Early* fuckin' November, he said.

—It's beautiful, said Aoife.

—Yeah. But. Work.

He had to go.

The last thing on the list of things he had to do.

Tell Noeleen, the boss.

Who wasn't really his boss.

—It never snows in November.

He'd been putting it off. The same question, every evening. Did you tell her yet?

—Will you be alright driving? Aoife asked.

—Yeah, no bother. It won't stick.

But it did. It stuck and it grew and now he was in work, stuck.

—Global warming me bollix, he said.

He pretended he was looking out the window.

—Yup, said Noeleen.

The boss. The senior partner. The owner of Jimmy's great idea.

There was no office; there were no internal walls. They were the team, the gang. The jacks and outside were the only escapes.

—Coffee? said Jimmy.

—If you go out to buy it, Jimbo.

—We'd both be goin' out, said Jimmy.—To over there.

He was pointing down, to the Insomnia at the far corner of the street.

—Oh, she said.—A date.

—Eh – yeah.

—I'll just get my coat.

—Grand.

He was stuck now.

He put on his jacket. He actually didn't have a proper coat. He couldn't think of the last time he'd wanted or needed a coat. He'd have to get one now. And fuckin' skis.

He met Noeleen downstairs at the door.

—Before we go, she said, just as his elbow started to push the glass.

He felt the cold lick his ankles.

—What?

—You're not thinking of leaving, are you, Jimbo?

That was a shock.

—No.

He had been – for two years now. It was a little dream of his, about the only one he had that didn't have tits or death in it. He fuckin' hated being called Jimbo.

—Ready? he said.

—Heave away.

He pushed open the door, out into the snow.

—It's lovely, she said.

—It is, he agreed.

It would be a while before it became a pain in the arse and dangerous. He knew already, he wouldn't be driving home. But he lived near enough to the Dart. Noeleen lived out in Kildare somewhere, in a house with a field. Her weekend was fucked. She'd never make it home.

He enjoyed hating her.

He didn't have a scarf or anything – it was only November, for fuck sake. The snow was getting in, down between his neck and collar.

—Any plans for the weekend?

He beat the snow off his head, and remembered. He had to get himself scalped. There was a barber a bit down from Insomnia. He'd trot down there after he'd told Noeleen he was dying.

—Yeah, she said.—We're booked into the Shelbourne tonight and tomorrow.

—Great.

—So we won't have to battle home in this.

—That's great, said Jimmy.

The other half of the we was Adam. Jimmy hadn't met him. The name had arrived about two months before.

—Great excuse, said Noeleen.—We can just stay in the room and fuck like little bunnies.

—Cool.

And actually, he did think it was a bit cool – the room in the hotel and the fact that she could tell him what she planned to do with it. He didn't really hate her. It was just easier pretending he did.

The café door was slowed by the soggy mat. He had to push it shut. He followed Noeleen to the counter.

—Your usual?

—I'm buyin', he said.

—Oh, I know.

He let her order his double espresso and her own super-frappa-chappa-whatever the fuck. That wasn't fair either. She ordered an Americano. And a bran muffin.

—You want anything to eat?

—No, he said.—Thanks.

They brought their coffees over to a corner. He waited till she was sitting before he did – he didn't know why. He didn't want to sit at all. He wanted to run. But he did – he sat.

—So, she said.

—So.

—Here we are.

—Yeah.

—What's on our mind?

She was taking over.

That wasn't fair.

Fuck it all, he was being too reasonable. He hated her. It was easier that way.

—I got a bit of news, he said.

—Oh yes?

She was in too early. Fuckin' typical.

—Yeah, he said.

He waited for her to jump in again.

She didn't.

—And you need to know about it, he said.—Because it's —

—Oh, Jimmy —

—I'm grand.

Fuck, fuck, fuck.

—I'm grand, he said again.

He sat up.

—I've got cancer.

She got up and went to the counter. She came back and handed him a tissue, a couple of them. Browny paper – the recycled stuff. She was sitting again.

He looked at the tissues in his hand. If he waited, would she take them back and wipe his eyes and cheeks?

—Alright?

—Yeah, he said.—Grand.

He held up the tissues.

—Thanks.

He rubbed his eyes. He put the tissues on the table, away to the side, so he wouldn't mess with them, shred them. He put his

44

hands on the table. He'd caught himself recently, a lot, finger in an ear, up a nostril. It wasn't good.

—I'm so sorry, she said.

—Thanks.

He was ready now, calm. It was his story – his.

—It's the bowel, he said.—Enjoy your muffin.

She looked down at the muffin. She hadn't touched it.

—I couldn't. Now.

—Go on ahead, he said.—What I mean is. It's not the lungs, or the brain. I'll be fine.

—What stage are you at?

A fuckin' expert – he should have known.

—Two, he said.—Stage Two. They think.

She looked at him like she doubted it, like she'd asked him how many drinks he'd had and he'd lied.

—Two, he said again.—Yeah.

—Okay.

She was nodding, measuring – businesswoman of the fuckin' year.

He got ready to give her the gist. The facts he'd learnt to go through. The reassurance that had started to bore him. He wouldn't do it again.

—I'll be out of action for a while, he said.—On and off.

—You'll need chemo.

—'Course, yeah.

He shrugged.

—It'll be fine, he said.—Radiation treatment as well, probably. Anyway.

He shrugged again. He was one big fuckin' shrug.

—I won't be around, he said.

And another shrug.

—Occasionally.

—Do you have dates? she asked.

—This week, he said.

—So soon? You could have —

—I'll be gettin' the dates this week.

—Oh. Sorry, yes –

—We'll have loads of time to sort things out.

—I didn't mean —

—Grand.

He shrugged. He smiled.

—So, he said.—Anyway.

—How's Aoife?

—She's grand. She's – well. Grand.

—The kids?

—They're grand. They don't – I don't know. I don't think they get it really. They know but—. So. Yeah, they're grand really.

He nodded at the window, at the snow beyond it.

—They'll be lovin' this.

—Yes.

Her hand was there, on his.

—And how are you, Jimmy?

—I'm grand.

—Everything's always grand in the world of Jimmy Rabbitte. Tell me.

—This is our gay moment, yeah?

—Yes.

—I'm fuckin' shattered, he said.—And frightened. And I keep adding bits to what's happening. Like a commentary, yeh know. My last fuckin' moments. I can't even watch ads on the telly. I start cryin'.

She patted his hand.

He was a fuckin' clown.

She was still there, smiling. Like she used to.

God, he was a sap.

—What caused it? she asked.

He shrugged.

—Don't know, he said.—They said it might be hereditary. Oh fuck.

—What's wrong?

—I forgot something, he said.—Completely fuckin' forgot.

He stood.

—I've to phone my da and my brothers.

—Oh Jesus! Jimmy! They'll have to be – is it, tested?

—Yeah, he said.—I forgot. Biopsies all round. Fuckin' hell.

They laughed.

—That's the Christmas presents sorted an' anyway.

She stood too. She hugged him.

—You never change, she said, to the side of his head.—I love you.

—Loveyoutoo, he said, like one of the kids.

He was a fuckin', fuckin' eejit.

—I'd better do it now, he said.

—You'd better.

He put on his jacket.

—Not here but, he said.—See you later.

—No rush.

He went out to the snow. He pulled up his collar and walked down towards the barber. He took out the phone. He found the number – he rubbed snow off the screen. He phoned Imelda.

He'd phoned Darren and his da. He'd told them they'd have to have biopsies, that the cancer might be hereditary. And he'd decided – again: he'd find Les.

He'd asked his da about his dead uncles, his grandfather.

—How did Grandda die?

—Stopped breathin'.

—Nice one. Why?

—Why? Look it, son, I know you've your problems. But I'll be honest. You're startin' to talk like a righ' little prick.

—Wha'?

—You've just told me I might have cancer, said Jimmy Sr.

—I didn't —

—Fuck off a minute. Yeh told me I'll have to have a biopsy but yeh didn't bother explainin' what exactly a fuckin' biopsy is. An' I don't like the sound of it. It's too fuckin' medical for me. Opsy.

—Sorry.

—I'm not finished.

—Ah fuck off, Da, would yeh.

He'd phoned back a few minutes later and apologised, and talked to him – finished up – properly.

This decision to find Les. It had been more than twenty years, and he'd let Les stay out there; he hadn't given a shite.

He was lacerating himself – he knew it. He didn't believe what he was thinking.

But here he was now, on Facebook. He'd signed up more than a year ago, nearly two; it was part of the job. And this was the first time he'd typed in Les Rabbitte.

He hit return.

Nothing. A few Lee Rabbittes, a Liz Rabbitte.

He typed Leslie Rabbitte.

Jesus. There he was.

No. There is no e at the end of this Rabbitt. There was no photo either, but the outline was female. It wasn't Les, unless he'd had a sex change.

The wife, a daughter. The Lee Rabbittes, or the Liz Rabbitte. Maybe all of them, some of them, were connected to Les. There were more than twenty years to fill.

His parents had sent Les over to England in 1989, to get him away from trouble and the law. He'd stayed with their auntie, his ma's sister – Jimmy couldn't remember the auntie's name. Then he was gone. Not a word since.

He typed in Imelda.

If Noeleen glanced over his shoulder when she was passing, she'd think he was chatting to Imelda May. She'd like that. There was money in Dublin rockabilly.

He left it there – Imelda.

He hadn't met her. The snow had saved him.

The twit beside him got up.

—Anyone want anything?

It was part of his job, keeping the team in coffee and hot chocolate, some bright idea Noeleen had brought back from a conference.

—You're grand, said Jimmy.—Thanks.

The coast was clearish. He typed in Quirk.

Nothing. She wasn't on Facebook. That was kind of comforting. He remembered his da telling him about Bertie's son picking up older women on Facebook.

Imelda was an older woman.

Anyway, the snow had stopped him – a few days before. He'd texted her. *I'm stuck*. And she'd got back, *Me 2xx*. He'd stared at the *xx*. He'd sent one back. *Another timexx*. And she'd got back to him. *Ah wellxxx*. Three of the fuckin' things.

—Who's texting you? Aoife had asked.

—Darren.

—What does he want?

—A new life.

It was an old joke.

—Say hello to him for me.

—Will do.

Not a second of guilt, sitting beside the woman he loved, texting the woman he probably wanted to ride. That was death for you.

Work.

He actually loved the job. And it was his own invention. Finding old bands, and finding the people who'd loved them. Loved them enough to pay money for their resurrected singles and albums.

Shiterock.com. His and Aoife's secret name for it.

He'd been rooting in the attic – this was about five years before – and he came down with a rake of old singles, and himself and Aoife started flicking through them.

—The Irregulars?

—They were good, said Jimmy.

—'Fuck England'?

—The B-side's better.

He'd gone up to get the old cot, so they could pass it on to one of Aoife's cousins. Some cousin Aoife was very fond of – they'd gone to the Gaeltacht together or some oul' shite that women insisted was important. Anyway, he came down with the cot and went back up for more of the singles. He passed handfuls of them down to Marvin.

—What are they?

—Just take them. I'll explain when I come down. Be careful with them.

—Why?

—Because I said so!

He'd heard them laughing.

He'd climbed back down. He took the risk; there was no one holding the ladder. They'd all gone down to the kitchen. They'd forgotten about him.

The singles were in piles on the table, four towers of the things.

—And you hung on to them all, said Aoife.

She'd guarded the records while the boys and Mahalia circled the table, dying to bring them out the back and throw them.

—Yeah, said Jimmy.—I did.

—They're lovely.

They were. A lot of them had picture sleeves. One of the singles on top was lime green.

—What are they? Marvin asked.

And Jimmy explained. Music in the grooves, the turntable, the needle – the stylus. The whole fuckin' history.

—But why are they so small? Marvin asked.—I've seen the big ones.

—LPs, said Jimmy.

—Yeah.

—These are singles, said Jimmy.—Only one song on each side. The LPs usually had ten tracks – songs, like.

—I know what a track is, said Marvin.

—Good man, sorry.

He took one of the records from its sleeve and showed it to Marvin.

—See?

Marvin put his hand out and Jimmy let him take the vinyl. Marvin held it exactly as he should have. There was religion in the kitchen. A *Lion King* moment. The other three had seen Marvin, how he'd held the little disc at its sides. They copied him. Jimmy let them.

—Body of Christ, he said, as he handed Mahalia hers.

—Stop that, said Aoife.

She was laughing.

—Would everybody be like you? she asked.

—Wha' d'you mean? A bit blasphemous?

—No, you eejit.

This was long before the cancer. She hadn't called him an eejit in ages.

—Would they have held onto all their old singles? she asked. —Like you.

—Some would've, said Jimmy.—I suppose.

—There's no need to be defensive.

—I'm not.

—You are, said Aoife.

He flicked through the singles.

—Well, said Aoife.—Are you going to answer?

—What was the question again, love, sorry?

—Would people like you, said Aoife,—collectors —

—I'll accept that.

—Would many of them have kept them, like you?

—Some, said Jimmy.

—But a lot wouldn't.

—No, said Jimmy.

—They wouldn't all be as obsessive as you.

—No.

And the idea was born in the kitchen. shiterock.com. Her idea – he'd stolen it quickly. But they'd done it together at first. A team – a real one. He'd tracked down old bands, phoned people

50

he'd known who might still know people. He became a private detective for an hour every night.

He'd never forget the first hit, the phone call.

—Hello?

The polite but wary voice at the other end, a man who didn't know who he was saying hello to.

—Is that Dessie Savage? Jimmy asked.

—Des, yeah, said the other voice.—It's a long time since anyone called me Dessie.

—Howyeh, said Jimmy.

He couldn't stay sitting.

He gave Aoife the thumbs up.

—Could I just check, so I don't waste your time? he said.—It's nothin' to do with tax or special offers, by the way.

He heard nothing from the other end.

—You still there, Des?

—Yes.

—Great, said Jimmy.—Yeah. I just want to check. Are you the Dessie – the Des Savage who played drums with the Irregulars?

The other voice laughed.

—God!

—It's you, is it?

—Yeah!

He laughed again.

—D'you know the last person to ask me that? he said.

—No, said Jimmy.—Who?

—My ex-wife, said Des.

He laughed again.

—She thought it was cool back then.

—It still is in my book, Des, said Jimmy, and immediately thought he was overdoing it. He couldn't even remember what Dessie Savage had looked like and he didn't want the man thinking he was stalking him or something.

—So, said Des.

—Yeah, said Jimmy.—Look it, my name's Jimmy Rabbitte. Yeh might remember. I managed a band called the Commitments.

—No.

—No? Doesn't matter.

Jimmy decided: his wife had been right to leave the cunt.

—Sorry, said Des.

51

—No worries, Des, said Jimmy.—This is about you. Have you kept in touch with the other lads?

—Well, said Des. Necko's dead.

—Shite, said Jimmy.—God, shite. I'm sorry.

—It was years ago, said Des.

—Sorry.

—No, said Des.—No. We hadn't been in touch for – fallen out of the habit, you know. Before mobiles and email, you know. He'd moved to Manchester.

—What was it? said Jimmy.—D'you mind – ?

—Cancer, said Des.

That was five years ago, and Jimmy would soon be phoning Des to tell him about his own cancer.

But that was just shite. More sentimentality. It was business as usual. Des would never have to know. Until it was too late, and he'd feel guilty.

—Sorry to hear it, said Jimmy, back then.—He'd a great voice.

—That's true.

—So, said Jimmy.—Look, I haven't explained why—. D'yeh have a minute, Des?

He felt great. Jimmy the salesman, Jimmy the manager. Talking his way to success.

Yes, Des had a minute and Jimmy filled it for him. The website, like iTunes – he could actually hear Des sit up. Anyone who googled the Irregulars —

—Even Dessie Savage, Des. Maybe even Des Savage.

They would quickly find www.kelticpunk.com, where they could buy and download – or upload, whatever the fuck – the long-lost song that had put the band into their heads in the first place.

—Still there, Des?

—Yeah, said Des.—Yes.

—How's that sound to you?

—Well, said Des.—Great. Great. It's been so long. We only ever had one single.

—I know that, yeah. 'Fuck England'.

Des laughed. Jimmy could hear the excitement, and something else, something a bit more.

—Great song, said Jimmy.—And the B-side. 'Fuck Scotland and Wales'.

Des laughed again.

—Happy days, said Jimmy.

—Yeah, said Des.—Yeah. I don't think I even have a copy of it myself.

Jimmy knew that probably wasn't true. The prick had an attic full of them.

—You can have mine, Des, he said.

—Thanks, eh —

—Jimmy.

—Great, yeah. But I think I gave one to my mother when it came out. She probably still has —

He was laughing again.

—She paid for the studio time, he said.—'Fuck England'. God love her – Jesus. What was I thinking? With the insurance money. My father died a few months before 'Fuck' —

He couldn't go on. He was laughing too much.

—So anyway, said Jimmy.—You're interested, Des.

—Yeah, said Des.—Yeah. Definitely. I'd have to contact the others – wouldn't I? I only co-wrote our songs. We did a lot of covers.

—'Walk On By', said Jimmy.

—Fuck, said Des.—Yeah.

—Before the Stranglers, said Jimmy.

He wasn't sure if that was true. He was betting it wasn't. He'd remembered the Irregulars' cover of 'Walk On By' while he was waiting for Des to calm down. It had been shite.

—Yeah, said Des.—But they had their label behind them.

—Yours was better, said Jimmy.

—I'm not sure, said Des.

Jimmy decided: he liked him.

—But, said Des.—You saw us. Back then.

—'Course, said Jimmy.—In the Magnet.

—God, said Des.—The Provos owned that place.

—We didn't know it at the time though, said Jimmy.

—No.

—Would you have cared?

—No.

—Same here.

—I would now.

—Same here, said Jimmy.

—But anyway, said Des.—God. I feel like I'm in a time machine.

—Same here, said Jimmy.

They met. They liked each other. They knew they would. It

was funny that, how you could just decide to like someone. They were home and dry before they were both sitting down.

—What'll yeh have, Des?

—Coffee, thanks.

—Anything with it?

—No.

They were men who didn't eat buns in public.

—So, said Des.—Tell me about celticpunk. Dot com.

Des was Southside. *Rednecks and southsiders need not apply*. But that kind of shite didn't seem to matter much any more.

—So, said Jimmy.—Here's what happens. Someone googles the Irregulars and —

—Who'd do that? Des asked.

—Well, I did, said Jimmy.—Before I came out. Did you?

—Yeah.

They laughed.

—There yeh go, said Jimmy.—People like us. Old heads, music fans. And actually. Kids. D'you have kids, Des?

—I do, yeah, said Des.—Well. One.

—Boy or —

—She's in Germany, said Des.—With her mother.

—That's messy, said Jimmy.—Is it?

—It is, said Des.—I try to get over every six weeks or so.

—Does she speak English?

—I speak German.

—Do yeh?

—I do, yeah. I lived there for a long time.

—Back to google, yeah?

—Okay.

—So anyway, said Jimmy.—We both googled the Irregulars and we got stuff about Irish history. No surprise there, that shite's never far away. And grammar. Verbs and shite.

—Yep.

—Nothin' about the band.

—Nope.

—We'll sort that, said Jimmy.—That's what we'll do. Get it up near the top of the list.

He hadn't a clue how that was done, but he'd find out – himself and Aoife would.

—You mentioned kids.

—Yeah, said Jimmy.—Yeah. I forgot. I got carried away. Yeah, so – kids. Teenagers, like. Like my own lads. They love the old stuff.

—Really?

—Oh yeah, said Jimmy.—Absolutely. And it's not just mine. All kids. Boys especially. So —

The coffee had arrived. They both drank it black.

—Our job, said Jimmy,—will be to push the Irregulars, the band like, up the charts. I mean, we get a Wikipedia page up and maybe a website, if the other lads are interested. Have yeh spoken to them yet?

—Not yet, said Des.—I wanted to hear a bit more first. To make it a bit more – less vague. And to meet you as well. And, well.

He picked up his cup.

—I haven't spoken to any of them in years, he said.

—I don't remember, said Jimmy.—Did yis break up, yeh know, dramatically?

—Not really, no.

—Good, said Jimmy.—That's probably good. My crowd but. The Commitments. Fuckin' hell.

—No, said Des.—Only, there's been no contact. So it would be a bit awkward, I suppose. But if I know a bit more, it'll make it easier.

He smiled.

—That's the theory.

—Grand, said Jimmy.—That makes sense. So. We build your presence there. Website, Wiki. Info, discography.

—It was only the one single.

—Doesn't matter, Des. It's still a discography. And here's the real trick. Links.

—Gotcha.

—Links. Wiki to the website. Website to Wiki. Wiki to us.

—celticpunk.

—Exactly.

Jimmy was giving Des Aoife's research. She'd done most of the early homework while he was at work selling cars.

—Where they'll find the single and the B-side for sale, upload or download.

—Great.

—Like iTunes, said Jimmy.—But boutique. More personal. Welcomin'. Not just buy or fuck off. There'll be pictures, info, a where are they now. A nice obituary for Necko.

Des nodded.

Jimmy rested for a bit. He was loving it, too much. He didn't want to get carried away. Or make Des greedy.

—And, he said.—But this might be a bit tricky. Given the fact that Necko's no longer with us.

—What? said Des.

Perfect.

—Reunion gigs, said Jimmy.

—Jesus, said Des.—I don't know. I haven't played in years.

Jimmy said nothing.

—And Necko, said Des.

Jimmy nodded.

—How would we manage it? said Des.

—Well, said Jimmy.—It's tricky.

—Tasteless?

That was a surprise.

—No, said Jimmy.—Well, I don't think so. There were four of yis. Is there a widow?

—There's, I suppose you'd call her an ex-widow.

—Grand.

—They had two kids.

—Grand.

—We ask her? said Des.

—I don't think yeh need to ask, said Jimmy.—Ask for permission. I don't think that'd be an issue.

He didn't know; he wasn't sure. He hadn't a clue.

—But it'd be nice to let her know, he said.—It'd be good. Get her to come along. What age are the kids?

—I'm not sure, said Des.

—Doesn't matter, said Jimmy.—It'd be emotional. And I don't mean that cynically now. I mean really. But then —

Des nodded.

—I know, he said.—Necko was the singer.

—There yeh go, said Jimmy.

Des shrugged. He was handing the problem over to Jimmy.

—Other bands manage it, said Jimmy.

—Yeah, said Des.

—Queen, said Jimmy.

—We weren't fuckin' Queen, said Des.

They both laughed.

—But you know what I mean, said Jimmy.—They have your

man, Paul Rodgers, instead of Freddie and no one complains or wants their money back because it's not Freddie. Or that's what I'm assumin'. Because I wouldn't be caught dead – sorry, didn't mean to be insensitive.

—No, no.

—I fuckin' hate Queen, said Jimmy.—Before and after Freddie. A glorified cabaret band. A bunch of fuckin' chancers. And I'm guessin' that you, as drummer of the Irregulars, agree with me.

—No, said Des.—I thought they were brilliant.

There'd never been an Irregulars reunion gig. The bassist wasn't dead but he was a born-again Christian.

—That's fuckin' worse.

He'd turned his back on the evils of rock 'n' roll.

—Fuckin' eejit.

Three-quarters of a band was a legitimate reunion, but half a band wasn't.

—Half the Who are dead, said Des.

—And the other half should just get on with their fuckin' lives, said Jimmy.

—You're probably right, said Des.

—So. Des. No reunion?

—No.

But the meeting with Des had been the start. When Jimmy had said –

—We'll look after you, Des.

– he'd wanted to whoop, because he'd believed every word. He'd found something great for himself – himself and Aoife had. They'd spent a night coming up with the proper name for shiterock. A cousin of Aoife's had a website that sold all sorts of Irish tack to the Yanks and Germans – bits of sod, teatowels, tins of stew —

—The Corrs' pubic hair.

—Ah Jimmy – stop!

Anyway, he – the cousin – told Aoife that the key word was Celtic.

—But we won't be sellin' stew.

—It's just the word, Aoife explained.—Typed into the search engine.

—Google.

—Yes, she said.—And Yahoo. All of them.

—But all we'll get is people lookin' for stew and Aran jumpers.

—Not if we – or they – put another word beside it, Aoife told him.—Celtic draws the business to us. And some other word —

—Punk, said Jimmy.

—Celtic punk, said Aoife.—That might be perfect.

—Celtic for the numbers, said Jimmy.—And punk for the attitude.

—www.celticpunk.com.

They'd grinned, they'd laughed. They'd leaned into each other and kissed.

But someone had got there before them. There was already a celticpunk.com.

—Fuck it.

—Ah well.

It looked like a fan site for people with tattoos who liked their diddley-eye music a bit mad.

—It's not even punk, said Jimmy.

He pointed at the photo on the homepage.

—That's a fuckin' banjo.

—Look, said Aoife.

She changed the c to k and that did the trick.

—What about gettin' rid of the k in punk.

—What d'you mean?

He typed it out. Kelticpunc.com.

—Too clever, said Aoife.

—Clever?

—Okay, said Aoife.—Stupid.

They were kelticpunk.com. The joy of it. The freedom. Tracking down old bands. Looking after them. And Jimmy had looked after them well. They'd seen a bit of life, the ones he'd found and adopted. They knew what a bit of extra cash meant, and what gratitude was. Some of them were still bastards, unchanged by the years, just wrecked. But even they were good crack. Jimmy and Aoife reared their kids and managed dead bands across the kitchen table and once every month or so they left the kids with the newest babysitter and went to one of their own reunion gigs, in Whelan's or somewhere else that made sense to people their age. And there was always something – good or bad, but always good – to bring home later.

—I said brown bread! Fuck!

They watched Barry Brown fling the tray across the dressing room. The room was about as wide as the tray, so the clatter

58

arrived while he was still swinging his arm and the tray came back off the wall and hit the side of his head.

Barry was lead singer with the Halfbreds. His drummer, a fifty-year-old girl called Connie Cunte, looked at the mess on the wall.

—It is brown bread, she said.

She was married to Barry.

—Stop being so fucking vain, Barry, she said.—Put your glasses on, dude.

They had two boys in Gonzaga and a girl in Alex, they'd told Jimmy and Aoife. The fees were killing them.

—What the fuck is Alex? Jimmy whispered to Aoife.

—A school.

—I thought they were after sendin' their young one off to Egypt or somethin'.

—It's Alexandra College.

—Mad pair o' cunts.

They'd been mad back then, before kids and fees – before Aoife – famous for it and not a lot else. And somehow they'd brought their madness with them into their current lives. Insanity cuddled up to respectability, in their clothes and on their faces, in everything about them.

—Mad as shite, said Aoife.

Jimmy loved the way she said that.

They watched Connie Cunte eat a brown bread sandwich straight off the wall, no hands. She was licking the paint.

—It's not the right brown bread, said her loving husband, Barry.

—Barry, said Jimmy.—Fuck off.

—Hey!

Barry pointed at Jimmy.

—Who's going out there tonight?

He pointed at the wrong door.

—I don't know, said Jimmy.

He felt Aoife's hand on his knee.

—I fucking am! Barry yelled.

They heard Connie swallow and laugh.

—So, Barry yelled, and took a breath.—No sandwiches, no show! Read the fucking rider!

Barry worked in the Department of Finance. He often had the Minister's ear.

—Will you go out there and tell the fucking crowd? he yelled.

—I will, yeah, said Jimmy.—No problem. There's only about

ten out there anyway. So I'll tell each of them individually. In fact —

He waited till Connie had turned from the wall and was listening properly.

—You not showin' up, said Jimmy,—is probably a much better night out than you actually goin' onstage.

—Fuck off!

—No problem, said Jimmy.

Barry and Connie huddled again. It was what they did. They huddled, then roared at each other.

—No!

—Go on!

—No! Okay, okay – fuck!

Aoife squeezed Jimmy's knee as Barry turned to them.

—I misunderstood, he said.

—I know, said Jimmy.—It's not a problem.

Jimmy put his hand out, and Barry took it.

—Is the Heineken okay? Jimmy asked him.—The cans are the right shape, are they?

—Fuck off.

—Grand.

Jimmy hadn't been accurate when he'd told Barry that there were only ten in the audience. There were twelve. But that figure grew to thirteen when the drummer left the band halfway through their crowd pleaser, 'Your Happiness Makes Me Puke,' but hung around for the rest of the gig so she could drive Barry home.

—I'm the designated driver, you stupid cunt!

It was a great night.

One of many.

Aoife did the sums – the accounts – one night. (Jimmy ran away from money and adding. Aoife did all that.) She looked across at Jimmy. This wasn't too long ago, although it felt like decades.

—D'you know what? she'd said.

—What?

—It's paying the mortgage.

—What is?

—shiterock.

—Go 'way.

—It is.

—That's brilliant, isn't it?

60

—It's fantastic.

They'd laughed; it just burst out.

It got better. It became their business, his job.

His company.

Their company.

He'd jacked in his old job. He'd hated it, especially after he'd decided to leave; the last few weeks had been hell. But if he hadn't resigned back then, he'd more than likely – almost definitely – have been out of a job eighteen months later when people stopped buying cars.

kelticpunk was suddenly their living. It was great, but frightening. There were great months and slow months, but the mortgage was always the same, hanging there, always more than they could afford. And the kids still ate the same amount. Actually, more. The first September had nearly creased them, with new school books and uniforms and black shoes, and the extra money for this and that. Football gear, a camogie stick, a deposit for a trip to Wales.

—Who in the name of Jesus'd want to go to Wales?

—Everyone else is going, said young Jimmy.

—Okay, okay.

And two ukuleles.

—Two?

—They're cheap, said Mahalia.

—Two but? said Jimmy.—And don't raise your eyes to the ceilin', May. Please.

—One for school, said Mahalia.

—For school?

—Yeah, said Mahalia.—Music.

—Thanks for the clarification.

He'd gone too far; he could see that on her face.

—Sorry. Go on.

—And the other one for home, she'd said.

—What? said Jimmy.—Do they make yeh leave the one for school in school?

—No, she'd said.—But music – double class, like – is the same day as camogie and I can't carry it all, like, the camogie gear and the ukulele and the ukulele would probably break, like, or get stolen.

So two ukuleles. Forty-four quid instead of twenty-two. It wasn't much but it was real. And it was coming up to Christmas.

61

Jimmy was getting Marvin a guitar and amp; he'd been in town with Marvin, and Marvin had stopped at the window of Music Maker, just down from the International, and stared at the electric guitars.

—Why not just get him an acoustic one? said Aoife.

—Cos he'll turn into a singer-songwriter, said Jimmy.—No fuckin' way.

Sales had gone up the year before, in October, November and December. But they'd sold nothing – almost literally – in the first two months of the new year. And this was before the recession, the crunch, the collapse – whatever the fuck they were calling it.

So they'd sold it. Most of it, seventy-five per cent. To Noeleen. They'd held onto a quarter – Noeleen's suggestion. And they'd got rid of the mortgage. They owned their own house, and everything was easier. They didn't know how much it was worth just before the crunch and they decided not to find out just after it.

—We don't need to know what negative equity means, said Aoife.

—You probably know already, do yeh?

—Of course I do, said Aoife.

Three years into a recession that still felt like it was just starting, life was a bit safe – if he forgot that he had cancer for a minute. He got paid every month and still owned a chunk of the business. He still ran kelticpunk, but Noeleen ran him. He worked where she could keep an eye on him.

That wasn't fair – it wasn't true. It was a chat they'd had before they'd signed. Where was he going to work? He'd opted for her office.

—Sure?

—Yeah, he'd said.—Makes sense. Is there room?

—Yes, she'd said.—Plenty.

The decision – all the decisions – had been his, and Aoife's. His – they'd been his. He'd always admit that. He had the safety of a salary, a pension, the VHI, a home he owned, and a bonus – so far – at the end of every year. The world was in shit but shiterock was making money.

And it killed him.

He liked Noeleen. He had to root through himself and pull out the resentment. Noeleen hadn't put her heel on his neck.

She'd made the offer and she'd left him and Aoife alone to pick at it.

They'd made the right decision and their timing had been accidentally perfect. They owned their house. The banks, the IMF, all forms of government could fuck off.

But it killed him. There was once – just once, and he never mentioned it to Aoife – the thought it had kicked off the cancer. He was literally going to end up what he was – gutless. And dead. He'd pushed the thought away. But the decision, the weeks leading up to it, had felt like physical pain, across his head, in his face, in his shoulders, through his stomach. They'd celebrated – they'd gone out to the Indian in Dollymount – after they'd signed the deal with Noeleen. He'd felt good about it, and right. But sad too. That was the word – sad. He'd had something special, and he'd lost it. He'd given it away.

He'd chickened out.

The anger never lasted. But the sadness, the grief, had never left. Like losing the kids, them growing up and away from him, one by one. This was the same feeling – grief. The risk, the excitement, at a point in his life when it would have been perfect, the two of them doing it together. But bills – fuckin' money – terrified him. The blood, when he'd noticed it first – and what the fuck had he been doing, examing the toilet paper? – when he'd watched it dyeing the water in the jacks, for a second, for a bit more than a second, it had made sense and he'd deserved it.

There was no photo, just a kid's drawing of a rabbit there instead. But the drawing was good – deliberately bad. There might have been an adult there, hiding behind the bunny.

Maisie Rabbitte.

Could he send her a message? Could he ask her if her dad was called Les? *Maisie only shares some information with everyone. If you know Maisie, add her as a friend or send her a message.* He'd do it, send her a message. But anything he wrote or thought of writing looked creepy.

He fired off a real message. *Hi Andrew. Got those snaps, ta. Any of the band post Eric? Raining here – as usual. J.*

Andrew – Andy Belton – had been lead singer and one of three guitarists with the Dangerous Dream, a prog rock group that, judging by the sales of their only album, *My Life on the Planet Behind You*, still had a following, and maybe a new following. Jimmy thought they were shite and he loved this – it didn't matter. It was business, and Andrew seemed sound. They hadn't met. Andrew lived somewhere near Nairobi – near in an African way. He worked for one of the Irish NGOs, and he was probably driving across a desert or something, boiling his head. Jimmy didn't know. But he knew this: the rain remark in his email made sound business sense. All his clients were middle-aged and most of them seemed to accept it, and they needed to know that the man who was looking after them was one of their own, another hip but middle-aged lad. And the weather did that. Information valuable to the middle-aged – *raining here* – handed over with a bit of timeless sarcasm – *as usual*. With clients he'd met, it could become *as fuckin' usual*. But Jimmy hadn't met Andrew.

He loved that too. The fact that he could find the man, excite the man, get the man to excite the other men, become a new big thing in their lives, without actually meeting them. He'd found Andrew on Facebook and Andrew had agreed to let Jimmy resurrect the Dangerous Dream, before Jimmy knew that Andrew was in Kenya. Jimmy had never heard Andrew's voice, except on his poxy record. And he loved that as well. He could like the man without liking the music, without actually knowing the man. And he knew: he'd never tell Andrew that his music was shite. Big Jimmy would tell the little bollix in Jimmy to keep all that to himself.

—You're maturing, said Aoife.

—Is that what it is?

—Yes.

—It took its time, said Jimmy.—And too fuckin' late.

—Stop.

—Sorry, he said.

—Okay.

—I didn't mean it. But – I don't know – I have to let it out sometimes.

—I know.

—Even when I'm only jokin'.

—I know. Just —

—What?

—Maybe be a bit careful of what you say, said Aoife.

—I know, said Jimmy.—The kids.

—No, said Aoife.—Me.

—Okay.

Hi. My name is Jimmy Rabbitte. I live in Dublin. Do you know anyone called Les Rabbitte? Or Leslie? Thanks. Jimmy.

He sent it.

He ran his fingers around the back of his head, from ear to ear. He hated it when he found a patch, a few missed bristles that felt like a harvested field. He leaned right over the sink, brought his face bang up to the mirror.

It looked alright; he'd done the job.

In the corner of the mirror – he saw something. He looked behind him.

It was Marvin.

Gone.

—Marv?

Marvin didn't answer.

—Alright?

No answer. And he couldn't hear feet on the stairs, or a door being opened or shut. But Marvin had definitely been there at the bathroom door. Looking at Jimmy shaving his head.

Rehearsing for the chemo.

He threw cold water over his head, bent down over the sink. He liked that. He felt wild, like he was out in the woods or something. He rubbed his head with a towel, looked at himself again. His eyes were tired, a bit dirty looking. He *was* tired.

He knocked on the boys' bedroom door. No one answered, but that meant nothing.

He knocked again. He waited, and went in.

Marvin wasn't there, or Brian. But young Jimmy was. Lying back, eyes closed – actually asleep.

Jimmy bent down and kissed his forehead. It was a while since he'd been able to do that. It was there for him now. The big, clear, beautiful forehead.

Something caught in Jimmy's throat. A sob.

He held young Jimmy's earphones and gently took them from his ears.

Young Jimmy's eyes were open.

—Alright? said Jimmy.

—Yeah.

—You were asleep.

—Yeah.

—You okay?

—Yeah.

—Just sleepy?

—Yeah.

Jimmy sat on the bed. Young Jimmy lay there, waiting for him to go. He would, but he wanted a few more seconds. He put the earphones into his own ears.

The Dangerous Dream.

Jimmy had emailed the album to the boys and Mahalia.

Our cool dad.

Another fuckin' sob.

He choked it. No way was he going to inflict it on young Jimmy. He took out the earphones.

—I'll leave yeh to it.

—Yeah.

—Later.

—Yeah, later.

—I want to show you somethin'.

He'd brought the laptop into the kitchen. He sat at the table and Aoife stood at his shoulder. He had it open on his Facebook page.

—You changed it, she said.

She pointed at his photograph in the left-top corner.

—Thought I'd better, he said.

—It's nice.

—Thanks.

It was him looking straight at the camera, the glass hole above the laptop screen. The shaved head, no smile.

—A bit fierce maybe, he said.

—No, she said.—Sorry to disappoint you. Serious. Interesting.

—Keep goin'.

—That's as far as I was going to take it, said Aoife.—Not fierce.

She patted his head.

He liked that.

—Anyway, he said.—This is – it might be – I don't know. Remember I told you I sent a message to someone called Maisie Rabbitte?

—Yes, said Aoife.—I do. What a name though.

—Yeah.

—She'd have to be lovely.

—Yeah. Look.

Aoife read it.

He's my dad.

—God, she said.

The sob again.

Aoife heard it. She put her hands on his head and pulled it back to her stomach.

—What'll you write back to her? she asked.

—I don't know, he said.

He was grand – he could talk.

—But I'm just after thinkin'. I changed my profile picture after I sent her the first message. I think I did anyway. So she sent her message to a man with hair and she'll be gettin' the answer from a fuckin' serial killer.

—Don't flatter yourself.

—Do I not even look a bit hard?

—No.

—Shite.

—Sorry.

—What d'you think though?

—About answering?

—Yeah.

—Keep it straightforward.

—Yeah. God, though. That's great news. I'm his brother. Somethin' like that?

—Yes. But you mightn't be.

—That's true, he said.—But. What're the chances of it not bein' Les?

—Small, I suppose. But I don't know.

—I don't either. So it can't be that fuckin' straightforward.

He typed.

Hi, Maisie. Your dad might be my brother. Will you give him my email address, please? All the best. Jimmy.

—Perfect, said Aoife.

—D'you think?

—Yes, she said.—Just send it.

He did.

—Now shut the laptop, said Aoife.

—Good idea – yeah.

He closed the laptop and pushed it to the centre of the table.

—Thanks, he said.

—Must feel strange.

—Yeah – yeah. How long will I give her?

—I don't know, said Aoife.—A day? Two? I don't really know.

—Yeah.

—She mightn't answer.

—She did the first time, he said.—I just hope—

—What?

—Well – I'm goin' into the Mater next week.

—And you'll wake up after the surgery, Jimmy.

—I know, he said.—I know that.

He stood up.

—I'm not bein' morbid, he said.

—You are.

—I'm not.

—I know.

She sounded angry. She wasn't looking at him.

—It would – Aoife?

—What?

—It would just be nice, he said.—Yeah, nice. Nothin' bigger. Nice. To contact Les. Even an email.

—I know.

—Before I go in.

—I know, she said.—I do.

—Let's stop sayin' I know. Will we?

—Okay.

—Grand.

He pointed at the laptop.

—This, he said.—I know it's been years.

—You said I know.

—I didn't. Did I?

—Yes, she said.—You did. But this.

And she pointed at the laptop.

—You didn't invite him to our wedding. That's how long it's been, Jimmy.

—I know, he said.—I know. I didn't know how – where to send an invitation. But I know. Fuck it.

—There are real people in the house, Jimmy.

—That's not fuckin' fair.

—Write an email, she said.—If it works, great. Just don't —

68

—Wha'?

—Just listen, Jimmy – for fuck sake.

—Go on.

—Don't make it bigger than it should be.

She was right, although he wanted to explode, throw fucks and froth around the room.

—Yeah, he said.—I know what you're sayin'. But fuck it, Aoife. It's – I don't know. It's excitin'.

—I know.

—Are there poppadoms? Brian asked.

—No, said Aoife.—No poppadoms.

—I said poppadoms, said Brian.—I told you.

He was talking to Marvin. Marvin had taken the orders and phoned.

—She censored the list, he said.

—She? said Jimmy.

—Mam.

—*She?*

—It's okay, said Aoife.

She looked at Brian.

—There was more than enough already, she said.—So I knocked a few things off the list.

—Bet you didn't, said Brian.—Did she?

—Stop this, said Jimmy.—Now. You listenin'?

Brian nodded.

—Okay, said Jimmy.—Good man. So look it —

He was wasting his time. The lids were off the cartons and they were all digging in. Mahalia was eating meat again. She seemed to stop being a vegetarian whenever they ordered a takeaway. Jimmy said nothing. He respected her principles and loved the way she could bypass them.

—So anyway, he said.

He tapped his plate with his fork.

—No speech, don't worry. Just —

They all looked at him. They were worried, even scared. He hated this – doing this.

—I'm goin' into the hospital.

They stared at him.

—And I'll be gone for a few days, said Jimmy.—That's all.

That wasn't all; they knew it.

—So, said Marvin.—Like – this isn't the last supper, no?

—Marvin Rabbitte!

God – fuck – he loved him. He loved them.

They looked at him and saw that they were allowed to laugh.

—Alright.

He looked at the guy, the anaesthetist, looking at his chart.

—Now, James.

He was looking at Jimmy's arm.

The cunt. With his James. He tapped Jimmy's shoulder.

—Count to ten for me.

Jimmy looked at the needle.

—One —

He came out of nothing.

No memory, image. Smell.

Nothing.

No name.

No idea where, who – nothing.

—Some of this?

The straw was at his lips. He knew what to do. He felt it. Water.
On his lip.

Gone.

He was alone. Blue curtain. Tray thing on wheels.

She was there.

—Aoife.

Her face was there. She couldn't hear him.

—Aoife.

—Hi.

She pressed. His hand.

—The drugs, he said.

—Shush, she said.—What drugs?

—Fuckin' amazin'.

—You can tell me later.

—Amazin'.

She held his hand.

—Later.

—Get the name.

They had him out of the bed.

—Fuckin' Lazarus.

It was his da.

—Fuck off, Da.

—So you're grand.

—Not bad, said Jimmy.—I've to drag this fuckin' thing around though.

He shook the IV stand.

—Not for ever but, said his da.—Am I righ'?

—A few days, I suppose. They told me but I forget. But I walked from over there —

He pointed to the bed.

—To here.

He pointed at his feet. He was at the door from the ward to the corridor.

—Fair play.

—An' I'm bollixed.

—It's a fair stretch, said his da.—Three beds.

—Twice.

—Six beds, said his da.—Good man. I know cunts wouldn't get past two.

He nodded at the only empty bed.

—This one dead?

—No, said Jimmy.—Gone home.

—Ah good.

Jimmy thought he was smiling but he wasn't certain. He was still a bit jet-lagged, behind himself. He wasn't sure where his face was.

—I'm fuckin' elated, Da.

—Good man.

—Really. I am.

His da stood back while Jimmy lowered himself slowly into the chair.

—Y'alrigh'?

—Grand, said Jimmy.

—Is it sore?

—Not really, said Jimmy.—Not yet, anyway. They said somethin' abou' that as well. But I forget. I'm tired just.

He watched his da grab the chair from beside the bed right across from him. The chap in the bed was asleep and restless.

—What's wrong with your man?

—Don't know.

He sat down just as Jimmy's eyes started to shut.

—Jimmy?

—Wha'?

—Alrigh'?

—Grand.

—Sure?

—Yeah.

The heat in the place. He hated it. He couldn't stay awake but they wouldn't let him get onto the bed. His head kept falling forward and he'd snap awake.

The nurses.

Wagons.

There wasn't a nice one among them.

There was.

One. She'd been there smiling when he'd woken. Was it this morning? Yesterday? He hadn't a clue.

It was hard to keep up. There was something he had to remember. He'd been grand a while back. Chatting to the fella across the way. A boring enough cunt. Going on about the horses. Trainers and jockeys, all the winners he'd nearly had, the fuckin' accumulators. The telly, the racing – the sound had been up full blast. It still was – Jimmy could hear it. It wasn't the horses now though. Australian voices. *Neighbours*. For fuck sake.

Jason Donovan.

Kylie Minogue.

Two names that fell neatly.

From way back.

Couldn't keep his head up.

Kylie. That was her name. Charlene. He thought. *Charleeeeene!*

—Sore?

—No.

—You're not just being brave?

—I am, yeah. I'm in fuckin' agony. No, I'm grand.

72

He was awake. Fully awake. Wide awake. He knew what day of the week it was.

—Wednesday.

—Thursday, said Aoife.

He sighed. It felt good. He could exhale without worrying. There was something; it was there now, something he hadn't told Aoife.

—The drugs, though.

—You told me, she said.

—No, he said.—I didn't. I don't think so.

—You said they were amazing, said Aoife.

—They were. Fuckin' amazin'.

—Okay, she said.—What was it about them?

She was sitting up on the bed. The kids had gone back down to the shop, Brian in charge of the tenner.

—Just, said Jimmy.—Your man, the anaesthetic guy. The anaesthetist. Try sayin' that when you're pissed.

—I'll give it a bash tonight. Go on.

—So he's there. All set, like. He was a bit of a cunt.

—Jimmy.

—Well, he was. Called me James.

—Then he was definitely a cunt, she whispered, and Jimmy loved her so much, so much, so fuckin' much.

—You've never been a James, she said.

He watched her mouth. The words were coming out – he could see them all. Eggs.

—The drugs, he said.

He held back the tears. He touched his face. It was dry. He was feeling strange again. Woozy. A bit not there.

She leaned down and took his hand. The tubed-up hand.

—Go on, she said.

—He tells me to count to ten, said Jimmy.

—Did you manage it? Aoife asked.

—I don't think I got to three. But the feeling, Aoife.

—What?

—It's impossible—. Heat, like. A rush. The nicest feelin' ever.

—For two seconds?

—Felt like much longer. Years. I don't know.

—You're crying.

—I'm not – am I?

She slid off the bed. She put her hands on his shoulders.

—I want to go home, he said.

—Me too.

—I don't like this place. It's a kip.

—That's my Jimmy.

—It's a fuckin' kip.

—Only a few days left.

—Okay.

Aoife looked up as she tied his lace.

—I'll have to get you a pair of shoes with Velcro.

—Ah Jaysis.

—Or slip-ons.

—No fuckin' way.

—Mind you, she said.—The Timberland boots go really well with your tracksuit bottoms.

He had to wear the bottoms, because of the stitches and that. Aoife had bought them for him. Blue with a yellow stripe.

He was standing now.

—Let's get out of here.

He grabbed his bag but she took it from him.

—Are you not going to say goodbye to anyone? she asked.

He was at the door.

—No.

—Ah Jimmy.

Outside at the ward station, he signed what needed signing, and got away to the lift as quickly as he could.

—Come on.

—God, you're rude.

—I just want to get out of here.

He was sweating, already wet.

—You didn't even say thank you to the nurse at the desk.

—I didn't know her, he said.—I just want to go.

The lift was right there, no distance away, but it took him all fuckin' morning to reach it.

Aoife pressed the down button.

—I wanted to do that, he said.

He could feel the sweat cooling. It reminded him of something, something that used to happen – he didn't know.

He hated not being able to remember. It felt like he was closing down. Songs, names, places – they were disappearing.

—How are you feeling? she asked.

—Grand, he lied.—I'll write them all a card, he lied again.—The nurses. To thank them.

—That's a nice idea.

No sign of the lift and there was none of the noise that meant it was on its way. It was one of those industrial-sized hospital lifts, built to accommodate three or four dead bodies on a line of trolleys. The real Jimmy wouldn't have waited. He'd have been down the stairs and out into the world by now.

—What did you say? said Aoife.

—Wha'?

—You said something.

—I didn't. Wha' did I say?

—I don't know. That's why I asked you.

—I didn't say anythin'.

—Are you alright?

—I'm grand.

The door slid slowly open and Jimmy walked in. They were sharing the lift with a fat guy in a tracksuit and a wheelchair. He seemed to be missing a leg but Jimmy wasn't sure. It was hard to tell where he started and ended. He was with his wife, or his life partner. Maybe his sister, or even his ma. The lift took forever. Jimmy wasn't even sure if it was moving.

—Cuntin' lift, said the chap in the wheelchair.

The sun was low and mean. It made his eyes feel old.

—Seatbelt, Jimmy, said Aoife.

—Oh yeah.

—And off we go.

—See the guy in the yellow dressing gown? And the baseball cap?

—Yes.

—Hit him, will yeh.

She laughed.

—Custodian of the remote control, said Jimmy.—You can see it in the pocket of his dressin' gown, look.

He was right. The ward remote was poking out of the pocket.

—Jesus, said Aoife.

—That's what I've been livin' with, he said.

Home was ten minutes away, even if all the lights went against them.

—How could Marv lose his fuckin' iPod? said Jimmy.

—What?

—How could he have been so fuckin' blasé?

She looked at Jimmy, and back at the road.

—Marvin didn't lose his iPod, she said.—He had it when he went to school this morning. I called after him because he'd forgotten his lunch but he didn't hear me.

—Are you sure?

She looked at him quickly again.

—Yes.

He dragged his open hand from his forehead to his chin. He looked at the sun through his fingers.

—Did I imagine it?

—I think so, she said.—You must have.

—I gave out shite to him.

—You didn't.

—I did.

—You couldn't have, Jimmy, she said.

He could hear the worry in her voice, and impatience.

—It didn't happen.

—I know, said Jimmy.—I can see that. But I imagined it did.

He looked at her looking at the road ahead.

—The only realistic thing I did imagine. Everythin' else was mad.

—It must be hard, she said.

He decided to say nothing.

There was a dog in the kitchen.

—Is that ours? said Jimmy.

—No, it isn't, said Aoife.

It was a tiny yoke with a face on him a bit like Gaddafi's.

—It's Caoimhe's, said Aoife.—We're just looking after it.

The thing barked. At Jimmy.

—It doesn't like me, he said.

—Don't be silly.

He sat down at the table and the dog jumped at his legs. He couldn't cope with this, Aoife's sister's dog pawing at him.

—See? said Aoife.—She does like you. She just wants to get up on a lap.

—She can fuck off, said Jimmy.

He pushed the dog's head away; he had to reach down to get at it. The dog skidded across the floor and came straight back at Jimmy.

—It's only for a few days, said Aoife.

The dog was scraping at Jimmy's tracksuit bottoms. Its claws were stinging the legs off him.

—Get down, Cindy, said Mahalia.

—Cindy? said Jimmy.—Wha' sort of a name is that?

—That's, like, a really stupid question, said Mahalia.

She picked up the dog and put it up to Jimmy's face.

—Say hello to Daddy, she said.

Jimmy fought the urge to grab the dog and throw it at the fridge door. He felt its tongue on his top lip. The fuckin' thing was trying to get off with him.

He pulled his head back.

—Enough, he said.

But the dog followed his head. Jimmy's eyes were swimming; he'd become allergic to dog hair or something.

—She really likes you, said Mahalia.

—May, please. Give us a break.

—Fine, said Mahalia.—Annyhoo. Welcome home.

—Thanks.

Her face had replaced the dog's. He kissed her cheek.

—You smell nice, he said.

—You don't, she said.

Brian was standing at the kitchen door, looking worried and eager.

—Alright, Smoke?

And Brian smiled. He'd put on weight. Jimmy would have sworn it.

—Yeh comin' in? he said.

Brian stepped nearer to him.

—Here, said Jimmy.—Give us a hug.

Brian laughed and came over to Jimmy. Jimmy held him and rested his head on Brian's shoulder. He didn't cry. It was the same Brian. Same size, same smell.

—It's good to be home, he said.

He thought of something. He looked at Brian and Mahalia.

—No school?

—Mam said we could stay at home till you came home, like, said Mahalia.

—Chancers, said Jimmy.—Usin' me as an excuse.

He had Brian laughing again.

—So I'm home, he said. So off yeh go, back to school.

—Can we have a takeaway —

—No!

Aoife and Jimmy shouted it together.

—I think that's a No, said Mahalia.

Brian got his schoolbag out from behind the door. He stopped, went, stopped. He turned to Jimmy.

—Are you finished?

—Finished wha'? said Jimmy.—The hospital, d'yeh mean?

—Yeah.

—I think so, yeah, said Jimmy.—I'll be in for the day just. Now and again. Once a week or somethin'. But I'll be home every night.

He looked at Brian's face and tried to take the worry off it.

—It'll be grand, he said.

He was exhausted. Wiped. The dog was back on the floor, scratching at the mat at the back door. He was surrounded by noise; that was what it was like.

He was fucked, shattered.

He smiled at Brian.

—How's school been since?

—Okay.

—Okay?

—A bit boring.

—How is it borin'?

—Just is.

—I'm flaked, he said.—I think I'll lie down for a bit.

He looked at the faces looking at him.

—I'll be up when you come home.

He stood up as sharply as he could manage and he made sure he didn't grunt or moan.

—It's great to be home.

He looked down at the dog. He smiled again. He fuckin' hated it. The sister's dog, a fuckin' spy.

—How long is a few days? he asked Aoife.

—Two weeks, she said.

—Fuck sake, he said.—Where've they gone?

—A cruise, she said.

—A cruise? he said.—Recession me hole.

—Mediterranean. Starting in Genoa.

—Grand, he said.—And endin' in acrimony. See yis in a bit.

He headed to the stairs.

—Will I wake you later?

No.

—Yeah, he said.—That'd be nice.

The light at the sides of the curtains wasn't as sharp. The sun had gone over the house.

He'd slept. Brilliant. He'd shut his eyes and he'd gone to sleep. Simple as that.

He could make out music, some shite downstairs. Hall & Oates, he thought it was. 'Maneater'. Aoife was listening to Nova on the Roberts. He'd give out to her later, wasting internet radio on shite like that. She loved what she called his musical fascism.

He could hear yapping now too. Caoimhe's excuse for a dog. Out the back. Although he couldn't be certain. The estate was full of yappers. If he'd ever needed to prove that this was a middle-class area it wouldn't have been the houses he'd have pointed at. They were just ordinary, three-bedroomed, with small gardens; reasonable at the time, ludicrously expensive for a few years and probably worth fuck all now. It wasn't the houses that marked the place, or most of the people. They were the same as everywhere. Although middle-class gobshites were a bit more complicated, harder to spot and easier to write off than the working-class ones.

—What school did you go to?

Jimmy had never been asked that question until the eejit next door, Conor, had asked him. Two or three years back, this was. Jimmy had had to think before he'd answered. He couldn't remember the name of the fuckin' place.

They were in Conor and Sinéad's front room, pretending they were relaxed and having a great time.

—Blackacres, said Jimmy.

Conor looked lost.

—The community school, said Jimmy.

—Ah, said Conor.

—It wasn't a bad oul' school, said Jimmy.—A bit mad.

—In Barrytown, said Sinéad.

Her face would have made more sense if she'd said, in Soweto. But she was trying her best.

—Blackacres was the name of the farm the houses were built on, Jimmy told her.—The barn was there for years after. The smell of pig shite – Jesus.

Sinéad and Aoife laughed.

—I think they called it Blackacres Community School to avoid callin' it Barrytown Community School.

—There's nothing wrong with Barrytown, said Sinéad.

—D'you know Barrytown, do yeh, Sinéad? he asked her.

Aoife's eyes were huge, charging across the coffee table at him.

—Yes, I do, said Sinéad.

—Do yeh?

—Yes, said Sinéad.—I'm from Barrytown.

Aoife grinned.

Jimmy looked at Sinéad and tried to recognise her.

—What part? he asked.

—Just Barrytown, said Sinéad.

—Old Barrytown? said Jimmy.—The part tha' was there before the houses?

—I lived in a house, said Sinéad.

Jimmy tried to see her twenty years before, or twenty-four or five. That was the thing: the young ones in old Barrytown, the ones from the older houses, the snobby houses, they'd all been rides, what every young fella in new Barrytown dreamt of. But this one, Sinéad, was too young. She was about ten years younger than Jimmy.

—D'yeh have any sisters? he asked her.

Aoife's mouth hung open, a bit.

—Yes, said Sinéad, and she left it at that.

He listened now for noise next door, in the bedroom beyond the wall. Sinéad was probably in there, somewhere in the house. She'd had the twins since that night. He often saw her pushing that double-decker buggy.

There was no sign of life in there. No sound.

His phone was in his tracksuit bottoms, zipped in safe like his lunch money. He'd left it off while he was in the hospital. He didn't have to lean too far. He grabbed a leg and lay back again. He was still comfortable, kind of half asleep. He got the phone out and turned it on.

Where he grew up, most of the dogs were huge. Their shite was mountainous, borderline human. Everyone he knew had been bitten by a local dog.

The phone started beeping as it rolled out five days' worth of texts. He didn't have an iPhone or a BlackBerry. Just an old-fashioned Nokia. He'd had a BlackBerry for a month but he'd got rid of it. There'd been no escape from work. Aoife had put it out on the windowsill one night.

The texts had stopped. He knew most of them were from his da, and the football scores. Liverpool had played while he'd been drugged. One text from his da would tell him the result. *For fuck sake.* They'd lost again.

The others could wait. He texted Darren. *Did u no Sinead Ni Cheallaigh?* The phone hopped on the pillow beside him. It was Darren. *Yes. How's the arse?* Apostrophe and all, the over-educated prick. *Still attached. Did u no hr well?*

The dogs in Barrytown hadn't yapped. They'd barked. They'd howled. If they started riding your leg, or even got up on your back, you didn't object.

The phone again. *Very well.* The bastard. He'd leave it at that.

The dogs here were small and mouthy. They were proper pets, extra children really. That was the indicator, the thing he'd have pointed out to any sociologist. Don't look at the houses or the cars or the schools. Look at the dogs.

He liked how he was now. Nice and lazy. A bit of fever, maybe. Nothing expected of him. He closed his eyes.

The phone again. *I fucked her til she begged for mercy in Irish.* Jimmy laughed. Darren never spoke like that. He was definitely spoofing. That was grand. He sent one back – *Good man* – and turned off the phone.

It was a bit darker now.

He could hear feet outside and young ones talking.

—Ohmyfuckingod, no way.

He heard the front door. He heard it slammed shut. Right under him.

He stayed where he was. He'd go down in a bit. Mingle. Meet and fuckin' greet.

—How's school?
  —Grand.
  —Grand?
  —Yeah. Kind of.
The ads were on, so the sound was down. They were all

81

watching *The Apprentice*, the Irish one. Jimmy couldn't remember the last time they'd all watched telly at the same time. They were sticking it out, staying together for the night. He liked that; he appreciated it. The couch was all his, and the remote as well. He could have switched to *The Frontline*, to the union men with beards discussing the Croke Park Agreement, and they'd still have stayed with him.

—How's the study goin'?

Marvin was on the floor, his head close to Jimmy's feet. He was staring at the silent Bulmers ad.

—Grand, he said.

—Doin' a bit?

—Yeah.

It was three weeks to Christmas, six months or so to the Leaving.

—Good man, said Jimmy.—Don't overdo it, though.

—Oooh, said Mahalia.—Sarcasm.

Brian laughed and looked up at Jimmy.

—I'm not bein' sarcastic, he lied.

Marvin was still staring at the telly.

—Yeh still there, Marv?

—Yep.

—Yeh don't want to peak too early, said Jimmy.—Yeh with me?

—Grand.

—Good man.

Why was he being like this, goading a kid he adored?

—Here we go, he said.—They're back.

He turned the sound up.

—It's a bit loud, said Aoife.

He turned it up a bit more, and down. Brian looked at him again. He winked.

He sat up a bit. *Don't fuckin' groan.* He leaned out and patted Marv's shoulder. Marv didn't move, didn't swerve out of reach. That was good. The shoulder felt big, hard; it belonged to a man.

That was the problem.

That was the thrill.

—Who'll be fired tonight? he asked.

—All of them, said Marvin.

—You're right, said Jimmy.—He should.

—Ah no, said Aoife.—I like the little fella.

—They're all, like, little, said Mahalia.—Which one?

—The young one, said Aoife.—The mouthy little fella.

—He'd drive me demented if I had to work with him, said Jimmy.—Look at the state of him.

—Well, I hope he wins.

—Ah Jesus, Aoife. Why?

—He reminds me of you.

They laughed. They all looked at him, even Marvin. He loved it.

He got up with the rest of them. He put bread in the toaster. He put bowls on the table.

He felt strange – kind of loose. He sat down.

No one noticed.

The fuckin' dog was there, clawing at the dressing gown, tearing holes in the fuckin' thing.

He gave up.

He bent down – he was grand. He got his hand under the dog and picked it up. It was nearly weightless.

Brian was watching.

—What's it called again?

—Cindy, said Brian.

—That's right, said Jimmy.—Stupid name.

He felt stronger now, more solid.

The dog turned a few times on his lap; she'd plenty of room. Then she lay down and curled up. He patted her back. The dog-in-law.

—What are you smiling at?

—Nothin'.

Hi.

He could feel his heart. Like he'd been running. He searched the rest of the page but he knew there was nothing else. No attachment, or a sentence pushed down to the bottom of the page by the Enter key. There was just the one word – and the name.

Les.

Christ. Oh, Christ.

His phone rang. It seemed to hop off the pillow as he was staring at Les's name. It was his da.

—Jimmy?

—Howyeh.

—It's me.

—Yeah.

—Your mother was wonderin' how yeh were.

—I'm grand.

—Good to be home, I'd say, is it?

—Great, yeah.

—Are yeh able to eat an' tha'?

—Yeah, no bother.

—Food, like.

—Yeah, I know wha' yeh mean.

—So, that's good, said Jimmy Sr.

—Yeah. No, I'm grand.

—How's everyone?

—Grand.

—Glad to see yeh home?

—Ah yeah.

—Great, that's great.

—Thanks, Da.

—I'll leave yeh alone. Good luck.

—Thanks for phonin'.

—No bother.

He didn't know why he hadn't told his da about Les's email. And his ma. He could phone them now; they'd be delighted.

No.

His heart was still hopping.

He had to get more from Les first. *Hi.* There had to be more than that.

He shut the laptop. He closed his eyes.

—He wants a sat nav.

—He doesn't have a fuckin' car.

—I don't think that's the point, said Aoife.

He watched her whisking the eggs. He'd woken up wanting scrambled eggs. And batch. There'd been eggs in the fridge and she'd gone down to the Spar for the bread.

—What use would a sat nav be to him? he asked.

—Why does it matter?

Brian's letter to Santa was on the table in front of him.

Dear Santa, I hope you are well. I want a Sat Nav. One that won't break easy. And a Xbox game that is appopiate for my age.

84

I'm nearly 11. Thank you very much. Yours sincerely. Brian Egan-Rabbitte.

He was crying again.

She didn't notice.

He was sick of the tears. He just wished the kids would stop growing up. Or, Brian anyway. He'd have been happy enough with one child to hold onto.

The dog-in-law was at him again, trying to pull the tracksuit bottoms off him.

—Will I cut the toast into soldiers for you? she asked.

—No, he said.—You're grand. Just dump the egg —

He looked across and saw her waiting, grinning. She'd caught him out.

—Ah fuck off.

He had the laptop with him. He was going to go back to work, in the kitchen. That was the plan. For a couple of hours. He'd get rid of some emails, have a look at what Noeleen had been doing to the homepage while he'd been under the knife.

He googled sat nav.

—A hundred and twenty quid, he said.—Or a hundred and thirty.

He scrolled down the PC World page.

—That kind o' range, he told her.

She was emptying the eggs onto the toasted batch. The smell was a killer.

—Would they be cheaper in the North? she asked.

—I'd need a sat nav to find the fuckin' North, he said.

She laughed.

He was happy. There was no escaping it. Happy and starving. And the starving – it was great. Like his guts were moving, waking up, demanding to be filled. There was nothing wrong or missing. He wanted food.

—So, he said.

He looked at the PC World page again and had a closer look at one of the sat navs.

—It's a rechargeable battery, he said.—As far as I can make out. So that's grand. He'll be able to walk around with it. Find his way to school an' that.

He pushed the laptop aside to make room for the plate that was coming at him. He pushed the dog aside as well, with his foot.

Aoife put the plate down.

—Thanks, he said.

She put her hand on his head, then pulled him gently against her. Just for a second.

Fuck, he was starving.

—But, he said.

—What?

She sat down beside him. She was going to watch him eat.

—Do we really want him walkin' to school with a sat nav? Holdin' it out in front of him. Do we want to expose him to the slaggin' he'll definitely get?

He could eat now.

—Maybe there are others in his class getting the same thing, said Aoife.

—I doubt it, said Jimmy.

—Yes, she said.—I know. We'd be seeing all the ads.

—That's right.

—But, she said.—Brian is Brian.

—True, he said – he knew what she meant.—This is exactly what I needed, by the way.

—Thanks.

He examined the toast. It was nice and soft. He rolled it into a cigar.

She was staring at him. She pointed across at the cooker.

—Have I just been your mother over there?

—Fuck off.

She nodded at the rolled-up toast on its way to his mouth.

—You've never done that before, she said.—Not in front of me.

—Lay off, he said.—It was just an idea.

—An idea or a memory?

—Okay, he said.—A memory. It's just the once.

He shoved the toast, the whole roll, into his mouth, and regretted it. He was stuck. Stuck and fuckin' choking. Being killed by a scrambled egg. In front of the woman he loved. One of the women he —

He was having a fuckin' ball.

He swallowed the mush. There was nothing to it.

—Brian is Brian, he said.—An' fuck the begrudgers.

—An' fuck the fuckin' begrudgers.

He laughed. A speck of the toast flew onto her shoulder. She didn't see it.

—That's not a bad impression of me, he said.

—It wasn't you, she said.—It was your father.

She leaned the small bit over and kissed him.

—There's nothing quite as sexy as scrambled egg on a man's breath.

—Okay, he said.—Okay. Never again. So.

He nodded at the laptop.

—That's a sat nav for Brian.

—And a few small things.

—Grand, he said.—I'll be able to go into town. Next week – I'd say. Or the weekend. We can do it together.

—Great.

—What about the others? he said.

There'd be no madness, no more requests for toys that didn't exist, or toys that every other kid in the country wanted and expected. Jimmy had driven to Belfast one Saturday, searching for a Buzz Lightyear. This was ten years ago, maybe more. When travelling north was still a bit of an adventure, when you knew you were crossing the border. He'd been going to stop in Newry but he was behind all these other Dublin registrations, hundreds of them, most of them turning for Newry, and he decided they were all on the hunt for a Buzz. So he kept going up to Belfast, and there wasn't a Buzz to be had, not even a Unionist one. He was in a cafe, just about to get dug into his – fuckin' hell, he remembered – scrambled egg on toast, when Aoife had called him. Her friend, Tara, had phoned and told her that there were Buzz Lightyears in Wexford, a consignment of them straight off the Rosslare boat. So he'd finished his egg and driven the length of the country to Wexford, and he'd got the Buzz Lightyear. For Marvin. He'd got to the Toymaster door about two minutes before they were closing for the day.

—Bollix, he said.

—What's wrong?

He'd gone on to Ticketmaster, to get an Oxegen ticket for Marvin.

—They've cancelled Oxegen, he said.

—Yes, said Aoife.—They announced it last week.

—Any idea what Marv wants instead?

—No, she said.—You can ask him later.

—Okay. Grand. If I see him.

He thought of something.

—Look at this.

He turned the laptop, so she could see the screen.

—What am I to look at?

—That.

She leaned forward. She squinted – a bit. He decided not to slag her about her eyesight.

—Is this from your brother?

—Yeah.

—God.

She looked at him, and back at the screen.

—Is this all there is?

—Yeah.

—God, she said again.—It's a bit – I don't know. Chilling. Is it? Only one word.

—I know what you mean, he said.—I'm not even sure it's him.

—Ah, it has to be him, Jimmy. There are too many coincidences for it not to be.

She looked at the screen again. Her face was right down at it.

—Do you think it might be someone else?

—No, he said.—Not really.

—Or someone messing?

—No, he said.—And I don't think it's another Les Rabbitte. But – this is a bit mad. When I read it—. Not that there's much readin' in it. I thought – I wondered. Well, it felt like maybe it was his ghost.

—Ghost?

—Contactin' me from, like – the afterlife.

—God, Jimmy. It's a fucking email.

—I know, he said.—It's just the way it feels. After so long, I suppose.

—Back from the dead.

—A bit, he said.

—Are you going to answer him? she asked.

—Yeah, said Jimmy.—'Course.

He typed. *Hi, Les. Great to hear from you. It's been too long.*

—Is that goin' too far? he asked Aoife.

—What?

—It's been too long.

—Well, it's true, she said.—And it's nice. But yeah.

—Grand.

He deleted it and typed his mobile number. *Phone me if you like. There's something I need to tell you. We should catch up.*

—Fuck it, he said, and typed. *It's been too long.*

She smiled, and kissed the side of his face.

—Life's too fuckin' short, he said.

And he sent it.

Jesus, it was cold. It was fuckin' freezing. The grass was solid under him.

He was putting out the bin. It was green wheelie day tomorrow. He'd forget the names of his children but he'd always remember the bin days. And he wasn't even ashamed.

God, it was cold but. The tracksuit bottoms were useless; he didn't know how homeless people managed in this weather. There was already ice on the handle of the wheelie. He'd have to be careful, or they'd be coming out to pour warm water over his fingers, to free his hands from the ice. Or he'd be found dead, stuck to the wheelie.

He wasn't alone.

He was out on the road now, lining up the bin at the edge of the path, and he saw Conor from next door. At his car. His jeep. Putting something in the back.

—Alright, Conor?

Conor's head was still buried in the boot. Counting party hats or something.

—That's a cold one.

Your man said nothing back. He stood up straight, slammed the boot shut, and headed for his front door. He didn't even look at Jimmy – and he must have heard him. It was a cold, clear night; Jimmy's words had felt solid coming out of his mouth.

He was shutting his front door, Conor was, when a hand came back out, holding the car key, pointing it at the jeep. It clicked shut – *tink tunk* – right beside Jimmy. Then the front door quietly clicked shut. Fuck him. *My brother rode your missis.* The ignorance of that, pointing the key. *Or so he says.* He must have seen Jimmy; he couldn't not have.

He'd locked himself out. Jimmy had.

—Bollix.

He had to ring the bell. Fuck, he was freezing now.

He rang again. They were all in the living room, watching the telly – with him. They thought he'd gone to the jacks or to fill the kettle; he'd stood up during the ads.

He rang again. They wouldn't have heard it. He knocked on the glass. He was shaking now. He leaned across – nearly fell over – and knocked on the living-room window.

His mobile started purring against his thigh.

For fuck sake.

He got it out. He could hardly press the green button, his fingers were so cold.

—Hello?

—Jimmy?

—Yeah.

—It's Les.

The door opened.

—What are you doing out there?

It was Aoife.

Jimmy pointed at the mobile up against his ear, with a free finger.

—Les, he said.—Howyeh.

—Okay. Fine. You?

The voice meant nothing. Jimmy didn't know it. He got the door shut behind him.

—I'm grand, he said.—Great.

—Good.

—Where are yeh?

—I'm at home.

—Yeah —

—England. Basingstoke.

—I've heard of it.

—Yeah.

—Listen, it's great to hear you. Thanks for gettin' back.

He could feel it. He was – they were running out of things to say. Already.

—That's okay, said Les.

—No, it's great.

—You said there was something you needed to tell me. In the email.

—Fuck, yeah. I forgot.

He looked at Aoife closing the living-room door. She picked up the dog as she did it. He kept going, down to the kitchen. It was warmer in there.

—Look, he said.—You still there, Les?

—I'm here.

—Grand, said Jimmy.—So look. I've had a bit of a scare.

There was nothing from Les.

—Cancer, said Jimmy.

—Oh.

—I'm grand. I'm just out of the hospital actually. The bowel. He couldn't stop.

—The cancer, like. Cancer of the bowel. So anyway, they removed the – yeh know – the tumours an' it's lookin' good. Fingers crossed now.

—Yeah. Sorry to hear that. Jimmy.

—No. Thanks, by the way. Les. But I'm grand. Home again an' back at work. I can do that, work at home. So I'm grand. I was just puttin' the wheelie out when you rang there.

What the fuck was he saying?

He couldn't stop.

—So anyway, they said – the specialists, like – they said it might be hereditary. So Darren an' Da had the tests done there, and they're grand. They're both great, by the way. Ma an' Da. Yeh there?

—Yeah.

—An' I wanted to tell you. So – cos they say you should get one done as well.

—Too late.

—Wha'? Les?

—I had a biopsy. Four years ago.

—Oh. Good. An' you were grand?

—No.

The silence was roaring at him now. But Les broke it.

—Same as you.

—Bowel? said Jimmy.

—Yeah.

—God. Fuck. Jesus. And are yeh alright now?

—Yes. Yeah. There's been no recurrence.

He used the word – recurrence – like a pro, like he knew exactly what it meant.

—Good, said Jimmy.—Great.

The man had been dying, over in England. Jimmy knew nothing about him.

—Hope it works out for you, said Les.

—Thanks, said Jimmy.—Thanks, Les.

—Bye.

—I'll phone yeh when 1 find out —

—Fine, yeah. Bye.

Jimmy sat down. He had to.

Aoife was at the door. Holding the dog like your man from the old Bond film.

—How was that?

—Weird, he said.—Great. Fuckin' awful.

—Do you want to talk about it?

—No, he said.—Tomorrow. It's too much.

—Okay, she said.—It must be strange.

—Yeah. Yeah.

—What were you doing outside? she asked.

—Wha'? Oh. I was puttin' the green wheelie out.

—Ah, Jimmy. For God's sake. One of us could have done that.

—I wanted to do it, he said.

It was true.

She smiled. She patted the dog.

—When's that thing goin' back to its mammy? he said.

—When its mammy gets home from its cruise. Sorry, her cruise.

—Heard yeh the first time.

—Fuck off.

—The fucker.

—That's a bit strong.

—No, he said.—Les. He's the fucker.

—Why?

He'd never told them – Jimmy, Darren or their da; the family males – about the cancer. They could all have had biopsies done back then. Four years ago. It could have been discovered, in him, way earlier.

And he wasn't even angry.

Something had woken him. Something outside.

It was quiet – no wind or anything. He looked at the clock beside him. He brought it a bit nearer. 2.43.

Then he heard it again, what he knew he'd heard. Metal bending, or buckling.

He got up. No bother. A bit stiff, a small bit sore. He went around the bed, to the window.

Someone was laughing now. Definitely.

He leaned over the dressing table and pulled back the curtain. There was a guy, a young lad, standing on the roof of Jimmy's car. And another lad at the gate, with a bike, one foot on the ground. Jimmy could tell, he was the one who'd laughed. He was nervous.

Your man on the roof was doing something. He'd started to pull down his tracksuit bottoms – they were like Jimmy's. And the fella with the bike had his phone out now – an iPhone, it looked like – and he was filming your man on the roof, and your man on the roof was bending his legs at the knees – the fucker was squatting and he was going to take a dump on the roof of Jimmy's car.

—Hey!

He wasn't loud enough – they hadn't heard. He pulled the curtain back properly. He pulled at the handle of the window. It was a bit stiff – he was sweating. The dressing table was in the way.

But he got the window open.

They looked up, the lads. They'd heard it.

—Fuck off out o' tha', he said.

He didn't shout. He wasn't outraged. He didn't want to wake the neighbours or Aoife. It was already becoming a story for his da – and Marvin and young Jimmy. He wondered if they knew this pair. It wasn't impossible.

Your man fell off – he slid off the roof. His pal on the bike was gone.

—Come here, said Jimmy.

Your man hesitated. He didn't stop. He was running, trying to run and pull up his bottoms. There was something about him; he wasn't all that worried. He looked back up at Jimmy and the window.

—Do it on the roof of the jeep over there. The green one.

But Conor's jeep wasn't there. It was gone. And so was your man with the shite. Jimmy could hear him and his pal at the end of the road, laughing. He stayed there a while longer but he shut the window. He looked across at Aoife. He hadn't woken her.

A pity about Conor's jeep.

Dying was great. No other consequences mattered. He didn't care if they'd heard him next door, if they were lying in the bed, appalled. It didn't matter.

93

He went around the bed, back to his own side. It was cold. He got in carefully, so his feet wouldn't wake Aoife.

Did he really believe that, that he was dying?

He did, yeah. Of course he did. He wasn't stupid.

—They've gone.

—Wha'?

—They've gone, said Aoife.—Just —

She shrugged. Then – she didn't start to cry. She was crying already. Her face was wet. He saw that now.

—What d'you mean gone? he asked.

He already knew what she meant. Conor and Sinéad next door had left. And the twins. During the night.

—Who told you? he asked.

She wiped her eyes with a sleeve. She was wearing one of his shirts.

—Angela.

—Who?

—Across the road.

—Who?

—Angela, she said.—You know. You hate her.

—Who? he said.—I don't.

—You said she's a fucking eejit.

—Doesn't mean I hate her, he said.—What did she say?

—Sinéad told her. They had to get out.

—They were fuckin' evicted?

—No, said Aoife.—I don't think it's that—. But they're in trouble. It's being repossessed. The house.

—Jesus.

—You never liked them, she said.

—That's not true.

—It is.

—It isn't, he said.—Anyway, you weren't mad about them either.

—That's not the point.

—Exactly.

—Well, they're gone.

She wasn't looking at him.

—It's sad, he said.

It was a lot more than that. It was becoming frightening, even before he'd had time to think properly about it.

—For God's sake, Jimmy.

—What?

—They're our neighbours and they had to run away.

—I know, he said.—I know. It's dreadful. I'm not even sure what havin' your house repossessed – what it involves. Do you?

—No.

—Thank Christ we actually own ours.

—Yes, she said.—But I think there was—. The business. Sinéad told Angela. Conor was struggling.

—What is it he does again?

—Catering, said Aoife.—Parties. Functions. I'm surprised you forgot that, Jimmy. Seeing as you sneered at him for it —

—I didn't.

—You did so.

—Okay, he said.—I had a go at him. But only after he'd made a big deal about me bein' from Barrytown.

—Sinéad's from Barrytown too.

Darren rode the arse off her.

—He was bein' a bollix, said Jimmy.—So, yeah. I was a bit snotty.

He'd asked Conor how he liked handing out cocktail sausages to the high-end cunts he'd gone to school with. And later, in bed, she'd laughed, Aoife had. Loud enough to be heard by Sinéad and Bozo through the bedroom wall. He decided not to remind her.

—But I'd nothin' against him, he said.—I didn't want his business to go belly up. For fuck sake.

He coughed.

—It's cancer of the bowel you have, Jimmy, said Aoife.—Not the lungs.

—I only fuckin' coughed.

She sighed.

—Sorry.

—Grand.

—You never liked them.

—You're wearin' my fuckin' shirt.

They stared for a while, but not at each other. Jimmy stared at the iPod dock on top of the fridge and she stared at the dog-in-law's basket.

—Sorry.

—Me too.

—It looks good on yeh.

—Thanks.

He sat down. She went to the fridge. He looked at the screen.

—What happens the house?

—Sinéad's?

—Yeah, said Jimmy.—I mean. Is it left empty or wha'?

—I don't know.

—Did they take their stuff? The furniture —

—I don't know.

She was away from the fridge, buttering slices of bread across at the counter. He looked at the clock. The kids would be in soon, early. It was clear in his head; their Christmas holidays started today.

—It looks the same, she said.—Exactly the same.

She was crying again.

—It's primitive, she said.—Isn't it?

—Yeah.

Aoife drove him in. He was going to the office do, his first time back since the operation. They didn't say much on the way but she kissed him before he got out of the car.

—Enjoy yourself.

—I'll try, he said.

He smiled, and she smiled. He opened the passenger door.

—The dog, he said.

—There's a truck behind me, she said.

The street was narrow and cobblestoned. It wasn't the spot for a conversation.

—She's home, isn't she?

Aoife was looking in the rear-view but she nodded. Someone behind the truck pressed the horn. The cunt thought he was in New York.

—So, said Jimmy.—The dog's ours, is it?

—Yep.

—And – ?

—Close the door, Jimmy. We can talk about this later.

He got out. He was okay – a bit stiff just.

—Did they even go on a fuckin' cruise?

—Think past the dog, Jimmy, for God's sake. Just shut the fucking door.

—Seeyeh.

He stopped on the steps before he went in. It was fuckin' cold. And dark. He had to bring the phone right up to his face. *What did u mean?* He fired it off to Aoife, and went in. He hated riddles, mysteries, answers that weren't fuckin' answers. She could fuck off.

He was wearing proper trousers for the first time since he'd got out of the hospital. They were a bit strange. Not tight – he'd actually lost a bit of weight. More, heavy. Like armour or something. And complicated.

It felt a bit weird being back. He wasn't ready to talk to the heads, to mingle, yet. He had a few quick glasses of mulled wine. *That'll teach her.* And he immediately had to go to the jacks. He'd been guzzling water all day. He was thirsty, dry-throated – all the time.

Noeleen was there when he got back.

—Either you hit the jackpot out there, Jimbo, or you just forgot, she said.

—Wha'?

—Your fly.

—Oh. Fuck. Thanks. It's got nothin' to do with the cancer, by the way.

What was he at?

—Must be Alzheimer's, she said.

—Probably, he said.—But it only happens when it's buttons. I never forget if it's a zip.

—Interesting.

A text went off in his pocket. It took him a while to get to the phone. He'd forgotten he was wearing trousers again, and the mulled muck had gone to his head. He'd burn the tracksuit when he got home. It was turning him into a toddler.

Noeleen was looking at him.

No. She wasn't.

It was just as well, because the text was from Imelda. Jesus Christ, he was fuckin' surrounded. He read it, brought it up to his eyes. *Wot do u meen wot did i meen?*

What was that about?

His head was swimming. Just a bit.

Now he got it. That text, the one he'd done outside on the steps – he'd sent it to Imelda instead of Aoife. He checked the Sent box and there it was.

Jesus.

He laughed.

The lad.

He'd have to be more careful. Conducting no affairs with a gang of women was a full-time job. He should have eaten before he came out. He shouldn't have come out.

But he was grand. He sat on his desk. He nearly missed it but no one noticed.

—Great to have you back, Jimmy, said the twit.

—Ah, thanks, eh —

He couldn't remember the twit's name.

—Are you back for good?

—Yeah, said Jimmy.—Yeah. I've the chemo to go. But fuck it. It's a man's world, wha'.

He slapped the twit's shoulder but kind of got him in the face instead.

—Fuck – sorry.

—No worries.

There was a new young one. The intern. She looked about ten. And forty. It was weird. She smiled at him. He thought he smiled back. He sat up straight. *I'm at work.* He stood up. That was better, more appropriate. More comfortable as well. *I'm the boss. Nearly the boss. I have trousers with buttons.*

Noeleen was beside him.

—So how's Jimbo?

—Jimbo's grand. How's Noely?

—She's savage.

—Grand.

His head had cleared a bit. He felt good again.

—How's it been? he asked.

—Well, *you're* fine, she told him.—You've seen that.

He hadn't, not really. But he nodded. Delight seeped through him – something like that. Or relief. He wanted to text Aoife. *We're fine.* He wanted to go home.

—Sales are holding up there, she said.—Well, they've dropped, but not drastically. The middle-aged are still finding the money to fund their nostalgia.

—It's kids that're buyin' the Dangerous Dream and the Legovers, said Jimmy.

She could shove her fuckin' nostalgia.

—True, she said.—But the Celtic Rock stuff.

98

Jimmy cringed. He actually did. The mulled wine was no protection. He had a stable of bitter old men who, forty years ago, had tried to fuse traditional music and rock. They'd failed, fuckin' miserably. But none of them knew it. Musically, they were dead by the time teenage Jimmy discovered the *NME* and started to eat it every week. These lads had never made the *NME*, or *Hot Press*. *Spotlight* had been their natural habitat, in beside the showbands. The Sons of the Fianna, the Minstrel Boys, the Bastards of Lir – Jimmy hated them all.

But they were his living – because Noeleen had told him to go after them. It was why she'd bought the site, or one of the reasons – she'd told him months later. For the Celtic part in kelticpunk. A portal to electrified diddley-eye. It had been hurtful, humiliating, just fuckin' desperate. But he'd done it. And he was selling buckets of their songs. They were helping him stand tall – kind of – beside his business partner. His fuckin' boss.

—They're our stars, she said.

—Jesus Christ, said Jimmy.—Don't ever tell them that.

He devoted one very long day a week to Celtic Rock. It was how he coped. The other bands were great, even the cunts – especially the cunts; the Halfbreds and some of the other old punks – because they knew they were lucky, even when they were complaining. They were having a great time. And they could all point to some contemporary sound or attitude and claim that they'd got there first.

—Who are your influences?

—The Legovers.

They were grateful to Jimmy, for the bit of recognition much more than the money. But the other fuckers, the Celtic rockers, all they could point to was the Corrs. Their struggle had been pointless. Pointless and just shite.

—But, said Noeleen.—Sales of anything recorded before 1982 have gone the same way as house prices. They've stopped. And with Oxegen cancelled —

—That's bad.

—The ticket to Oxegen isn't the Christmas present from Mummy and Daddy any more. And to think, it was a stocking filler three or four years ago. To go with the car or the pony.

—Not in our house, said Jimmy.

—I've four great new bands, said Noeleen,—and nowhere to send them next July. There'll be no giddy boys and girls on

99

Phantom or Spin telling the kids at home how hot they are. No displays in Tower. It's back to the drawing board, Jimbo.

—Don't worry about it, said Jimmy.

He gave her the *Apprentice* line.

—We'll hit the ground runnin'.

He hadn't a clue; he really didn't give a shite.

—It's the new austerity, Jimbo, she said.—Youth has been cancelled.

—Ah cop on, Noeleen, said Jimmy.—We'll be grand.

His sons would never get to Oxegen. That was a bit sad. It had been the twenty-first-century Irish kid's initiation, a weekend on a racecourse in Kildare, getting pissed and stoned, sleeping it off in a 15-euro tent while some of the world's biggest bands shook the place deeper into the muck. But now they'd never get there. And Mahalia – she wouldn't be going either. That was a relief.

Jimmy was going to cry. He couldn't drink; he was a fuckin' eejit.

The intern and the twit were working their way through the room with trays of cocktail sausages. Pity it wasn't Conor.

—What's funny?

—Nothin'.

He needed blotting paper, the bit of grub inside him. He'd learn the intern's name, and the twit's. He knew the twit's already; he'd been sitting beside him for more than a year. He'd remember it. He was back at work.

Noeleen was still there.

—Your optimism is infectious, Jimbo, she said, although she sounded like she was telling him the jacks was blocked.

—That'll be the drugs, said Jimmy.

He lifted his glass.

—Or this.

He knocked back the bit that was left, and swallowed a couple of cloves. He was sending darts down through the remaining twenty per cent of his bowel.

—There'll be no bonus this year, I'm afraid, said Noeleen.

Jimmy shrugged. Smiled. Shrugged.

—For either of us, she said.—Just so you know.

—Grand. Okay.

It was too late to bring back the Christmas presents. To un-buy them.

They'd be okay. They were making money. *He* was making

money. Jesus though, he hated money, thinking about it – the consequences. He'd have to tell Aoife. Of course, he would. Anyway, she missed nothing. She could read bank statements like they were novels.

The sausages gave him something to do. He grabbed three from the intern's plate.

—Thanks.

—You're wel-com!

She was American. How did that happen?

—What's your name, by the way?

—Ocean!

—Which one?

She said something back but he didn't hear her. He was busy with the sausages. He was fuckin' starving. It was amazing. He could feel them working, soaking up the poison. He wiped his mouth – missed it the first time.

The arse on Ocean.

Noeleen was still there.

—When does the chemo start? she asked him.—Do you mind my asking?

—No – you're grand, he said.—Middle of January.

The room was fuller. A lot of skinny young lads and the odd fatso – usually the drummer – in skinny jeans. Noeleen's new bands. And the skinny girlfriends. He saw some of his people as well. The Halfbreds – Connie (aka Brenda) and Barry – were over where the water cooler used to be, before it became unnecessary. They were hissing at each other. Jimmy waved. Connie waved back but Barry didn't. There was no sign of any of the Celtic Rock pricks. But Des Savage was there, the oldest drummer in the room. He liked Des. He'd go over to Des. He'd fill his glass on the way, or see if there was anything better. Beer or something.

—The bonus thing, he said to Noeleen.—That should've been a joint decision.

—You weren't here.

—Actually, Noeleen.

Think like Aoife, think like Aoife.

—That's no excuse, he said.

Perfect.

*   *   *

Then he woke up.

There was daylight – tomorrow. He was at home.

Thank fuck.

He couldn't remember anything. Not a fuckin' thing. His head – his brain – was dry, shrivelled, killing him.

Great.

He'd had a normal day. He was dying now, in a pre-cancer kind of way. Being punished for it. And it was great. He turned the pillow – he could manage that, just about – and lowered his head back down onto it.

He still couldn't remember a thing.

It was Christmas Eve. Loads to do.

Bollix to it. He didn't care. The big things were sorted.

There was the turkey – sorted.

He'd ended up in a Chinese place. There was a gang of them – he thought.

And the ham. It was in the fridge.

He could hear the telly under him and the dog yapping, and feet – Aoife's shoes, maybe Mahalia's. The fuckin' dog. He remembered now. It was theirs. He couldn't even remember its name. What was the story with the sister? Break-up? Money trouble?

He'd stood up and left the Chinese restaurant. He'd eaten a spring roll or something like a spring roll – he could taste it now – and he'd stood up. He remembered, the backs of his legs against the chair. He'd just walked away. He'd check now, in a minute, make sure he'd brought home his jacket and his wallet.

The phone. He lifted his head. It wasn't too bad. He leaned out. He usually left it on the floor beside him. It was there. He grabbed it and lay back. He wrote – he *composed* – a text. *Do I owe anyone money?* He fired it off to Noeleen.

He heard someone on the stairs. He listened to the door being opened quietly, slowly. The hinge needed oil.

—Awake?

—Good mornin', he said.—Is it mornin'?

—It's not that late, said Aoife.—It's eleven or so.

—I didn't wake anyone when I was comin' in, did I?

It was gloomy but he could see that she was smiling.

—Wha'?

—You really don't remember?

—What?

—We were all watching telly, she said.

102

—Oh.

—Do you remember now?

—No, he said.

—You were lovely.

—Was I?

He could feel himself getting hard. An erection! Christ. A blast from the fuckin' past.

He grabbed her – he grabbed his wife. She didn't object.

—Are you sure? she said.

It wasn't an objection. And she didn't object to him taking off her shirt – his shirt. He gave up on the buttons. She lifted her arms. Fuck, she was lovely when she did that. He sat up properly – he had to – to get the shirt over her head.

—The door.

He watched her stand and go to the door. For a horrible second, he thought she was going to keep going. But she was back on the bed, in beside him.

—Are you sure? she said.

—You asked that already.

—And you didn't answer me.

—If the stitches burst, or whatever, it might be manslaughter but definitely not murder.

—Oh, fine.

—I'll die happy.

—Stop.

—Why —

—No, not that! Don't stop.

—Make your fuckin' mind up.

—Was that your stomach? she asked.

—Ignore it.

—I am.

—I'm still alive, he said.

—Damn.

—You thought you'd ride me to death.

—That was the evil plan.

—I love you.

—I love you too.

—The dog —

—Forget about the dog.

—Okay.

—It's ours.

—Grand.

—You'll love it.

—Yeah.

The phone hopped. She leaned out and grabbed it. She brought it right up to her eyes. They were going blind together.

A name roared across him. *Imelda.*

—Noeleen, she said.

She handed it to him. He held it so she could read it too. *Not money but u owe someone apology. X*

—What does that mean? Aoife asked.

There was no edge in her voice.

—Fuck knows, he said.—I was locked.

—You're never drunk.

—I know.

—It was lovely.

—Grand.

—You were funny.

—Hang on.

He wrote one back. *Why?*

—Don't forget the X, said Aoife.

—Oh yeah. *X*

He fired it off.

He was falling asleep. She was so warm beside him, hot.

She sighed.

—What?

—I was just thinking about Sinéad.

He edged away from her, slightly. He was wide awake and getting hard again. Women's names – Christ. They were the best thing about them.

—It's bad, he said.

Broken glass, Mother Teresa.

—The worst thing about it, said Aoife.—It's selfish but – Sinéad.

Enda Kenny, broken glass.

—She told Angela. Not me.

—You didn't know her that well, he said.—Did you?

She didn't answer.

—Are you cryin'? Aoife?

—No.

The phone hopped again.

—Why? said Aoife.

—Why what? said Jimmy.—I don't follow yeh.

He was nervous now. Words were dangerous.

—Why didn't I know her that well? said Aoife.

—I don't know, said Jimmy.—Yeh can't know everyone.

—For God's sake.

She was moving, getting up.

—Hang on, he said.—Am I bein' blamed for this?

She was standing now. She was putting on his shirt. The door was open. She was gone.

He'd get up.

He could see her point of view. He thought he could. But they'd both agreed, Conor was a wanker. It had been a joint agreement.

He found the phone and read the text. *U kept callin Ocean Atlantic. X*

Is that all? X

He'd had sex. He'd just made love. He was still alive.

The phone again. He unlocked it. *No.*

It could wait. It, she, fuckin' they. He'd remember what he'd done and he'd deal with it.

He got out of the bed and found his tracksuit bottoms. He went across to the bathroom.

Brian was on the stairs.

—Alright, Smoke?

He was standing there, waiting for Jimmy.

Waiting for his dad to be his dad.

—What'll we do today?

—Don't know.

—Excited?

—Yeah.

—It doesn't do upstairses.

—What?

Jimmy had been dropping off to sleep again. He couldn't believe he was up this early, although it happened every fuckin' Christmas.

—It doesn't show you when you're going up the stairs, said Brian.

—The sat nav? said Jimmy.

—Yeah, said Brian.

He sounded disappointed.

—Well, look it, said Jimmy.—It's designed for cars. It's rare enough you'd need to be drivin' upstairs in a house.

—S'pose.

—Why are yeh dressed like that? The heat's on, isn't it?

Brian had his jacket over his pyjamas and – Jimmy saw now – he was wearing his school shoes.

—I'm going out to test it.

He was holding the sat nav in both hands, like a steering wheel. Jimmy looked at his watch.

—It's only half-five, Smoke. You'll have to wait till it's bright outside.

—That's not for ages.

—No.

—Please.

Aoife was behind Brian now.

—Why don't you ask your dad to go with you? she said.

—Okay, said Jimmy.—I give up.

He stood up, no bother.

—Come on, Smoke.

—No, you don't, said Aoife.—Open your present first.

—I thought I did, said Jimmy.—Did I not?

There were socks, a box set – *The Killing* – and a Liverpool mug. A crumby enough haul.

—No, look, she said.

She leaned across the back of the couch and found another package under the pile of wrapping paper. She handed it to him.

—Thanks.

It was soft. A jumper or something. She'd never done that before, bought him clothes, tried to dress him. He tore through the wrapping paper, the way real men and boys did it.

It was a tracksuit.

A fuckin' tracksuit. It was purple, and some sort of velvet – the word popped up: velour.

—Do you like it?

—Eh —

—I thought you'd like another one. So you can wash the other one now and again.

She was slagging him, the bitch, and telling him to start dressing like an adult again.

—It's lovely, he said.

—You can wear it out now.

It was dark outside – safe.

—Great idea, he said.—I'll break it in. Actually, I might wear it to mass.

Jesus, it was cold but. He walked down the road with Brian and got excited with him when they came to the first corner, and there it was, on the sat nav.

—Brilliant.

They took the left and watched themselves taking it.

—Coolio.

—Here, Smoke, tell it where we're goin' and it'll tell us where to go.

Brian impressed Jimmy, the way all his kids did, with his ability to negotiate the buttons, the confidence, the effortless speed. No grunting from this boy.

—Where're we goin'? he asked.

—The Spar, said Smokey.

—It's only over there.

—Drive forward, said the sat nav.

The voice was posh and reassuring, like an Aer Lingus pilot's.

—Can you choose the voice? Jimmy asked.

—Yeah, said Brian.—Think so.

—Bob Dylan did it, I think.

—Who?

—Oh God. D'yeh have to pay for a different voice?

—Don't know.

—I'll pay for Dylan if you want.

They'd found the Spar and were going on to Brian's school. Jimmy looked at his velour legs. He was going to tell her the truth: they were comfortable.

Brian turned right.

—The wrong way, Smoke.

—I know.

—Turn left, said the voice.

Brian kept going.

—Turn *left*, said the voice.

Brian looked down at the sat nav.

—Fuck off, he said, and laughed.

He looked at Jimmy. And Jimmy laughed too.

—It's brilliant, Dad, said Brian.

Six in the morning, out with his youngest, disobeying a brand new sat nav. And none of it had been his idea. He breathed deep; he hauled the tears back in. This was his Christmas present.

—Turn *left*.

—Will it break if you keep pissin' it off?

—Don't be stupid, Dad.

—About turn and proceed.

—That's more like it, said Brian.—It's really cool.

They turned back and proceeded.

The phone gave him a jolt. He'd been falling asleep.

He found the zip – another zip; for fuck sake – and got the phone out.

—Hello?

—Jimmy?

—Yeah. Is that Les?

—Yes.

—Great. How are yeh, Les?

—Fine. I'm good. You?

—Good, yeah. Grand. Happy Christmas.

—You too, yeah. Merry Christmas. To you and your family.

—And yours, said Jimmy.—How's your day goin'?

—Good, yeah, said Les.—Fine.

—How's the family?

The line wasn't great. There was a bit of a buzz. Les wasn't answering.

—Was Santy good to yeh, Les?

—I did alright, said Les.

Jimmy thought he heard him laugh, but he wasn't certain. The line was shite.

—How's Maisie?

—She's fine, said Les.—Look, I've to go.

—Okay, said Jimmy.—Great to hear your voice, Les. Happy Christmas. Tell your —

—Bye.

He was gone. The prick.

No.

It was brilliant. It was. Distressing and brilliant.

*   *   *

He was the dad, not the cancer patient. He couldn't be the first to go up to bed. But then Brian fell asleep during *Downton Abbey*. What a load of shite that was; he didn't blame Brian for passing out. He was doing the same, except the dog kept at him, wanting Jimmy to pick up its present, a pig with a squeak, so it could bark and demand it back, the fuckin' eejit. Then young Jimmy surrendered and went upstairs, and Jimmy decided it was okay for him to stand up —

The dog landed on its back.

—Jimmy!

—Wha'?

—The dog – for God's sake!

—Is it not supposed to land on its feet?

—That's, like, cats, said Mahalia.—Hello.

—He's grand, look.

—She.

—Wha'ev-errr, said Jimmy.

That got a laugh, so he didn't feel too much of a cripple as he kissed the women goodnight and put his hand on Marvin's head as he passed him. But he felt like one by the time he got up the stairs. Not in the legs. They were grand. It was the breath, the lungs – he supposed. He was puffing.

He'd been warned about it – by one of the Celtic Rock wankers, Ned O'Hanlon. He'd told Jimmy. He'd held onto Jimmy's elbow all the time he'd spoken to him, his face bang up against Jimmy's. He'd told Jimmy that he'd been through it himself. This was at the office do; Jimmy remembered this bit.

—I thought it had gone to the lungs, Ned had told him.

—Yeah.

—But it was the anxiety – the breathlessness. Because, let's face it, you're fighting for your life. Aren't you?

—Yeah.

—It has to come out somewhere.

—Yeah.

—Don't worry about it.

—No.

Jimmy's eyes were swimming a bit; your man's face was right up against his.

—You'll be fine, said Ned.—You have the spirit.

He let go of Jimmy's elbow and put his hand, palm open, on Jimmy's chest, where his heart was – Jimmy wasn't sure. It was terrible. It was fuckin' excruciating.

Ned was looking at something over Jimmy's shoulder. Jimmy looked. It was the intern, and she'd rescued him.

—Her name's Ocean, he told Ned.

—Yes, said Ned.

—Some arse on her, wha'.

—Steady on, Jimmy.

Anyway, that was the breathlessness sorted. And he needed exercise. The specialist – Jimmy couldn't remember his name – the doctor who was a mister, had told him. He had to stay fit, or get fit for the first time since he'd given up the football thirty years ago. Mister Dunwoody.

The cunt.

He slid out of the velour and climbed into the bed. He lay back. But something stopped him. Something hard hit against his feet. He tried pushing it off the bed but it wouldn't budge. It was tucked in, tangled in the duvet.

—Fuck it.

He leaned across, turned the light on. He sat up and pulled off the duvet.

It was a suitcase. That was what it looked like, black and rectangular. But it was too narrow, like a suitcase had been sawed down the middle. He pulled it towards him. It wasn't heavy but it didn't feel empty. It was quite thick, deep – like a suitcase again. He opened it, pulled the zip across the front.

—Fuckin' hell.

It was a trumpet. A fuckin' trumpet. It was a beautiful thing, shining brass, in its red plush coffin. He picked it up. It felt heavier than the case had. It was cold too. He put his cheek against the horn – he caught himself doing it. It was amazing, though, the most beautiful thing he'd ever held. It was definitely a woman.

—Do you like it?

It was Aoife. He hadn't heard her.

—Is it mine?

He knew he sounded stupid, but it was hard to think that he could actually own one of these.

—Yes, she said.—It's yours. Keepies.

—It's gorgeous.

—Yes, she said.

He'd seen a trumpet before, of course. An oul' lad in his first band – Joey the Lips Fagan – had been a trumpet player, and there'd been a trumpet in two of his later bands. But he'd never held one. He brought it up to his mouth.

—Where's the yoke? The mouthpiece.

It wasn't there. The trumpet looked unfinished, a bit useless, without it.

—It's separate, said Aoife.

She pointed at the case.

—See? It has its own little space.

Jimmy took the mouthpiece from the case.

—He said to be sure not to put it in too tightly, said Aoife.

—Sound advice.

He put it to his mouth.

He changed his mind. He took it away.

—Are you not going to give it a go?

—No, he said.—Not now. It'll be terrible. Tomorrow, I'll try it. But not now.

He looked properly at her.

—Jesus, Aoife. Thanks.

—You're welcome.

—It's just – amazin'.

—I know.

He pulled out the mouthpiece and put it back in its hole.

—It's funny, he said.—I don't even know how to hold it properly.

—You can have lessons.

—Yep.

He put the trumpet back into the case.

—He said you —

—Who?

—The man I bought the trumpet from. He said you'd be able to play a tune by next Christmas.

—Great.

He looked at her.

—Brilliant.

He closed the case and zipped it.

—You like it, so?

—It's—, he said.—Well – it's perfect.

—Good.

—And it looks perfect.

—It does, doesn't it?

—Yeah.

—And sexy.

—Oh yeah.

She picked up the velour.

—So, she said.—Do you like your new cancer trousers?

—Fuck off now.

He'd whacked Ned.

That fact whacked him at his mother's. It shook him. He couldn't remember ever hitting anyone. Anyone else – ever. He'd always avoided fights, and no one had ever really started on him. In a pub or club, or a taxi rank – the usual places – the queue in the chipper. He'd never picked a fight that needed a boot or a fist.

But there it was.

He looked at his right hand. There were no marks or cuts, no sudden pain to match the clout of the memory.

But he'd whacked the man. Outside, after the office do. It was there in his head, something that had definitely happened.

The house was packed. It was the same every Stephen's Day. All the kids and grandkids, the wives, husbands, and the latest life partners. It had started years ago, when Jimmy and his sister, Sharon, had first moved out. They'd eat the stuff left over from Christmas Day. Now though, there weren't enough leftovers. It was a whole new turkey, more spuds, ham, the works and the leftovers. They ate in shifts or standing up, or on the stairs. A couple of the kids even ate on the street, holding their plates and kicking a ball.

—This is our big day now, his ma had told him.

She spoke quietly.

—How are yeh, love?

—Grand.

—No, she said.—Listen to me. I've been livin' too long with your father. How are you – really?

His ma had shrunk. She was in under his chin, a hand on his chest and a hand on his back, the way he'd often held onto his own kids.

—Really, he said.—I'm grand.

—Grand, she said.—I hate that bloody word.

His da was pretending to count the grandkids.

—You're new, he said to Brian.

112

—I'm not, Grandda.

—Well, yeh weren't here last year.

—I was.

—And which one is your da?

Brian pointed.

—Him.

—Far as yeh know, said Jimmy's da.

His ma let go of Jimmy.

—In you go. If you can find a bit of space.

His sisters and brother – *No Les!* – and the other adults all hugged him carefully or shook his hand, carefully, and gave him enough space to park a car. They were just being considerate but he found himself in front of the only empty chair in the house, probably in Barrytown, and surrounded by loved ones who were waiting to see if he'd manage to sit without his guts spilling onto the carpet.

He stayed standing.

Ned had been walking ahead of him. Jimmy had held back, just for a few seconds. He was getting used to the air, and waiting till he thought he'd be able to walk without strolling out onto the road. But he was fine, he was grand. He was getting the hang of simple things again, how to walk with people close to him, how to talk to more than one person at a time, how not to panic, how not to give up and just go home, how not to worry about the taste of the mulled wine that kept coming back up at him.

He was grand. He was grand.

—Alright, Jimmy?

—Grand, yeah. I'm just waitin' on Des.

—He's ahead of us, look.

—Oh, grand.

He could walk. He was fine.

—Sorry.

He'd bumped into someone – the twit.

—No worries.

He'd been walking. There'd been nothing to it. Easy.

There were women ahead. He'd catch up. He'd soak up their sympathy and love. The mulled wine was there again, a ball of it bursting at the top of his throat. He kept going, though. He was grand. There was Noeleen. And girlfriends and wives. He'd nearly caught up. And he saw Ned's hand. Sliding down the back of your woman Ocean's jacket, down towards her arse. And Jimmy grabbed Ned's arm, kind of leaned forward – he remembered this – like he was crossing a finishing line or something. Ned turned and Jimmy thumped him – no, slapped him. That was it – he'd slapped Ned across the face. Jimmy could feel the beard on his open hand.

He squeezed his eyes shut.

—You alrigh'?

It was his da. Worried. Quiet.

—Yeah, said Jimmy.—I'm grand.

His eyes were open again. He looked at his da.

—I just remembered somethin', he said.

—Oh-oh.

They were side by side at the table.

—D'yeh know wha'? his da said now.

—Wha'?

—I see a man cringin' like tha'. The way you were now. Yeah?

—Okay. Yeah. Go on.

—Well, I say to myself, there's a man who's nearly back to normal. He's done somethin' stupid. Am I righ'?

—Yeah.

—I knew it, said his da.—An' between you, me an' the fuckin' wall —

He looked around, like he was in a shite film, checking to see if anyone was earwigging. Then he leaned in, even closer to Jimmy.

—I'm delighted, he said.—That's all I'll say.

—Thanks.

—Is it serious?

—No, said Jimmy.—No. Not really.

—It won't kill yeh?

—No.

—Grand.

He'd slapped the cunt twice. At least. He remembered being pulled away, and someone getting between the two of them. It was the father in him. He'd explained it – he'd tried to, to Noeleen.

—When I saw his hand.

—Okay, listen —

—I just saw red. He's twice – he's fuckin' three or four times her age.

—I know, she'd said.—And here's what, Jimbo. It's exactly where you wanted to put your own hand. Now, for God's sake, listen —

He smiled at his da.

—I'll mingle, he said.

—Good luck, said his da.

He didn't know how many were in the house. He actually didn't know how many there were in the family. There were his sisters, Sharon, and the twins, Linda and Tracy. There was his brother, Darren. *Where's Les!* There was his gang, the kids and Aoife. There was Sharon's young one, Gina, tall and gorgeous and twenty-one, and Sharon's other kid, Craig. Her husband, Martin, had become her ex-husband since last Christmas, so they wouldn't be seeing him again. Martin had seemed alright when Jimmy had met him the first few times, but he'd turned out to be a bollix. Mean with the money, and just plain mean. But Sharon had stuck with him for a while – a good while. Craig must have been fourteen now, and Martin had only left some time in the summer. Anyway, he was gone, so that was one less.

—What're yeh doin'?

It was his da again.

—Countin' the family, said Jimmy.

—Why?

—Just curious.

—How many is there?

—I'm not finished, said Jimmy.—Eleven so far.

—Did yeh subtract tha' culchie cunt?

That was Martin.

—I did, yeah.

There was Darren's pregnant Melanie, and their two, Fay and Fergal. That brought it up to fourteen. Should he include the unborn kid? Better not, he decided. Just in case.

—What're you smilin' at?

—Nothin'.

There were his ma and da. Sixteen. Melanie was already huge, even though she wasn't all that pregnant – Jimmy wasn't sure. Time had gone weird on him. It was the way she was moving, and the colour of her face. She looked colossal. And lovely.

There was his other sisters, the twins. They were identical but one of them had five kids and the other was a lesbian. How had that happened? They'd been mad about the same boybands and real boys when they were thirteen or so, the last time Jimmy had really known them. Anyway, there was Tracy's five, Glen, Alex, Shauna, Jordy and he couldn't remember the name of the youngest, the bullet-headed little bastard who'd charged into him earlier.

Five kids, and she was only thirty-three or so. The young one, the only girl, was following Mahalia everywhere, holding onto Mahalia's new H & M hoodie. There was Glen Sr, Tracy's husband. He was usually out the back, smoking and avoiding everyone. He was okay, the few times Jimmy had actually spoken to him. That made twenty-two – he thought. Then there was Linda's partner, Louise. This was her third Stephen's Day, so she qualified.

—She's sound enough, his da had said once, when Jimmy had asked him what he thought.

—You've no problem with her?

His da shrugged.

—No, he said.—I wish she was better lookin'. A bit more – yeh know. I'd love to be able to flirt with my daughter's wife, yeh know. But she's grand. She's good for Linda.

—What does tha' mean?

—I don't know, to be honest. Your mammy said it. So that's the line. I'll tell yeh but. She plays a great game o' pitch an' putt.

—Wha'?!

—Wha' d'yeh mean, Wha'?

—You play pitch an' putt with a lesbian?

—I'll play pitch an' putt with annyone. Is there a rule tha' says I can't?

So Louise made it twenty-three.

The twins weren't nearly as identical as they used to be. There was more of Tracy, but she looked happier, or at least smilier. Linda didn't look unhappy, and maybe she'd just had less to drink than Tracy. Glen Sr must have been the designated driver, wherever he was. Out in their mini-van, waiting for it all to end.

Anyway, Louise had two kids, Max and Faith, and she'd brought them with her. They were both adults, and they lived in New York – or they used to – with their dad. This was the first time Jimmy had seen them.

Darren was beside him.

—What d'you make of Mad Max?

—He hasn't said a word.

—Gas, isn't it? His mother's gay, his father's a vegan and he thinks he's walked into a house full of weirdos. He's terrified.

—Your woman can't be a vegan too, can she?

—Faith?

—Yeah.

—Doubt it.

116

—She's a big girl, said Jimmy.—It's a nice name, isn't it? Faith.

—She's an atheist.

—I wasn't watchin' them eat, were you?

—I was, yeah, said Darren.

—Did they eat the turkey an' ham?

—Well, Beyond the Thunderdome ate nothin'.

—At all?

—At all.

—Jaysis. An' Faith?

—She ate her own and his.

—Excellent.

It was the strange thing about being in a packed room. You could talk away and no one heard you.

—His first.

—Wha'?

—She wolfed Max's dinner first, said Darren.—Took a breath, then went down on her own.

—Brilliant. How's Melanie?

Darren looked at Jimmy over the top of his glasses.

—She's fine.

—Good. She looks great.

There was a scream. The house was full of screams. No one really gave a fuck. Even the women had copped on. The kids would sort themselves out.

—How are you? Darren asked him.

—I'm grand, said Jimmy.—I got a trumpet for Christmas.

—I got a train set, said Darren.—But I don't have cancer.

—Neither do I, said Jimmy.

Darren was looking at him over his specs again.

—Why don't yeh get lenses, Darren?

He was a superior little cunt sometimes.

—D'you even need those fuckin' glasses? You spend most of your time lookin' over them.

—You don't have cancer? said Darren.

—No, said Jimmy.—I don't. I used to. That's the way I'm lookin' at it.

—When does the chemo start?

—Couple of weeks.

—What does it involve?

—Happy Christmas, Darren.

—Okay, said Darren.—Sorry.

117

—Grand, said Jimmy.—What d'yeh think but? Do I include Faith an' Thunderdome in the family?

—I'm not with you.

—I've been countin' everyone, said Jimmy.—Kind of a census, like. Like Bethlehem – is tha' the place?

—No room at the inn.

—So I was just countin'. Seein' how many are actually in the family. Martin's out, yeah?

—Okay.

—An' Louise is in.

—Agreed.

—But what about her kids? Are they family?

—No.

—Why not?

—Well, okay.

—You understand my predicament.

—There's no blood connection, said Darren.

—Okay, said Jimmy.—But what if one of us was adopted? Would we be turfed out?

—No.

—So?

—Well —

One of Darren's kids was beside Darren. Jimmy hadn't seen him arriving.

—Howyeh, Fergie.

—Hi.

—What's up, Fergal? said Darren.

—Can I have another Coke?

Darren looked a bit embarrassed. Jimmy loved that. And he wouldn't be telling Darren that it was a reasonable and regular question in his house too.

—Did you ask Melanie? said Darren.

—She said No.

—And I'm saying No, said Darren.—But I won't be going into the kitchen any time soon.

—Cool.

Fergal was gone.

—You handled tha' well, Darren.

—Fuck off, said Darren.

—So, said Jimmy.—Seriously now. Are Faith and Max family?

—No.

118

—Ever?

—Not yet.

—I'm with yeh, said Jimmy.—A few more years, a few more visits.

—Yeah, said Darren.—That seems to make sense.

—That's twenty-three so, said Jimmy.—I'm surprised. I expected more.

—Yeah, Darren agreed.

Jimmy made his mind up.

—I wonder how many kids Les has, he said.

—One, said Darren.

—D'yeh think so?

Darren looked at him over the specs – then properly.

—I know, he said.

—Maisie, said Jimmy.

—Yeah.

—Lovely name.

—Yeah.

—How did yeh know? Jimmy asked.

He didn't know what he felt – how to feel. Robbed. Guilty. Relieved. Fuckin' useless.

—We've been in touch.

—You an' Les.

—Yeah.

—Me too, said Jimmy.

It had never occurred to him that Darren and Les would have been talking to each other, that Darren would have contacted Les, or Les would have contacted Darren. It made sense. It made sense! They were brothers, for fuck sake, closer in age than Jimmy was to Les.

—Have you seen him? Jimmy asked.

Darren didn't answer quickly.

—No.

—Phone?

—Yeah.

—Me too, said Jimmy.

He hated hearing himself.

—Is he alright? he asked.—D'you think?

—Yeah, said Darren.—Yeah.

He wasn't holding anything back; Jimmy didn't think he was.

—Is he married?

—No.

—That's twenty-five so. In the family.

—Right.

Mahalia was passing through, with Tracy's Shauna and Darren's Fay hanging onto her. And, he saw now as well, Mahalia was trailing Sharon's Gina. And – Jesus – Gina was following Max.

—Christ, Mahalia, said Darren.—You're taller than your mother.

—That's, like, no big achievement, said Mahalia.

Darren laughed – he burst out laughing. Jimmy wanted to hug Mahalia.

He put it to his mouth, and blew. But nothing came out. Just the sound of his breath.

He tried again. Deep breath.

Nothing.

He'd watched a guy on YouTube explaining how to get sound from the trumpet. It was the lips – the aperture. Say M, your man said, then smile. Then blow.

—Mmmmmm.

Nothing.

Maybe his smile wasn't convincing enough. He was faking it.

—Mmmmmm.

There were white spots, and he had to sit on the side of the bath till they went.

He was grand again; he wouldn't be fainting. The smile had been too big, too desperate, like your man's in Wallace & Gromit. He made it smaller, take it or leave it.

He blew.

He heard a cheer from downstairs, and applause.

He phoned Des. But Des had been ahead of the rest, and he'd changed his mind about going to the Chinese. He'd got into a taxi instead, and gone home.

—Alone?

—Unfortunately.

—So you saw nothin'?

—Saw nothing, heard nothing.

—Okay, said Jimmy. You don't know anyone that teaches trumpet, do yeh, Des?

—No.

He phoned Noeleen.

—Jimbo.

—Howyeh.

—How was Christmas?

—Grand. Great. Quiet. You?

—Same here. So.

—Do I have to phone Ned?

—Strange question, Jimbo.

—I know. But. Did I apologise to him?

—No.

—How was he?

—Angry.

—Okay.

—Phone him.

—Okay.

—It's been nearly a week.

—I know. I'll phone him.

—And you're in tomorrow?

—Yeah.

—We'll talk.

That sounded a bit ominous.

—Yeah.

He sat on the bath, the trumpet in one hand – it was so fuckin' cool – and his phone in the other. He found Ned's number.

—Hello?

—Ned.

—Yes?

—It's Jimmy. Rabbitte.

—Ah.

—I owe you an apology.

—Ah.

—I'm sorry, said Jimmy.—I was out of my face. I'm not excusin' myself now. I shouldn't've hit you.

He shouldn't have said that, reminded the poor man that he'd given him the slaps.

—So look it, he said.—I'm sorry.

—Thank you, Jimmy, said Ned.

—Yeah, well, said Jimmy.

He looked at himself holding the trumpet. He liked what he saw. The chemo could fuck off.

—I meant to phone you earlier, he said.—But it took—. The drugs, yeh know. The painkillers.

Shut up, for fuck sake.

—I probably shouldn't have been drinkin' at all, he said.

—Forget about it, said Ned.—It never happened.

—Fair play, Ned. Thanks.

—But, said Ned.—I'm just thinking. It might be an idea to apologise to Ocean too.

Fuckin' why?

—I'll do that, Ned. Good idea. I'll do it when I see her.

—Hold on, Jimmy. I'm just passing the phone over to her now.

—Hi, Jimmy!

He hung up and got out of the bathroom. It was becoming a David Lynch film in there. He went into the bedroom and lay back on the bed.

Aoife was sitting beside him when he woke and knew he'd been sleeping. It was cold, and dark.

—Jesus, it's freezin'.

He was trying to climb in under the duvet.

—Your shoes, Jimmy.

He got them off, dropped them on the floor.

—Get in with me.

—Dinner's ready.

—I'm your starter, said Jimmy.

He moved across the bed, onto the trumpet.

—Fuck, sorry – me trumpet.

—God, you're sleeping with it now.

—I'm not.

—I don't know, she said.—I'm jealous.

—No need to be, he said.—It's a hard oul' hole.

—Ah Jimmy!

—Only messin'.

He held her.

—Warm me up, nurse.

Her arse was in his lap. He put an arm around her and pulled her nearer.

—It's pizza.

—Lovely.

He pulled her even closer. She didn't object. He could feel the material; she was wearing one of his shirts again.

—Listen, he said.—I'm in a bit of a moral dilemma.

122

She didn't move but she definitely seemed to be further away.

—It's not what you might think, he said.

—I've no idea what I might think, she said.

—I want your advice, he said.

—Go on.

He told her what he'd seen on the street after the do, and how he'd whacked Ned. He said whacked, not slapped. He told her about the call to Noeleen and the call to Ned.

—And she was with him.

—Who?

—The Ocean one, said Jimmy.

—With this Ned guy?

She started to sit up.

—Yeah, he said.—He handed the phone to her.

—God, said Aoife.—The fucking monster. What did you say to her?

—Nothin'. I just hung up.

—You should have told her to get out of that man's house as quickly as possible. Where does he live?

Quite close was the answer but he wasn't going to tell Aoife that.

—The thing is though, he said.—It isn't illegal.

—It should be, said Aoife.

—Why?

—It's obvious. The age difference. He's exploiting her.

—How do we know?

—What?

—It's horrible, said Jimmy.—No argument. He's more than twice her age.

And so was Jimmy.

—Way more, he said.—Must be nearly three times more.

—Spare me the maths lesson, Jimmy, said Aoife.

She was getting out of the bed.

—Hang on, he said.—Please. Aoife.

She stayed put.

—It's not illegal, okay?

—Okay, said Aoife.

—They're both consentin' adults.

—Don't rub it in.

—Well, okay. Sorry. But they are. An' he's one of our clients. A bit of a big one. So what do I do?

—Ditch him.

—Okay. Why?

—He's a pervert.

He took a breath.

—Not really, he said.—But okay. And his back catalogue's shite. That's two good reasons not to like him. Which is easy enough anyway. He's a prick. But do I drop him because o' that?

—I would, said Aoife.

—Would you?

—Yes.

—Would you, though?

—Is there any way we could kill him?

—There's plenty, said Jimmy.—But I don't think we'd get away with it.

—And your motives would be ludicrous, said Aoife.—You'd kill him because he played a banjo in one of his songs.

—Fuckin' sure, said Jimmy.—And it wasn't just one of his songs.

He sat up.

—So anyway, he said.—I'm stuck with him, yeah?

—It's disgusting, said Aoife.—But yes. I'm glad you hit him.

—Well, I'm not sure about that.

—What?

—When I apologised to him —

—What?! You didn't tell me this.

—Yeah. Earlier. I told you.

—You said you spoke to him. You said nothing about apologising.

—Well, I didn't phone him to talk abou' the football, said Jimmy.

—Go on.

—So when I said sorry and then he passed the phone to your woman —

—The child.

—Ah stop.

—The orphan.

—Grand. The thought struck me. That me hittin' him had brought them together.

—No.

—No?

—No. No, said Aoife.—It's too weird.

—She fell into his arms, said Jimmy.—Felt sorry for him. No?

—No.

—It's impossible, is it?

—No.

—So it's possible then. She's a Yank.

—Oh.

—So do I apologise?

—You did already.

—Again.

—Why should you?

—For hangin' up on her.

—No.

—Sure?

—Yes.

—There's Noeleen as well.

—Ah, you didn't hit Noeleen?

—No, said Jimmy.—No, I didn't – relax. But she was talkin' a bit at the do. Things aren't goin' too well, and we can't really afford to be leakin' clients.

—At his age, I'm sure he's leaking.

Jimmy laughed.

—That's very good.

—Oh, thank you.

—So anyway. Do I apologise again – more?

—No.

—How come?

—See what happens.

—Fine. Grand.

—Should we be worried, Jimmy?

—What about?

—Business, she said.—Your job.

He felt it; he knew. This was what he'd been wanting.

—Probably, he said.—I'm not sure. Maybe.

She sighed. So did he.

—On top of everything else, she said.

—Yep, he said.—But I think we're okay.

—I'm sure it's fine.

—Yeah.

★　★　★

125

A note this time. He held it. As long as he could.

The dog downstairs howled.

—You're upsetting Cindy!

Grand.

—Ned.

—Ah.

—It's Jimmy.

—Ah.

—It's a few days early, I know, said Jimmy.—But Happy New Year, Ned.

Nothing came back from Ned. The beardy bollix.

—Listen, Ned, said Jimmy.—I think I owe you another apology. No, look it, I know I do. So, sorry. Yeh there, Ned?

—Yes, said Ned.—I'm here.

—No excuses, said Jimmy.—I'm sorry.

—Okay.

—Thanks. You still there, Ned?

—I'm here, said Ned.

Jimmy heard one of those theatrical sighs – the only type the prick at the other end was capable of. Then a different, chirpier prick spoke.

—Thanks for phoning, Jimmy.

—No, I had to. Listen, we'll meet. Go through stuff. A few gigs in the spring.

—Sounds good.

—Germany.

—Great.

—Denmark.

—Great.

—Norway, said Jimmy.—But anyway, I'll leave yeh. I just wanted to —

—No, said Ned.—Thanks for phoning.

—No, you're grand, said Jimmy.—Always a pleasure. Anyway, so – you're a lucky man.

—I know.

—I'm glad yeh realise that, said Jimmy, and he laughed.—Anyway. Next time, give her one for me.

—Bye.

—Good luck, Ned.
Fuck off, Ned.

—The Pope? said Noeleen.

He'd had the idea that morning, listening to the news on the way in.

—Yeah, said Jimmy.

He grinned; he actually laughed – just a burst.

—Tell me again, said Noeleen.

She did her businesswoman thing, put one foot up on her chair.

—Right, said Jimmy.—In 2012 – the day after tomorrow. There's a thing – it's called the Eucharistic Congress. Here in Dublin. And it's the first time since 1932.

—And?

—It was huge back then.

—But not this time.

—Wait, said Jimmy.—Just wait. If they were havin' it tomorrow, I'd agree. But it's later in the year an' this is the Catholic Church, remember. They'll get a crowd.

—It won't be Oxegen, Jimmy.

Her foot was still up on the chair.

—No, said Jimmy.—It'll be bigger.

—How – ?

—Just listen, Noeleen, for fuck sake.

He was grinning.

Her foot came down off the chair – the oul' muscles weren't what they used to be. But she was still listening.

—They're invitin' the fuckin' Pope, he said.—It was on the news this mornin'. Remember the last time?

—Not really, she said.

That was right; she was younger than him. He hated that – he fuckin' hated that.

—It was mad, he said.—The whole country shut down. The year after there were tons of babies called John Paul.

—What's the current pope called?

—Don't know, said Jimmy.—And I know what yeh mean. The times are different. Benedict – that's it. But you're right. But so am I.

—Benedict the what?

127

—Haven't a clue, he said.—There's probably about three people in the country that know or give a shite. But —

He was loving this.

—It's still not the point.

—Go on, said Noeleen.

He had her by the entrepreneurial curlies.

—So, he said.—There's big religion rollin' towards us.

—It's not rock 'n' roll.

—Everythin's rock 'n' roll.

He'd no idea what that meant.

—It'll all be back to 1932. People will be cryin' for it, rememberin' their parents and grannies talkin' about it.

—Faith of Our Fathers.

—Exactly, said Jimmy.—All that shite.

—It's been done.

—The CD, I know. And it proves my point. It was only a few years back, wasn't it? A CD full of hymns outsold every legitimate album released that year. Bang in the middle of all the child abuse inquiries. And people bought it anyway, even though they hated the Catholic Church.

—Nostalgia.

—It was deeper than that, but yeah.

He loved that – it was deeper than that. He was a philosopher, a theologian. He'd ride the Sisters of Mercy, every fuckin' one of them, to sell a record.

—So, said Noeleen.

—So, said Jimmy.—The songs of 1932.

—More hymns?

—Hymns an' everythin', he said.—Every song we can find that was recorded in 1932 – in Ireland. We'll root through them all and come up with an album's worth.

—Are you sure about this, Jimbo?

—I am, yeah, he said.—Look it. It's 1932. If it was America, it'd be speakeasies and the Great Depression. The archives – for fuck sake, Noeleen. Jazz, country, prison songs, gospel, the blues. Some o' the coolest stuff that was ever recorded. Alan Lomax an' his da. And your man, the other archive fella – Harry Smith. There's box sets. iTunes sells them. We'll do the same. We could trace the roots of punk to some whistlin' bogger in 1932.

—How would you go about it?

—No idea, said Jimmy.—Not yet. I only thought of it this mornin'.

The office was filling again, as much as it ever did. Lunch was over.

—It's possible, he said.—Listen to this. It's possible we could find someone still alive who recorded a song in 1932. For the radio. Even just into a tape recorder or on acetate.

Acetate. He loved saying that.

—RTE will never give us their archive, said Noeleen.

—Fuck RTE, said Jimmy.—We'll go after tapes. Parish stuff, family stuff. Lost records. Someone who sang – some teenager back then is ninety-four or five now.

They both smiled; they grinned.

—It's so cool, said Noeleen.

—It fuckin' is, he agreed.—There'll be no blacks, fair enough. But even then, you'd never know. But anyway, it could nearly be as cool as an American archive. Why wouldn't it be? I've a feelin' already. I think —

The twit was beside them, watching his bosses. He'd never really seen them like this before, the way they'd been back before they'd solidified.

—What? said Noeleen.—What do you think?

—I think – , said Jimmy.

Ocean was there now too. Looking on.

—I think, he said again,—we might find somethin' we were never supposed to find.

—What?

—Somethin' hidden, said Jimmy.—Music that never made it onto the radio. Our own blues, say. Suppressed – deliberately forgotten. Cos it didn't tally with De Valera's vision for Ireland.

What a word. Suppressed. Commercial fuckin' dynamite. Suppressed nostalgia? For fuck sake.

—You're losing the run of yourself, Jimbo, said Noeleen, but she approved.

—Probably, said Jimmy.—But who knows? The official picture is never the real one.

Jesus though, he was impressing himself again. It was years since he'd felt like this.

They'd moved away from the others. They looked out at the street.

—Will you be able for it? said Noeleen.

—What? said Jimmy.—Oh. With the chemo an' that?

—Yes.

He gave it a gap. He actually gave it thought.

—I should be, he said.—I don't see why not. *Mister* Dunwoody said I'd probably be grand. But we'll see. Alright?

She nodded, smiled. He knew: she wanted to hug him. He liked her, he liked her.

—But a bit of help wouldn't be any harm, he said.

—Ocean, said Noeleen.—She'll stomp up to every door in Ireland and smile.

—Grand, said Jimmy.—Okay. Would she be up to it but?

—What d'you mean? said Noeleen.—She's beyond efficient, Jimbo. She's actually amazing.

—Great, said Jimmy.—But, being American, like. Does she know the place well enough? The culture, like.

—Of course she does, said Noeleen.—With a father like Ned. Jesus, she'd have to.

—Wha'?

The chemo saved him.

—I can't phone him again, he told Aoife.—I just can't.

—Noeleen can, said Aoife.

—No, said Jimmy.—I don't want that. Like she's my boss? Moppin' up after me or somethin'.

—Well, it needs a mop, Jimmy.

—I know.

—Jesus, Jimmy.

—I know.

—I'll do it, said Aoife.

—No.

—Yes.

—Why?

—If it'll help.

—But it's my mess, said Jimmy.

—That's right. But it's ours really, said Aoife.—We both reached the same nasty conclusion about Ned.

—True, said Jimmy.—But it doesn't mean he actually isn't —

—Don't.

—Only messin'.

—I know. But anyway, I'll do it. We're both shareholders.

—True, said Jimmy.—It's ours. We should never have sold. Sure we shouldn't?

—Not now, Jimmy. We did well out of it.

—Okay.

They were in bed. It was a strange new world. Brian was the only other one in bed. The others were still up, moving around downstairs, homing in on the fridge.

—So I'll phone him, said Aoife.—Alright?

—Okay.

—I'll explain who I am and then I'll play the chemo card.

—He's been through it himself, said Jimmy.—He's been through chemo.

—Great, said Aoife.—So he'll understand.

—He might.

—Ah, he will. But, God, you're stupid.

—I know.

—And you can apologise to his daughter.

—Okay, righ'.

—Just say sorry, said Aoife.—Don't elaborate. Don't attempt to justify it.

—I hear you.

—Don't joke. Are you listening to me, Jimmy?

—Yeah, he said.—They suit yeh.

She was wearing her new reading glasses.

—Thanks.

—What's that you're readin'?

—A book about cancer, she said.

—Is it any good?

—Yes, she said.—It's very good. It's a history —

—It has a fuckin' history?

—Yes, of course. Attitudes, beliefs. It's really interesting.

—Oh good. I'm glad it's interesting —

—You've had your quota of sympathy today, James.

—Okay.

—Asking a man to – what? – give her one for you. Jesus – with his own daughter.

—You'd want to have been there, said Jimmy.—There was a context.

—Don't laugh.

—I'm not.

—You are.

131

—So are you.

—You're such an eejit, she said.—Seriously though, you should read this.

—I'll bring it with me to the chemo, said Jimmy.—Don't tell me the endin'.

He picked up his own book, Jah Wobble's autobiography. He put on his own new reading glasses.

—Do they suit me?

—Do you remember Harry Worth?

—Ah fuck off now. I only got them to keep you company. I don't really want to know.

—What?

He pointed at Aoife's Kindle.

—I read the first page there. When you were brushin' your teeth.

—And?

—A quarter of all deaths in America are caused by cancer.

—I know, she said.—It's frightening.

—Yeah, said Jimmy.—But actually, really – it's not. The figures mean nothin'. But it's supposed to be the history of cancer, yeah?

—Yeah.

—But it's still killin' a quarter of all Yanks, said Jimmy.—So it's not history at all.

—It is.

—And the chemo's a waste of time.

—No.

—Because nothin' works.

—That's ridiculous. Jimmy —

—I know, said Jimmy.—I agree with yeh. But if I read that one, or the others you're hidin' there in your Kindle —

—I'm not.

—I'm only messin', he said.—But even the *Chemotherapy for Dummies* one you gave me. If I read too much of it, I start havin' doubts. More doubts than I have already. Cos the optimistic stuff is just fluff, and I'm better off not knowin' the pessimistic stuff. Cos it's way more believable.

—Okay, she said.—That makes sense.

—The fuckin' *Dummies* book would tell me to love my tumour.

—Probably.

—I'd have to bend over and shout it up my hole. I love you, little tumour!

—Play your trumpet to it.

—That'll definitely kill it.

—You're doing very well.

—The trumpet?

—Yes.

—No, he said.—It's shite.

—Well, I like hearing it.

—Thanks, he said.—Good. Thanks.

They took off their reading glasses. She turned off the light. They lay in the dark, said nothing for a while. They listened to the sounds downstairs. They listened to the feet on the stairs, Mahalia using her cop-on, going up to bed at just the right time. They heard her in the bathroom. They heard her bedroom door. Then there was nothing.

—No sign of life next door, said Jimmy, softly.

—No.

—Any word there?

—No.

—Is it still cold out there?

—It's been cold since November, said Jimmy.—Have you not been out since then?

—Oh God, said the nurse.—A character.

He watched her work. The saline bag, the stand, the red digital numbers going on, off. Why did they have to be fuckin' red? She hooked the bag to the top of the metal stand.

—Can I've ice an' lemon with that? he said.

—You're gas.

He turned on the radio. Joe Duffy. Good, he could get annoyed. Joe was doing one of his poxy polls. Should the Pope visit Ireland?

—Fuckin' hell.

The lights ahead were red. He texted Noeleen. *Joe Duffy poll. Shud pope vist. Txt yes. Get evyone.* Green again, mission accomplished. He was delighted. He'd just been nuked and he was still working.

He was down near the Grand Canal Theatre. He didn't really know this part of the world but the new corners and blocks seemed to have been finished just in time, seconds before the bust. He found a parking spot and texted Aoife. *Chemo was grand X.*

The cold was good. He was walking fast, cutting through it. He'd felt a bit shiny leaving the hospital, but this was great.

The phone buzzed in his pocket.

It was Noeleen. *Poll says yes to pope.*

Brilliant.

That was his job now, saving the Catholic Church.

He found the door, a windowless slab of grey-painted iron, and the line of buzzers, more grey against the grey of the cement. He could hardly read the signs. He needed the light on his phone. Live Studios. He pressed.

—Yeah?

—Howyeh. Can yeh hear me?

—Yeah.

—Is that Lochlainn?

—Yeah.

—It's Jimmy Rabbitte.

—They've gone.

—The Halfbreds?

—Yeah.

—Can I come in anyway?

He heard the buzz, and a slight click. There was no handle on the door but there was room for his fingers, so he pulled it back and found the light switch before he pulled the door shut again. The switch was on one of those timers. He had thirty seconds, and a set of concrete steps in front of him. He was Tom fuckin' Cruise. He went up, no bother, onto a landing, a turn, and more steps, and another switch. He gave it a thump and kept going, and came to another iron door, this one painted red with a single badly painted eye staring at him. He knocked, and stepped back as the door slowly came at him.

—Lochlainn?

—Yeah.

—Jimmy.

—Hi.

It was disappointing, even before he saw anything. Lochlainn obviously lived there, but it wasn't like one of those New York lofts. This was a tiny kip. The studio was a corner of what might have been the bedroom – Jimmy wasn't sure.

—They've gone, you said.

—Yeah.

These guys were always fuckin' autistic; he'd forgotten.

134

—But they recorded the song? said Jimmy.

It was a prayer more than a question.

Lochlainn shrugged.

—Yeah.

—Is it anny good?

He shrugged again. Or at least his Nine Inch Nails T-shirt moved.

—Can I hear it so? said Jimmy.

—Yeah, said Lochlainn.—But.

—But?

—They only did one take.

—Is that a problem? Jimmy asked.—There was only ever one successful take of 'Like a Rolling Stone'. Did you know that, Lochlainn?

—They, like, said Lochlainn.—I think they broke up.

—Ah Jesus, again?

—He – eh —

—Barry.

—Yeah. His phone rang before the end.

—Of the first take?

—Yeah.

—The only take?

—Yeah.

—Ah shite.

Lochlainn shrugged. He drew breath and spoke.

—She —

—Brenda.

—She said Connie.

—Same woman, said Jimmy.—Go on.

—She shouted.

—I'd better hear it, said Jimmy.

Bollix to it.

But he'd come this far. He wanted something to attach to the day, his first day of chemo. And he was curious.

—They're old punks, he told Lochlainn.

—Maybe, said Lochlainn.—But he left because the Minister needed a file for questions in the Dáil tonight, yeah? And she had to pick up their daughter from hockey.

—And you reckon they broke up?

—Looked like that.

—That's just their way, said Jimmy.—They love each other, really.

—Cool.
Can I hear it?

Lochlainn shrugged again.

—It's yours.

Jimmy looked around for somewhere to sit, but changed his mind. He was too giddy to sit. And Lochlainn had the only chair.

It was rough.

—I'M DOWN ON MY KNEES —

It was dreadful.

—A MUNCHIN' MUNCHIN' MUNCHIN' —

It was brilliant. Lochlainn was yawning but he hadn't a clue.

—AND THE GIRL DON'T KNOW —
I GOT ERECTILE DYSFUNCTION —

Jimmy was listening to the howling kid inside every middle-aged man, and Brenda on the drums was the howling middle-aged woman.

—OH YES SHE DO —
—OH NO SHE DON'T —
—OH YES SHE DO —
—OH NO SHE DON'T —

—Was their bassist with them? Jimmy shouted.

—No, said Lochlainn.

—I didn't think so, said Jimmy.—Just the two of them, yeah?

—Yeah.

—They fill the room but, don't they?

—SHE'S SMILIN' BACK AT ME —
SHE'S SHOWIN' ME HOWTH JUNCTION —
AND THE BITCH DON'T KNOW —
I GOT ERECTILE DYSFUNCTION —

There was no getting away from it, the senior civil servant could sure make that guitar scream. There wouldn't have been room for the bass.

—OH YES SHE DO —
—OH NO SHE DON'T —

This was the scream of a shocked and angry man. And Brenda's drums boomed, brutal as ever. Waiting, wanting, wanting, wanting. Waiting, wanting, wanting, wanting. It was fuckin' wonderful.

—BUT NOW SHE KNOWS —
—I GOT ERECTILE —

The phone – Barry's phone – went off. 'Ace of Spades'. It was perfect and it sounded distant, fading. And Barry's voice.

—Sorry.

And Brenda's.

—Ah, for fuck sake!

—I'll have to take it.

Brenda kept at it. Waiting, wanting, wanting, wanting. And stopped.

—Then fucking take it, Barry!

—Stop it there, Lochlainn.

Brenda's shout was still in the room.

—Exactly there, said Jimmy.

—What?

—I want it to end on Barreeeee – the way she says it, okay? Jimmy loved this.

—Make the eeee hang there, he said.—Three beats. No, four. Then done. Can you handle that, Lochlainn?

Lochlainn shrugged – no problem, no interest, your funeral. He hadn't a fuckin' clue. And Barry and Brenda. They hadn't a clue either. They'd left, gone back to their other lives. It was a classic, and Jimmy was the only man in the world who knew it. He'd probably need the rights to 'Ace of Spades', even that poxy phone version. But that was grand, easily done – he thought.

What a day.

He watched Lochlainn fiddling away.

—D'yeh suffer yourself, Lochlainn?

—Sorry?

—The erectile dysfunction.

—No, said Lochlainn.

—No, said Jimmy.—Me neither.

He sipped.

—Jesus.

He tried it again. He'd never tasted anything like it. That was the chemo – he'd read about it, before he'd stopped reading. How his taste might become heightened.

He sipped again. It exploded – it just exploded – upwards, straight into his brain. He shook. *Coffee tastes amazin. X* He fired the text off to Aoife. She'd like that.

He looked around. Everything else was normal. The Brazilian young one behind the counter still looked nice, but not as nice as she should have looked, being from Brazil. But she was the same young one – that was the point. Everything was the same. It was just taste; it was exact, scientific. He wasn't going mad.

Aoife's text arrived. *Great. X.* And another one. *Will u be wanting cancer trousers when you get home?* He fired one back. *Fck off.*

Barry's phone was off. But Brenda answered him immediately.

—We're not paying for the studio.

Jimmy could hear kids – girls – shouting, behind Brenda.

—Who's winning?

—We are, bitch. My girls are pussy-whipping Mount Anville. She wasn't whispering.

—Great, said Jimmy.—Ra ra ra.

—We're not paying.

—I wouldn't expect you to, Connie.

—It wasn't my fault, said Brenda.—Hey, fat girl! Try chasing the ball!

—It was nobody's fault, said Jimmy.

—Bloody Barry, said Brenda.—*So* fucking important. Good block, honey!

—I think it's saveable, said Jimmy.

—We're not paying.

—No one's askin' you to pay, said Jimmy.—I'm happy to cover it. That's what I do.

—Yeah, yeah. Suck my cock.

—Here's what I'm thinkin', Connie, said Jimmy.—I'm goin' to run it past some people and see wha' they think. Some market research, but nothin' too formal.

He'd play it to the kids – the older pair – when he got home. And Aoife – she'd love it.

—You're serious? said Brenda.

—Yeah, said Jimmy.—I am.

—Yessss!

—Did we score there?

—Yes!

—Ah great.

He didn't tell Noeleen. He kept the song in his pocket. He wanted to live with it for a day.

—How was it? she asked.

She knew it was chemo day.

—Grand, he said.

—That all?

—Yeah, he said.—It was fine.

He kept going. Ocean was waiting in the meeting corner. She looked too young sitting there.

—Hi.

—Hi.

He sat. He stood.

—Back in a minute.

He walked to his desk. He looked at nothing on his screen. He went back. He sat.

—Listen, he said.—Before we start.

She looked even younger. Bambi's sister.

—I owe you an apology, he said.—Sorry.

—Thank *you*.

—No, he said.—I'm sorry. So. Did Noeleen mention anythin' to yeh?

—Yes, she said.—It's so cool.

—Great. So.

He wished he had a cup or something, anything he could hide behind.

—Where do we start?

—We-*ellll*, she said.

She looked at the iPad on her lap.

—I, like – okay. I did some brainstorming of my own, with some of my girl*friends*.

She looked at him, and did the huge-eyes thing.

—I'm sorry, she said.—Was that okay?

—Yeah, yeah. Grand. No – go on.

—Soo*oo*. Here's what we came up with. My girlfriends are Irish, by the way. Just in case – I'm sorry. You know, not an invading force of American postgrad chicks kind of thing.

He felt useless, superfluous. But it was great, like being shown the insides of a clock or something – how everything turned.

He leaned forward, and she showed him the list. The archives, the collections. It was brilliant. And the other stuff too, the Irish links. The friend with the uncle in the UCD Folklore Department; the dad who was going through bankruptcy proceedings with another man, who was president – or whatever – of the John McCormack Appreciation Society; the mother with the *friend* who played golf with the bishop.

He pointed at *friend*.

—Why the italics?

—They fuck.

—Oh. Grand, go on.

It was all there, on one page of an iPad. A roomful of Southside girls had given Ocean everything she needed.

He was getting an iPad. They were fuckin' brilliant.

—This is great, he said.—Thanks very much.

—My pleasure.

—It's so fuckin' Irish but, isn't it?

—How so?

—Someone knows someone.

—Yes, she said.—Very. But hey, it's an awesome project, so I'm willing to go native.

—Grand, he said.—These will give us the expected sounds. They'll be great but – official. Expected. You with me, Ocean?

—Yes.

He pointed at the iPad.

—Middle-class Ireland will give us the sounds of middle-class Ireland. The country they created and then fucked up. You don't mind me sayin' this?

—No, she said.—It's cool.

—Grand, he said.—Good. So where'll we find the surprises?

He met Marvin in the hall.

—How're things?

—Grand, said Marvin.—How was the – ?

—Not too bad, said Jimmy.—Nothin' to it really.

—Cool.

Marvin was moving to the stairs.

—How's the band?

—Grand, said Marvin.

—Great, said Jimmy.—I must hear yis some time.

—Cool.

—What's for dinner?

—Don't know.

He watched Marvin disappear up the stairs – his head, then his shoulders, bent a bit as if he was too big for the house. There was music on in the kitchen. Fuckin' hell, it was Steely Dan. It must have been for him. That was lovely.

—'Home at Last', from *Aja*, 1977. Where's the dog?

—Hi, said Aoife.—She's taken her back.

—Your sister?

—Caoimhe, yes, Jimmy. On a trial basis.

—The dog – ?

—Yes, said Aoife.

She wasn't looking at him. She was stabbing some big potatoes.

—Sorry, she said.—How was it? I mean, you said in the texts —

—No, it was grand, said Jimmy.—I'm great. But she took the dog?

—Yeah.

—On a trial basis?

—Yes.

—What does that mean?

—I'm not sure, said Aoife.—She used the term, not me. But you know Caoimhe.

—What're we havin', by the way?

—Chicken.

—Lovely. Go on.

—No, nothing. Just, you know the way she is. She always assumes you know what she's talking about. Anyway, they're back together.

—Her and the dog.

—And Tom.

Tom was the husband.

—On a trial basis as well, yeah?

—I think so, said Aoife.

Jimmy looked down at the corner.

—She took the basket as well.

—Yes.

—How're the kids about it?

—Well, actually, said Aoife.—There now, it's lovely.

—Lovely?

—They're more worried about how you'd react, said Aoife.
—They know you love Cindy.

—I hate Cindy.

—Yeah, yeah, we know.

—Stupid fuckin' name.

—We know that too, said Aoife.—We all heard you calling her Imelda.

For fuck sake.

—Imelda May, he said.

—We guessed.

—That's 'Josie' now, by the way. Steely Dan.

—I know, said Aoife.—We can get another one.

—A dog?

—Yes.

—No way, said Jimmy.

His phone hopped and rescued him. When had he called the dog Imelda? *Why* had he called the fuckin' dog Imelda? It must have been just after he'd got back from the hospital, when he was still a bit out of his tree. That made some kind of sense. Nothing else did.

—Des?

—Jimmy, hi.

—How's it goin'?

—Not too bad. How are you?

—Grand, grand.

—Did you start the chemo today, or when – ?

—Today.

—Jesus. I can phone back —

—No, it's grand. So far, anyway.

The line went bad; Des's voice slid away.

—I didn't catch that, Des, sorry. I lost yeh there.

—The trumpet, said Des.

—Yeah, I got one.

The day was beginning to catch up with him. He could feel it in his eyes – behind his eyes.

—I know, said Des.—You told me.

—Grand.

—D'you have a teacher yet?

—Not yet, no, said Jimmy.—I need one.

—Yeah, you asked me if I knew anyone. And I said No.

—Gotcha, said Jimmy.—I remember now.

He didn't.

—But there is someone, said Des.

—Great, said Jimmy.—Who?

—Me.

—D'you play the trumpet, Des?

—No, said Des.—No, I'm joking. I do.

—Great —

—I did it when I was a kid, said Des.—But I stopped then, for years. But then when you asked me if I knew anyone – . I thought about it later and I dug it out. It was in my mother's attic. And, well. I love it – it all came back.

142

—Great.

—So, said Des.—If you're still interested –

—No, yeah. Brilliant.

—I'm not qualified or anything.

—Who gives a shite?

—It wasn't too bad so?

—No, said Jimmy.—No.

—Great.

—Not so far anyway.

—Fingers crossed so.

—Yeah, said Jimmy.—Yeah. When were yeh born?

—Jesus, said his da.—1941. I think. Yeah, 1941. Why?

—Was there much talk about the Eucharistic Congress when you were a kid?

—God, yeah – Jesus. Big time.

—Wha' was it?

—Big mass, all sorts of processions.

—No pope.

—No, said Jimmy Sr.—No. A raft o' fuckin' cardinals. My parents talked about it all the time. I think it was kind o' like 1990, for their generation.

—Wha' d'yeh mean?

—Well, 1990 was unbelievable – remember?

—I do, yeah.

—It was just the football to start with. But then, when it took off. The penalty shoot-out an' tha'. The country was never the same again. It was the beginnin' of the boom.

—D'yeh think?

—Yeah – I do. I mean, I had tha' chipper van at the time. With Bimbo, d'you remember?

—Yeah.

—An' it was a bit of a disaster, tha'. But I was never unemployed again – after Italia '90. I wouldn't let myself be. I was always doin' somethin', even before the buildin' took off. Because – an' this is true. We felt great about ourselves. For years after. An' tha' only changed a few years back. Now we're useless cunts again.

—Thanks for the analysis.

—Fuck off. You asked.

—An' 1932 was like tha', was it?

—Yeah, said Jimmy's da.—A bit. The country was only ten years old, remember. An' dirt poor. Then, like, the man in the flat next door to my mother's gets a radio – a big fuckin' deal. An' everyone bails in to hear it. She always spoke about hearin' your man, John McCormack, singin' live on the wireless. At the mass. Like he was Sinatra or – I don't know – some huge star today. The Bublé fucker or someone. My father said it was like the whole world was listenin' to somethin' tha' was happenin' here in Dublin. An' it probably was as well. Why did you ask?

Jimmy told him.

—An' you came up with that idea, did yeh?

—I did, said Jimmy.—Yeah.

—It's a winner.

—D'yeh think?

—Fuckin' sure. If you do it properly.

—I will.

—Oh, I know, said his da.—D'you remember my cousin, Norman?

—No, said Jimmy.—I don't think so.

—He'd be your cousin as well, I suppose. Second cousin, or first cousin twice removed or tha' shite. Anyway, he has a huge collection of old 78s an' stuff.

—Great, said Jimmy.—From back that far?

—I'd say so, yeah, said his da.—He wouldn't throw out his shite, Norman. He's a bit older than me as well. An' he's a real collector, yeh know. Goes to meetin's an' all. So I'd say he could help yeh.

—Brilliant, said Jimmy.—Will yeh introduce me to him?

—Does tha' mean I have to go with yeh?

—Just the once, said Jimmy.—Till I get me foot in the door.

—Okay, said his da.

—Come here, said Jimmy.

He leaned to the side.

—Don't fart, said his da.—Not so soon after the chemo.

—Fuck off, said Jimmy.—I'm just gettin' my iPod out. Here we go.

He untangled the earphones and handed them to his da.

—Here, he said.—Yeh know where these go.

He watched his da shove one into each ear, like he was trying to make them meet in the middle. Then he – Jimmy – turned on the iPod.

—What the fuck is this?! his da roared.

But he kept the earphones in, and laughed once, and kept smiling for most of the two minutes and twenty-three seconds.

Jimmy turned it off, and his da unplugged himself.

—What was tha'?

—The Halfbreds, they're called.

—There's no way they're from 1932.

—No, said Jimmy.—It's a different thing. A different project.

—There's no stoppin' ych.

—You're beginnin' to be too nice, Da.

—Okay, said Jimmy's da.

—They're the Halfbreds.

—They fuckin' sound it.

—A husband an' wife combo. They're old punks. From way back. But they recorded that one last week. An' everyone loves it. Marv, young Jimmy, Aoife, all the gang at work. They all think it's great.

—Specially the endin'.

—Tha' wasn't rehearsed.

—You could tell, said Jimmy's da.—Howth Junction, wha'.

—Yeah.

—Always my favourite Dart station.

—Windy oul' place.

—Great view but.

—Anyway, said Jimmy.—Everyone loves it. But d'you know how many will actually buy it?

—Go on.

—No one, said Jimmy.

—Why's tha'?

—Would you buy it?

—No.

—Why not?

—It's shite.

—You just said you loved it.

—Yeah. Because it's shite.

—Ah, for fuck sake, listen. Nobody's buyin'. The kids don't think they have to.

—They download it for nothin'.

—Yeah, said Jimmy.—Exactly. My age group an' a bit younger, we still buy. But they don't buy much. An' very little that's new.

—Make a video.

145

—We're goin' to —

—A good one, said his da.—Make us laugh. Get your woman from the Rubberbandits video.

—You know the Rubberbandits?

—Of course I know the fuckin' Rubberbandits.

The Rubberbandits were a pair of clever lads from Limerick who wore SuperValu bags over their heads, and rapped. Their song, 'Horse Outside', was the new national anthem. Jimmy hated them.

—More than eight million YouTube hits, said Jimmy.

—Twice as many as live in this poxy country, said his da.—It's the way to go.

—But only about nine thousand bought the song, said Jimmy.

The misery in that statistic pleased him, all the noughts in the millions falling away – the state of the fuckin' world.

—Beats a kick in the bollix, said his da.—An' listen. I remember when you were a kid. You sat on the floor in front of the telly when *Top o' the Pops* was on – don't fuckin' deny it. An' yeh held up a microphone and taped every song yeh liked, an' played them all on your little cassette recorder. For nothin'.

—That was —

—No, it wasn't different. There were thousands of yis, doin' the same thing, all over Ireland and over in England. Robbin' the artists. An' the artists were still multi-fuckin'-millionaires.

—You might be right.

—I am right. I know more than yeh give me credit for.

—I know, said Jimmy.—Sorry.

—So, said his da.—Make a fuckin' video an' get the young one from the Rubberbandits one – with the dress an' the eyebrow, yeh know her?

—'Course.

—Or someone like her, said his da.—Shoot it at Howth Junction station. On the platform. Northbound or southbound, I don't mind. An' when your man there sings, *She's showin' me Howth Junction*, just get her to point at the sign an' raise her eyebrow, the way she does for the Rubberbandits. Then stick it up on YouTube an' see wha' happens. An' don't worry, I'll phone Norman for yeh.

Des was sitting on the bed.

—Sorry there's nowhere else, said Jimmy.

—It's fine, said Des.

—I didn't realise the house would be full, said Jimmy.—There's usually an empty room at the weekends.

—Jimmy, said Des.—You're just looking for excuses not to start. Go on.

—Am I standing right?

—It's not a photo shoot.

—Fuck off, Des. The hernia.

—What hernia?

—If my stance is wrong, I could give myself a hernia. I saw it on YouTube.

—You're fine, said Des.

He looked behind him, like he was checking the distance to the pillows. If he lay back there on the bed, Jimmy would sack him, or fuck the trumpet at him. He was already a shite teacher.

This was terrible.

He looked at the window. He put the trumpet to his mouth. He blew.

—There now, said Des.

—Wha'?

—It's not about force, said Des.

—I know.

—It's the buzz.

Des pursed his lips.

—My cheeks didn't fill with air, he said.—Did you notice?

—Yeah, Jimmy lied.

—Take two breaths, said Des.

Jimmy looked down at him.

—First one, said Des.—Then the extra one.

—Tell yeh wha', Des. Stand up and show me.

—Oh, said Des.—Sure.

He stood up, and stood beside Jimmy.

—So, he said.—Breathe in. Fill your lungs.

Jimmy did.

—Now, said Des.—The bit extra. Imagine you're filling your stomach with air. I think that's how we imagine it anyway, filling our stomachs, not our lungs. You can exhale now.

—Thanks.

—Put the mouthpiece to your lips. Purse the lips, good and tight. Breathe in. No – keep the lips tight. Yeah – and breathe. And blow. Release the air. You're in control. Just—blow – . Great. That was a G.

147

—Was it?

—Not really, said Des.

It was fuckin' freezing. The station platform – southbound – was the most exposed place on earth. Fuckin' Attenborough hadn't a clue.

—Has there been a murder, love?

—No, we're filmin' a video.

—Ah, lovely. Is the young one in it?

—She is, yeah.

—She's gorgeous, isn't she?

—Yeah.

—She must be petrified though, God love her.

—It's only for a bit. She'll have her coat back on in a minute.

—Ah grand.

He hunched down, and looked at it framed in the monitor. Barry standing like Elvis Costello *c.* 1977, Brenda standing behind the drums like Moe Tucker *c.* 1967, the Dart crawling past them as Barry roared it for the fourth time.

—SHE'S SMILING BACK AT ME —

AND SHE'S SHOWING ME HOWTH JUNCTION —

He was singing straight into the weather, sweating, losing weight on one of the coldest days of the winter.

—Happy?

The director, Pete, was hunched beside Jimmy.

—Yep, said Jimmy.

—Cut! That's our take. Now's your moment, Avril!

Jimmy stood up straight, and felt fuzzy, weak, just for a moment. But the cold quickly fixed him. He watched the cameraman lift the camera and bring it closer to the station sign. He watched the young one, Avril – she was a model, one of those glamour ones. She usually did photo shoots in a bikini, launching new sewerage schemes with county councillors. Jimmy watched her point at the sign, at the Junction in Howth Junction, and raise her eyebrow – exactly as the script demanded.

It was a different batch of people this time. Different patients, different nurses. This new one smiled when he asked for ice and lemon.

Still the same terror as he watched the bag of poison being hoisted. He'd never yawn when that happened. He'd never feel like a veteran.

There was a fella beside him who was obviously up for a chat. Jimmy put in his earphones and headed him off at the pass. He didn't turn on the sound; he couldn't have coped. But he scrolled through the bands and chose the songs for his funeral.

—I was fine for two days after. But then – Jesus, Les.

—It's the steroids, said Les.—They mask the nausea. But they wear off.

—It didn't happen the first time but.

—No, said Les.—Same here.

—Horrible.

—Yeah.

—Thanks, by the way.

—It's fine, said Les.—Any time you want to talk —

—Thanks.

—No problem.

—I don't want to worry Aoife or – or – the kids. Sorry.

—Fine.

—I'm out in the fuckin' garden.

—Just remember, it's normal.

—I know.

—And it stops.

—But it fuckin' comes back.

—I know.

—And I can't even vomit.

—Yep.

—How're things with you anyway, Les?

—Fine.

—Thanks for this.

—It's fine.

The barman told him to go back outside and around to the basement. That was where the gigs were.

He waited at the top of the stairs. He could hear the music – he could feel it, coming up from the wooden steps. He went down

149

the first six or seven, to the turn. The heat came up at him – it felt like a crowd. He stayed there a while, a few seconds. He was hoping Marvin wouldn't see him. He hadn't told him he'd be coming – he hadn't asked. He didn't want to embarrass him. He'd only stay for half a song.

He made his move.

It got hotter every step down. It was ages since Jimmy had felt crowd heat like this. The gigs he'd been organising were usually a couple of dozen middle-aged people, looking awkward, trying to remember what they were supposed to do.

The beat became real sounds as he got to the bottom of the stairs, and his head dropped below the top of the door at the same time that a kid on the platform – it wasn't a stage – grabbed the mic off its stand and screamed.

—He was incredible.

—Did he see you?

—I only stayed for a bit.

—It's great you saw him.

—Ah Jesus, Aoife. I'm so fuckin' proud.

—Tell him.

—I will, don't worry. The place was jammered.

—Great.

—It only fits – it couldn't be much more than a hundred. But it was packed. Teemin'. But you should've seen him. D'you remember Jason an' the Scorchers?

—No.

—Country-punk. No?

—No.

—They were brilliant. Mad live now – mad. All over the stage. And the guitarist used to spin around while he was playin'. An' Marvin did that – exactly like it. He nearly decapitated a few o' the punters at the front.

—Great.

—I'm goin' up to play me trumpet.

Norman lived just off the New Cabra Road.

Jimmy waited for his da to park his van behind him. He looked at his da checking that he had the right house, squinting a bit.

He looked a bit uncertain, even unhappy. Then he saw Jimmy's car in front of him.

—Here's my da now, he said, and he opened his door.

The fuckin' nausea – it was lurking, waiting for him. He needed air. He needed his da.

He got out of the car. Fuck the nausea.

—How's it goin'? he said.

His da was out of the van, hitching up his jeans.

—Howyeh, he said.—How're things?

—Grand, said Jimmy.

He stepped back, and to the side.

—This is Ocean, he said.—From work.

—Hii*ii*.

—Ocean, he said.—This is my dad. Jimmy – as well.

—Howyeh, Ocean.

—Ocean is – she's coordinatin' the project, Jimmy told his da.—Does that sound okay, Ocean?

—That sounds great, said Ocean.

His da was staring at her a bit. Jimmy hadn't told him she'd be with them.

—We might as well go in, said his da.—He knows we're comin'. I had to shout a bit on the phone. He's gone a bit deaf, I think.

He pushed the gate. He had to give it a lift too, to get it open.

—Tragic really, he said.—Goin' deaf in a house full o' records. I'll oil his gate while we're here.

He stepped onto the porch and rang the bell.

—Did yis hear tha'? he asked Jimmy and especially Ocean.—I couldn't hear annythin'.

He put his ear to the pebbled glass and pressed the bell again.

—You'd want to be a dog to hear tha' fuckin' bell, said his da.

He ran his hand down the side of the glass, along the paint and wood.

—Needs a bit o' work, he said.

—Here he comes, said Jimmy.

They saw the shape, then the man behind the glass, and the hand going to the lock.

—Here we go, said Jimmy's da.

The door was opening.

—There y'are, Norman.

—Is it Jimmy Rabbitte?

—It is, said Jimmy's da.

—There's no need to shout, said Norman.

He was a small man, and kind of papery. Jimmy didn't think he'd ever met him before. He couldn't remember a younger version. He was smiling, but unfriendly. He took something out of his waistcoat pocket.

—Look.

He was talking to Jimmy's da. He'd paid no attention to Jimmy or Ocean.

—See here? Three settings.

—What's tha', Norman?

—Stop shoutin', I told yeh. It's my hearin' aid.

—Should it not be in your ear or behind it or somethin'?

Jimmy and Ocean followed his da and Norman into the house.

—Christ.

—Oh my God.

Every wall they could see was covered in shelves of records. Jimmy stopped to look, to slide a few from their perches. But something stopped him: *Don't touch till you're let*. He kept going down the hall – made narrow by shelves – to a big bright room that was, after he'd spotted a kettle and the fridge, the kitchen. He heard Ocean behind him shutting the door.

His da was looking at the ceiling.

—Spot of damp there, Norman, he shouted.—Look it.

—Where?

—There.

—That's been there for years, said Norman.—That one up there?

—Yeah.

—It looks like Perry Como.

—Does it?

—Oh, it does.

—You've a fair few records here, all the same, Norman.

—Hold on a minute, said Norman.—I have to adjust me yoke here. When I move from a low ceilin' to the high one.

—Will I say it again or wha'? said Jimmy's da.

—Say what?

—You've a great collection o' records.

—I know.

—That's why I brought young Jimmy with me.

—I know.

—And – what's your name again, love?

—Ocean.

—An' Ocean, Jimmy's da told Norman.—She's here as well.

—I can see that.

If the room had a middle, Norman was in it. He was moving no closer to the shelves; he was telling them nothing, and showing them nothing.

—Norman, said Jimmy's da.—The Eucharistic Congress.

—What about it?

—You heard me?

—Every word.

—Grand. Sorry if I seem—. Annyway, Jimmy's lookin' for music from 1932.

Norman looked at Jimmy.

—1932?

—That's right, said Jimmy.

—Is it in here, Norman? asked Jimmy's da.—Or in one o' the other rooms?

—Is what in here?

—1932.

—Why would there be a year in my kitchen?

—Your 1932 records, said Jimmy's da.—Are they in here?

—Hold on here, said Norman.—Do you think I catalogue the records by the year?

—Well —

—Are yeh mad? said Norman.

—I'm open to persuasion.

Norman pointed at a wall.

—So that's supposed to be 1947, is it? Or 1583?

—I think I left somethin' in the van, said Jimmy's da.

He walked past Jimmy.

—I'll be back with a spanner, he said.—We can beat the information out o' the fucker.

He hitched up his jeans and kept going. Jimmy looked around. He did the full turn.

—This is amazin', Norman, he said.

Norman nodded.

—I've never seen anythin' like it, said Jimmy.—Have you, Ocean?

—No, said Ocean.—It's like the Smithsonian.

—Exactly, said Jimmy.

—It's *such* a thrill, said Ocean.

Norman was listening.

Jimmy met his da at the hall door.

—I had to get out before I smacked him, said his da.—I'll go back in now an' get him movin'.

—Stay here a bit, said Jimmy.—Ocean's chattin' to him. He's givin' her the tour. I thought I'd leave them to it.

—Usin' her feminine charms, yeah?

—Yeah. Spot on.

—She's wastin' her time, said Jimmy's da.

—Wha'?

—Norman, said Jimmy's da.—Did yeh not notice?

—Notice wha'?

—He's gay, for fuck sake.

—Norman?

—The Norman in there, yeah.

—He's gay?

—Yeah.

—Since when?

—Wha'?

—Like, he's old, said Jimmy.

—It's not a recent thing, if that's what yeh mean, said his da.—I don't think it works tha' way. Yeh don't wake up thinkin' you're gay at the age of seventy-eight or nine.

—But – , said Jimmy.

—I fuckin' hope not, an'anyway.

—But—. I mean – how long have yeh known?

—Always.

—All your life, like?

—Yeah, said Jimmy's da.—Norman was always Norman.

—Even way back?

—All I can tell yeh is tha' he was always Norman. In the family, like. An' no one gave much of a shite.

—He was openly gay, like?

—Jesus, man. Go back sixty years. D'you think those words meant annythin'? 1952. Here's Norman Rabbitte. He's openly gay. For fuck sake.

—Okay.

—No one was openly annythin' in 1952, Jimmy's da told Jimmy.—But as near to fuckin' open as he could be, Norman was open. An' it was all grand, in the family. As far as I ever knew. But relax, don't worry. He was probably miserable.

Jesus Christ, my da's becoming me.

—There now, said Jimmy.—Listen.

154

They heard music coming from the back of the house.

—Ocean's worked her magic.

They went after the noise, and found it.

—Jesus.

It was ceili music, but wilder and rougher than Jimmy thought was normal. And there was something else in it, something that made him want to laugh.

—Is tha' feet?!

Norman turned to look at him. He was holding the cover of an old Parlophone 78.

—Dancing, he shouted.—They're all dancing!

The room was full of the sound of dancing feet, dozens, maybe hundreds, of pairs of shoes landing on a wooden floor.

—What year is that from, Norman?!

—Wha'?

—Wha' year – ?

—1932!

—Brilliant!

Jimmy could feel the feet beneath him, coming up from the floor. The dancers on the record were all long dead – they had to be – but he could feel them in the room. There were moments when they were all in the air, then – bang – down, they hit the floor together.

The nausea could fuck off, and the diarrhoea.

—What's it called, Norman?!

—'Kiss the Bride in the Bed!'

Jimmy looked at his da, and at Ocean.

—Track One! he shouted.

—What's this?

—That's the second time in the last few months you've looked at a dog and asked, What's this?

—It's a dog.

—Yes, said Aoife.

—Is it ours?

—Yes.

—I don't want a dog.

—Yes, you do.

—Okay.

* * *

155

Shepherd's pie – Jimmy's choice. He could only manage baby food and he didn't want the kids to see that even the thought of most food made him want to be sick.

But the nausea – he hated the fuckin' word – seemed to be gone. That feeling that made him snap his eyes and even his head – his mind – shut.

—Any gigs comin' up, Marv?

—No.

—How come?

—Dunno.

—Grand, said Jimmy.

He could eat. He could look properly at the kids, even the ones who wouldn't look at him. It didn't upset him. It was temporary.

—So, he said.—The dog.

He put some mince in his mouth.

—Delicious, he said, to Aoife – to all of them.

Young Jimmy thought of something; his head was up from his plate.

—Hey, Dad, he said.—That sounded like you said the dog is delicious.

The laughter filled the place.

—All these years, said Jimmy.—And you never knew what went into shepherd's pie.

—That's, like, gross, said Mahalia.

She was eating beans and mashed potato.

—Anyway, said Jimmy.—We've a dog. That right, Smoke?

Brian nodded so much his face had problems keeping up.

—Well, said Jimmy.—I want the right to name him.

There was silence, except for the cutlery.

—What's wrong?

—Nothing.

—Does he have a name already?

—No, said Mahalia.

—Then wha' then? said Jimmy.—There's somethin' wrong. What?

—There's nothing wrong, said Aoife.

—It's the way you said it, said Mahalia.

—Said what?

—I want the right to name it.

—How did I say it?

156

—Like it was your last wish, like, said Mahalia.

—Did I?

Aoife was looking at Mahalia.

—You're amazing, she said.

—I'm just saying the truth, said Mahalia.

—Yes.

—Did I though? said Jimmy.

A chair scraped, not very dramatically. But Brian was standing, wet-faced, heading for the door to the hall.

—I'll go after him, said Jimmy.—God, Jesus – I'm sorry.

—Leave him a minute, said Aoife.

—I was jokin', said Jimmy.

—We know.

—I'm sorry.

The self-pity felt a bit like the nausea – but only a bit.

He whispered, to all of them.

—I wanted to call him Chemo.

—Cool.

—Savage.

Jimmy kept whispering.

—But I don't suppose I can call him that now.

—No, said Aoife.—Anyway, look at him. He's gorgeous.

The new dog – he was only a pup – was asleep, beside his basket.

—What is he? Jimmy asked.

—He's a bit of an omelette, said Mahalia.

—Wha'?

—Cocker spaniel, like, poodle and greyhound.

—Jesus, said Jimmy.—How did the greyhound get down – ?

—Don't.

—I'll tell yeh but, said Jimmy.

He looked across at the pup.

—It'll be like bringin' a wheelbarrow for a walk.

He stood up.

Don't hitch your jeans.

—I'll go up to Brian.

—Bring up the rest of his dinner, said Marvin.

—Don't start. Leave Brian alone.

The radio, the Roberts – great fuckin' invention. It was on, low. Jimmy could tell – there was something about the voice, the news being delivered.

—Hang on.

157

He turned it up.

—What's happened?

—Shush – listen. Ah, no.

—What's wrong?

—Whitney Houston's after dyin'.

He sat beside Brian on the bottom bunk.

—Alrigh'?

Brian nodded.

—I'm sorry, said Jimmy.

He put his arm around Brian's shoulders.

—I just – , he said.—I joke about these days. It's my way.

—It's funny.

—But I go too far.

Brian was crying now. Jimmy loved it and hated it. Loved it, because one of his children needed him; hated it, for the same reason – and the fear that he wouldn't be able to help.

—Are – , Brian started.—Are—.

Jimmy let him try again.

—Are you – ?

It was too much for the kid; it would take forever.

—Am I goin' to die? said Jimmy.

Brian nodded. He was humming now. That was how his crying sounded. A steady hum, like the washing machine going through its last spin.

—No, said Jimmy.—At least – . We could both be hit by a bus the next time we go out. Even with our sat navs.

—No – no mocking.

—Sorry. You're right. But you know what I mean. I could trip on the dog. Or – a dog could fall out of the sky and land on our heads.

A laugh got out.

—Good man, said Jimmy.—But this chemo thing. It's short for —

—Chemotherapy.

—Exactly – great. It's a precaution. The cancer's gone. The operation before Christmas. You remember —

Brian nodded. His face, the left side, was up against Jimmy's chest, and Jimmy's shirt was soaking. It felt like wet paint was being lightly smeared across his skin.

—Well, he said.—It was a complete success. You know that.
Another paintbrush up and down his chest.
—The cancer, the tumour, like – it's gone.
—Forever?
—That's the plan, said Jimmy.
He was crying now too. He didn't want to – but he did. He was still able to talk.
—The chemotherapy will kill any little cancerous cells that might be still in there. Chemo – chemicals. It's really strong medicine.
—I read about it, said Brian.
—Did yeh?
—Yeah.
—Where?
—Downstairs.
—I mean, what did you read?
—Wikipedia, said Brian.
—And you understood it?
Brian's hair painted a shrug onto Jimmy's chest.
—It's easy.
—Good man.
—But it makes you sick.
—For a while, just. Till it's over.
—I know.
They weren't crying now.
—I don't like the jokes, said Smokey.
—Okay, said Jimmy.—No more jokes.
—Only sometimes.
—Thanks, said Jimmy.—How's school?
—Okay. It's a bit boring.
—It hasn't changed, so.
—That's a joke.
—No, it isn't.
—Why are we laughing then?
—Cos it's nice and we love each other and we like bein' together. I'd say that covers it.
Brian nodded again.
—I like laughing, he said.—Just not jokes about you.
—I hear you, said Jimmy.—So has anyone been sayin' things in school?
—What things?

—About chemotherapy – .

—No.

—Or cancer.

—No.

—Grand, said Jimmy.—What'll we call the dog?

They had two tracks now, two days before Jimmy's next session of chemo. 'Kiss the Bride in the Bed', and a real showstopper, 'The House On My Back', sung by a wild woman called Dolores McKenna.

—Can we do something with the name? he asked.

—The name? said Ocean.

—Can we call her Weepin' Dolores or somethin' like that?

—I guess.

—Make her more interestin'.

—Interesting?

—Yeah, said Jimmy.—It's a bit dull – just plain Dolores. If we – wha'? – embellish the name a bit, people will hear more in the song.

Ocean didn't get it. She even looked a bit hurt.

—But don't get me wrong, said Jimmy.—It's brilliant. An' well done, by the way.

He was talking too much. He could hear himself but he couldn't do anything about it.

—Let's hear it again.

He watched Ocean, Norman-trained, bring the stylus to the edge of the record. He could tell she loved what she was doing. She brought the stylus down like she was being talked through it by air traffic control.

They'd keep the crackles. It was like the sound was battling its way through the eighty years since Weepin' Dolores and the piano player had been in the studio.

It was simple, heartbreaking, the song of an emigrant who knew she'd never escape.

—THERE'S THE HEARTH STONE —

AND THE BELLOWS —

AND THERE'S MY OLD DOG—JACK —

It had none of the Paddy, none of the dishonesty at the core of every Irish song Jimmy had ever heard, except 'Teenage Kicks' and maybe 'The Boys Are Back in Town'.

—OH—I'M TRAIPSIN' THE WORLD —
WITH THE HOUSE ON MY BACK —

He lifted the stylus. It came back immediately, the delicacy and importance of the movement. He didn't have a record player. They'd been waiting till the kids grew up.

Norman walked in.

—You're back, Norman.

Norman looked a bit lost.

—How was that? Jimmy asked him.

I'm worse than my da. I'm my da's fuckin' da!

—Fine, said Norman.—Grand.

—We were talkin' about Dolores McKenna there, said Jimmy. —D'you know annythin' about her, Norman?

—There's no need to keep repeating my name, said Norman.—I know who I am.

—Grand. Great.

—That's her only record, said Norman.

He looked pleased, then anxious.

—That's – my God, said Ocean.—Her only recording.

—No, said Norman.—Only record. It's the only one in the world. As far as is known.

—Oh – my God.

—Jesus, Norman.

Jimmy went to lift Dolores off the turntable.

—No!

He stopped.

—Let Ocean do it.

—Okay, said Jimmy.—Fair enough.

He got out of her way.

—Anyway, he said, to Ocean.—That line, I'm traipsin' the world.

—I love it.

She slid the record into the purple sleeve.

—Me too, said Jimmy.—But – here's why I was wonderin' about adjustin' her name a bit.

—What? said Norman.

—Well, said Jimmy.—If she was American. A blues singer.

—Black?

—Is there any other colour? said Jimmy.—Anyway, when she sang that word traipsin', we'd know she meant a bit more than just traipsin'. Walkin' around, like.

There was no distance between his brain and his mouth; that

161

tube had come out with the surgery, into the bucket with the bowels. And the smile – the grin. He could feel it in his skin. It belonged to a man who knew he'd be wanting to vomit and die in less than forty-eight hours.

—What're you talking about? said Norman.—Are you talking about sex, by any chance?

—Yeah, said Jimmy.

—And you think that line is about sex?

—No, said Jimmy.—It's what can be suggested.

—It's a girl with a lovely voice who misses her dog.

—I know.

—And her mother!

—I know. I know. Just bear with me.

He talked to Ocean.

—A blues singer in America in 1932 could sing the word traipsin' in a way that hid meanings from official America. She could have been singin' about sex or —

He looked at Norman – he tried to.

—missin' the sex.

—With her dog?!

—No, not with her fuckin' dog. Jesus, Norman, I'd have thought that you of all people would've —

—What? said Norman.—Would've what?

Ocean rescued him.

—An Irish woman sings traipsing in 1932, she means, I guess, moving along slowly with a bundle on her back. An African-American woman sings it in 1932, and she means, okay, moving along slowly. But she also means fucking. That, I think, is what Jimmy is saying. Right, Jimmy?

—No. Yeah. No.

He took a breath.

—No, no. Listen. Ireland in 1932 was a miserable place. That's my guess, and I bet I'm right. Kids with no shoes, hunger, bad housin', the Church supervisin' everythin'. But the official picture was different. Happy peasants, glad to be rid of the Brits.

He was loving this.

—So anyway. One of the few escapes, beside real escape – emigration, like – was music. It's always been like tha'. Music is the great escape. In the words an' the rhythm. You could do things an' say things that weren't allowed. And not just sex now. Although everythin' is sex.

It was hard to look at both of them, at either of them. But he did.

—But anyway. The music. Happy when times were bad. Or laments when they were bein' told that things were lookin' up. They could tell the priests an' the politicians tha' they'd do whatever seemed natural an' they wouldn't be askin' for permission. Inside in the song. In Ireland, in 1932.

Norman and Ocean stood side by side, almost touching. They looked like a strange but happy couple.

—So, said Jimmy.—Dolores there. She's singin' about carryin' the weight of her memories wherever she goes. And it's brilliant. Thanks, Norman.

Norman smiled.

Norman fuckin' smiled.

—It's a sad image and it's a very sad song. But where's the defiance?

They were still glued to him.

—Where's the fuck-you to the dump she's had to leave? It's when she sings about traipsin' —

—Bellows, said Norman.

—Sorry, Norman?

—Bellows, he said again.

—What about it?

—I think it might mean the mickey, said Norman.

He took the hearing aid yoke from his waistcoat pocket, and put it back in.

—You mean it's phallic? said Ocean.

—That's a better way of putting it, said Norman.

—That's *interesting*, said Ocean.

—It's the way she stresses it, said Norman.—The word. I think she might have winked there.

—The hearth's the vagina, said Ocean.

—And Jack?

—He's not really a dog, said Norman.—And he has the bellows.

—In 1932.

—July the 17th, said Norman.—To be exact.

—But it's hidden, said Jimmy.

—Oh, it is, said Norman.—It's still a song about emigration.

—And it's brilliant, said Jimmy.—But I'd love to find – what we need is a singer who hides nothin'. Is he here, Norman? Or she.

—No, said Norman.—No.

—Well, said Jimmy.—I'm goin' to find him.

—The cancer trousers are back.

—Lay off, Aoife.

The nights were the worst. When he couldn't sleep and he knew he wouldn't be able to – until he woke up.

Two nights to go.

—What're you doing?

—Oilin' the valves, he said—I'm not sure if I'm doin' it properly.

—It looks complicated.

—Not really.

She picked up the bottle.

—Blue Juice Valve Oil, she read.

—Yep.

She let him take the bottle. She watched him as he dipped the nozzle against what must have been one of the valves and let a few drops roll out onto its side – it looked oily already – before putting it down, on top of the bedroom radiator.

—Jimmy, she said again.

—Wha'?

—Can I say something?

He couldn't hear her. He could – but he had to try hard. It was like trying to follow what someone was saying in a packed pub.

—Go on.

—Look at me.

—Hang on.

He lowered the valve back into the cylinder, or whatever it was.

Go away, go away.

He jiggled it till he thought he heard a click and a tightness – the valve was home – and he screwed it down. He put fingers on the valves, and lowered them. He lifted the fingers and watched the valves rise.

—Done.

—I'm still here.

The way she'd said it – she was lovely.

—Sorry.

—Nervous?

—Not really. Yeah. Very.

He put the trumpet in the case.

—I'm terrified, he said.

Now he looked at her.

—Not the chemo, he said.

—I know.

—The nausea.

It felt good to say it.

—It's like puttin' your hand on a hotplate, he said.—Deliberately. Why would you fuckin' do that?

—Do you want to stop?

—No. You mean call it off?

—Yes.

—No. Yeah, I'd love to. I'd – I'd faint with happiness if I was told – if they rang now an' told me it was over.

Her arms were around him.

—But no.

She pulled at the waistband, and let it go.

—Lay off.

—Sorry. I'm listening.

—I'm finished, he said.—And sorry about the cancer trousers. I know you hate them.

—I want you to hate them.

—I do.

—Not really.

—No, I do. It's just – the tension, I suppose.

He tried to show her.

—It's all around my stomach, like it's in it. Have I put on weight?

—No.

—It feels that way. With proper jeans on.

—Will you come downstairs?

—Yeah, yeah. In a minute.

—No, listen, she said.—I don't know what you're going through. Don't take this wrong – but you're frightening the kids. Even Marvin. Especially Marvin. When you're like this. And I know – . But – do you understand, Jimmy?

—Yeah.

He nodded.

—Yeah.

His eyes were wet. So were hers.

—I'm tryin'.

—I know.

He wasn't sure the bed would still be there when he moved, whether they were right at the edge of it and he'd end up face-first on the floor; he didn't know where he was here. His feet were tangled in – it might have been a dressing gown, or a towel.

He was freezing.

—Are you in a hurry? said Imelda.

—No, he said.—No.

—Liar.

—I'm not, said Jimmy.—Seriously.

He'd walked in earlier, into the kitchen. He'd looked at Aoife. He'd smiled. Brave man, only one night left to chemo.

—How are you? she'd asked.

—Grand.

—How was the day?

—Grand, he said.—Not too bad. Shifted a few units.

—Good.

He'd gone upstairs. He'd sat on the bed. He'd thought about leaving, sliding out of the house. Driving to Howth Head. Stepping off it. Onto the rocks and into the sea.

It wasn't real thought. He was messing.

He walked back into the kitchen. He looked down at the dog.

—Do we have a lead for this thing? he said.

—In under the sink, said Aoife.—But he's a bit small for it, I'd say.

She was right. The lead was a thick length of rope, probably made for a harpoon. And, now that he thought of it, the dog didn't have a collar yet.

—Do we have any string?

—No way, like.

It was Mahalia.

—Why not?

—You'll strangle him.

—Only if I want to.

—Not funny, she said.—Hang on.

She was gone – he had to wait. But it was fine; he wasn't panicking.

Mahalia was back.

—There.

She handed him what looked like the cord of a dressing gown.

—Grand, he said.—Hang on, this is mine.

—Tough shit, Sherlock.

He tied the cord around the dog's neck, not too tight. He stood up and gave it a little tug. The dog yelped, and skidded. It was the shock, not the tightness.

Jimmy had to get out. He felt devastated, and fuckin' great. He didn't trust himself.

—I'm gone.

—We'll eat when you get back.

If I get back.

Gobshite.

—Grand. Come on, Messi.

—Bring this.

Aoife handed him a SuperValu bag.

—Why?

—Poo.

—I'll wait till I get home.

—You're hilarious, she said.

He put the bag in his pocket.

—See yeh in a bit.

—Has he been wormed, by the way? he shouted back from the hall.

—Keep him off the grass!

That made about as much sense as anything did these days.

—Grand.

He slammed the front door. It was expected; everything was normal.

He gave the cord a bit of a tug. The dog didn't budge. He actually did look a bit like Messi, the hair and the front legs. But not nearly as cheerful or enthusiastic.

—Come on, for fuck sake.

He took a few steps but the dog didn't go with him. He didn't realise it – the dog was so light – until he heard a knock on the window behind him, and he looked back and saw Messi on his side, claiming a fuckin' penalty. He laughed, although he wanted to kick the dog down the road.

—Come on, stop messin'.

He picked him up and put him back down when he got past

167

the car and the gate. The dog pissed, then stood in the piss and shivered.

Jimmy pulled the dog out of the puddle, but any more pulling would have been cruel. He picked him up again, held him out and shook some of the piss off him. He took the SuperValu bag from his pocket and shook it open with his free hand. Then he put Messi into it.

That was the dog's first walk, up to his neck in a SuperValu bag. His feet never touched the ground but he went as far as the coast, through the last of the daylight, across the wooden bridge to Bull Island.

Jimmy hadn't walked this far in ages. But, then, he hadn't committed adultery before. The word meant nothing. The sex felt like an achievement. The day before his third session of chemotherapy, with memories of the second one still raw enough to make him cry, he'd managed it. Simple as that. There were all sorts of reasons why he shouldn't have done it, and all sorts of reasons why he shouldn't have been able to do it. But he'd put his hands on the skin of a woman he didn't really know, didn't know well, and he'd pushed all the worries and doubts away. He'd given Imelda the best five minutes she'd had all week.

There were people staring at him.

Fuck them.

They could see the guilt on him.

That was just stupid. And he didn't feel guilty.

He'd come too far, but he wanted to go to the end of the Wall. They'd be starving if they were waiting for him at home. He'd see if he could get a taxi when he got back onto the main road.

He should have told Imelda about the cancer. She'd liked his head; she'd said so. She'd run her hands over the stubble. His hair hadn't fallen out – not yet. He was just a man with a shaved head. The excuse hadn't been there to tell her.

You've no eyebrows, Jimmy.

But that was shite.

He'd been afraid of tears and sympathy. He'd wanted her to sit on him because he was a man, not because he was dying.

He believed that.

—So, she'd said.—Are we going to do this again?

—Yeah.

He'd been dying to go, to get the fuck away. But he'd have stayed. She was still gorgeous. *Still*? He'd fancied her – and he'd liked her – for more than a quarter of a century, and he'd have kissed her neck again, while her kids came skipping up the garden path. Were her kids still kids? Her garden path was a three-minute walk from his parents' garden path.

He was heading into chemo in the morning and three hours ago Imelda Quirk had groaned when he'd entered her. A woman fancied him. Simple as that. An attractive – that was the word – an attractive woman looked at him and saw someone, a man, she wanted to ride.

It was great.

There was rain in the wind now. He'd turn back in a bit. There were car lights behind him. His shadow stretched way ahead of him.

What a fuckin' mess.

There was a cop car down on the beach, to his left, just below the embankment. It was going at a fair clip, over the sand. It stopped and the front doors opened. They must have been looking for someone. He kept going – he wasn't interested.

He'd be able to face Aoife when he got home. There was nothing telling him he wouldn't be.

The hand came down on his shoulder just as he saw the two cops coming up off the embankment stones and running at him.

—Where're you going?

He was surrounded by big men half his age.

—What's wrong?

—Where're you goin' with the dog there?

—A walk, said Jimmy.—I'm goin' for a walk.

Then he saw it – what they saw. A man with a pup in a plastic bag, walking to the end of the Wall, the pier, whatever it was, with the tide coming in.

—Oh, hang on, he said.

They were young lads, probably fuckers, but they were questioning a middle-aged man in good clothes. So they listened to him.

—He went for a piss and stood in it. He's only a pup. And I didn't want to get the – eh – urine on my jacket.

Thank fuck he hadn't worn the cancer trousers.

—And I had the bag with me, for his poo.

He remembered the faces now, those people staring at him back there, when he'd been walking past the golf club.

—Did someone phone you?

—Someone did, yes.

—Look, said Jimmy.—The dog's name is Messi. If I went home without him – .

They believed him – the pricks.

They started to back away.

—Right, said one of them, the spokesman.—Just be careful. The fuckin' clown.

They were nearly off the embankment now, heading back to the squad car.

—Lads, he shouted.

They stopped.

—You couldn't give me a lift, could yeh?

The thing he really hated about this place was the fact that he was so near people with cancer. Women with wigs like crash helmets, men who should never have been bald. Pinheads. He only felt dangerously sick when he was here. (The nausea wasn't sickness. It was catastrophic but it ended, even if he couldn't believe that while it was destroying him.) Some of them – women and the men – arrived, wandered around like they were all set for a day at the beach. Bags full of stuff. Someone had left a cake on the counter beyond, and it had been rancid-looking chocolate-chip muffins the last time he'd been in. There was a guy a bit down from Jimmy, in cargo shorts and – Jimmy couldn't believe it – a Choose Life T-shirt. He kept looking around for someone to smile at.

The cancer community. Jimmy wanted nothing to do with them. They probably felt the same way about him. He didn't give a shite. At least he hadn't brought togs and a towel with him, pretending he was in Wexford or Majorca. All he had was his iPod.

Aoife was doing his worrying for him.

That wasn't true. He was worried. Although all of his worry – he couldn't think further than two or three days from now when the nausea would haul him out of his life.

Something by Ennio Morricone. 'The Good, the Bad and the Ugly'. For when they were carrying the coffin. But it would just get a laugh, and he didn't want that. He wanted the song that would make them say, That's Jimmy. His last moment in the present tense.

For fuck sake.

He was done, finished, out on parole. He put on his shoes. He smiled at the nurse, the sarcastic one. He turned his phone back on. Three texts. Aoife. *How was it? X*. He texted back. *Boring X*. She'd like that.

There was one from Des. *Are we still on for 2moro, Jmmy?* The trumpet lesson. He'd be fine. *If its ok wth u Des*. The polite middle-aged men. There'd be six or seven texts when one would have done the trick.

And one from Imelda. *Whenll I see u agen? 2 many precious moments*. Oh Christ. What had he fuckin' done? But he knew what had happened. She'd written the first bit, recognised the lyric – the Three Degrees, September 1974 – and she'd written the rest of it. For the laugh. It wouldn't be a bad song for the funeral, now that he thought of it.

He didn't know how to answer her, what to write. He deleted the text. Then he put a reminder into his calendar: *Text Im*.

The lift was taking forever. As usual.

Another text. From Aoife. *Lunch X*. She was reminding him. Lunch together straight after the chemo, so she could witness him tasting food and coffee like it was the first real time in his life. *On way X*. They were meeting in a place near work. The Dog's Lunch. He'd just pretend, if the taste thing didn't actually happen this time. He'd let her think it had. He owed her that.

Fuck the lift. He'd attack the stairs.

There was a guy right beside him, against him. If they'd been out on the street Jimmy'd have thought he was after his wallet. A small, wiry cunt; rough looking – losing the fight. Jimmy had to go around him, to get to the stairs. He glanced at the little cunt's face.

—Outspan?

The little cunt looked at him.

—Jimmy Rabbitte?

—Yeah, said Jimmy.—How's it goin'?

But he could see for himself. It was going horribly.

—Grand, said Outspan.—Not too bad.

—What're yeh doin' here? Jimmy asked him.

—Stupid fuckin' question, Jimmy, said Outspan.

The lift door had opened but they stayed where they were.

—An' yourself? said Outspan.—The chemo as well?

Jimmy nodded.

—Yep.

171

—Fuck sake, said Outspan.—The both of us.

Outspan had been in the first band Jimmy had managed, the Commitments. He'd been in Jimmy's class in school, in secondary and further back, to the first day of primary.

—What's your one? said Outspan.

—Bowel, said Jimmy.—Yourself?

—Lungs, said Outspan.

—Okay.

—I'd better be goin'.

—Grand, said Jimmy.—Okay. An' look it. It was great seein' yeh again.

—Yeah, said Outspan.—An' yourself.

—Good luck, Outspan, said Jimmy.

He headed for the stairs.

—No one calls me tha', said Outspan.

Jimmy stopped.

—Wha'?

—No one calls me that anny more, said Outspan.—D'yeh remember my real name, do yeh?

—Liam, said Jimmy.

—That's righ', said Outspan.

—D'you want to go for a pint or somethin'? Lunch?

—Lunch?

—Yeah, said Jimmy.—Lunch.

—Okay, said Outspan.—I can't manage the stairs but.

He pressed the lift button.

Jimmy stood beside him.

—I'm still called Jimmy, by the way.

—Fuck off.

There were other people, healthy and dying, waiting for the lift. They were staying well back from the two old friends.

—Derek, said Outspan.—Remember?

—Derek? said Jimmy.—Yeah. 'Course I remember.

Derek was another Commitment, another lad from school, and Outspan's best friend.

—Well, said Outspan.—He moved to Denmark, yeah?

He waited a while, took in breath.

—An' he was the last one tha' called me Outspan.

Another wait.

—An' now no one even knows wha' Outspan means.

The lift door – there was only the one – slid slowly open.

172

—Not since they released fuckin' Nelson Mandela.

They walked into the lift. It always reminded Jimmy of a butcher's fridge.

—Derek's in Denmark?

—Yeah.

The lift was filling behind them. Jimmy could hear Outspan's breathing.

—What's he doin' there?

—Pullin' his wire.

Jimmy hated himself for feeling embarrassed.

—He's married to a Danish bird, said Outspan.

—What about yourself?

—Married?

—Yeah.

—She was Irish.

—Was?

—Is, said Outspan.—An' part fuckin' Martian.

—Yis aren't together?

—No, said Outspan.—She fucked off with a Klingon.

Jimmy heard a snort. Someone in the lift was trying not to laugh.

Jimmy could never tell if the lift was moving or not. But the door opened, and there were people waiting to get in. He got through the crowd in front of him.

—Hang on, for fuck sake.

Jimmy was tempted to keep going. To pretend he hadn't heard him, to lose him and have his excuse ready in case they ever met again, upstairs in Chernobyl or anywhere else. But he turned and waited, and watched Outspan coming towards him. It was definitely Outspan Foster. The head – the look – was there; he still looked like Jiminy Cricket with a hangover.

—Alrigh', Liam?

—You're grand, said Outspan.—You've what again?

—Bowel.

—The guts.

—Well spotted.

—Fuck off. The lungs here – . Walkin' an' tha'. I can't keep up.

—Okay, grand.

—Havin' a shite now. I'd beat yeh hands down.

—I've to phone the wife, said Jimmy.

—Hate tha'.

—I'll only be a minute.

—Bet yeh won't.

They were still in the building; it would be easier than out on the street. He leaned against a wall, beside a noticeboard, and dialled Aoife.

—Hi.

—Howyeh, listen. Have yeh left the —

—I'm just off the Dart.

—Listen —

—And it was fine this morning?

—Yeah, said Jimmy.—Grand. Listen —

He did it. He looked across at Outspan, and lifted his eyes to fuckin' heaven.

—Is anything wrong?

—No, said Jimmy.—Nothin'. I've met someone.

Someone I knew years ago. We had sex yesterday afternoon.

—Up at the chemo. A guy I went to —

His voice jumped away, and he was suddenly right on the edge of crying.

—Jimmy?

He took a breath.

—Jimmy?

—I'm grand, he said.

His voice was back – his.

—What's wrong?

—I, said Jimmy.—I met an old friend. From way back. Up in the chemo. I can't really talk. He's here – near, like. Outspan Foster. Did I ever mention him? He might've been at the weddin'.

He was okay now. He could talk. He could trust himself.

—And he's – he's in a bad way.

—God.

—Lungs.

—Oh God.

—Anyway. I said I'd buy him lunch.

—Okay.

—Sorry.

—No —

—I'm really sorry.

It was true. He turned a bit, so he knew Outspan couldn't see his mouth.

—Life hasn't been kind to him, he said.

174

—Go, she said.—Have lunch.

—I'm —

—I'll see you later.

—I love you.

—I love you too.

—What ages are your kids?

　—Twenty-two an' seven, said Outspan.

　—Jesus.

　—Wha'?

　—The gap.

　—What about it?

　—It's wha'? – fifteen years.

　—I know.

　—Two women?

　—No, said Outspan.

　—Fair enough, said Jimmy.—Mine are eighteen, sixteen, fourteen an' eleven.

　—Four women, yeah?

　—Fuck off.

They'd found a Costa.

　—This do us?

　—Yeah.

There was a fair-sized queue.

　—D'yeh want to sit down over —

　—No.

　—Okay, said Jimmy.

　—She left me before this, said Outspan.

He hit his chest with his open hand.

　—Yeh know?

Jimmy nodded.

　—Just so yeh know, said Outspan.

Jimmy ordered the coffee and Outspan's tea and a couple of sandwiches in boxes, nothing that had to be made there and explained. They got a corner of a table, and sat with their knees and elbows banging.

　—Fuck off.

　—You fuck off.

　—Where're yeh livin' these days?

　—Swanbrook.

—Posh.

—No, said Jimmy.—Not really.

—G'wan, yeh cunt.

—What abou' you?

—Wha'?

—Where are you livin'?

—Back in me ma's, said Outspan.—It's not too bad.

—Yeah.

—Life is simple, yeh know.

—Yeah.

He had to pack the good days. But he'd started to love the race.

They'd two new songs. They'd found no more hot ones in Norman's house but Norman had put on his coat and brought them to other houses, and other men – they were all men – who collected old records.

'Eileen With the Smileen' would have been filthy sung by Muddy Waters.

—SHE MOVES THROUGH THE FAIR —

AND THE CHAPS DO STOP AND STARE —

Even sung by Billy Maguire and His Fermanagh Fiddles, you could tell the chaps were looking at her arse.

—THEY'VE NEVER SEEN ANYTHING LIKE IT —

OH – A SIGHT SO RARE AND FAIR —

—Brilliant.

—One of the fiddles is out of tune.

—That makes it even better.

Jimmy couldn't sit down.

—Good work, Ocean.

He could never sit down. He felt like that madman who'd produced *London Calling*, Guy Stevens, the guy who'd thrown chairs and swung ladders in the studio. Jimmy threw nothing but, still, he felt a small bit out of control.

—THEY DOFF THE CAPS AND SET THE TRAPS —

SHE'S A SIGHT SO RARE AND FAIR —

The song was a great find but it wasn't *the* song. It swung and charmed, but it didn't shock. And Jimmy, more than anything else – he wasn't sure why – wanted to shock.

The other one, the fourth, was a murder ballad. It was a song he knew from primary school, when he was younger than Brian.

They'd all stand and sing it, like a funny hymn. *There was an oul' woman and she lived in the woods – weile, weile, wáile*. He remembered Outspan standing somewhere near him in the room, and Derek. But even though the words – the lyrics – had been there, he'd never paid much attention to them.

This though – this version was different. The oul' woman was a young woman, and she was singing it.

—SHE HAD A BABY THREE MONTHS OLD —
WEILE WEILE WÁILE —

—Fuckin' hell, said Jimmy.

Norman was right beside him.

—The hair – on the back of my head, he said.

—I know, said Jimmy.

—It's terrifying, said Ocean.—Truly.

—SHE STUCK THE PENKNIFE IN THE BABY'S HEART —
DOWN BY THE RIVER SÁILE —

It was the voice and nothing else. And they knew it: they were listening to a confession. The woman in the record had murdered her baby. She'd given birth to her illegitimate child in among the trees, and she'd stabbed it.

—THEY PULLED THE ROPE AND SHE GOT HUNG —
WEILE WEILE WÁILE —

No one spoke for a while. Ocean lifted the needle.

—I googled executions in Ireland, she said.—In, like, 1932.

—And?

—No women.

—I'm surprised, said Jimmy.—She had me convinced. Who is she again?

Ocean held up the record, showed him the label.

—Mary McCrone.

—Can't be her real name, said Norman.

—No, Jimmy agreed.

—So, Jimmy, said Ocean.—Is this *the* song?

—No, said Jimmy—It isn't. It's the song tha' was written after *the* song.

—So, said Des.—Got that?

—Think so, yeah.

—You imagine your throat expanding as you breathe in. And when you exhale, the quality of the sound – it's already better.

—Yeah.

—You've been rushing —

—I know.

—Charging to the end.

—I know, yeah.

—Because you're scared you'll run out of breath.

—I know.

—But you won't.

—I know.

Jimmy hated being the student, hearing himself – *I know, I know* – the teacher's pet. But he loved what he was learning. Now and again, once or twice each time he played, he got a note that sounded right, a lovely thing that filled the room and the house. There was something great, a bit brilliant about sending the sound out, anticipating it, then blowing and getting it exactly as he'd wanted, and expected.

—This is great, Des. Thanks.

—No, said Des.—You're doing well.

They were chest to chest in the space between the bed and the wall.

—Your money, said Jimmy.—Hang on.

—Thanks.

Jimmy put hands into both pockets, found two euro, some copper and a memory stick.

—Shite, Des, he said.—I've no money.

—Don't worry, said Des.—You can get me the next time.

They were out on the landing.

—Sure?

—Yeah, yeah.

—If that's okay with you.

—No problem.

Des was ahead of Jimmy on the stairs. He stopped, and turned.

—Actually, no.

He spoke quietly. Jimmy was two steps above him, so Des had to look up a bit.

—I need it, he said.—Sorry.

—No problem, said Jimmy.

—I'm broke.

—It's okay, said Jimmy.

The urge was to push Des gently down the rest of the stairs, and out the door. Follow him, grand, but get him out of the house.

—I'll go with yeh to a pass machine. There's one in the Spar up the way.

—Thanks, said Des.—I'm sorry about this.

He was shaking. Jimmy could see it in his hand as it went for the banister. Jimmy could've dipped into the kitchen and seen if Aoife had the money. She probably did. But no. He'd go up the road with Des. Twenty-five fuckin' euro!

The dog was at the door. He'd heard Jimmy coming down. He stood there, the tail doing ninety, looking up. *Give us a walk!* Jimmy got his foot under the dog – it was easily done – and gently slid it out of the way.

He opened the door.

—Quick, Des, before Steve McQueen gets out.

—Lovely dog.

—The kids love him.

It was dark now, coldish, but Jimmy wouldn't go back in for his jacket. They were only going up the road. He looked at Des unlocking his bike from the front gate. The girl's bike – a woman's bike. Aoife had pointed that out the first time Des had come to the house. He wrapped the chain around the bar under the saddle. He wheeled the bike out to the path.

—Down this way, Des, said Jimmy.

He turned left at the gate and waited for Des to turn the bike his way. He smiled.

—Alright?

—Yeah, said Des.—Sorry again —

—You're grand, said Jimmy.

What would he say? He hardly knew the man.

—I need to get some cash for one of the kids anyway, he said.—A school trip or somethin'.

Rub it in, yeh stupid cunt. He could throw money at his kids without knowing what it was for, and probably more than he'd be throwing at Des. But that was ridiculous. He wasn't sure how, but it was just sentimental.

They walked beside each other.

—Winter's over I'd say.

—Yeah.

—Thank Christ.

—Yeah.

—Easier goin' on the bike.

—Yeah, yeah. Much easier.

179

—Did you sell the car, Des?

—Yeah, said Des.—I couldn't – I had to.

—That's bad, said Jimmy.

—No, it's actually grand.

—No, it's not grand.

He wished Aoife could have heard him say that. He'd tell her later.

—I meant, said Des.—I don't really miss it.

—I don't use mine much, said Jimmy.

That wasn't true. It used to be truer, but not since the surgery and the chemo.

—But yeah, said Des.—It was hard having to decide to get rid of it.

—Did you get a decent price for it?

—No.

They walked past three gates before they spoke again.

—The bike, said Jimmy.

—It's my daughter's, said Des.—When she's over.

—Christ.

—She's tall, at least.

—What happened?

—No work.

Jimmy didn't know what Des did – had done – for a living.

—Just disappeared, said Des.

He rang the bell on the handlebar.

—That was an accident, he said.

—What do yeh do? Jimmy asked him.

—Landscaping, said Des.—Gardens mostly.

—Southside?

—No, said Des.—Fuck off.

He smiled.

The Spar was right in front of them. They stopped walking.

—Everywhere, said Des.—You'd be surprised.

—I probably wouldn't.

—I put fountains and ponds into council-house gardens, said Des.

—I bet.

—Anyway, said Des.—Small jobs were the first to go.

He shrugged.

—No real problem, he said.—I'd four or five lads working for me. Lithuanians. Great heads. But that became two or three. Then the

180

big jobs became smaller. But they've stopped too. All these people have suddenly learnt how to cut the grass. That's not fair. But —

He rang the bell again, on purpose this time.

—It's rough, said Jimmy.

They just stood beside each other for a bit.

—I'd never have guessed tha' that was what yeh did, said Jimmy.—Landscapin'.

—Why not?

—Well, you're always dressed – dressed to kill, my ma would say. And your hands —

—I wash myself, said Des.

—Sorry.

—You've got some stupid notions, Jimmy.

—I didn't mean anythin'.

He looked at Des.

—Sorry, he said.—I'm a twat.

—The real killer, said Des,—was two big jobs I never got paid for.

—Fuck. Really?

—And I know – I know for a fact that at least one of them is well able to pay. Just won't.

—The cunt.

—You said it.

Jimmy nodded at the shop.

—You comin' in?

—No, said Des.—I'll only be tempted to spend money I don't have.

—Grand. Won't be a minute.

Jimmy knew: Des really couldn't spend money he didn't have. It was that basic. He didn't have a working bank card, let alone an overdraft or a friendly manager. Jimmy's eldest two had their own bank cards; their pocket money went straight to their accounts. They withdrew fivers, and they couldn't actually spend money that wasn't there. But they were in better shape than Des. He was back where he'd started, somewhere in the late '70s. But, of course, he wasn't. That was just sentimentality too.

The sentimentality – it was fuckin' everywhere.

He took out a hundred and headed for the door, then changed his mind. He didn't want to hand Des a fifty, didn't want to tell Des it was fine, it could cover the next lesson as well. He didn't want to hear himself say, You're grand.

He went to the counter, picked up a packet of Doublemint, handed it with a fifty to the young one behind the counter. He took the change from her.

—Thanks.

He put twenty-five into a pocket and went back out to Des.

—There yeh go.

—Thanks.

It was fuckin', fuckin' dreadful. But he liked Des and it felt good to be with him now. Neither of them wanted to go. He knew Des would say no to a pint. Anyway, he didn't want one himself. But he did something a bit clever. He anticipated the chat later that night with Aoife; what she'd ask, how she'd look at him.

—Is your apartment okay, Des? he asked.—Safe?

Jimmy knew that much; Des had an apartment. Somewhere off the Stillorgan Road. Jimmy had envied him – just a quick stab. The familyless life. The step back into happiness. Jesus.

—Yeah, said Des.—Yeah.

—D'you own it? Sorry if I'm —

—No, said Des.—No. My aunt owns it. I've been renting.

He shrugged.

—I'm her godson.

—Nice.

—Awful.

—Yeah.

—But yeah. I'm lucky.

—If you say so, said Jimmy.—But look it. Any time. You know.

—Thanks, said Des.

—I'm not just sayin' that, said Jimmy.

—I know.

—If I can help – . Sorry. I mean it.

—I know.

—It's a ceili band playin' 'Black an' Tan Fantasy', said Jimmy.

—My God, said Aoife.—In 1932?

—Yep, said Jimmy.—It's a Duke Ellington song. But they didn't call it that. These guys here.

—What did they call it?

—Liscannor Bay Fantasy.

—Brilliant.

They listened to an accordion doing what should have been done by a trumpet.

—Did you recognise it?

—Nope, said Jimmy.—I fuckin' hate jazz.

—I forgot, said Aoife.—Sorry for asking.

—You're grand, said Jimmy.—No, it was the young one.

—Ocean?

—Yeah. She spotted it immediately. Turns out she knows her onions. Whatever that means.

They said nothing for a bit while they both enjoyed the madness of it.

—How are you feeling? she asked him.

—Grand, he said.—Really. Grand.

—It mightn't happen this time.

—It will, said Jimmy.—But it's okay. I'll survive.

He paused the song.

—And you know what's good?

—What?

—This, he said.—The searchin'. The Eucharistic Congress is in June an' we've still only got about half an album's worth o' songs. But she's brilliant. Ocean.

—And she's the girl you thought was being seduced by her father.

—Same one, he said.—Seems like ages ago. Fuckin' hell.

They laughed.

—Anyway, said Jimmy,—we need about five more songs and we might be able to get away with four.

He held up the laptop, just before he put it on the floor beside the bed.

—It's good though, isn't it? The latest one.

—Yes, she said.—It is.

—I love that, he said.—Ceili lads listenin' to nigger jazz, down a boreen somewhere.

—With the sound down low.

—Very low. Huddled around the gramophone, like. And hidin' the record. Passin' it around. In a different cover. It might even've been illegal. Banned.

—Different times.

—The good ol' days, he said.—They must've been lookin' for new music.

—And they found it.

183

—Yeah, but they had to disguise it.

He slid down under the duvet.

—I want to find somethin' that wasn't disguised.

—What?

—Don't know.

She slid down beside him.

—Do me a favour, she said.

—Wha'?

—Concentrate a bit on the kids.

—I took Brian and May to my parents —

—The other two.

—They hardly know if I'm here or not.

—They're worried. Just like the younger ones.

—They've some way o' showin' it.

—Ah Jimmy.

He knew he was being a prick. A complete one.

—Sorry.

—It's okay.

She was still right in against him. It was great but it made him nervous. He was sure there was a smell of something off him – guilt, or fuckin' stupidity. That was just stupid, he knew. But he couldn't believe he'd get away with it. And he kind of didn't care.

He turned in the bed, to face her properly. He bent his legs, so one of his knees touched her thigh.

—Tell me one thing, he said.

—What?

—If they're so worried, if Marvin's so worried – . This is a real question now. It isn't self-pity.

—Go on.

—Right, said Jimmy.—The last time I was sick. An' they all saw the state of me —

—You shouldn't feel bad about that.

—Easily said.

—Jimmy, I'm tired of this. I really am. You're flogging yourself. But, actually, you're not. You're flogging us. Me.

—Okay, he said.—Sorry. I hear you. You're right. Just – Marvin.

—Go on.

—He sees me, he sees you gettin' me up the stairs. And he leaves – he goes out the fuckin' door, to a party.

She sighed, but she didn't move.

184

—Yes.

—So, said Jimmy.—What? He's goin' to a party because he's upset?

—Jesus, Jimmy. Use your imagination.

—I know. I do. I just wish he'd be a bit more conventional. I wish he'd fuckin' hug me.

—When was the last time you hugged him?

—Okay – yeah. Yeah.

He closed the curtains. He got onto the bed. He sat back against the wall.

It was coming. He knew it was coming.

Oh God.

Oh fuck.

The house was empty.

Just him.

He listened again, the same voice, the exact same unbelievable message.

—Okay, he said.—I'll have to – . Did you phone my wife, by the way?

He listened carefully.

—Okay.

He looked across at Ocean and Noeleen.

—Okay, he said.—Grand. I'll be there as soon as I can.

He was finishing the call, about to press the red button. Then he thought of something.

—Thanks.

He inhaled, and slowly exhaled. He looked at the women, and stood up.

—Sorry, he said.—A family thing. I've to go.

—Is everything alright? said Noeleen.

—Yeah, he said.—It'll be grand. I just have to – . Sorry about this.

He was on his way.

—Jimbo?!

—Yeah?

—Is there anything we can do? A phone call or anything?

—No, he said.—Thanks. It's under control.

Jesus.

Down the stairs, out to the street, and the two corners to the car park at the back of the building. He had the key out, all ready to point at the car.

Nearly there – he was sweating like a bastard.

The code, the code – the car-park gate. He hit Cancel. He'd been punching in his bank card number. He had the right one now. 1977. How could he have forgotten that? *Heroes, Exodus, Lust for Life*. Maybe that was the steroids too – forgetting simple things. He'd ask Aoife. She'd know.

His heart – he could feel it.

He had the car going. On his way. He'd be there in twenty minutes.

—Mister Rabbitte?

—Yes.

—Mahalia Egan-Rabbitte's father?

—Is something after happenin'?

Mahalia had gone back to class after the lunch break, drunk.

He checked his hands, loosened his grip on the wheel. They were fine – no shakes.

Pissed in home economics.

Mahalia – May. She was brilliant in school. She always had been. Since day one. Drunk as a skunk while making a swiss roll.

It wasn't funny.

He was over the East Link now, past the O2.

Aoife had told him to concentrate on the kids. Well, her wish was coming true. Her wish and his. He'd be well able for this.

He'd texted Des as he went down the school corridor. *Might hve to cancel trumpt. I'll get bac.* He'd texted Aoife too. *On way. X.* He'd been tempted to call her but he'd thought it would've looked bad, arriving at the Principal's door with the phone to his ear.

—Where is she now? he asked.

He was in the Principal's office, sitting in front of her desk. Missis Halpin. He thought her first name was Fionnuala.

—Sickbay, she answered.

—I want to see her, said Jimmy.

—Of course, she said.—We'll just wait till Miss Traynor joins us.

Miss Traynor was the Year Head. He'd met her before – he

thought. At one of the parent–teacher meetings. She'd been alright.

—I need to see her, said Jimmy.

—Mister Rabbitte.

—Jimmy.

—There are ten girls in sickbay.

—Ten?

—Ten, yes. Mahalia's in good company. She's being well looked after.

—I know, said Jimmy.—And I'm really sorry about this. We don't have drink in the house —

—I'll stop you there. This isn't some fitness-for-parenthood test. That isn't why we're here.

—I know – thanks.

—I don't doubt that yourself and Missis Egan-Rabbitte – . Is she on her way, by the way?

—I think so, said Jimmy.—Yes.

—Fine, said Missis Halpin.—Good.

—How long will she – Miss Traynor – be, d'yeh think?

—Classes end in —

Missis Halpin lifted her sleeve and took a look at her watch.

—Ten minutes.

—Ten – I can't wait till then, sorry.

He stood up.

—Where's the sickbay?

—Mister Rabbitte —

Where the fuck was Aoife?

—Sorry, he said.—I don't mean to be obstructive or anythin'. We'll back whatever the school decides to do. I'm sure we will. But I have to see May.

He went to the door.

—I'm her dad.

His voice wobbled a bit, shook, like a bubble had passed through it. But he was grand.

—Mister Rabbitte.

She was standing too now.

—I'll go with you.

—I just want to see her, he said.—Let her know I'm here. She's probably feelin' —

He said it; he got over it.

—Nauseous.

They were on the corridor.

—This way.

Don't look at her arse.

They turned on to a different corridor, and another one. They didn't speak.

—Here we are.

They were in front of a door with no window. She held the handle. She seemed to be listening. Her ear was an inch from the green-painted wood.

She opened the door.

It was a small room and it was full. He couldn't see Mahalia – there were ten Mahalias. The air was damp with old tears and sweat. He could feel it. And the smell of puke and something sharply sweet, some sort of cleanser or spray. There were two of the girls – no, three – lying down, and the rest were sitting in a row.

She was sitting between two orange girls – it was the fake tan, and she probably looked even paler than she was because of that.

She saw him.

—Hiya, love, he said.

He saw her eyes fill. She smiled – it wasn't easy.

He went further into the room.

—Mister Rabbitte.

He went across to Mahalia. There was a woman he saw now, to his left. She was smiling but she looked worried. He kept his eyes on Mahalia. God love her, she looked desperate. White, blotchy skin, panda eyes; her lips were dry. A confused little girl.

He kneeled in front of her. The oompa-loompas on each side of her stared at him.

—Alright?

She nodded. He put his hand to the side of her head, over her right ear. She tilted her head to meet it, the way she'd always done, since she was a little thing. Her head felt hot, the hair was a bit sticky.

—Want to go home?

She nodded again.

—Come on.

He stood up, and so did she. She looked okay; she was steady enough on the pins. He walked back to the door and Missis Halpin. He spoke before she did.

—I'm bringin' her home. I'll come back.

—Alright, she said.

And he saw: she smiled at Mahalia as Mahalia went around her. Mahalia didn't look at her.

—But could you sign her out at the office, please?

Jimmy was heading for the door at the end of the corridor. He waited for Mahalia. He held out his hand. She took it.

He pointed at the exit door.

—Is this the quickest way out, love?

—Yeah.

He turned as he walked.

—I'll be back.

He couldn't fuckin' believe he'd just said that.

—Where were you?

—The vet, said Aoife.

She was holding the dog.

He was coming down the stairs. Mahalia was in bed. She'd puked again, and said Sorry so many times it had stopped being a word.

—You're home early, said Aoife.

Something thumped Jimmy.

She looked guilty – caught. *Is she doin' what I've been fuckin' doin'?*

—I phoned you, he said.

—I left my phone here.

—I texted you.

—My phone – I told you. What's wrong?

He told her.

—I don't believe it.

—I know, he said.—But I saw it. She's grand now.

Aoife went past him, up the stairs. She was still holding the dog. He followed her.

She was sitting at the side of May's bed. Jimmy could hear May sobbing, and Aoife whispering.

—It's okay, it's okay, it's fine.

—I've to go back, he said.

—What?

—To the school. I've to go back.

—Oh, she said.—Why?

—Face the music, I suppose.

He heard Mahalia moan.

—It's okay, love, he said.—It's grand. You'll be fine.

He went out to the landing. He came back.

—What's wrong with the dog?

—Nothing.

She hadn't looked at him. She was gazing down at Mahalia.

—Okay, he said.—See yeh later.

—Okay.

The dog was her fuckin' alibi.

Cop on.

He drove back to the school and found he'd missed his place in the queue. He sat beside a woman who seemed to have been crying – she'd definitely been. She had that blotched thing, and she looked angry and confused. Like her daughter, probably. She wasn't interested in talking. There was a man to his right. He'd arrived just after Jimmy. He'd smiled, raised his eyes to heaven, shrugged, but didn't seem to speak any English. He was standing. They'd run out of chairs. The secretary, across the way, kept looking out of her hatch. She might have been the woman who'd phoned him earlier; she had the head to match the voice.

There were five people ahead of him.

He got his phone out.

He texted Des. *Cant make it. Srry. Truble wth kids sch.* He deleted the last bit, and sent it. He texted Aoife. *How is she? x*

The door opened. A woman came out, with one of the orange girls. They left without glancing at anyone. They'd both been crying. Jesus. He thought he recognised the ma. Someone he'd known years ago, when they were kids – teenagers. He wasn't sure. The phone shook in his hand. It was Aoife. *Fine. Asleep. Messi ate my knickers. X*

The phone hopped again. Des. *No prob. Tues?* He'd pay Des for the missed lesson. *Cant. Chemo. Wed?*

He could get through a few bars of 'Abide With Me', and he thought it sounded okay, sometimes, when he didn't panic and rush. He was thinking he'd record himself, for when they carried the coffin. That would be dramatic – heartbreaking – the man himself playing at his own funeral. Such a fuckin' loss. *Who's tha' playin'? It's Jimmy himself. He was shite, wasn't he?*

His life was an awful fuckin' mess.

Des again. *Ok.*

Even texting – it was a nightmare. He'd send the wrong message

to the wrong person. The wrong woman. A good name for a film.
Starring Jimmy Rabbitte. Fuckin' eejit. He'd fuck up, fire off the
wrong text, call her the wrong name.

It was fuckin' great.

—Mister Rabbitte?

—Wha'?

It was your woman, the Principal. He was next – he hadn't
noticed.

—Sorry, he said.—I was —

He held up the phone.

—Work.

—I know.

He followed her into the office.

—When the word expulsion was mentioned —

—Oh Christ no. Expulsion?

—Yep.

—Oh God – Jimmy – ! They can't —

—Hold on, he said.—It's not too bad. She was just tellin' me
they *could*. That the offence justified it.

—That's ridiculous.

—I know, yeah. But I didn't argue with her. I heard someone
doin' that – before me, like. It didn't last long. Anyway, look,
they're not goin' to expel ten girls all at once. It'd be a national
scandal. The press would jump on it. Joe Duffy. It'd take their
minds off Anglo an' the fuckin' Household Charge —

—Jimmy, tell me.

—I let her have her say. Expulsion, suspension, all the options
and procedures. And then I told her I had cancer.

—You – ?

—So it's grand. She's not bein' expelled.

—Because you told Fionnuala Halpin you had cancer?

—No, he said.—But I told her before she said what they'd
decided to do. Just to be on the safe side.

The dog was beside him, at his leg. He picked him up and
parked him.

—Suspended, he said.—For a week.

—That's not too bad.

—Includin' today.

—We'll ground her.

—Yep.

—Take her phone.

—No pocket money.

—Yes.

—I'm to phone her tomorrow, said Jimmy.—To let her know what we're doin' from our end.

—And a letter of apology, said Aoife.

—Good idea. An' I'll send her an mp3 of 'Erectile Dysfunction' as well.

Aoife smiled.

—Maybe this is – .

—What?

—To do with you.

—Wha'?

—Mahalia, said Aoife.—She's never as much as got a negative remark in a Christmas report. Ever. And now – this.

—Because of me?

—Don't dismiss it, she said.

—I'm not, said Jimmy.—But no – fuck it. There were ten o' them. I only recognised one. Shannon I think her name is. She's been in the house. But, like – they didn't all get pissed because they're worried about me.

—Forget the others —

—You should've seen them, by the way. In the sickbay. Jesus, it was chillin'.

—Just think about it.

—Okay.

The dog's front paws were on his chest.

—Vodka, he said.

—They drank?

—She had – your woman, Nuala —

—Fionnuala.

—She had the empty bottle on her desk. Exhibit A.

—They didn't drink it neat?

—No, said Jimmy.—That was Exhibit B. A Coke bottle, one o' the two-litre jobs. Oh, and that's another thing.

—What?

—She wants to know who brought the bottle into school.

—That's fair enough.

—I told her we don't have much drink in the house.

—I could do with one.

—We'll have to interrogate May.

—Tomorrow.

—Could they all have got hammered on one bottle of vodka?

—Well, it wouldn't be easy. But there's the context. Where were they?

—Behind the gym.

—In the right circumstances ten girls together could probably get drunk without actually drinking anything at all. They're amazing things really, teenage girls.

—They're terrifyin'.

—Probably.

—I'll go up to her and say hello.

—She'll like that, said Aoife.—She feels wretched.

—Good.

They smiled – grinned.

—But anyway, said Jimmy.—I thought I handled it well. The school.

—Calling in the cancer was a masterstroke.

—I thought so.

—Did she ask for a doctor's cert?

He laughed. She loved that, making him laugh.

—And this fella, he said.

He held up the dog.

—The vet. Another of today's shocks.

—God, yeah, said Aoife.—I'd forgotten.

—What happened?

—He was lying on the floor, she said.—Over there. And he wouldn't move his eyes or respond. I called his name and he wouldn't wag his tail. But it was his eyes really. They were – dead.

—Christ, said Jimmy.

—So I just picked him up and ran. There was no one else in the vet's, thank God, and Eamon —

—Who's he?

—The vet – hello.

They laughed at her Mahalia impression.

—So he put Messi down on the table. The stainless steel one he has. And he felt Messi's tummy. Then —

She started laughing.

—He put his finger —

She couldn't talk for a while. He was laughing now as well.

—Was he wearin' rubber gloves?

—Yes! But he put his finger up poor Messi's bum and said, Aha, and pulled out something. It was horrible at first. I thought it was a worm or a lizard. But then I knew.

She wiped her eyes.

—I think I recognised them before Eamon did —

—I fuckin' hope so.

—Stop, she said.—I mean, I knew what they were before he did. But he was still pulling away when Messi stood up and —

She was laughing again.

—started —

She couldn't stop. She waved a hand, like she was surrendering to it; she'd be back in a minute.

—No hurry, said Jimmy.

—He started —

—Go on.

—He started wagging his tail.

—The vet?

—Messi, she said – she actually screamed it.—While Eamon was still pulling them out! Oh God —

He wondered if Mahalia could hear them laughing. The boys – all three of them – had wandered in. That often happened when they heard their parents laughing. They hovered around the door and the fridge.

—You must've been pleased, said Jimmy.

—Relieved, she said.—Mortified.

—Still, said Jimmy.—Your knickers able to fit inside a dog this small. At your age.

—Fuck off.

They loved hearing their mother use bad language.

—Poor May, said Jimmy.—I'll go on up and say hello.

He handed the dog to Brian.

—Here yeh go, Smoke. Mind he doesn't eat your jocks.

It was always a surprise to know he'd been asleep. He hadn't been breathing; he'd been holding his breath, smothering – he didn't know. And quickly enough, he didn't care. He was up and out, trotting ahead of the dark thoughts.

He got up before the gang. He let out the dog, he fired off a few emails, he let the dog back in. The Halfbreds were demanding a meeting. They wanted to know why more than three hundred thousand YouTube hits had produced less than two thousand sales. They were entitled to an explanation. But they had kids, so they knew that kids didn't buy the vital musical moments they'd be bringing with them for the rest of their poxy lives; they expected them all for nothing. And their parents were beginning to share the attitude. Mammies wearing Uggs, dads in skinny jeans – they were stealing their music now as well. Anyway, two thousand – so far – was very good. This was Ireland, a small country on the brink of collapse. Barry and Connie could fuck off.

The Dangerous Dream's coast-to-coast return tour had to be sorted. The middle-aged prog rockers were refusing to stay in B&Bs, and they wouldn't accept that they could drive home after most of the gigs. Their main man, Andrew Belton, had been living in Kenya for the last twenty years, so Jimmy didn't know what his problem was. Sleeping in the van should have been a fuckin' luxury. But *My Life On the Planet Behind You* had been Jimmy's solid seller all year, and he'd made the big mistake of telling Andrew. A nice enough head was becoming a bit of a bollix. Jimmy would have to book a couple of rooms in a hotel beside one of the roundabouts outside Athlone – the same hotel every night, even for the Dublin gig.

He had to lavish emails on the clients he'd been neglecting since the chemo started, especially the Celtic Rock brigade. And he had a mobile number for a chap he thought had once been called Brendan Goebbels. He was the founder, if it was the right guy, of a Dublin punk outfit called the High Babies. Jimmy'd read somewhere – it might have been in *The Ticket* – that the Edge and Bono were doing the soundtrack for a new HBO series, set during the hunger strikes, starring Colin Farrell and Bono's daughter. And he'd remembered a song the High Babies used to do, around the time of the hunger strikes, called 'Snap, Crackle, Bobby'. *Eat your Krispies Bobby – Or you're goin' to die*. He didn't know if they'd recorded it. But if they had, he knew someone who knew the Edge's cousin, who might get the song to the Edge. If this was the right man, if Jimmy could grab the man's interest, and if the other man could grab the Edge's interest. If, if, fuckin' if. On the good days, Jimmy loved that word.

He'd phone Les. He'd phone Darren. And Des. And Imelda – instead of just texting. He'd talk to her properly. He'd phone Outspan.

He still didn't have the song.

But he had an idea.

He was at chemo, scrolling through the iPod again.

He'd make it up.

It was there, as solid a thought as he'd ever had, already a fact, as if he'd made the decision months ago. He'd invent the song.

He attacked the iPod again. It was different now, though. It wasn't cheerful self-pity. This was research.

He looked up.

The knitting, the books, the fuckin' eejit over there with his iPod. Jimmy knew what that poor cunt was doing.

He was nearly done here. Then he'd be running again, charging. There was no stopping him.

—We've no money, she told him.

—Wha'?

They weren't broke like Des, just normal broke. They'd insufficient funds. Aoife hadn't been able to take any money from the Pass machine in the Spar. They were paying for the lunch with her credit card.

—My treat, she said.

It was nothing to worry about.

But it was.

Jimmy remembered a conversation he'd had with Noeleen that had shocked him. But he'd forgotten about it – he couldn't believe it.

They were all taking a pay cut.

—How much? said Aoife.

This was before they'd started eating, just after she'd asked him how the chemo had gone.

—I think she said 30 per cent, he said.

—Jesus.

—Yeah, he said.

It was like news he'd just heard.

—Jesus, Jimmy.

—I'm sorry.

—We'll cope, she said.

She was talking to a man who'd just come from chemotherapy. But he knew she wanted to kill him.

—And Noeleen, she said.—And is she taking the pain as well?

—Yeah, said Jimmy.

He thought he remembered Noeleen telling him that.

—An' we've some interestin' stuff comin' up, he said.—So we should be okay – . D'you remember the Halfbreds?

—God, yeah.

—I've to meet them in a bit, said Jimmy.—Want to come?

—No.

—Ah, go on.

—Okay, she said.

—Great.

—Why?

—Why what?

—Why do you want me to come? she asked.

—It'll be good crack, he said.—An' they might be less obnoxious if you're with me. Anyway —

He looked at her properly.

—It was always us, wasn't it? You an' me. We did it, not fuckin' Noeleen.

—Leave her alone.

—I know. But you know what I mean.

And he told her about the song he was going to write. He got a bit worked up as he heard himself tell her, afraid it sounded infantile and silly. They were skint and he was going to mess with history.

He finished telling her, and she told him she'd an idea as well.

—No.

—Why not?

—D'yeh think?

—Why not? she said again.—You've seen him.

He thought – he didn't; he didn't have to.

—Okay, he said.

His eyes were watering.

—Fuckin' hell, Aoife.

He walked into the kitchen. He was struggling a bit, a bit drowsy. He saw Marvin at the fridge, or young Jimmy. It was still dark. There was something not right – he turned on the light.

He roared – it wasn't a word, or a howl.

It was a kid, a young lad, a fuckin' burglar. Gone. Out the open window. Jimmy hadn't seen him get there. There'd been no sound on the floor and he'd knocked nothing over as he slid out.

Jimmy went after him.

He was gone – the kid was gone. Over the back wall. Or the wall beside him, into the empty neighbour's. He didn't know. He wasn't even certain now he'd seen him.

He went back into the kitchen.

The window was open. It was nearly a welcome sight, proof. He'd seen the kid.

—You, he said softly, to the dog.—You're a useless shitebag, aren't yeh?

Jimmy picked the dog up. His arms were shaking. He could feel it before he took the dog's weight. His heart was hopping. He was surprised, though; he wasn't angry. He felt nothing about the kid.

His roar had woken no one. He listened – no sounds from upstairs.

He brought the dog over to the door, and shoved him out the back for his piss.

They'd left the kitchen window unlocked. They never used the alarm.

They were broke.

They weren't.

They were – they were squeezed. They were in the club.

He let the dog back in.

There'd been something about the kid, the glimpse he'd had of him. Standing at the fridge, like one of his own.

He didn't phone the Guards. He wasn't going to. He was telling no one.

He shut the fridge door. He made the coffee.

She sat on the bed. She looked back at him and laughed.

—Fuck off, Jimmy.

—Look, he said.

—No, she said.—You fuckin' look.

She hadn't moved.

—This stay away from each other shite, she said.—We're not married, Jimmy. There's no arrangement. That I'm aware of. A kiss an' a cuddle now an' again. That was always it.

—I know.

—So grand. You know. Fuck off.

This hadn't been the plan.

—You don't get to decide, Jimmy, she said.—There's no fuckin' decision. If you want to stay away, then stay away. I couldn't care less.

—Listen —

—Don't fuckin' listen *me*, Jimmy Rabbitte.

She stood up.

—I'm not your fuckin' wife.

She walked out of the room. Two steps did it. But the way she did them – fuckin' hell. He heard her put down the toilet seat – she didn't bang it. Was he supposed to go while she was in there? She'd told him to fuck off. And she'd meant it – he thought she had.

He'd get fully dressed, no rushing down the stairs with his jeans and shoes in his arms. He didn't want to leave like this. He didn't want to leave at all. He wanted to change his mind, get back into the bed, roll back five minutes and shut his fuckin' trap.

But he was up now, buttoning his shirt. He heard the flush, the tap.

—Where're yeh goin'?

—I'm just goin', he said.—Work.

—Ah. And I was goin' to put you in my mouth one last time.

—Really?

—No. Fuck off.

—Can I say somethin'?

—Go on, said Imelda.—But keep puttin' your trousers on.

She sat back into the bed.

—I've – , he started.

Don't!

—I've —

Fuckin' don't.

—I've cancer, he said.

She laughed. Her head hit the wall behind her.

—Sorry, she said.—I don't mean I don't care.

She smiled.

—I'm really sorry.

—It's okay, said Jimmy.

She looked very calm. Kind of flat – neutral.

—When did you find out?

—A while back, he said.—I should have – .

—Bowel, she said.

—Wha'?

—Your cancer.

—How did yeh know tha'?

—The scar, Jimmy.

He looked down to where it was, hidden behind his clothes.

—I've had my face up against it quite a lot over the last few months, she said.—I could see it was newish. Tuck your shirt in, Jimmy. You're not a teenager.

He smiled. They were over the hump.

—So anyway, he said.

She sat up a bit straighter. She was pushing a pillow behind her when she spoke.

—And that's the excuse, yeah?

—Wha'?

—Your escape route, she said.

She let go of the pillow and looked at him.

—You tell me you have cancer. After you fucked me, mind you. Thanks very much, by the way. You were magnificent.

—Look, Imelda —

—Every grunt was music to my ears.

She wasn't angry, or sarcastic. She wanted him to laugh – he thought she did.

He sat on the bed and put on his socks and shoes.

—So, she said.

She tapped his back with her foot, kind of kicked it.

—Go on, she said.

—Wha'?

—You've got cancer, she said.

—Yeah.

—And?

—I need —

He was putting on the wrong sock. It was one of her husband's, from under the bed. Blue. His were black.

—What? she said.

She nudged him again with her foot.

He couldn't tell her about the sock. They'd never spoken about the husband, or Aoife. Steve. That was all he knew. He travelled a lot. That was all.

He did his laces.

—I have to spend time with the kids.

She laughed again.

—Lovely, she said.

—Serious, he said.

—As cancer.

Had she always been that quick?

—So, she said.—Like – . You've suddenly got cancer.

—Yeah, he said.—Not suddenly, no.

—You're – you must be, wha'? Jesus, it's like measurin' a pregnancy. You're havin' chemo by now. Are yeh?

He nodded. He thought she shivered. But she was naked and it wasn't warm.

—Look it, he said.—I couldn't tell you.

—'Course yeh couldn't, Jimmy. You haven't gone bald or anythin'.

—No.

—Lucky, she said.—So. I'm just curious. When we finally *met*. Had the chemotherapy started?

—Yeah.

—Grand.

—Just.

—Wha'? The same day?

—No, he said.—Once. But not then – the first time.

—Go on, Jimmy, she said.—Hop it.

—Sorry.

—For what?

—I should've told yeh.

—Yeah, she said.—But it's no odds, really. I kind of knew anyway.

—Did yeh?

—Not really, she said.—That's just tha' women's intuition shite. I don't believe in it. Unless it suits me. Go on.

—I'd better.

—Yep, she said.—Fuck off.

—An' I'm sorry —

—Jimmy. I'm not givin' you the satisfaction. Go on. Fuck off.

He'd been dismissed. Already gone; it was like he'd never been there.

He was downstairs, at the front door. He felt exposed – he even checked his fly. He'd liked it that they'd never spoken about the families. He'd started once, to tell her about May and the drinking. But she'd stopped him. *I don't want to know.* He'd loved it. He'd laughed. Except.

He wanted her to show something.

He could creep back up the stairs. Open the door here, close it loudly, go back up and catch her. Crying? Not a hope. He didn't know. He knew nothing about her.

He had to go. *Cop on, cop on.*

He'd parked the car at the Hiker's. He was meeting his da.

For fuck sake.

He'd go on up to the main road and walk back down to the pub from that direction.

It was unfinished. Unstarted. There'd been nothing to it, except the sex and the bit of chat. Every man's fuckin' dream. Every man in Barrytown would have envied him, if they'd known. Maybe that was the problem.

He didn't trust himself. He'd tell his da – or Aoife. The way he was.

He took the phone out. *Thanks X*. Proper spelling. He fired it off. She wouldn't answer. He didn't know why, or why not. He knew nothing. He hadn't a clue.

—Did you talk to Noeleen?

—No. I forgot.

—Jesus, Jimmy.

—Sorry.

—We need to know.

—I know.

—D'you want me to talk to her?

—No.

—It's a simple question.

—I know, he said.—Tomorrow. I swear.

—It's humiliating.

—Yeah. But it's grand. Has to be done. It's grand.

—What're you reading?

—This.

—*Just Kids*. Patti Smith. Oh, we like her, don't we?

—Fuck off.

—Have you spoken to Marvin yet?

—Tomorrow, said Jimmy.—I've an appointment. He's agreed to meet me at six.

—Jesus, said Aoife.—What are we like? He's a schoolboy.

—He's a fuckin' rock star.

★   ★   ★

—Cool.

—Yeh like the idea?

Marvin nodded.

—Yeah.

Jimmy spoke to young Jimmy.

—And yourself?

Bringing in young Jimmy had been Jimmy's idea.

Young Jimmy shrugged, looked at his brother, shrugged again.

—Yeah.

—Great.

It was a fuckin' miracle. He was sitting with his sons and they had this thing in common.

—Will what we're doing, said Marvin.—Will it, like, be illegal?

—Christ, said Jimmy.—I never thought – . I suppose it will.

—Cool.

—You alrigh' with that? he asked young Jimmy.

Young Jimmy shrugged.

—Yeah.

—Great. So.

He caught himself rubbing his hands together. He hated that; it was oul' lad behaviour.

—I've chemo tomorrow, he told them.—Last session.

—Nice one.

—Yeah, said Jimmy.—So after that – the sick days, yeh know – I'll book the studio.

—Cool.

—I'm delighted, said Jimmy.—Thanks, lads.

—What about royalties?

—Feck off.

—Seriously, said Marvin.—You warned me about being exploited.

—Good point, said Jimmy.—Here's what. We're recordin' a song that never existed. Yeah?

He saw young Jimmy sitting up, as if he was just now really getting it.

—Really, he told the lads.—It's fictional. You're with me?

—Yeah.

—An' so are the royalties.

—No way —

—I'm not pullin' a fast one, Marv, said Jimmy.—If we go claimin' royalties, the whole thing falls apart. I'll look after yis, don't worry.

But the royalties thing. I'm glad yeh brought it up. An' Jim – you as well. It brings home the point. Nobody is to know about this.

This appealed to them – he could tell. It appealed to him too. The international man of fuckin' mystery.

—Just the three of us, he said.—And your mother.

—And Mush and Docksy, said Marvin.

They were the two other lads in his band.

—Yeah, said Jimmy.—But not yet. Till we're ready. An' not the full story.

They liked that too.

—What'll I do, though? said young Jimmy.

—Give me a hand, said Jimmy.—Produce it, engineer it. And we still have to write the fuckin' thing.

—What sort of music was there in 1932? said Marvin.

—We'll decide that, said young Jimmy.

—Wha'?

—We'll decide what sort of music there was in 1932.

Jimmy stared at him, just for a bit.

—Good man.

—Les?

—Yeah. Hi.

—Great to hear yeh.

—Yeah.

—Thanks for phonin'.

—It's okay.

—How's Maisie?

—Good.

—Great. Tell her I was askin' for her.

—Yeah.

Ask about mine, yeh cranky monosyllabic prick.

—Les?

—Yeah.

—You're still there.

It always felt like a fight. Trying to get words – anything – out of him. Jimmy always became the interrogator, the sarcastic bollix – *You're still there.*

—Yeah, said Les.

Jimmy sometimes wondered if it actually was Les.

—I just phoned to say good luck, said Les.

—Thanks – eh —
—I knew it was coming up.
—Yeah —
—The last session.
—Yesterday, said Jimmy.
—Oh. Great.
—Yeah.
—Like the school holidays then.
—You were never in school, Les.
He heard Les laughing.
—That's true, said Les.
Jimmy wanted to cry – again.
—Thanks for phonin', Les.
Say something else, get him to stay on the line.
—Bye.
—Bye.

He heard the slap of something hitting the hall floor. He looked, and turned it over with his foot. It was that mad thing, *Alive!*, the free Catholic paper. Normally, he'd have walked out to the green wheelie with it – even this early. But he read the headline; he couldn't avoid it. DEATH, JUDGMENT, HEAVEN AND HELL.

He picked it up, and saw the two smiling girls on the front page. Normally they'd have been promoting a new app or a beer festival. Here though, they were advertising the Eucharistic Congress.

He took it with him into the kitchen. He shoved the dog out for his piss and put on the coffee. Then he opened page 12: *Are You Ready for the Congress?*

No, he wasn't.

It was starting on the 10th of June. That was less than two months away.

He read on down the page, looking for hints that the Pope might be coming. There weren't any. The oul' prick was staying put. He wouldn't risk the country's indifference. But the Congress was going ahead, with or without the headline act. It even had a theme: 'The Eucharist: Communion with Christ and with One Another'. Jesus, they'd be riding in the bushes after that session. Events, workshops, keynote addresses; ecumenism, marriage and the family; priesthood and ministry; reconciliation. It wasn't what

205

Jimmy'd expected. Where was the big stuff – the crowds? Only seven thousand had registered. They were coming from Kazakhstan, El Salvador and Uganda. These would be hardcore fuckers; they'd be walking all the way, over the water and all. And they wouldn't be buying Jimmy's album.

What fuckin' album?

Ocean kept bouncing up to him with another 78 or spool of tape. She'd found him about twenty songs. She often had Norman with her. Jimmy half thought she might have moved in with Norman.

—Stranger things have happened, said his da.

—Fuckin' name one. Go on.

And Jimmy had rejected them all. Too pious, too bland, too familiar, too slow. He hadn't told Ocean, or Noeleen, the real plan. He didn't want to be confronted with boring fuckin' questions about cost and legality. He wasn't going to listen.

He picked up the *Alive!* The coffee had done its job. It was time for the morning dump and survival test. Every time he wiped his arse he half expected bad news. *One day at a time, sweet Jesus.*

He preferred to get this done before the rest were up and scratching at the bathroom door. If he found blood, he wanted to be back downstairs, getting the breakfasts and lunches ready, smiling at them as they shuffled into the day.

He looked at the front page again. DEATH, JUDGMENT, HEAVEN AND HELL. He had the four walls of his song.

He was tempted to stop the car; he thought he'd have to. Get off the road, up onto a path.

Noeleen could fuck off. Marching around with the accountant – her fuckin' cousin, for Jesus' sake.

—Got a minute, Jimbo?

No, he fuckin' didn't. He wasn't taking the blame for whatever the accountant had lined up there on his iPad. Gavin was his name. Middle-class culchie cunt. Jimmy wasn't going to give her the chance to tell him she had no choice, and blah fuckin' blah.

He'd start all over again if he had to. Him and Aoife.

He had to stop. He put on the hazards – there was a van too close behind him. The driver put his fist on the horn. Fuck him. Jimmy saw a place where the kerb was a bit low. He aimed at it, got up on the path. Stopped the car. Left the hazards on. Got the phone out. He couldn't read the names on the screen. He closed his eyes. He remembered her number – he thought he did. He found the digits.

—Hi.

He couldn't talk.

—Jimmy?

She sounded frightened now. This was fuckin' dreadful.

—Are you alright?

—I —

—Jimmy?

—I can't drive.

—Where are you?

He knew the answer. But he couldn't look – he didn't know.

—Jimmy, I'm getting a taxi. If I phone you in a minute, will you be able to tell me?

What she'd said – what was it?

—Jimmy?

—No. I —

—I'll leave the phone on. I'm calling the taxi with the landline. Jimmy?

—Yeah.

—I'm phoning for the taxi. Try to see where you are. I'm coming.

He could hear her. Moving in the kitchen.

It was shifting, receding – the wave. He could breathe. He knew where he was – he couldn't remember the street. But he saw the sign.

—Mattress Mick.

—Jimmy?

—Mattress Mick.

—Great. Brilliant.

She knew what he meant. They'd seen the billboard the first time together. The sham with the glasses and the '70s footballer's hair.

—Mattress Mick.

—You're great, she said.—I'm on my way.

He heard her shoes in the hall. Heard the front door opening – closing. He read the billboard.

—The Mattress Pricefighter.

He read another bit.

—Finance available.

207

—A few minutes, Jimmy, she said.—I'm on my way.

She was outside. The sounds – the wind.

—Here's the taxi now. I told them it was an emergency. They're brilliant. Remember with the kids? When we had to get them in to Temple Street? They were always here in a few minutes.

He heard her getting into the taxi. He heard her door close.

—Aoife?

He heard her talk to the driver.

—Do you know the Mattress Mick sign? I can't remember the name – .

He couldn't hear the driver.

She had the phone up to her mouth again.

—I'm in the taxi. Jimmy?

—Yeah.

—We're moving. He knows the sign. Seville Place. How long?

She spoke again.

—We'll be there in a few minutes.

—I love you.

—Oh, Jimmy.

—I'm sorry.

—There's no need.

—I'm sorry.

—Stop saying that.

He was frightening her.

—Jimmy?

—Yeah.

—Have you any money? I came out without —

—Yeah.

—Great. Phew.

He could hear the radio in the taxi. Nova. Fuckin' Genesis.

—Aoife.

—Yes?

—Tell him to put on Lyric, will yeh. John Kelly's on.

He heard her asking him to change the station.

—Blues, Marv.

—Too American, said Marvin.

He was right.

—Yeah, said Jimmy.—Good man.

He was sitting on a couple of pillows with his back to the cold radiator. He could manage it that way; he was fine. He was wearing the cancer trousers. He knew there'd be no slagging or objections, not the way he was, his face the colour of rain.

The boys were sitting on the bed, making sure their toes didn't touch him. It was awkward, fuckin' excruciating. But – strangely, and brilliant; he couldn't wait to tell Aoife – the fact that he was sick was an advantage. It kept him back, stopped him taking over, smothering the thing before they got going – taking out his fuckin' trumpet.

He was getting the hang of terminal illness. Fuckin' typical too, just when he was getting better.

—But maybe, he said,—we could give our man some blues records.

—No, said young Jimmy.

—Why not?

—Modern Irish music tries too hard to be American, he said.

—That's right, said Jimmy.

Brilliant.

—Where'd you hear that? he asked.

—You.

—Oh.

—When I was about five.

—Oh. Did you understand?

—I do now, said young Jimmy.

He was saying more than Jimmy had heard from him in years.

—You were slagging U2, said young Jimmy.

—When you were five.

—I might've been six.

—Grand.

—And you were shouting at the car stereo.

—Oh yeah, said Marvin.—I remember that.

—Why is he pretending to be American?! He's from fuckin' Glasnevin!

—Why were you always playing U2, Dad? You hate them.

He took a deep breath – *scare them a bit.*

—I don't hate them, he said.—They disappoint me.

—But why – ?

—I was educatin' yis, said Jimmy.—I did it for you.

They were smiling. Beginning to enjoy this new thing.

—Anyway, said Jimmy.—You're right. He can't be too American.

He closed his eyes. They were looking at him, he knew. This was madness.

—Just give me a minute.

Marvin strummed away.

—TODAY – IS GONNA BE THE DAY —

—No fuckin' way, Marv.

He could hear them laughing. He really had educated them. They knew exactly what chords and poxy lyrics could make a dying man feel even worse.

He heard young Jimmy.

—What's he called?

—The 1932 man? said Marvin.

—Yeah.

—Don't know.

—Kevin something.

—Kevin – why?

—Don't know, said young Jimmy.—It's just   I don't know – it sounds right.

—Kevin what? said Marvin.

—O'Leary.

—No way.

—Kevin Keegan.

—There's a real one of them.

—Is there?

—Football. ESPN.

—Pity.

—Yeah.

—Kevin Tankard, said young Jimmy.

—Unreal.

The boys tested the name, with different voices and accents. Jimmy let them at it. He kept his eyes shut.

—With yis in a minute, lads.

—D'you like the name?

—Love it.

He pushed through the last of the nausea. That was what he actually did. He felt it coming up on him and he shoved it away, the plunge, the sweat.

He just kept going.

It was all fuckin' mad.

Kevin Tankard became a man. He stopped being a joke, although he looked at the boys sometimes and they burst out laughing.

—I WANT HER ARMS —

I'M GOIN' TO HELL —

They'd be sneaking into the studio in a couple of days. He wasn't sure if he'd told Aoife. He thought he had; he'd tell her again.

—I WANT HER LEGS —

I'M GOIN' TO HELL —

Now, Noeleen was saying something.

—I'd say you were drunk.

—What?

—Are you drunk?

—No, I'm not.

She was smiling. It couldn't have been too bad.

—Painkillers?

That would get him out of jail.

He nodded.

—Go on though, he said.—I'm grand.

They'd gone through the list – the Electric Picnic, the other festivals, the Eucharistic Congress. They'd agreed things, deferred a few things. He'd told her he was on to a song. He agreed, they were running out of time. He'd agreed, it was a pity the Pope was playing chicken, and that no one seemed to know about the Eucharistic Congress. They'd plough ahead. He'd deliver the song by the end of the week, or they'd just go for one of the ones that Ocean had brought in.

That was it – the meeting. He thought he'd read it right. Where was Gavin the accountant? He hadn't asked. He'd looked for anger, or anxiety, eyes about to give him bad news. He was awake, aware, especially after she'd asked him if he'd been drinking – at half-nine in the morning.

But this was the thing: he wasn't sure. Hours later, he wasn't convinced. He wasn't certain if it was that meeting or another one he'd been to. It was mad – he knew that. But it didn't worry him.

—I WANT THAT PLACE —

He'd be grand. He'd never felt better.

—I'M GOING TO HELL —

—Sing like a man who really would take eternity in hell for – yeh know – .

—What?

—You know. A girl.

—You hate songs about girls, Dad, young Jimmy reminded him; the little prick had a memory like a fuckin' PowerBook.
—Remember when you played the Rolling Stones?
Jimmy listened to young Jimmy doing a good impression of Jimmy.
—Hear that, lads? It's women – *women!* Honky tonk women.
—What age were you tha' time? Two?
—Eight, said young Jimmy.—And you were wrong.
—How was I?
—Simple. The song says honky tonk girls as well. Honky tonk *girls*.
—Yeah, said Jimmy.—But you knew what I meant.
Young Jimmy and Marvin answered him together.
—We do now.
—Leave the girls to the boybands. You said.
—Well, I was right, said Jimmy.—Go on, Marv.
Marvin sang like a man who'd have sawn off his one remaining arm for a ride. Because his dad had told him to.
—I PROWL THE STREETS —
I'M GOING TO HELL —
Jimmy felt like a bit of a pimp. He worried that he might be polluting the boys, shoving their faces into stuff they weren't ready for.
—I KISS HER FEET —
I'M GOING TO HELL – I think I should say lick there.
—Lick her feet? said young Jimmy.
—Good idea, Marv, said Jimmy.
—Why would he want to lick her feet? said young Jimmy.
Marvin shrugged.
Aoife told Jimmy he'd put on weight. She said it the way women do, pretended it was a question.
—Have you put on a bit of weight?
—No.
—It suits you.
—It can't fuckin' suit me. It isn't there.
—Just saying, she said.—Take a chill pill.
He didn't see it. The weight. He didn't feel it. A bit puffy around the face. That was how his da had described it.
—It suits yeh.
—Fuck off.
He was paying for the studio time himself. He had to. There was no way of avoiding it, if the scam was going to work.

—An' your hair never fell ou'.

—No.

—Will yeh keep shavin' it?

—Don't know – probably.

—I WANT HER NOW —

I'M GOIN' TO HELL —

He hadn't a clue how much they had in their account. He hadn't gone onto banking 365 in months. And he hadn't had that chat with Noeleen. He'd kept waiting for Aoife to tell him they were skint again. It would have been the trigger. But she hadn't, so he hadn't. So they were grand.

—WON'T SAVE MY SOUL —

—I'M GOIN' TO HELL —

It was a song now, a real thing. Marvin had gone off with it, to batter it into oldness with his buddies.

—DON'T HAVE A SOUL —

I'M GOIN' TO HELL

He'd got the all-clear. Himself and Aoife sat there, at the victim side of Mister Dunwoody's desk. The prick glanced down at the file before he looked at them and smiled. He told Aoife. Jimmy watched the fucker flirt with Aoife as he told her that her husband's biopsy specimen had presented negative margins, how he'd gone up her life partner's arse and come back empty-handed. They'd promised each other they wouldn't cry, if the news was good. They thanked Dunwoody and went for a pint.

—He was tryin' to get off with yeh, said Jimmy.

—No, he wasn't.

—He fuckin' was.

—No.

—He never looked at me.

He loved the way she drank her pint, like a man.

—Why? she said.—Are you jealous?

—No.

—No?

—No, said Jimmy.—If I was ever gettin' off with a man, it definitely wouldn't be him. I'm fuckin' starvin'.

—D'you think I've put on weight? he asked.

—Big time, said Imelda.

—But it suits me.

213

—Ah yeah.

This was – this was mad now – outside his parents' house. She'd been driving past, and she stopped when she saw Jimmy getting out of his car. He watched her get out of her Punto. There was a chunk off the side of it – useless prick she was married to, couldn't get that sorted. She seemed a bit shy and that made him want to run at her – and run away, up to his parents' front door. God, she was lovely. She'd always be lovely.

—Hiya.

—Imelda, he said.

—I saw yeh there, she said.

—I was hopin' you'd stop, he said.

—And I did.

—D'yeh miss me?

—Ah yeah. Fuck off.

She was smiling.

—How are yeh? she asked.—I'd been meanin' to ask, to phone yeh, like.

—I'm grand, he said.

He told her the news, the all-clear; he even mentioned the negative margins.

She put her hands on his shoulders and kissed his cheek, and stayed there for a while.

—Brilliant, she said.

He stepped back – impressed himself. And fuckin' cursed himself.

—I've to go in, he said.

He nodded sideways at his parents' gaff, kept his eyes on her.

—How are they?

—Grand.

—So. Anyway. That's brilliant news.

—Yeah, thanks, he said.

She stepped back, and turned, and turned again.

—Give me a bell, she said.

She knew he was watching as she climbed back into her car. She flung back one last word.

—Whenever.

And she shut the door.

He wouldn't. Whenever.

There'd been a bit of grief at home about the studio date. He'd booked a different day – today, now that he thought of it

– and then found out that Marvin had his Irish oral – the Leaving Cert. Marvin hadn't told him. Aoife had hit the fuckin' roof.

—Your oral, Marvin!

—I'll fail anyway.

—You won't! Jimmy!

—What?

—Did you not think of checking?

—He never —

—It's May! He's doing his Leaving.

—Okay, grand. I can change it, it's not a problem. For God's sake, Marvin.

He looked at his watch. He was still at work. Marvin would be finished by now. He took out the phone. He'd text him.

Hows it goin?

But he sent it to Imelda.

Fuck, fuck, fuck – fuck fuck. Eejit, eejit. He double-checked that it had gone to Imelda and not someone else. And, yeah, it had gone to the right woman, the wrong woman, and, actually, he didn't feel like an eejit at all.

For fuck sake.

Hows it goin?

He fired it off to Marvin.

He'd had enough – he was going home.

All these posters. Yes, No, Yes, Yes, No. There was another referendum coming up. Stability, austerity. Say yes to Europe. Tell Europe to get fucked. He'd no real idea what it was about. But he'd educate himself.

He'd ask his da.

His phone buzzed in his pocket. Two messages. One from Marvin – *Grand.* One from Imelda – *Grand X.* He was a sick cunt, all the same. Trying to think of more messages that would produce the same answer from his eldest son and his floozy.

Glad it went well. X He sent that one back to Marvin. A proper dad message. He really didn't want to destroy his life.

He texted his da. *Pint?*

He'd meet up with his da or go straight home. The phone hopped. *What kept u?* That was that. A pint on the way home. A bit of reality. *There in hlf hr.*

—Y'alrigh'?

His da was looking at him. He felt like he'd been caught.

—I'm grand, he said.—Why?

—Yeh seem distracted or somethin', said his da.

—No, I'm grand, said Jimmy.—A bit – eh – jumpy, I suppose.

His da was talking again – he had to concentrate.

—Wha' has yeh tha' way?

—Don't know, said Jimmy.—I think it might be the news.

—More news?

His da looked scared.

—No, no, said Jimmy.—No. Sorry. The same news. The all-clear, like.

—Grand.

—I'm – I don't know. I've to get used to – I suppose – normality. Again.

—It's borin', said his da.—I don't know if you remember tha'.

—I do, yeah, said Jimmy.—No, but – I'm grand.

—How's Aoife?

Did his da know something?

—Grand, said Jimmy.—Great.

—Good, said his da.

—Marvin did his oral Irish today.

—How'd tha' go?

—Grand, I think, said Jimmy.—We'll have the autopsy when I get home. Actually —

He dug out his phone.

—I'll text Aoife, he said.—He'll be home by now. She'll've got more out of him than I could.

How did he do? X – and an extra one – *x*. He didn't like the way his da kept looking at him.

He read out Aoife's answer.

Ok – he says. X

—Tha' sounds righ', said his da.—He's too brainy to say it was easy.

—Talkin' about brains, said Jimmy.

He told his da about the song. And he watched his face start to relax. He wasn't examining Jimmy now. Jimmy was over the hump – whatever it was. Whatever his da had seen and hated.

—So, he said.—We're in tomorrow.

His da sat back.

—Brilliant, he said.—I love tha'.

Jimmy had been able to feel it, the pull on his lip, his da dragging some kind of confession out of him. But he'd let go – his da had let go. Jimmy wasn't going to be stupid.

—Can I come? said his da.

—Maybe not, said Jimmy.

It wasn't a bad idea.

—It might freak out the lads.

—You're right, said his da.—No, you're right.

—Maybe though, yeah, said Jimmy.—Fuck it, yeah. Why not?

—Great, said his da.—I'll behave meself.

—Yeh'd better.

—Is there somethin' wrong with tha' cunt?

—Shut up, for fuck sake.

—He can't hear me.

—It's a studio, said Jimmy.—It's designed for fuckin' hearin'.

—Well, is there?

—Wha'?

—Somethin' wrong with him.

He was talking about Lochlainn.

—Leave it, said Jimmy.

—It's a medical question, said his da.

—Shut up.

—Okay.

He'd seen the grandsons looking at him. The boys weren't sure they liked their granddad being there, with Marvin's pals there too. No harm. It would keep them focused.

Marvin's pals, the rest of the band, seemed fine. They were all shifting around – there wasn't much room – all trying to be cool, and succeeding.

—We ready, Lochlainn?

Lochlainn shrugged.

—D'yeh have Auto-Tune, Lochlainn? Jimmy's da asked.

—No way, Granddad, said young Jimmy.

—No, no, said Jimmy's da.

He raised his hands, like he was surrendering.

—I'm with yeh, he said.—It's an awful invention. A fuckin' sin. I was just curious. Is it a thing, like? Or is it just inside in the computer? An app, like?

—Da?

—Wha'?

—I'm payin' by the hour.

—Sorry. Grand. Fair enough.

—Righ', said Jimmy.

—No Auto-Tune, said Lochlainn.

—Good man, said Jimmy's da.—Back to mono.

—Right, said Jimmy.—D'yeh want to run through it, lads?

The drummer – Jimmy couldn't remember whether he was Docksy or Mush – started tapping the side of the snare. It was a bit daft, but immediately true. It sounded right; it sounded historical. And the rest of it – Christ.

Jimmy looked at young Jimmy. He was sitting beside Lochlainn, watching every move.

It was the magic Jimmy had wanted all his life. A small gang of men, there because he'd brought him there, strumming, tapping and groaning –

—I WANT HER LEGS —

I'M GOIN' TO HELL —

They were making something new. It was perfect – maybe perfect just this once. Was Lochlainn even recording it?

He was – or he seemed to be. The lads kept rolling. It was 1932.

He delivered the song. He told them the lie.

—An oul' lad my da knows from pitch 'n' putt. He told my da he had all these ol' tapes in the attic, his own da had collected.

He smiled.

—So there yeh go.

—Are there more? said Ocean.—Oh my God.

—Most of the tape was melted, said Jimmy.—Like – solid. Baked. Right in under the eaves. South-facin'.

He was a fuckin' estate agent.

—But there was this one saved.

He nodded at the iPod dock.

—And the scratches —

—Don't touch them, said Noeleen.—They're amazing.

—Yeah, said Jimmy.—It's like he's already in hell or somethin'.

—Exactly, said Noeleen.—Singin' up from the pit.

Lochlainn had done a great job.

Jimmy couldn't sit – he couldn't stay still. They'd catch him if he stayed there. But they wouldn't. They couldn't. He was way ahead of everybody.

He'd cancelled the trumpet. He'd texted Des. He hadn't been practising. He couldn't concentrate on the thing. But he'd changed his mind; Des needed the money. Then he got the text from Aoife, because he hadn't answered the phone. *Des is here.*

—Jimmy.

—Wha'?

—There's nothing worse – from the lady's point o' view now. There's nothin' worse than the man answerin' a text. Is it your wife?

—I've to go, he said.

—That's tha' question answered, said Imelda.

—Trumpet lesson.

—Lovely, she said.—Double-booked, are yeh?

—I suppose so, he said.—Sorry.

They were sitting in his car.

—Someone else to blow yeh, said Imelda.

—You're gas.

—Oh, I know, she said.

—We weren't doin' anythin', said Jimmy.

—Jimmy, said Imelda.—We were fuckin' talkin'.

—Yeah.

They were on top of Howth Hill, in the car park.

She opened her door.

—So anyway, she said.

—Sorry about this, he said.

—No problem.

—I enjoyed it, he said.

She looked at him.

—So did I.

She was still looking.

—We're friends, aren't we?

—Yeah, he said.—Yeah.

—It's kind o' surprisin', tha', she said.—Isn't it?

—Is it? he said.

—Yeah.

—I suppose so, he said.—I think I know what yeh mean.

—I like it, she said.

She got out of the car – she groaned.

—I like it too, he said.

—Grand, she said.—No more sex, so. That's a relief, isn't it? Seeyeh.

She took the three steps to her own car. He waited till she was in before he started the engine. He waited till she was looking, then smiled, waved, and reversed.

What sort of a fuckin' eejit was he?

They'd done nothing. He didn't have to check his face in the mirror. They never were going to do anything. Not in the car. It was still bright, and they were two good-sized middle-aged adults.

He was down the hill now, driving through Sutton. Still miles from home.

He remembered once, him and the lads on Bull Island. This was when he was fifteen or sixteen. At night. They used to creep up on a bouncing car, two of them on each side. They'd wait till the chap inside's arse was in the air, then they'd shake the car till the screaming stopped and the chap was trying to get out. And there was once, they were shaking the car when one of the lads, Softy Brennan, recognised his da in the fuckin' car.

They ran back up into the dunes. Jimmy remembered deciding not to laugh.

—Did yeh not see it was your da's car?

—It's dark! said Softy.—There's no colour!

—Wha' abou' his arse? Did yeh not recognise tha'?

That was Outspan.

—Fuck off!

Imelda was right; they were friends. Although he was fairly certain she'd been joking there, about the sex.

She was lonely.

He'd have to contact Outspan.

—He had to go.

—Shite. Sorry.

—It's not me you should be apologising to, said Aoife.

—I know.

—He cycled across the city.

—I'll phone him.

—Where were you?

—Work.

—Jimmy, she said.—You came home from work.

—I went back, he said.—Had to. Artwork for the Eucharist Congress album.

—Is it still *Faith of Our Fathers Me Hole*?

—No, said Jimmy.—That was just the workin' title.

—Good.

—No, he said.—It's – you listenin'?

—I am.

—*1932: More Songs about Sex and Emigration*. Wha' d'yeh think?

—Great.

—Really?

—It's very good.

—Would you buy it?

—I'd be curious.

—Is that all?

—It's enough, she said.

—You're right.

—Phone Des.

—I will.

But he didn't. Not then.

He went upstairs.

There was no interest in the Eucharistic Congress. That was the problem. Noeleen had sent him a link to an article in the *Irish Times*, the Bishop of Dublin defending the money they were spending on it, saying that there'd be a big mass in Croke Park but admitting that it wouldn't be full. She'd put a line of ?????s and !!!!!s above and below the link. And *We need to talk* at the bottom. He agreed, but he hadn't – talked. Not yet.

Money, money, fuckin' money.

He went into the bathroom. He looked at his face. He looked okay. The heat behind his eyes – it wasn't there, he couldn't see it. But it was bad. It had started just when he was parking the car, outside. It wasn't too bad. It made him blink – that was all. He turned on the cold tap, got his hands under the water. He bent down and drenched his face. He looked again. He looked fine.

* * *

She found him.

Something had happened. He'd sat down on the bed – he'd had to. His legs were buckling, going from under him; he could feel it happening. The feeling behind his eyes spread out and down. Through his head, his gums, down, his shoulders. He was your man at the end of *Blade Runner*. Sitting there, cross-legged, frightening as fuck, then gone – switched off. That was Jimmy.

She came looking – where was he? And she found him.

—Jimmy?

He could hear her but he couldn't answer. He literally couldn't answer. She pushed him back gently onto the bed. She pulled his shoes off.

That was all.

She told him later that that wasn't true, that he'd functioned properly.

—Functioned?

—Yes.

—Like, went to the jacks an' tha'?

—Like, asked Marvin how his exams were going. You even joked about it.

—Did I?

—He was a bit upset after English Paper Two.

—Was he?

—Well, he was fine, she said.—But he said – he shouted, Fuckin' Seamus Heaney didn't come up! And you said, I didn't know we knew Seamus Heaney.

—Did I?

—He laughed. It was lovely.

—Good. Good.

But he'd no memory he trusted. He'd brushed his teeth, he'd shaved. He'd moved around. He'd gone out with the dog.

—I brought you.

—Brought me?

—To Dollymount, she said.—I left you there and collected you.

—God.

He remembered slobbering. Feeling drool on his face, his chin. He remembered the surprise, and the shame, and how it took ages for the back of his hand to arrive so he could wipe it off.

Solid tears, too big and hard to get out. They pressed back into his head. He could only breathe with his mouth open.

They were waiting for him. All of them. Noeleen, the bank, the bands, the kids, Imelda, everybody – Aoife.

—The cancer trousers again, Jimmy?

He didn't hear her. He did – he did. But only after. Questions he didn't know were questions, until he saw her waiting for the answer. Or for his face to change.

Most of the time, he slept. That was what he remembered. That was when he was nearly happy and they left him alone.

It wasn't dark.

He wasn't by himself. He didn't look, but he knew it. There was someone there, beside him.

He – whoever it was, a man – coughed.

Jimmy moved. He tried to make it seem like he was stretching, just shifting in his sleep.

There was a chair beside him. One of the chairs from the kitchen. Someone sitting on it.

Jimmy's neck hurt. So did his eyes. They were dry, stinging.

—Outspan?

—Howyeh.

—What're you doin' here?

—Lookin' at you, yeh shiftless cunt.

—Who let you in?

—Eve.

—Aoife.

—Yeah.

—Her name's Aoife.

—Grand.

Jimmy rubbed his face with both hands. Outspan was still there.

—So, well. How're yeh doin'?

—Not too bad, said Outspan.

—How's the health?

—Same as ever, said Outspan.

He didn't look too bad – no worse anyway.

—Gas, isn't it? said Outspan.

—What's gas?

—Eve downstairs thinks yeh need cheerin' up. You're a bit depressed. So she phones me. An unemployed man with terminal cancer, who has to live with his ma.

—Brilliant.

223

—It's nice to be fuckin' needed.

—Did you say Aoife phoned yeh?

—Yeah.

Jimmy looked down, beside the bed. His phone wasn't there, where he always put it.

—When did she phone yeh?

—She phoned a few times.

—You didn't drop everythin' an' come runnin', no?

—I did actually.

—Did yeh?

—Yeah. I didn't run but.

Jimmy wasn't sure about this. He felt too okay. Like nothing had happened. Like what he'd gone through was ridiculous.

—So, he said,—Outspan. Cheer me up.

—Fuck off, Rabbitte.

That worked. Being called Rabbitte.

—Here, he said.—I was thinkin'. Remember the time in Dollymount, we caught Softy Brennan's da ridin' your one from the Mint?

—Colette.

—That's righ'. Colette. With the limp. D'yeh remember it? Creepin' up on the car?

—It wasn't Colette, said Outspan.

—Yeh sure?

—It was another one.

—Could've sworn it was Colette.

—Tha' was a different time.

Aoife was there now. Right behind Outspan. She looked anxious and too happy. Desperate. He'd never seen her like that before – he didn't think he had.

He wanted to sink back. He didn't want her thinking that all it had taken was a visit from Outspan. That it had been that easy. That false.

—He's awake, she said.

—Yeah, said Outspan.

She had a mug with her. Tea for Outspan.

—Now, Liam, she said.

—Sound, said Outspan.—Thanks, Eve.

Jimmy watched her face. She was happy enough being called the wrong name.

—How're you feeling?

224

She was talking to Jimmy – it took a while for him to know that.

—Grand, Eve, he said.—Not too bad.

There was no going back. She smiled – she grinned. She was close to crying.

He dressed properly. Trousers with a zip. A shirt with buttons. Tucked in.

—Your dad phoned.

—Did he?

—He said something about a drink.

—Let me know if he ever says nothin' about a drink.

She smiled. He watched it change her face.

—I'll drive you there if you like, she said.

—No, he said.

—Sure?

—Yeah. Thanks.

He was at the fridge, looking in. Like one of the boys.

—Hungry?

—No, he said.—Not really.

He wanted to sit on the floor. He didn't know why. It was nearer than any of the chairs. The dog was at his feet, trying to trip him. The dog – he'd forgotten the dog. He'd forgotten all about the dog.

—Messi. Good man.

Now he could get down on the floor. He had his excuse. He pressed the side of his face against the dog. He felt the tail walloping his arm.

—He's grown, he said.

That sounded odd, like he'd been away somewhere.

Aoife was still smiling. But there was a bit of that thing, the desperation he'd seen when Outspan had been in the house.

But it was true; the dog was bigger. Still a pup, though.

—How're things? he asked the dog.

—Anything you'd like?

For a second – was that the dog? But it was Aoife talking to him. Of course it fuckin' was.

—Not really, thanks.

—Scrambled egg?

—Oh yeah.

She laughed. It was easy.

—And you're sure about meeting your dad?

—Yeah, he said.—No. In a few days maybe.

He wasn't sure about that.

—Kids in school?

—It's July.

—Yeah.

He was glad he was on the floor.

—I could text him, he said.

—What?

She was bullying the eggs, chasing the yolks around the mixing bowl.

—I could text my da, he said.—Arrange somethin'.

He wanted his phone but he didn't want to ask for it.

—After I've done this, she said.—I'll get it for you. I think I know where I left it.

She was playing with him.

The dog was lying on his back, in Jimmy's lap. Jimmy had to remind himself: you rub the stomach. He watched Aoife pour milk into the bowl. She put the bowl down and took his phone out of the cutlery drawer.

She bent down and left it on the dog's stomach.

—There.

—Thanks.

It slid off, onto the floor.

He could smell the eggs now, becoming food. He texted his da. *Alright?* He knew Aoife was watching him. He didn't look at the texts in the Inbox, or Sent. He put the phone beside him on the floor.

She'd known his code. But she'd always known it. He'd been using the same one for years, from phone to phone, way back to the first one. The same digits as his first bank card.

The phone buzzed and Messi was up off Jimmy's lap and barking at it.

—Shut up, yeh fuckin' eejit.

—Poor Messi.

It was his da.

Grande. Yrself?

Jimmy sent his answer.

Not 2 bad.

—Your dad? said Aoife.

226

—Yeah.

—Oh, she said.—I forgot.

—What?

—Toast?

—Brilliant, yeah. Lovely.

His da was back.

Grate.

He'd started spelling the words wrong when he texted.

—I'm enterin' into the spirit of the thing, he'd said a good while back.—LOL.

Another one followed.

Pynte?

Jimmy didn't answer. He would, but he didn't know when he'd be ready to have a pint, or to leave the house on his own. The trip out to the wheelie – he knew he could get there but he wasn't as confident about making his way back.

He heard the toast hop in the toaster. He stood up. His eyes danced, swam a bit. Low blood pressure – he thought he remembered being told he had it. He went to collect the plate from her.

—Brilliant, he said.—Perfect.

There were two plates, two mounds of scrambled egg on toast.

—Are you eatin' as well? he asked her.

—Is that okay?

It wasn't a real question; she was slagging him. But it took him a while.

—'Course.

He took both plates from her.

—Yeh deserve it.

—Fuck off, Jimmy.

He liked the sound of that. He put the plates down on the table, no bother, and sat.

—Knives and forks, he said.

—I'm ahead of you, said Aoife.

She sat beside him, not at the other side of the table. Strange, he thought. She slid the cutlery at him.

—There you go, she said.

She was sounding a bit like his da.

—What's funny?

—Nothin', he said.—I just – I don't know. I'm happy.

It was true. But the phone. The phone. He got a mouthful of the egg into his mouth.

—Lovely.

He cut some of the toast, brought it up to his mouth.

—Really lovely, he said.

—It's not bad, is it?

—Fuckin' lovely.

—Pepper?

—No.

—What's the magic word?

—Thanks.

She nudged him. Some egg fell back onto his plate.

—Sorry.

—No problem, he said.—Did you phone Imelda?

He'd never felt more alive – *low blood pressure me hole*.

—Yes, she said.

—Yeh did?

—Yes, she said.—I phoned everyone.

—Okay.

He got egg to his mouth.

—I was worried, Jimmy, said Aoife.—Jimmy.

—Wha'?

—I was really worried.

—Okay.

—I still am.

—Okay.

He decided to speak before he took another mouthful.

—So am I, he said.

—Okay.

He ate. So did she.

—I think I'm better.

—You're fine. Oh —

—Wha'?

—I have something for you.

She stood up and went to the fridge. She stretched and took down a bag from the top of it – an Eason's bag. She handed it to him.

—There.

—What is it?

—It's in an Eason's bag, Jimmy. Chances are it's a book.

She is *my fuckin' da*.

He took the book from the bag. *Adventures of a Waterboy*, Mike Scott's autobiography. He hated the Waterboys, but he wasn't going to tell her that. Anyway, it probably wasn't true. He was quite fond of the Waterboys.

—Thanks, he said.—Brilliant.

—I bought it a while ago, she said.—I read a review. But I thought I'd hold onto it till —

—I know. Thanks.

—You like them, don't you?

—God, yeah.

—Who is Imelda?

—Old friend, he said.—Lovely cover.

—How old?

—Same age as meself. Remember the Commitments?

—I didn't know you then —

—But you remember me talkin' about them?

—God, I do.

—Fuck off, Aoife. She was one.

—One what?

—One of the band, he said.—Singer. Like Outspan – Liam. He was in the Commitments as well.

—She sounded nice.

—She is, he said.—She's sound. She lives near my folks.

—She sends her regards.

—I'll phone her. You'd like her.

He patted the new book.

—I have *This Is the Sea* on vinyl.

He didn't.

—Up in the attic.

He polished the plate. There was no evidence that there'd ever been food on it.

—Any news? he asked.

—Well, we won't be going to Syria this year for the holidays, she said.

She is so my fuckin' da!

—Where are we goin'? he asked.

She looked at him.

—You tell me.

It was July. Was it late July?

—Where're the kids?

The house was empty, except for them and the dog.

—May stayed in Lauren's house last night, said Aoife.

—Cocktails at sundown.

229

—Stop, she said.—Jesus. Lauren's parents are good. They're terrifying. I think they're Christians or something. So I think she'll still be teetotal when she gets home.

—Grand. Brian?

—Football camp.

—Great, said Jimmy.—I'll collect him.

—He wants to come home on his own.

—Great.

—And Jim's *out*, said Aoife.—Whereabouts unknown. I think there's probably a girlfriend.

—Great.

—But I'm not sure.

—You didn't check his phone, no?

She looked at him.

—Are you letting your hair grow? she said.

He rubbed a hand over his scalp. There was a couple of weeks of hair up there.

—I suppose so, he said.—Yeah.

—Good, she said.

He checked his face. He'd shaved earlier – he remembered.

—Why is it good? he asked.

—You look less like a drugged convict, she said.

—Jesus.

—The shaved head only suits you when you're healthy, she said.

—I am healthy.

—Good.

—I am.

The new him.

—Where's Marv?

—Bulgaria, she said.

She was looking at him again.

—That's right, he said.

He remembered saying goodbye to Marvin, holding his shoulder, whispering something about Bulgarian women; he couldn't remember what. But he'd felt poor Marv's embarrassment coming up through his T-shirt.

—How's he gettin' on?

—Fine. He says.

—Good.

—It's all he says.

—What's he doin' in Bulgaria anyway?

—He did the Leaving, she said.

—Yeah, said Jimmy.

—And it's become normal for kids to go away together and destroy a foreign country after they've finished.

—Yeah, said Jimmy.

—Look, said Aoife.—How much do I have to tell you?

—Better give me the lot.

—Okay, she said.—So one of his friends. Ethan.

—Ethan?

—You know Ethan. He's ludicrously tall. And a bit gorgeous.

—Gotcha.

—His aunt has an apartment in Sozopol and she must be lovely or a bit naive. Because she's letting them all stay there.

—How much is all?

—I don't know, she said.—His band buddies, and Ethan, and probably twenty-seven others.

—Grand, said Jimmy.—I'll text him.

—Phone him.

—Yeah.

—Do.

—Oh my God!

—Hey there.

—What're you doing down there, like? Mahalia asked.

He was on the kitchen floor.

—Chattin' to the dog, he said.

—You're hilarious.

She went to the fridge and stood in front of it the way her brothers did. She was taller. She opened the fridge door, looked in, closed it again.

—D'you want me to make you a pancake? said Jimmy, and the thought of it delighted him.

—No, she said.

—Okay.

She opened the fridge door again and took out the milk. He stood up, felt a bit wobbly. Mahalia moved away as he approached.

He opened the fridge door. There was the usual amount of stuff in there, half-eaten, uneaten. It looked like it always did – no less. There was nothing in there he wanted.

—Sure about the pancake, May?

—Yeah, she said.—I'm not hungry, like.

—Are you okay? he asked.

She looked a bit caught.

He said it again.

—Are you okay?

He smiled.

—Yeah.

Her eyes were huge and watery. She looked like she wanted to run.

—What's wrong? May?

—Are – like – ? Are you better?

Oh Jesus. He wanted to die.

—Yeah, he said.—I'm grand – I'm fine. I don't think – . I'm not sure what was wrong. But I'm better. D'you want a pancake?

—Yeah.

He texted Des.

Up to a lesson?

He texted Outspan.

Hows it goin?

He texted Noeleen.

In 2moro. Thanks. X

He couldn't phone her. Couldn't face it.

He took out the trumpet. He blew. Not too bad. He held the one long note – no valves. He couldn't remember which it was, C or G. He tried another. It slid away from him. He heard clapping from downstairs. He blew again.

Shite. Yrsefl?

That was Outspan. He sent one back.

Want to meet?

The phone hopped again – Des this time.

Cool. Friday nite?

He went back downstairs. He left the phone on the kitchen table, so Aoife and the kids would notice the blips and buzzes, the social interaction.

—We heard you playing the trumpet.

—I've a lesson on Friday.

—Great.

The air was full of wet hope.

He started to fill the dishwasher. He remembered now, he enjoyed it. Fitting everything in. All the things he did in the house, the washing, the hanging up. He enjoyed it all; he always had. Except ironing.

There was no word back from Noeleen.

His phone rang.

—Hello, he said.

—Where?

It was Outspan.

—Howyeh, Liam.

—Where'll we meet?

—Pub.

—No.

—Starbucks.

—Fuck sake, said Outspan.—Which one?

—College Green.

—Grand.

He looked around casually, hoped Aoife was listening. The room was empty.

—I'm going back in to work tomorrow, he said.

—Lucky cunt, said Outspan.

—Fuck off, Liam, said Jimmy.—After work? Five or so?

—Okay.

He felt wobbly going in. Nervous, like he was going in for a job interview.

He probably was.

—Did you talk to Noeleen? he'd asked Aoife the night before.

—When?

—Well. Recently.

—Yes, she said.—I did.

—Okay.

—I had to, Jimmy, she said.—You weren't going to work.

—Grand.

—She was worried too, you know.

—Okay.

—She phoned me every few days.

—Great.

—And we went out a couple of times.

—Out?

233

—Yes, said Aoife.

She pointed at the bedroom window.

—Out there, she said.—We had a drink. And an early bird.

—Wha'?

—Something to eat.

—Early.

—Smart boy.

Noeleen's car wasn't in the car park. He was ahead of her, back in action.

Maybe she'd offer him a lump sum. Maybe he'd take it.

July, but it was freezing. It had been raining for days. There'd been spectacular stuff in England. Flooding and chaos, the roof on at Wimbledon. He thought about phoning Les.

He got down to the emails. He watched them pour in. 97 became 167, became 298, became 407. They were still coming. He'd wait till they'd all arrived before he'd start to delete them.

There was something else Aoife had said to him last night.

—When I went through your phone.

Here goes.

—Yeah?

—Your address book, she said.

—What about it?

—You've no friends.

He looked up from the Mike Scott book. He kept having to start it again, even though he liked it.

—I've a few, he said.

—Not many.

—No, he agreed.

—It made me sad, she said.

—I'm grand.

—How can you fucking say that, Jimmy?

He slid through the emails now and deleted the ads and spam, the daily stuff he had sent to him but never looked at, StumbleUpon, RCRD LBL.com, PledgeMusic. All that shite. He was down to less than two hundred.

He was finishing a reply, just the one, to the Halfbreds' sixty-two messages when he knew Noeleen had come into the room.

—Barry and Connie want to support the Stone Roses at the Phoenix Park, he told her.—No – hang on.

He read their last one again.

234

—They want the Stone Roses to support them. Are they too late?

—That was last weekend, she told him.

—Okay, he said.—I'll offer them the Ballybunion Arts Festival.

—When is that?

—Doesn't exist, said Jimmy.—Yet.

—Welcome back, said Noeleen.

—Thanks.

He actually wrote that he was looking into a slot at the Electric Picnic for them, apologised for the delay in answering – holidays, kids, family bereavement, no mention of health or the state of his head – and finished up with the hope that their eldest got the points she needed for veterinary – he remembered Connie saying something about it. *JXx*. Then he hit Send, and listened to the whoosh.

—Good to be back?

—Yeah.

He stood up and they hugged. She held his shoulders and looked straight at him.

—How are you? she asked.

—Grand.

—Great.

It was a bit awkward, a bit embarrassing. But she wasn't sacking him.

—You can unfold your arms now, Jimmy, she said.—You're safe.

It occurred to him now, properly; she'd been talking to Aoife. They'd been swapping the notes. Aoife was always on about him folding his arms. He even did it in his sleep, apparently.

They sat in the meeting corner. She'd brought him a coffee from across the street. They were the only two people in the place.

She looked at him, and laughed.

—Where will I start?

—Give me the bad stuff first, he said.

—We're fucked.

She laughed again, sent her hair behind her head.

—No, she said.

She put a hand on his knee, and took it away.

—It's not too bad, she said.—And it ain't too good.

She had her own iPad now, and she started flicking through pages. He'd have sold the house to buy an iPad, the way she was using it there.

235

—So, she said.

The news was actually dreadful. He hated spreadsheets; they made him dizzy and useless – the numbers never stayed put. But he was able to listen, and every aspect of the business was being hammered.

—So, she said.—There you go.

—Jesus.

He didn't feel too bad.

—You said it wasn't too bad, he said.—All bad.

—It could be a lot worse.

—Could it?

—We're still here, Jimmy, she said.—We're surviving. Sales are down but they're not gone, totally. We just need a haircut. Actually, needed.

He looked around.

—There's no one else comin' in, is there?

—No, she said.—Sorry. I didn't want to tell you – to start with that. I let them – I had to let them go. It couldn't wait.

—Okay.

He'd always been on his own, his own branch of the business. That wasn't going to change. But it was bad. He'd loved the fact that he'd made some of those jobs. It had been one of the measures of the thing. When Jimmy had been the same age as the twit – he couldn't even remember the poor kid's name – he'd never had a proper job. He'd always done stuff, sold things that needed selling, organised gigs, done a bit of band promotion. He'd sold sandwiches at the early festivals – sandwiches and toilet paper. He'd hired a taxi for himself and about two thousand egg sandwiches, all the way to Lisdoonvarna, with the windows wide open all the way, and he'd still made a fuckin' fortune. And T-shirts – always weeks ahead of the official merchandise. He'd sold Smiths T-shirts, printed by a chap called Smelly Eric, outside the Smiths' first Dublin gig at the SFX, long before the Smiths copped on that selling their own T-shirts might be a good idea.

When things picked up in the country, he'd ignored it. All the pyramid schemes, timeshares in Bulgaria, 'it'll pay for itself' deals, the no-brainers – he hadn't been interested. It had always been about music – even the egg sandwiches; he'd sold them to people like himself. There'd been guys making fortunes selling ad space on the jacks walls of pubs, an idea Jimmy had every time he went for a piss. They were welcome to it. Because it was boring. He'd taken the old records down from the attic because he loved music. They'd invented shiterock because of the music. It had made work for him, a good income, jobs for others – success.

The times had caught up with him.

Fuck it.

Fuck them.

—What's the good news? he asked.

—Well.

She started doing the flick thing with the iPad again. Then she stopped.

—You might have seen this already, she said.

—What?

—Our big success story, she said.

—What?

—*More Songs About Sex and Emigration*, she said.

He'd nearly forgotten about it.

—Really?

—It's done okay, she said.—We won't be retiring on it. And we still have to move.

—Hang on, said Jimmy.—We're movin'?

—Did I not mention it?

—No.

—Sorry. Yes.

—Shite.

—Agreed. But it has to be done. But – now. This.

She still wasn't offering to show him what was on the screen – the tablet – in her hand.

—This is where we're going to make money, said Noeleen.—Just look at this.

She moved, and sat beside him.

—Can you see?

—Yep.

It was YouTube – hard to make out. A low-roofed room, a lot of crowd noise, a whoop. The camera was all over the place; it never settled.

—Is it a gig?

—Watch.

She pointed to the title under the screen. *I'm Goin' To Hell*.

—Jesus.

She pointed to the views. 5,237,016.

He began to understand it. The camera, more than likely a

phone, was being held over people's heads. The guy holding it was moving through the crowd, pushing. The guy – the camera – turned. And Jimmy saw it – him. His son. He saw Marvin.

He said nothing.

The camera got no closer.

Marvin stood sideways to the microphone stand, and sang.

—I WANT HER ARMS —

I'M GOIN' TO HELL —

Marvin's pals, the other lads, were there too. Mush and Docksy – the rest of the band.

—I WANT HER LEGS —

I'M GOIN' TO HELL —

He sat back a bit. The screen swam when he was too close to it, and he wanted to get a look at Noeleen looking at it. She loved it. She was melting there, listening to a great song. And watching the handsome man singing it. *For fuck sake.*

—I PROWL THE STREETS —

I'M GOING TO HELL —

He tried to remember when Noeleen had last seen Marvin. It would have been years ago, when she'd bought into shiterock. There'd been a barbecue, a few things like that. They'd been friends, partners. There'd been genuine affection. Actually – he looked at her now – there still was. Looking at her there, leaning into the sound. She hadn't a clue who she was watching. That was Jimmy's guess. Kids grew so quickly; Jimmy himself could have been persuaded that it wasn't Marvin.

But it was.

He wanted to cry.

—Who's that? he asked.

—A Bulgarian band, said Noeleen.

—Bulgarian?

—Yep, she said.—It's the bomb. Isn't it?

—Fuckin' amazin'.

—That's a club in Stara Zagora, she said.

—That's in Bulgaria, is it?

—According to Google.

—I'LL GET MY HOLE —

—I'M GOIN' TO HELL —

—Oh my fucking God.

That was Noeleen, and Jimmy wasn't sure she knew she'd spoken. He decided to step out on the ice.

—He sounds very like —

He couldn't remember the name – the guy who'd recorded the song in 1932.

Noeleen rescued him.

—He sounds exactly – *exactly* – like Kevin Tankard.

—Unbelievable, said Jimmy.

The three minutes were up.

Noeleen sat back.

—Well?

—I don't know wha' to say, said Jimmy.

It was the truth.

—It's so great, said Noeleen.—So – just exciting. You found this song and a few months later there are kids in Bulgaria playing it. And more kids all over the world watching them. Millions of them. How does that make you feel, Jimbo?

—Great.

—Ah, come on! Give us a bit of the old Jimmy.

—Fuckin' great.

He grinned.

It was fuckin' unbelievable. But he couldn't tell anyone. Except Marvin, when he got home. If he got home. He was obviously a superstar over there. He'd be Marvin Rabbeettski or something. And young Jimmy – he could tell him. If he didn't know about it already.

—So, said Noeleen.

She stood up.

The place was a bit ridiculous with just the two of them in it.

—They're ours, said Noeleen.

—Who?

—We're going to sign them.

—The Bulgarian lads? said Jimmy.

—Yep.

—Great, he said.—Good idea.

He stood up too.

—Have you made contact with them yet? he asked.

—No.

—I'll do that, he said.—What're they called? I didn't notice there.

—Moanin' At Midnight.

—Great, he said.

—Wild.

—It's a Howlin' Wolf song, by the way, he told her.

—What is?

Their name, he said.—They know their stuff.

An hour back at work, and he was already ahead of her. They hadn't been called Moanin' At Midnight when Jimmy had seen them months – a year – ago, or when they'd recorded the song. They were untouched and untraceable, until Jimmy decided to find them.

—Did you look for a website? he asked her.

—No, she said.—I only saw it on Friday.

—Who told you about it?

—My niece, she said.

—What age is she?

—Sixteen.

—She liked it, yeah?

—Oh God. Jimmy. We have to sign them. This isn't just a bit of crack, like the Halfbreds. It's the real deal. It's rock 'n' roll.

He grinned – he couldn't help it. This was all mad and brilliant.

—Leave it with me, he said.

—I'm phoning John Reynolds, she said.

—The Electric Picnic chap?

—Yes.

—To get them on the line-up, yeah?

—Yep.

—Good idea, he said.—Great idea. Bulgaria's in the EU, isn't it?

—Yes, she said.—Why?

—Visas, said Jimmy.—They won't need them. They can come over whenever we want them. And come here. Put a word in for the Halfbreds as well, will yeh?

—I'll mention them.

—Thanks, he said.—There might be a cancellation or somethin'. And while you're at it —

—You're back.

—I am. Ned – the Bastard of Lir.

—Still feeling guilty, Jimbo?

—You said it.

He needed to get out – just get out, move, march the excitement off himself. But he couldn't. He had to sit down now and search for Moanin' At Midnight. He couldn't disappear and come back with them, delivered. Noeleen had to see him working for it.

—There's no point in googlin' Moanin' At Midnight, he told her.

She was behind him somewhere.

—Why not?

—The song, he said.—Thousands of blues sites.

—What about Bulgarian Moanin' At Midnight?

—Leave it with me.

He texted Marvin while he spoke.

How r things? X

—Where're we movin' to, by the way? he asked.

What was the time difference, between Dublin and Bulgaria? Marvin wouldn't get back quickly anyway; he never did.

—Well, she said.

She was sitting now too, with her back to him. Just the two of them in a space made for twenty. Although there'd never been more than twelve. Still though, it was sad. And it was frightening. Things were shrinking. It was the same all over Dublin. People wandering around empty spaces.

He missed her answer.

—Sorry?

—My mum's back garden, she said.

—You're jestin'.

—She's letting me build a Shomera, said Noeleen.

—A fuckin' prefab?

—They're lovely, she said.—The one I chose. I'd have included you in the decision if —

—Grand.

He said it nicely; he hoped he did. It couldn't have been easy for her, moving from here to her ma's back garden.

—Two rooms, she said.—Offices.

—Jacks?

—God, yes.

He wouldn't have to be banging on the oul' one's back door, walking across her kitchen with *Mojo* or the Mike Scott book under his arm.

—Where does she live?

—Clontarf.

—That's handy.

It was nice, tapping away, throwing the chat over their shoulders.

—Why your ma's?

—What?

—Why not get the Shomera installed in your place? I know it's a good bit out —

—I've moved back.

—Oh.

—It's okay.

It wasn't. It was shite, having to move back to her mother's house.

—I'm sorry about that, he said.

—It's fine.

He hated asking but he thought he'd better. He did the Aoife test: would she be furious if Jimmy told her that Noeleen had moved back home but he didn't know why? Yes, she would. Although she probably knew already. But that probably didn't matter.

He stopped typing. He rolled back his chair a bit, so she'd hear it move. He swerved, so he could see her.

—What happened?

The phone hopped. It was Marvin.

Grand.

He put the phone back down.

—One of the kids, he said.—Sorry.

—Can't afford to keep it, said Noeleen.

She shrugged, smiled.

—Same old story, she said.—I'm supposed to think I was greedy.

—Don't see why.

—I don't either, she said.—I could afford it at the time. We could.

—Is Adam in your ma's as well?

She smiled, and shook her head.

—Nope.

—Jesus, he said.—It's rough.

—Ah well.

He texted Marvin. *Ok if I phone u later? X*

Outspan had a latte and skinny blueberry muffin. Jimmy had a double espresso.

—Yeh not eatin'?
—Not hungry.
—Hard on the hole?
—Just not hungry.
—Yeah, maybe.

They found a table in among the young and the healthy. Jimmy couldn't look at Outspan properly; he could feel his neck rip when he forced himself to keep his eyes on him. They'd nothing in common, especially now that Jimmy wasn't dying. He liked Outspan but, really, he was there because he wanted Aoife to know he was there.

—How's your ma? he asked.
—Same as ever, said Outspan.—I seen your parents there.
—Yeah?
—They're lookin' great.
—Yeah.

The coffee was muck. Jimmy pointed at Outspan's cup.

—How's yours?
—Grand, said Outspan.—Not too bad.

The phone hopped in his pocket.

It was Marvin, back.

Grnd. 7?

Perfect.

He thought of something now – shocking – and perfect again.

—Are yeh still into the music? he asked.
—A bit, yeah.
—D'you want to come to the Electric Picnic with me?
—No way.
—Why not?
—Hippy shite.
—Ah, for fuck sake.

This was more like it; now they could talk.

—Grow up, man, said Jimmy.—You're talkin' shite.
—How am I? said Outspan.—I went to an outside gig once. Brought me daughter – the older one, Grace. She likes Coldplay. Don't fuckin' ask. Annyway, it was crap.

Jimmy texted Marvin. *Great.*

—Coldplay won't be at the Picnic, he said.
—Not Coldplay, said Outspan.—They weren't too bad. It was the whole thing. Fuckin' eejits hoppin' around. No one listened to the music. The Coldplay fella – he seemed like a nice enough

head. Yeh can kind o' see wha' your woman, Gwyneth Paltrow sees in him. Annyway, he says, We're goin' to play 'Yellow', or somethin'. An' the young ones around us go mad. Oh I love this one!

His Southside girl impression was brilliant, but eerie. Several Southside girls stood up and went to a free table outside. Inhaling the taxi fumes was preferable to witnessing Outspan's performance.

—An' then they'd just start chattin' to each other again. There's no way! Fuck right awf! He's the focking bomb!

—The Picnic's different, said Jimmy.—It's for people who know their music.

—You've been there yourself, have yeh?

—No, said Jimmy.

He hated outdoor festivals. Outspan was bang-on.

—But I'm goin' this year, he said.—Will yeh come?

—No.

—Go on, yeh cunt.

—Okay.

He couldn't resist.

—See now, he said.—I have friends.

She smiled – she grinned.

—Fuck off, she said.

Then she looked a bit more serious.

—Is it not – is it not a bit strange that the friend you asked might not be alive by the time it starts?

—That's a bit pessimistic, said Jimmy.

—I suppose.

—Look it, said Jimmy.—You were the one who got the two of us together again.

—I know, she said.—It's great.

They were alone in the kitchen. Even the dog was missing.

—What's the noise? said Jimmy.

—What noise?

—Outside, he said.—In the back.

—It's Jim, she said, and she looked out the window to check.—I asked him to wash the brown wheelie.

—Asked him?

—Told him, she said.—It was stinking.

244

—Grand.

—Oh God.

—What?

Jimmy stood beside Aoife and watched young Jimmy vomiting on the patio. It was hot out, no sign of a cloud for once, and the air around young Jimmy was packed with flies. It looked like they couldn't make up their minds between Jim's puke and whatever was left at the bottom of the wheelie.

Jimmy had his second great idea of the day.

—I'll give him a hand.

The stench grabbed him before he was even out the door.

—For fuck sake.

He waded through solid stink, across the patio to young Jimmy.

—Y'alright there?

Young Jimmy stood up, wiped his eyes.

—I can't do it, he said.—Sorry.

Jimmy looked into the wheelie.

—Oh fuck!

They stood there laughing, disgusted, delighted. The dog pissed against the side of the wheelie, and that got them going again.

—It can't be easy, said Jimmy.—Vomitin' and laughin' at the same time.

He was rubbing young Jimmy's back, thrilled to be having the opportunity. He tried to remember when the brown wheelie system had been introduced, when the Council had thrown one of them at every house, before the whole service was privatised.

—I think I've gone blind, said young Jim.

Jimmy patted his back.

—Good man.

It must have been four or five years. He wasn't positive, but he didn't think the brown wheelie had ever been washed. He'd never done it; he'd have remembered. There was stuff at the bottom of that bin that they'd eaten in the middle of the last decade.

—I'll give you a hand, he said.

—Thanks, said young Jim.—I'll hose the puke.

—Grand, said Jimmy.

He looked.

—Fuck.

—What?

—I think Messi's after eatin' most of it.

That got them going again.

—Don't tell your mother.

A disgusting job, but Jimmy wasn't sure he'd ever been happier.

—Breathe through your mouth, that's the trick.

They hosed, brushed, sweated, gagged, laughed, and shovelled years-old rot into a black plastic sack. The only thing was the flies – and especially the maggots. There was no laughing at them. They were serious.

—There now.

They were finished.

—Yeh proud?

—No.

—You could eat your dinner off tha' wheelie.

I am my da.

—D'yeh fancy goin' to a film? he said.

—Eh – what – what film?

The cosy bit was over.

—No, it's grand, said Jimmy.

And it was. It was funny.

—Only if you want, he said.—I thought the Batman one.

—I've seen it, said young Jimmy.

He looked so relieved.

—Twice, he said, just in case.

—Grand.

Jimmy thought of something.

—Did you see Marvin on YouTube?

—Yeah.

—Good. Isn't he?

—Yeah.

—Does anyone know? About the song.

—No.

—Sure?

—Eh – no.

—Okay.

He went back in through the kitchen. The last of the flies went with him. Brian was home, head coming out of the fridge.

—Want to go to the Batman film, Smoke?

—*The Dark Knight Rises?*

Jimmy loved that, the precision, the literalness of kids that age – still that age.

—If that's what it's called, he said.

—Cool. Yeah.

—Great. How was the football?

—Okay.

—It was good, yeah?

—Yeah.

Mahalia was in at the computer.

—Hey there.

—You smell, she said.

—I know.

—There are, like, flies flying around your head.

—I'll deal with them, don't worry.

She looked back at the screen.

—D'you want to come to *The Dark Knight Rises*?

—I've seen it.

Ah shite.

—Twice, she said.

—Grand.

She stayed staring at the screen.

—Seeyeh, he said.

It was sad but grand. He'd make it something nice to tell Aoife.
They got out of the house before she could object to them
going to the Batman film so soon after the shootings in Colorado,
and drove up to Coolock. And it wasn't too bad, the film. He
stayed awake through most of it. It was entertaining enough and
he didn't want to miss any of Anne Hathaway. He'd definitely
watch all of *The Devil Wears Prada* the next time Mahalia was
watching it.

He'd timed his phone alarm to go off at seven.

—Back in a minute.

—Okay.

—You're alrigh' by yourself for a bit?

—Yeah.

—Good man.

He went out to the car park because the foyer was full of mad
kids and their mas. The rain was back, so he tucked himself in
against the wall of Burger King. There was a longer delay than
usual, the signal heading to Bulgaria, he supposed, and the dial
tone was different, foreign. He half expected Marvin not to answer.

—Hey.

—Marvin?

—Hey.

—How are yeh? It's Dad.

—Yeah.

—Yeh havin' a good time?

—Yeah.

—An' is the weather good?

It was an oul' lad's question. No answer came back.

—So things are good, yeah?

—Grand, yeah.

—Great.

—Yeah, it's good.

—Come here, said Jimmy.—Your gigs.

—Yeah?

—Moanin' At Midnight.

Marvin laughed. Jimmy loved that sound.

—Great name, he said.

—Yeah, thanks, said Marvin.—It's a Howlin' Wolf song.

—I know.

—Cool.

—I saw the YouTube thing, said Jimmy.

—Yeah?

—The song.

—Did you see the number of hits it has?

—It's supposed to be a fuckin' secret, Marv.

Stop!

—But it's brilliant, he said.

—Cool – thanks.

—But the secret.

—It kind of still is a secret, said Marvin.

—I know.

—People think the song is really old. Traditional, like.

—No, it's great, said Jimmy.—And the record's sellin' really well. Probably because of you. I owe you a pint or somethin'.

—Cool. I've to go –.

—Okay, grand. But —

—We've to do a soundcheck.

—You've another gig?

—Yeah.

—Great, said Jimmy.—I'll let yeh go. There's another thing but.

—What?

—They think you're Bulgarian.

—Who?

—Everyone.

—No.

—Far as I know, yeah.

He could hear Marvin laughing. He could hear him – he swore he could – waving his arm, getting his buddies to come over and hear the news.

—Marvin? Yeh there?

Marvin's voice was deeper.

—Yesss.

Jimmy copped on: he was pretending to be Bulgarian.

—Good one.

He laughed.

—Listen, he said.—I'll let ych go. But my boss – my partner. Noeleen – do you remember her?

—Think so.

—The way the video is cut – your one, like. With no intro or anythin', just the song. She thinks you're Bulgarian. And she's not the only one. So.

—D'you want us to pretend we're really Bulgarian?

—No, said Jimmy.—Yeah. But no. Listen. Be a bit mysterious. Don't say anythin' between songs. Don't say anythin' at all. It'll be more convincing than puttin' on an accent.

—Okay.

—Can you follow the logic?

—Yeah. Think so.

—And listen. I'll let yeh go now. But —

He was drenched, the side of him leaning against the Burger King window, right through to his skin. The water was running straight into his clothes. He hadn't noticed and he didn't care.

—Yeah? said Marvin.

—You're Bulgarian, said Jimmy.—But you're mysterious Bulgarians. You're like guerrillas. You strike, an' disappear.

Jimmy remembered Joey the Lips Fagan, the Commitments' trumpet player, saying the same thing, back in the days when Jimmy was Jimmy.

—We hit an' then we sink back into the night.

—We?

—You, said Jimmy.—I meant you. But listen. Final thing.

—Yeah?

—I'm supposed to be searchin' for you, said Jimmy.—To get you to come over to Ireland for a few gigs.

Marvin's laugh became a howl.

—The Electric Picnic, Marvin, said Jimmy.

The howl became something even madder.

—We can plan it when you get back, said Jimmy.—Properly, like.

—Cool.

—Good luck tonigh'.

—Thanks.

—Be mysterious.

—Yeah. Yeah.

—I love you.

—Yeah.

—Seeyeh.

—Yeah, seeyeh.

On his way back in to Brian and Anne, Jimmy's phone buzzed in his pocket. It was Marvin.

Tanx. X

—A nice enough lad, he told Noeleen.—The manager. His English is excellent.

—What's his name?

Oh fuck —

—Boris.

—Great, she said.

—He's in the band as well, actually. The drummer.

—It's fantastic, she said.—We're doing business with a man called Boris.

—Yeah, said Jimmy.—Gas, isn't it?

He googled Bulgarian Male Names, looked over his shoulder, scrolled down through them. Too fuckin' late – he was stuck with the name. There was no Boris but there was a Borislav. Boris was definitely short for that. He was grand – safe.

He'd have to be careful. He'd have to keep ahead of Noeleen and, now that he thought of it, everyone else, including himself. He was making it up, and he'd have to keep reminding himself of that.

Fuckin' hell though. It was brilliant.

—Phone me tomorrow at about midday, he told young Jimmy.

—Okay.

—I'll be callin' you Boris.

—Eh – why, like?

Jimmy told him.

—Cool.

—Don't tell your mother, said Jimmy.

He was saying that a lot these days.

—And come here, he said.—I'll text you first. Just to make sure Noeleen's there and she can hear a bit of the conversation.

—Should I be a prick? said young Jimmy.

—I told her you were sound.

—Oh. Okay.

—We'll keep it simple, said Jimmy.

Outspan phoned him.

—Me ma's organisin' a fundraiser for me.

—For an operation?

—No, said Outspan.—The Electric Picnic thing.

—Really?

—Yeah, said Outspan.—Upstairs in the Hiker's.

—Brilliant, said Jimmy.—Or is it?

—Ah yeah, said Outspan.—It's grand. A bit embarrassin'.

—What'll it be? Jimmy asked.

—Wha'?

—The fundraiser.

—Race nigh' or pole dancin'. She can't make her mind up.

—You're jestin'.

—Yeah, said Outspan.—There's no pole in the Hiker's.

—Do they do pole dancin' for charity?

—They do annythin' for fuckin' charity.

He'd sent the text.

Phone.

And, fair enough, the phone rang.

—Hello?

—It's, like, Boris.

—Boris! said Jimmy.—Hey!

—Fock thees hey.

—How did the gig go last night?

—Fock thees geeg.

—Great, said Jimmy.—Brilliant.

He stood up. He didn't look at Noeleen. He strolled nice and slowly out to the stairs.

—Is this okay? said young Jimmy.

—So Boris, said Jimmy.—Have you spoken to the band?

251

Every word was clear and separate, so Boris in Bulgaria could understand him.

—Are you still there, Boris?

—Yeah. Sorry if I messed —

—And they're happy?

—Yeah.

—Great. Great. Great. It's a great line, isn't it? You sound like you're only down the road.

—I am, said young Jimmy.

—Down the road, said Jimmy again.—Yes – no. It just means very near. Anyway. The band is happy. Yes?

—Yes.

Jimmy kept going down the stairs.

—I'll look at dates and venues and put something together. Do the lads – ? Sorry. Do the guys in the band have jobs? Are they students?

—Students.

—Students. Great.

He was down the stairs, out on the street. He was crossing, to Insomnia. But he kept it up, in case Noeleen was looking out at him. Method management – it was the only way. He just hoped he wasn't frightening young Jimmy.

—Great. That's useful to know. We'll make sure they are back in time for the start of college.

He pushed the door, got in.

—Jim?

—Yeah.

—Thanks, said Jimmy.—See yeh later.

—Okay.

—You were brilliant, thanks, said Jimmy.—I owe yeh.

—Big time, said his son.

He got coffees for himself and Noeleen. He was happy. But something was pulling him back. His cop-on had grabbed hold of his shirt. He remembered how elated he'd felt, how fuckin' high and powerful, before he'd crawled into bed. This was different though – it had to be.

He was back out on the street. That was it. Earlier in the year he'd have been striding out, indestructible. Now though, he looked left and right and made sure he didn't spill the coffee over his fingers.

Aoife came with him. A tenner each, and up the stairs. Outspan was at the bar, looking miserable.

He looked at Aoife.

—Howyeh, Eve.

The place was full of people Jimmy used to know, bald men he'd gone to school with, fat oul' ones he'd kissed or wanted to. They'd all paid their tenners for Outspan.

—Howyeh, Missis Foster.

—Ah, Jimmy.

—Great night.

—Massive, said Outspan's ma.—I had a bit of a blubber earlier.

She must have been over seventy, like his own parents. But she looked exactly the same, the only one in the room who did.

—An' come here, she said.

She grabbed Jimmy's shoulder and pulled him down so her mouth was at his ear.

—You're a great lad, doin' what you're doin' for Liam.

—I'm doin' nothin'.

—Fuck off now, said Missis Foster.—He won't let yeh know, but he's delighted. An' come here.

She grabbed Jimmy's hand and pulled him through tables and familiar faces. The men were in suits or football jerseys. Jimmy in his jeans and a shirt was under-dressed and over-dressed.

Missis Foster was still holding his hand.

—Howyeh, Rabbitte.

—Here, Jimmy! Don't let her drag you ou' to the jacks!

—Fuck off now, you, said Missis Foster.

They were heading for a corner. And the thought hit him. Imelda! She'd be here. She lived just down from Outspan's house.

Grand, grand. He'd introduce her to Aoife. Christ, his life was full.

—He's droppin' the hand, Missis Foster!

—It'd make my night, said Outspan's ma.—Don't mind those fuckers, she told Jimmy.

She'd dragged him right across the lounge. There was no sign of Imelda.

—Here now.

Outspan's ma let go of his hand. She was beaming at a kid, a little young one, in her party dress. She was seven or eight, a beautiful little thing.

253

—This is Alison now, said Missis Foster.—Say hello, Alison. This is your daddy's friend, Jimmy.

Jimmy held the kid's hand.

Outspan's daughter.

Has she won?

—I don't know, I don't know.

They were all in the room, waiting for the result.

—What's keeping them?

They watched Katie Taylor and the Russian young one, the ref between them holding their arms, down.

—Did she win?

—I don't know – Jesus, wait.

They were all there, the whole family, Marvin as well; he was home. It was the first time in ages – since Christmas – that they'd been like this.

It was agony.

—The poor girl.

Jimmy Magee, the commentator, was going mad now, but it was hard to tell with that gobshite. Then the ref lifted Katie's arm.

—She's won!

—Oh God, she's won it!

—Cool.

—She's fuckin' won – sorry!

They were up out of the couch, off the floor, hugging, laughing.

—Kay-tee! Kay-tee!

—God is my shield!

The dog was barking and jumping at them but he seemed happy enough.

—God is my shield!

—She's brilliant.

—God is my shield!

—Jesus, Jimmy, said Aoife.—If you keep saying that, I'll think you're serious.

—God is my shield!

He didn't know why he was so happy. It was just a young one after winning a medal. She was barely older than his own kids. But that was it – that was it. An Irish girl had won an Olympic gold. She'd done something brilliant and now, today, it meant everything.

A text from his da.

Its 1990 over here!

—Kay-tee, Kay-tee!

He sent one back.

God is my shield.

He could hold his kids for as long as he liked. He could love being Irish. There'd be Chinese tonight, thanks to Katie.

—Jimmy.

Aoife tried to hold onto his new hair. Her mouth was in his ear. He was on top of her; she'd wanted all of his weight. He had Katie Taylor to thank for this as well.

—Jimmy.

—Yeah?

He lifted his head, so he could look at her. She'd have wanted that.

—It was funny the first time, she said.—It really was. But if you whisper God is my shield once more, I'll pack a bag and never come back.

—Sorry – okay.

Her hands were back in his hair.

—Say something else, she said.

—Okay, yeah. Good idea.

They had a Wikipedia page ready, himself and young Jimmy.

Kevin Aloysius Tankard (1905–unknown) was an Irish musician and singer. He is thought to have been born and lived in the Liberties area of Dublin, although little is known of his early life.

It looked good, the real thing.

There is only one recording known to exist, the recently discovered I'm Goin' To Hell *(1932).*

—It's a bit short, said Jimmy.

—Yeah.

—How did he die?

—A pact with the devil.

—No, said Jimmy.—People will start thinkin' of Robert Johnson.

They'd kept looking at the Robert Johnson page while they constucted Kevin's.

—Plane crash?

—Too modern.

—Drug overdose?

—Might ring true, said Jimmy.—Google old-fashioned drugs there, till we see.

They looked through the lists.

—Opium.

—It's hard to imagine opium in Dublin in the '30s or '40s, isn't it?

—Who says he stayed in Dublin? said young Jimmy.

—I do, said Jimmy.—But it's a good point. What else have we?

—Peyote.

—Too Mexican, said Jimmy.—How would it've got here?

—Okay, said young Jimmy.—Heroin.

—There's a thought.

Young Jimmy pointed at something on the screen, a date.

—It's been around since 1874, he said.

—Cool, said his father.

They built up a history of questions, a long paragraph, and shortened it. They sat side by side at the kitchen table and forgot where they were.

—Someone claims they saw someone like him in – say – Argentina.

—Brilliant.

—There's a graveyard in – what's a city in Argentina?

—Buenos Aires.

—Cool. There's a stone – like tombstone, like. With K.T. carved on it.

—Yeah, yeah.

—Leave it with me, said Outspan.

—Sure?

—Yeah, he said.—What's the word again?

—Yurt, said Jimmy.

—An' that's a posh tent, yeah?

—Yeah, said Jimmy.—So Noeleen says – in work. An' they're in a quieter camping site, she said. Away from the fuckin' madness.

—Grand.

—They're supposed to be comfortable.

—An' fuckin' waterproof, yeah?

—Yeah, yeah, said Jimmy.—An' they give yeh inflatable mattresses as well.

—An' inflatable women – for tha' fuckin' money.

Jimmy didn't think he'd ever heard Outspan sound really excited before.

—So – a yurt, yeah?

—Gotcha, said Outspan.—An' come here.

—Wha'?

—The night in the Hiker's. We took in way more than I need. So. Is there annyone else we can ask?

—Well, said Jimmy.—Brilliant, yeah. What abou' Derek?

—Asked him, said Outspan.—He started his usual, yeh know. Ah, I don't know, would we have to camp, will there be toilets? A pain in the fuckin' arse.

He was talking so much, Jimmy began to wonder about his lungs. But then there was a noisy pause. It lasted a while. Then Outspan spoke again.

—So I told him to fuck off.

—Fair play, said Jimmy.—Is there annyone else?

—No one I know, said Outspan.

Jimmy said nothing. It was probably true. He was like Jimmy there. There were loads of people who wished him the best – the Hiker's had been packed – but he'd no real friends.

—There's a guy, said Jimmy.—Des. He's sound.

—Ask him.

—Okay. Sure?

—Yeah, go on. We need to fill the fuckin' yoke.

—The yurt.

—Yeah.

A thought fell through Jimmy.

—D'you remember my brother, Les?

—The mad cunt.

—He's not mad these days – I don't think.

—Is he still a cunt but?

—I don't know, said Jimmy.

He didn't mind saying that.

—He lives in England, he said.

—That's not fuckin' promisin'.

—Will I ask him?
—Fire away.

—Did it – ?
They were in the bed. Aoife waited till he noticed she'd stopped talking.
—Yeah?
—I don't mean this nastily, she said.
He sat up a bit. Mike Scott would have to fuck off again.
—Go on, he said.
—Well. Did it ever occur to you that I'd like to go?
—To the Picnic?
—Yes.
Jimmy went for honesty.
—Yeah, he said.—'Course.
—And?
—Well, he said.—I'm guessin' you'd probably like to.
—I might, she said.
—But I'd asked Outspan – Liam. And I'm askin' Les.
—Are you?
—Yeah.
—That's lovely.
She meant it. She was delighted, and that delighted him. It really did.
—So I didn't think you'd want to share the tent with us all, he said.
He said tent instead of yurt, in case she thought a yurt would be big enough for everyone.
—But I want to see Marvin, she said.
She knew about the Bulgarian scam. She had to; he couldn't have hidden it. Although he hadn't told Noeleen, and he'd told – asked – Aoife not to. Till he'd figured out the consequences.
—There are day tickets, he said.
—I know.
—We can get a few.
—I know.
—Great.

—I was thinkin', said Jimmy.
—Yeah?

258

—Maybe we could give Kevin a few more songs.

—No, said young Jimmy.

—One, even.

—Don't wreck it, Dad.

—You're right.

—Les?

    —Jimmy.

    —How are yeh?

    —Fine. You?

    —Fine, grand, yeah. How's Maisie?

The usual little pause.

    —Fine.

    —Great. The Olympics went well.

    —Yes.

    —Did you get to annythin'?

    —No.

    —Watched it on telly, yeah?

    —Some.

Jesus, what was he doing?

    —Come here, he said.—Do yeh like your music?

    —What do you mean?

    —Do you follow the music, yeh know – go to gigs, ever?

    —Not really.

    —No?

    —No.

    —Well, listen.

Jimmy told him about the Picnic. The yurt, Outspan, Des. The Cure. Elbow. Dexys Midnight Runners. The free ticket. He could give it the full Jimmy because he knew the answer was going to be No.

    —So. Would you be up for it?

    —Yes.

    —Yes?

    —Yes. It sounds great.

    —Great, said Jimmy.

He meant it, and that was a shock. It was like something warm flowing down through him – the anaesthetic he'd had when he'd had the bowel whipped out; that same rush.

    —Jimmy?

—Yeah.
—Still there?
—Yeah.

The house was calm again.

Marvin had gone down to the school. He'd said he'd text when he got the news, but he hadn't.

—Send him a text, said Jimmy.

—Why me? said young Jimmy.

—You're not me or your mother. He'll answer you.

—Go on, Jim, said Aoife.—Please. The tension's killing me.

They watched young Jimmy pulling his phone out of his pocket, like he was pulling barbed wire from his hole. They watched him compose the text and send it.

—What did you say? Aoife asked him.

—It's private.

Marvin didn't text back.

—Will we phone him? said Jimmy.

—Yes. Maybe.

—He's only been gone half an hour. How far is the school – to walk?

Young Jimmy had disappeared. So Jimmy went up to Mahalia's room and woke her.

—How long does it take you to walk to school?

—What?

He asked her again.

—Like, I haven't walked to school in, like, months. It's the holidays, like.

—How long though – about?

—I don't remember.

—A rough guess.

—Ten minutes. Go away.

—Okay. Thanks.

He went back down. He hadn't noticed Marvin actually doing the Leaving in June. Now but, he was shitting himself. Jimmy hadn't done the Leaving. He'd left school a few months before the exams.

They felt a shift in the air inside the house before they heard the front door closing. And they were up and out, skidding into the hall to get at Marvin.

—Well?

—Three hundred and forty points, said Marvin.

—Is that good?

—Of course it's good, said Aoife.

—Brilliant, brilliant. Will it get you what you want?

—Think so, said Marvin.

He wanted to do Arts or something, in UCD.

—If it's the same as last year, said Marvin.

There was the hugging.

—Proud of you, son, said Jimmy.—Always.

The excuse was great, the fuckin' window. He could gush and let himself go. Maybe exams weren't such a bad thing. Marv's arms were around him too.

—I'm proud of you too, Dad, he said, the sarcastic, wonderful little prick.

Now he could phone the Halfbreds. Barry or Connie?

He went out to the back garden.

Connie.

He didn't think the phone rang even once.

—Five hundred and sixty points, motherfucker!

—Congratulations, Brenda.

He seemed to remember Connie screaming something about the points her daughter would need to earn the right to shove her hand up donkeys' cunts.

—Five hundred and sixty!

—Great stuff, said Jimmy.—So she's all set to become a vet.

—Oh yeah!

Connie was never going to ask him why he'd phoned.

—I've some more good news for you, Brenda.

—What?

He'd got them – Noeleen had got them – a Picnic gig, half an hour in one of the tents, to replace Little Whistles, two girls with guitars and flowery dresses. Their auntie had died; she'd been the inspiration for their big song, 'Forget Whatever'. So they'd cancelled all gigging till the new year.

—I've a gig for you, Jimmy told Connie.—The Electric Picnic.

—We're not going on before the fucking Cure!

He took a quick breath.

—Or Patti Smith! said Connie.

—Christ, said Jimmy.—Will Patti Smith be there?

—Not on my fucking stage.

261

Jimmy could hear a girl crying happily behind Connie. That would be the kid with the points, the donkey lover.

—I'll make sure Patti stays away, said Jimmy.

—G.L.O.R.I.A. spells fuck off, bitch!

—Good one, said Jimmy.—So you're up for it, yeah?

They'd been screaming at him for a decent gig, for months – for years.

—I'll think about it.

—Grand, said Jimmy.

Aoife needed the car.

—Why?

—I'm going too, she said.—Remember?

—Shite, yeah – sorry. Can yeh not get the bus?

—Jimmy.

—Grand, okay. Shite. Not you – life in general.

Des had sold his car and Jimmy was fairly certain Outspan didn't have one.

Do u own car?

Xwife says its hrs.

—Da?

—Jimmy.

—Howyeh.

—We've Leslie here with us.

It was Wednesday night and Les was staying at the folks' until they headed down to Stradbally and the Picnic on Friday.

—Great, said Jimmy.

Slap the fatted calf onto the fuckin' barbecue.

—I'll be over tomorrow night.

—Wha' time? his da asked.

—Why?

—We're goin' out for a meal, said his da.—Leslie's treatin' us.

—Brilliant, said Jimmy.—But come here. Can I've a lend of your car for the weekend?

—'Course.

—It's to get us to the festival. Aoife needs ours.

—No bother, said his da.

—Thanks very much.

—Delighted to be of help.

His da sounded so happy. He told Aoife about it.

—Because Leslie's come home, she said.
—Yeah.
—And why's that?
—Because —
It hit him.
—Because I asked him.
She laughed.
—And how does that make you feel?
—Eh – good, he said.

—Where's tha' Swiss Army knife?
—You're not serious.
—I am.
—It's two in the fucking morning, Jimmy.
—Exactly the time o' day when you'd need a Swiss Army knife.
I didn't mean to wake you, by the way.
—Why would you need a knife?
—Cuttin' rope, self-protection, killin' Outspan.
—Come back to bed.
—Okay.
She pulled him tight to her.
—You're going to have a great time.
—I know.
Her knee whacked his arse.
—Sound convincing.
—I *know*.
—That's a bit better. Stop worrying.
That annoyed him.
—I'm not worried, he said.
He didn't think he was lying.
—What's the worst that can happen?
—Listen, he said.
He tried not to push away from her.
—I'm not one of the kids.
—I'm just —
—Stop fuckin' patronising me.
She said nothing. Her knee was gone. But her arm was still there.
—Listen, she said.—I've been doing it a lot. Since your diagnosis. Which wasn't even a year ago, by the way.

—I know, he said.—Mad.

—I've tried to imagine what the worst thing is that can happen. The worst conclusion.

—My fuckin' death.

—Yes, she said.—That was one of them. And very upsetting. Usually.

—Fuck off.

She squeezed.

—But after the surgery and chemo, she said.—Money, next door —

There was still no one in there, behind their bedroom wall.

—All the worrying things. Genuinely worrying. I'd ask what the worst outcome was.

—And?

—It's usually not that bad, she said.—Not good either. Shite actually. But not devastating. So.

—So?

—What's the worst that can go wrong? she asked.

—We won't be able to stand one another.

—And you come home?

—I suppose.

—It's not that bad, she said.—Is it?

—No, he said.—I suppose not. I'm not sure I even want to go.

—Ah Jimmy.

—I do – but. And it's not that I'm worried that somethin' will go wrong. Do we have any babywipes in the house?

—Why?

—It'll be easier than washin' an' whatever.

—Jesus, she said.—You really are thinking ahead, aren't you?

—There's another thing.

—What?

—What if somethin' happens to Outspan?

—It won't.

—You can't say that, he said.

—Then you'll need more than babywipes.

She started laughing first.

—Jesus, Outspan.

—It's grand.

—It's fuckin' Darfur.

—Okay, said Outspan.—Okay. But it's kind o' Southside Darfur.

He had a point. It looked like a refugee camp but it was filling up with blonde girls in shorts and flowery wellies. None of them looked hungry. It wasn't too mucky yet but it had been pissing down all the way from Dublin and Jimmy could feel the months of rain just under his feet, waiting to fuck up the weekend.

—I want me yurt, he said.

They'd come in Outspan's ex's car. He'd phoned Jimmy that morning, to tell him.

—I hacked up blood in front of her, he'd said.—An' she relented.

—My da's happy enough to give us his.

—No, said Outspan.—I have it now, so we may as well run the arse off it.

Jimmy didn't want to be involved in some kind of marital vendetta. Outspan's ex was bound to be a hard woman. But —

—Okay, he said.

—One thing but, said Outspan.

—Wha'?

—Can yeh drive us?

—Okay, said Jimmy.—No bother.

—I'd do it meself, said Outspan.—But I can't.

—Cos o' your meds?

—No, said Outspan.—I'm banned.

—Grand, said Jimmy.

Des had cycled to Jimmy's, and Aoife had given them a lift to his da's. Les had been waiting for them, dressed like a man who did some serious walking.

—I bet he has a Swiss Army knife, said Jimmy.

—Shut up, said Aoife.

—And a fuckin' compass.

The three of them had walked down to Outspan's. Past Imelda's. Her car wasn't there.

Outspan was standing in the garden.

—Will it rain?

—Between now an' Sunday night? said Jimmy.—Bring your fuckin' coat. This is Les an' Des.

He only copped on now how stupid that sounded.

—Leslie an' Des, he said.

—Leslie an' Dezlie, said Outspan.

Outspan didn't do smiling, so it was a good few seconds before

265

the four of them were laughing together. Then they were all in the car, and gone.

It was a bit awkward at first. Les in the back said nothing to Des, and Des said nothing to Les.

Outspan had the atlas.

—Left or right here, Outspan?

—Do they do left an' rights down here?

Jimmy said nothing about the rain, even when he'd had to slow down because he could see fuck all through it. He could already imagine it seeping through his clothes. Before he'd heard one note or eaten a chip. He'd be soggy for the whole weekend; he wouldn't be able to bend his legs because of all the water in his jeans.

—They say it'll be nice tomorrow and Sunday, said Des.

—Cunts, said Outspan.

It was just four men who didn't know one another, including – especially – the two brothers. They were going through Kildare before they laughed again, when they passed a dead fox at the side of the road.

—Left or righ', me bollix, said Outspan.

They'd parked in a field that must have had hay in it the day before. They followed the line of cars, further and further in. The ground felt solid enough under the car.

—It's well organised, isn't it?

That was always a surprise.

—Should be an Olympic event. Synchronised parkin'.

—We'd be in with a shout.

They were really starting to enjoy themselves, until they got out and opened the boot.

—Tents, said Jimmy.

—Yeah, said Outspan.

—We don't need tents, said Jimmy.

—We kind o' do, said Outspan.

—What abou' the yurt?

—Too dear.

—You said it wasn't a problem.

—Well, it was, said Outspan.—I did me sums wrong.

If the other two lads – the pair of liggers who were getting in for nothing – were embarrassed, they weren't showing it.

—Why didn't yeh tell me? said Jimmy.

Outspan looked at Jimmy like he was going to jump on him, or sink into the ground. *What's the worst that can happen?*

—It's fine, said Des.

Les took a tent out of the boot.

—Sorted.

Jimmy took the other one – it was very light – before Des or Outspan could grab it. He pushed a blanket to the side and saw the oxygen.

He thought he'd fuckin' die.

—It's just in case, said Outspan.

—Will we bring it?

—No, said Outspan.

Jimmy knew now why Outspan had borrowed the ex's car. Or stolen it. He could have done with a blast of the oxygen himself, and so could Leslie and Dezlie, judging by the pair of earnest heads on them.

The slabs of beer saved them.

—Never heard of this one, said Jimmy.—Excelsior?

—It's not the worst, said Outspan.—An' it was good value.

—Where?

—Lidl.

—Grand.

—I got the tents there as well, said Outspan.

—How much?

—Seventeen euro.

Les laughed. He looked at Outspan.

—You're serious.

—Each, said Outspan.

Les hoisted a tent onto his back and got one of the slabs out of the boot. And that was a new worry. Jimmy thought there might have been a bit of history there, Les and the drink. It might have been something his mother had once said. Or just something he'd imagined; there was something too careful about the way Les carried himself. But, fuck it, he grabbed a slab – or he tried to. It was heavy. He got it up onto his shoulder but it was immediately awkward, and sore. He'd his bag as well. He'd never make it.

—Let's go.

Now they stood at the edge of Darfur. Jimmy was sweating like a bastard. The walk from the car to the gate – the wrong fuckin' gate – to the right gate, to here, had killed him. He was glad he'd let the hair grow because the sweat – the fuckin' lard – would have been running straight down his face, into his eyes.

But he'd made it and he was happy enough. His breathing would be normal again in a minute and the breeze was already working away at the sweat.

They weren't ready to go in deeper yet, although the sun was out and the field of tents looked quite pleasant.

—Jesus, men, said Des.—We're old.

The truth of that was funny. It loosened them up, made them feel a bit brave. A steady line of kids kept passing them, to grab their places further in. It was early afternoon – Jimmy checked his watch – only just after two.

—We're missin' Joe Duffy.

—Who's Joe Duffy? Les asked.

—Cunt on the radio, said Outspan.—We righ', lads?

They picked up the gear, the tents, the bags, the sleeping bags, the slabs of beer, the wellingtons, and got ready to walk into the heart of darkness.

Les led the way. Jimmy could see none of the young Les in him. There was nothing of the kid left. Young Outspan was still in the current Outspan. But young Les was gone. It made Jimmy sad – and guilty. He couldn't really remember what Les had been like. When Jimmy had met him the night before, the only reason he'd known it was Les was the fact that he was standing in their parents' kitchen and he couldn't have been anyone else. But it wasn't like he was damaged, or twitchy or anything like that. He seemed grand. He was fit. He didn't have much to say. But that was alright too. He'd gone ahead a bit and Jimmy wanted to run after him, chat to him – ingratiate himself, make up for the decades.

—Look.

It was someone their own age.

—That's a fuckin' relief.

There were more, over near the edge of the camp. Normal-looking people. The Picnic was supposed to be for the more mature music lovers, and there were about nine of them here. There'd be more arriving later, Jimmy supposed, after work.

Outspan was struggling.

—Alrigh'?

—Grand.

—D'yeh want a rest?

—No.

He stopped. He looked lost for a second, gone. Then he was

alive again. It was fuckin' madness, though; he was going to die. Here.

Les had found them a spot. Himself and Des were sitting on the tent packs by the time Jimmy and Outspan got there, and Les had opened a can. Outspan dropped – *dropped* – beside them and grabbed a can too, before he slipped back into his little coma, and woke again.

—The business, wha', he said.

He was some boy.

They clinked cans.

—We're here.

—We fuckin' are.

—I like this, said Les.

—Jesus, said Outspan.—Over there, over there, look – quick!

They looked.

—D'yis remember when tits used to look like tha'? said Outspan.

They weren't alone now. In the minute they'd been sitting there, they'd gone from outer suburbs to inner city. Girls pulling wheelie suitcases and boys hauling two-wheeled trolleys with multi-storey slabs of drink were surrounding them, claiming their space. The girl that Outspan was pointing out had just gone past in a wheelbarrow, pushed by two young guys who looked like they played serious rugby. Outspan's mouth was about a foot away from her ear.

—Shut up, for fuck sake.

—Wha'?

They sat there for a bit, and relaxed.

—Ground's damp.

—Stop whingein'.

—I don't hear any music.

—It hasn't started yet.

—So we paid a fortune for fuckin' silence?

—Fuck off, said Jimmy.—It'll kick off at four – I think.

He took the programme from his back pocket. He'd printed it out the night before. He had to bring it up to his eyes; he hadn't brought his reading glasses.

—A quarter to four, he said.

—Who's on tonight?

—Sigur Rós.

—Who?

—The xx.

—Fuckin' who?

—Christy Moore.

—Ah, for fuck sake.

—I like Christy Moore, said Les.

—We all like Christy Moore, said Outspan.

Jimmy hated Christy Moore.

—But it's like havin' one o' the neighbours gettin' up onstage, said Outspan.—Who else? Someone we know – come on.

—Well, I'm going to Christy Moore, said Les.—A good old sing-song.

—Grand, said Jimmy.

Maybe Noeleen was right; he just automatically hated everything Irish.

—Why Christy? he asked Les.

—What d'you mean?

—Is it cos you live in England?

—Come on, said Les; he looked happily angry.—You think I cry into my pint, pining for home?

—No.

—He's good, Jimmy.

—Okay.

—You haven't changed.

How could he tell? How could Les know what Jimmy had been like twenty-five years ago, when Jimmy hadn't a clue what Les had been like?

—I'm happy enough, said Jimmy.—I'll watch Christy too.

—He'll be fuckin' delighted, said Outspan.

—Fuck off.

—He'll write a fuckin' song about yeh.

—Fuck off.

—Will we put up the tents?

—In a minute.

—Annyone hungry?

—No.

Jimmy could feel the heat now, on his neck and hands. The ground was cold under them though, even under plastic.

—When's it open? Des asked.

—Three – I think.

—You didn't answer me question, Rabbitte, said Outspan.

—Wha' question?

—Who else is playin'? said Outspan.—That we've heard of.

—Tonigh'?

—Tonigh'. Come on.

—Grizzly Bear.

—Never heard of them.

—I have, said Des.

—Anny good?

—I don't know, said Des.—I know the name. But I don't think I've actually heard them.

—Ah now, Dezlie. For fuck sake.

—Dexys Midnight Runners, said Les.

—Tomorrow, said Jimmy.

—Fuckin' brilliant, said Outspan.—Thirty thousand cunts singin' 'Come On Eileen'.

They were on their second cans.

—We should o' brought some o' those fold-up chairs.

—We might be able to buy some.

—My arse is numb.

—Like your fuckin' head.

It was a great few hours. Doing nothing, getting to know the other lads. Jimmy liked Les. He liked being with him. He texted Darren. *At the Picnic wth Les. Hows the baby?* Les was a can ahead of the others but Jimmy made himself relax. Some of the passing kids stared at them, like they were afraid they'd find their parents with them.

—We'd better get the tents up or there'll be no room.

—Good thinkin'.

It was hard standing up –

—Fuck.

– but good crack erecting the tents. Although they seemed a bit light and small, and useless.

—We should've brought some of those inflatable mattresses.

—Not at all. We'll be grand.

They watched Les unrolling a rubber mat.

—Do we have annythin' like that? Jimmy asked Outspan.

—What is it?

—A yoga mat.

Aoife had one like it, except hers had the dog's teeth marks on it, and a corner missing.

—No, said Outspan.

—Wha' have we?

—Wha' d'yeh mean?

—To lie on.

—The fuckin' ground.

Jimmy tapped the roof of the tent. It was like tapping a stretched silk shirt.

—Hope it doesn't rain, he said.

—You're startin' to annoy me, Rabbitte, said Outspan, although Jimmy could tell that Outspan wasn't annoyed. And he liked that, that they were slipping into their old selves, the way they'd known each other years ago.

—Just fuck off whingein', said Outspan.—It'll keep the rain ou', no bother. Most of it, annyway.

—Grand.

—We'll go for a wander, will we?

—Okay.

They threw all the stuff into one of the tents.

—Will it be safe?

—Probably not.

They followed Les. The grass was intact nearly everywhere. The boggier patches had been filled with wood chippings and bark, small bits of tree. There were people cooking, a gobshite playing a guitar, a few lads already skulled. Jimmy always thought of his own kids when he saw other kids drunk. But he'd park that for the weekend; he'd try to.

—Any sign of the jackses?

—The middle-aged bladder.

—Fuckin' terrible, isn't it?

—Over there – look it.

The muck looked more sinister as they got nearer the toilets, a line of plastic, windowless phone boxes that looked like they'd already taken a hammering. There was a urinal too, a long yellow plastic trough of a thing that was probably used for feeding cattle when the field wasn't full of teenagers from Dublin. It was up against a wire fence, so they pissed while gangs of young ones and lads passed on the other side of the fence, and a group of older women who looked like they were normally a book club.

Outspan had gone into one of the phone boxes and he'd been in there for a fair while.

—Is he okay?

—He's dyin'.

—Not now though – is he?

—Will I knock?

272

—Don't know.

But Outspan spared them the decision. He climbed out of the thing, like he was getting out of a car. The kid who was next in line for Outspan's jacks waited till Outspan had gone past, then moved to the back of a different queue.

—Alrigh'? said Jimmy.

—Grand, yeah, said Outspan.—That'll do me till Sunday, I'd say.

—Ah good.

—Look.

Darfur had grown four or five times bigger since they'd arrived. The average age had gone up too, and some of the tents had seen serious use – these were people who'd brought families camping. There was movement; the kids were starting to migrate towards the stages and the main arena.

—I've changed me mind.

—Wha'?

—We're not the ugliest nation in the world.

—Some of them are lovely, aren't they?

—Most of them.

—Fuckin' all o' them. 'Cept your woman over there in the Donegal jersey.

—Were their mothers as good-looking?

—No way.

—Yeh sure?

—Positive, said Des.—I'd remember.

They could hear a band tuning up now, the noise drifting across at them.

—Who's that?

—Don't know, said Jimmy.

He hated having to admit it.

—Sounds shite anyway, he said.—Are we righ'?

They went back across to their tents. They packed jacks paper, rain jackets, middle-age hoodies, and Ambre Solaire –

—You're fuckin' optimistic.

– into two backpacks. They left everything else. The sun came out, sudden and strong, and Jimmy could see right through their tents. If the sun could do that what would the fuckin' rain do?

—Will we bring the wellies?

—Fuck the wellies.

There were two young lads sitting on folding chairs outside

their tent, a better-looking tent than Jimmy's. Les turned to them.

—Gentlemen.

—What's the crack, man? said one of the young lads, a bogger. They were both wearing Kilkenny jerseys.

—You staying here for a while? Les asked – actually, he said it; it wasn't a question.

—Probably.

—Keep an eye on our stuff, a'righ'.

—Oh. Right.

They wouldn't budge for the night, the poor fuckers. Les wasn't big or muscle-bound or anything like that. But there was something about him – certainty, solidity. And the English tail on his accent – it made him a bit of a Kray twin. The drink was safe. They could have left their watches and wallets.

—Thanks, lads.

—No bother, man.

They were on their way. Back through expanding Darfur, back past the jacks. They'd been given wristbands at the outside gate and now they had to show them again to a stoned-looking security man – and they were through, in. At the Picnic.

—Brilliant.

It was, immediately. It was like someone's huge mad back garden. There was a helter-skelter and a ghost train, and Jimmy could see four big tents, and the outdoor stage was off to the right somewhere. There was a row of great-looking food places, and a bar or something that was already hopping, even though nothing had really started yet. And as they walked further in, they could see huge wooden sculptures and all kinds of hippy stuff going on in under the trees.

But Outspan was struggling again. They'd had to slow down. The year's rain was right under them, sloshing at their soles.

—Alrigh'? Jimmy asked Outspan.

—Grand, said Outspan.

It was as if he'd got over some sort of obstacle, and he started to look around again.

—I wasn't expectin' this, he said.

—It's cool.

—Body an' Soul, said Outspan.—Wha' the fuck is tha'?

—Yoga an' knittin'.

—At a fuckin' rock festival?

274

—Just ignore it.

They stood at what seemed to be a corner. Four men – one decision.

—How many stages are there? Des asked.

—Five, said Jimmy.—I think. More.

—Five gigs at the same time?

—Think so.

—Brilliant.

—Hungry, lads?

—Starving.

—Wouldn't object to a nibble, said Les.

Outspan had the money. Or Jimmy hoped he did. Des hadn't a bean, and Jimmy hadn't a clue about Les. He had a couple of hundred quid himself.

—Liam?

He spoke quietly.

—Wha'?

—You know – the yurt an' tha'. And how you were short o' funds?

—Yeah?

—Are we okay?

—We are, yeah, said Outspan.—I just thought we could put it to better use.

—Grand.

—What do we fancy? said Outspan.

—Burger.

—Excellent.

Outspan and Les queued at the Gourmet Burger, and Jimmy and Des went across to another queue, to get the beer.

—It's Heineken, Heineken or fuckin' Heineken. Or look – Tiger.

—Fifty cent extra for the Tiger.

—Then fuck it.

There was no change out of twenty quid and they spilt about a fiver's worth on the way back to Outspan and Les. They were sitting on a plastic poncho under a tree. There were no real sounds, no songs, coming from any of the tents, or the main stage. Just the occasional chord, or a testing one, testing two.

Outspan looked angry and happy.

—Enjoy these burgers, men, he said.—They're the last you're gettin'.

—What's up?

—Price o' the fuckin' things.

—Steep, said Les.

—Fuckin' criminal.

—Are they anny good but?

—That's beside the fuckin' point.

—Okay. The beer's dear as well, by the way.

—Good burger.

—Great burger. Good chips.

—Great fuckin' chips.

—They're hand-cut, said Outspan.—An' the burger's organic.

—Hand cut?

—So it says on the van.

—How else would they be fuckin' cut?

—Fuck knows, said Outspan.—Unless it's Christy Brown. Left-foot-cut. Ah fuck it, I'm after gettin' goo on me front.

—There's jacks paper in the backpack there, said Jimmy.

—Sound.

They watched Outspan dipping a wad of paper into his Heineken and rubbing the ketchup off his hoodie. It came off without a struggle.

—Jesus, said Des.—What's it doing to our insides?

—I couldn't give a shite, said Outspan.—I'm not even sure I have any fuckin' insides.

He looked around for somewhere to put the wad. It was funny how they'd all been tamed by age. Making sure they didn't get damp, looking for places to put the litter.

Outspan dropped the paper beside him.

—Here, he said to Jimmy.—You never told me Leslie was in the club as well.

—The club?

—Cancer.

Des's mouth stopped working, even though he was dug into his burger.

Something – some band – started in one of the tents.

—What's tha'?

—Don't know, said Jimmy.

—The fuckin' expert.

—Fuck off, said Jimmy.

He got the programme from his pocket.

—It might be Gypsies on the Autobahn.

—Sounds more like Gypsies on the M50.

—They'll survive without us.

—What's the first band worth seeing, Jim? said Les.

—Grandaddy, said Jimmy.—I'd say.

—One of the tents, yeah?

—Tha' one over there – I think.

—Great.

—All tha' way?

—Fuck off.

—What sort o' stuff do they play?

—It's kind o' unique, said Jimmy.

—Oh fuck.

Des needed rescuing. He was eating again, but he didn't look like he was enjoying himself.

—You're the odd man out, Des, said Jimmy.

—Far as he knows, said Outspan.

Les laughed.

—Les had the same version as me, Jimmy told Des.—But he's grand now. Righ', Les?

Les nodded.

Des would be fine. He'd already known about Jimmy, and Jimmy had warned him about Outspan – although a warning could never come close to meeting the man himself. So Les was the only surprise addition.

It was getting cold. Jimmy could feel the damp pawing his arse, and he was ready for another piss. But he felt great. The anxiety had gone out of his neck and shoulders and the burger was probably the best he'd ever eaten. He didn't give much of a shite about food. But it was the context – the time, the place, the company, the hand-cut chips.

—Could've done with a bit more salt, Liam.

—Fuck off.

None of Jimmy's acts were on till the next day, the Saturday. He had the Halfbreds and the Bastards of Lir, Ocean's da's poxy band, and the one he was planking about – and giddy about – Moanin' At Midnight. He was a free man till then.

He smiled at Des. He lifted his beaker.

—Another?

—Go on.

Outspan threw his empty beaker across at Jimmy. Jimmy waited for him to send a twenty across with it. But not for long – Outspan's hands didn't go anywhere near his pockets.

Des stood up with him.

—I'll give you a hand, he said.

—I'm going via the jacks, said Jimmy.

The place – the park, whatever it was; the grounds – it was really filling now. Going anywhere in a straight line wasn't an option. It was vast, it really was. But they spotted a sign for the jacks. They sank a bit, but they were grand – they were okay. It was a bigger version of the jacks back in Darfur, and already well broken in. They got places beside each other at another yellow urinal. Jimmy held the empty plastic beakers high in his left hand.

—The Olympic torch, said a young lad on the other side of him.—Cool.

—The Paralympics, said Jimmy.

Des laughed. So did the young lad. This was the life. Des held the beakers while Jimmy did his buttons.

—You enjoyin' yourself, Des?

—Watching you doing your fly?

—No, I was takin' that for granted, said Jimmy.—I mean – overall.

—Yeah, said Des.—But —

—Go on.

—I can't pay for anything. I've enough for a couple of rounds —

—You're covered, said Jimmy.—That was always the deal.

—Thanks.

—No. But actually, it's Outspan – that's Liam – you should be thankin'.

—I like him.

—Yeah.

—Is he definitely – ?

—Yeah, said Jimmy.—There'll be no happy ending there.

—Fuck.

—Yeah, said Jimmy.

The queue for the drink still wasn't too bad. It was hardly a queue at all, more a slow walk. Out of Darfur, the average age had shot up. Jimmy and Des might have been the oldest in the line, but not by too much. Women too, hitting the forties.

They were closer now to two of the music tents.

—That's the Crawdaddy, I think, said Jimmy.

He pointed at the one on the left.

—A lot of the good stuff, our kind o' music, yeh know. It'll be in there.

—Ol' lads' music.

—Discernin' oul' lads. Exactly.

He handed over the beakers to the young one behind the counter. He didn't even have to tell her what he wanted, and she never asked. He had to hand over the twenty before she went off and filled them. He didn't thank her and she didn't thank him.

—A bit soulless, isn't it? said Jimmy.

—Fuck it, said Des.

They got back to Outspan and Les. It felt good, seeing them there, sitting side by side, staring out at the world. It was like he hadn't seen them in ages, years, and – in a way – it was true. It was just a sentimental thought. But grand. His head was nicely fuzzy.

They sat and watched the world wade by.

—Jesus, the height of her.

—My God.

—Is she WiFi enabled?

It was time to move, stretch the legs – Jimmy was numb. They all were.

—My leg's gone dead.

Les held onto Jimmy's shoulder while he shook blood back down through his leg.

—Fuckin' oul' lads, said Outspan.

He looked like the only one ready to bop.

They liked being the oul' lads. It was safe, relaxing; nothing was expected or demanded. They could go spare or give up; it didn't matter. No one would give a shite, especially them.

Maybe.

They gathered up their rubbish and found a bin.

—Goes against my fuckin' principles, said Outspan.—So where're we goin'?

They strolled across towards the Crawdaddy tent. It looked a bit like something out of a children's book – the candy-stripe roof – and they weren't the only people heading into it.

—It's like the end of *Close Encounters*, said Jimmy.

They walked into the dimness of the tent and the smell of dead grass. The ground was wet but it was fine. The feet weren't sinking.

But something wasn't right. The people around them were too young. They weren't Grandaddy people. Grandaddy had been around for years, long enough to break up and re-form. Their one great album, *The Sophtware Slump*, had been released around the time Mahalia had been born, maybe a bit after. Jimmy got the programme out of his back pocket.

—Sorry, lads. Wrong tent.

—Ah, yeh fuckin' eejit.

They got out and moved across the field, to the Electric Arena. They had to go at a stroll, to let Outspan keep up with them, but they got into the tent – it was huge – in time to see a big gang of beardy lads walk onstage.

—This them?

—Yeah.

—Who are they again?

—Grandaddy.

A few people whooped, a few more clapped, and the usual eejit started shouting the name of a song.

—'The Crystal Lake'! 'The Crystal Lake'!

There was no messing or tuning. The band got going and the tent quickly filled and warmed up. They were great. They were brilliant. There was no encore. The band bumped to a good end and walked off.

—What did yeh think?

—Shite, said Outspan.

—Good, said Des.

—Not my kind of thing, said Les.—But they were thoroughly professional.

They went back out, for a piss and a drink, and back in for Grizzly Bear.

—What did yeh think? said Jimmy.

—Shite, said Outspan.

—Yep, Jimmy agreed.—I expected more.

—Yeh poor naive cunt.

They were outside again, and across the field to the bar. Les bought the round.

—Fucking expensive this side of the pond.

Fuckin' eejit, Jimmy thought, but he wasn't sure why. Because it was fuckin' expensive. No one was tearing off to the jacks this time.

—We're gettin' the hang o' this.

—Becomin' acclimatised.

—Jesus, lads, said Jimmy.—Two gigs down an' it's still daylight.

—Marvellous, said Les.—What's next?

Mark Lanegan, in the Crawdaddy.

280

—Fuckin' who?

Jimmy gave Outspan the history – Queens of the Stone Age, The Gutter Twins, Isobel Campbell, Soulsavers. Lanegan walked out and he was immediately their man. In a dirty black suit he stood at the microphone, held it, looked at the ground when he wasn't singing and said nothing between songs. And the songs were great – straightforward, hard, three minutes. Jimmy could feel the sound as a physical thing, thumping his chest, even flapping the sleeves of his hoodie. Lanegan had pulled the crowd in; the tent kept filling. There was a fair bit of good old-fashioned head banging going on around them. Jimmy looked at his own gang. They were loving it.

—What did yeh think?

—Shite, said Outspan.

—Ah, for fuck sake.

—What's next?

—Need a break?

—No – fuck it.

—We'll have a look at the main stage, will we?

—Who's on?

—Sigur Rós.

—I like them, said Des.

—You know them?

—I think so.

It was cooler now and the sun had dropped behind the trees. One man stopped to zip up his hoodie – all the men stopped and zipped their hoodies. Then they were on the move again. It was much busier, a bit chaotic, but they weren't in a hurry. That was the trick, Jimmy decided; not really caring if you missed the start of a show, or stayed for the lot. It was like watching telly, except you were your own remote control. Or something.

Some of the women were unbelievable. They were dressed for the clubs in the middle of a field. Jimmy wondered were they cold, then wondered why he wondered.

—Would you dress like tha'? he asked Outspan.

—Depends.

—On wha'?

—I'll get back to yeh.

The main stage was right ahead of them.

Outspan stopped.

—You alrigh'?

—Yeah, said Outspan.—Not too bad.

—Are yeh enjoyin' yourself?

—When did you become my fuckin' ma?

—Grand – sorry.

The other two ahead of them had stopped. They came back.

—Alright? said Les.

—Yep.

Outspan pointed.

—Them.

It was a line – two lines – of girls. They'd a chair each and they were standing behind them. Their tight T-shirts said Mobile Massage.

—Wha' about them?

—Massage, said Outspan.

The girls were busy bullying the necks and shoulders of people, mostly women, in the chairs in front of them.

—You want a massage? said Jimmy.

—No, said Outspan.—But.

—Wha'?

—Massage, said Outspan.—It's usually a wank, isn't it?

—Do you see annyone bein' wanked there, Liam?

—No, said Outspan.—But.

—Wha'?

—I'd love a tug, said Outspan.

—Will a pint do yeh?

—G'wan.

—My twist, said Des.

He looked at Jimmy.

—Grand, said Jimmy.—Thanks, Des.

—Good man, Dezlie.

Les went up to the bar with Des.

—See, if this was a film, said Outspan.

—Wha'?

—Yis'd arrange a wank for me cos I'm dyin'.

—True.

—You'd go up to the big bird there an' whisper in her ear.

—That's righ'.

—An' next of all we'd be back at the tents an' she'd be in one o' them.

—Yeah.

—She's gorgeous, isn't she?

—Yep, said Jimmy.—But Liam?

—Wha'?

—It's not goin' to happen.

—Ah, I know, said Outspan.

The other two came back with the beer, and they made their way along the side of the field, and down, nearer to the stage.

—She was gorgeous though, wasn't she? said Outspan.

He looked back, and Jimmy waited for him to start moving again.

—Alrigh'?

—Ah yeah, said Outspan.—A bit sad. Come on so.

—She's a real masseuse, Liam. She doesn't —

—Fuck off, Jimmy, for fuck sake. I'm not stupid.

They kept walking.

—I know, said Outspan.—Even if I wasn't in the state I'm in. An' if I was twenty years younger. I still wouldn't have a fuckin' hope.

—In shite.

—I agree, said Outspan.—I fuckin' agree. It's just – . Remember Imelda Quirk?

—Yeah, said Jimmy.—'Course I do.

—We all fancied her, remember?

—Yeah.

—An' we all knew we hadn't a hope.

—Yeah.

—But we could still hope. You with me?

The band – Sigur Rós – were coming onstage, but they were easy to ignore because Jimmy and Outspan were standing a good bit back and on their own. Anyone near them was moving closer to the stage or away from it.

—Yeah, said Jimmy.—I know what yeh mean.

—An' listen, said Outspan.—It isn't the young one. I wouldn't – I don't think I would. But, say, she was older – her ma, say. Sometimes things like tha' – seein' a beaut like that. It just reminds me that I'll be dead in a couple o' months.

Jimmy said nothing. He put his hand on Outspan's shoulder. Outspan didn't object. He stared at the stage as he spoke.

—Give us a wank later, Jimmy, will yeh?

—No problem.

Jimmy didn't know much about Sigur Rós but he liked what he saw and heard. It was slow, songless stuff, like classical music by men who wanted to be in a band, not an orchestra. He liked that. The singer – Jimmy thought his name was Jonsi – had a voice so unlike Mark Lanegan's it was nearly hard to accept that they were both human. Actually, there was something not quite human about Sigur Rós, and he liked that too. They were David Bowie's foster kids or something. They'd have been better under a roof but, still, Jimmy liked them a lot.

But they were losing the crowd. There were dozens of people walking away, back past them.

—Wha' d'yeh think? Jimmy asked.

—Interesting, said Des.

—Utter shite, said Outspan.

It was cold now and dark. Outspan had a black cap pulled down past his eyebrows – where his eyebrows used to be.

—Where next?

Jimmy got the programme out of his pocket. He couldn't read it.

—Can't fuckin' see.

—Here, said Les.

He took the paper from Jimmy and held it up and at an angle.

—Ah yes.

—Who?

—Christy Moore.

—Let's go. Where?

—Crawdaddy.

They were veterans now. They knew where to go.

Jimmy wanted to lead the charge into the tent, to get over the hump, the fuckin' barbed wire fence that was his snobbery. His head was well up for it but his body was holding him back. He could feel it, just above his kneecaps, around his waist, pulling the back of his hoodie. He was fighting himself to stay up with the lads and have a good wallow in Christy. And he was fighting everyone else at the Picnic as well. All thirty thousand – whatever the number was – the population of Darfur and the other Darfurs, the posh tents and the yurts; there were kids dashing to Christy who hadn't been born when Christy was starting to think about retirement. It was a good-sized tent but it hadn't been built for a population this size.

—Fuckin' hell.

Les kind of gathered them up. He wasn't a big man – no bigger than Jimmy – but he seemed able to shield the other three and push backwards through the entrance, and in. Jimmy wondered – the thought popped up – if Les had served time in the army, the British Army. There was something so efficient about the way he moved and commanded the bodies to get out of his way without a word or an elbow.

They were in now and sweating in honour of Christy.

—JOXER MET A GERMAN'S DAUGHTER ON THE BANKS OF THE RIVER RHINE.

They'd arrived in the middle of 'Joxer Goes to Stuttgart'.

—AND HE TOLD HER SHE'D BE WELCOME IN BALLYFERMOT ANY TIME.

And it was great to be there, to be right in there, in all the love and the steam. Jimmy hadn't been in as packed a crowd as this since – he couldn't remember – years ago, the ska days. And it was the only gig he'd been to so far where no one around him was talking. All eyes, all mouths, were on Christy.

It was over. They stayed put. They held one another's sleeves like kids on a school trip while the solid mass around them loosened and they could get back out into the cold.

—Wha' did yeh think? Jimmy asked Outspan.

—Brilliant.

—You actually liked somethin'?

—Fuck off, he was fuckin' brilliant.

Jimmy took a breath and crossed the line.

—Yeah, he said.—He was incredible.

He wanted to cry. The rest of his life was going to be great.

But Outspan looked bollixed.

—Nightcap? said Les.

—Back at HQ, said Jimmy.—Sound.

—Are there any more gigs? Des asked.

—Just DJ stuff, I think, said Jimmy.—Dum-dum, fuckin' dum–dum.

—Oh fuck, come on.

They grabbed a few hotdogs on the way.

—For fuck sake – look.

There was a photograph pinned beside the hatch; the pigs on the organic farm before the organic farmer knifed the poor fuckers.

—Here, said Jimmy to the lad with the ponytail in the truck. —Which pig did ours come from?

The lad leaned over the hatch and put his finger on a pig. He was wearing dentist's rubber gloves.

—That one.

—Did he have a name? said Les.

—Janice.

—Brilliant.

—Worth the seven euro.

They went slowly – the ground, the food, the crowds, the dark, Outspan. There were parents shoving buggies through the muck and trying to keep count of the kids on legs. The music from the funfair bashed against the techno coming from one of the tents. They weren't the only ones going back to Darfur but there were as many coming at them, heading back in.

—Fuckin' eejits.

Les led the way to the jacks. There was a watchtower to the left, and two lads in reflective jackets on a wooden platform, a spotlight above their heads. The field was well lit.

—It's like a fuckin' prisoner-of-war camp.

—Not really, said Les.

They could feel the ground clinging to them as they got nearer to the urinals. Jimmy slid, but stayed up. They stood in a line.

Jimmy saw it – a lump in the corner, just past the urinal. It looked like a pile of clothes but it had two heads. It was a couple, a boy and a girl, sitting close; their hair looked tangled together. They would have looked lovely on a beach.

—Are yis okay?

—Hi, said the girl.

—Are you alright?

—Fine, said the boy.

—Grand, said Jimmy.

—Bye.

—Bye.

He caught up with the others. He could hear Outspan's breathing.

—Alrigh'?

Outspan nodded.

They looked out for the guy ropes. The spotlight was behind them and sprayed the roofs of all of the tents ahead. But their bodies made long shadows and even in the light the ropes were tricky – thin and glassy. They tripped over a few but nearly all the tents were empty.

—Look where you're going!

—Fuck off.

Les knew exactly where their tents were. Definitely, thought Jimmy; he'd been in the British Army. He'd found tents and loojahs in Iraq and Afghanistan.

The two young lads were still minding the tents and the gear.

—Alright, gents?

—Grand.

—Have a good night, lads?

—Great, said one.—Not a bother.

—D'yis want a few cans? said Outspan.

—We're grand.

They were gone, away, tripping over the ropes.

—Poor cunts.

They sat on their jackets.

—It's fuckin' cold enough now, isn't it?

—Cuddle up here, look it.

—Fuck off.

—Well, said Les.—I enjoyed myself tonight. Thanks, Jimmy.

—What're yeh thankin' tha' cunt for?

They opened cans, and tapped them against the other cans.

—Cheers.

—Great night.

—Who was the best?

—Christy.

—Lanegan.

—Fuck off. Christy.

—I liked Sigur Rós.

—You fuckin' would.

—What about tomorrow?

Jimmy told them about his own bands.

—They sound like shite, said Outspan.

But they all seemed happy, even a bit excited. Jimmy took a breath, felt himself go over another hump, and told them about his Bulgarian son.

—Brilliant.

—Fuckin' brilliant.

—Just – fucking brilliant.

All four of them were fathers. Jimmy realised it for the first time. They grinned and laughed and loved the thought of one of their kids up on a stage.

—I'll finally get to see my nephew, said Les.

Jimmy could see Des and Outspan looking at Les, trying to work out the story. He was Jimmy's brother; that was all they really knew about him. They said nothing.

Jimmy looked at Des, and felt a bit bad – a bit guilty. The Irregulars, Des's band, had been his first clients.

—If your vocalist hadn't died, Des, he said.

—Selfish prick, said Des.—It should've been me, men.

Les put his head back and roared.

—It should have been Des!

They joined him for the second shout – even Outspan.

—It should have been Des!

No one objected.

—Where is everybody?

—They're at the dum-dum dum-dum.

—Young people, wha'.

—They haven't a fuckin' clue.

—There was no fuckin' dum-dum dum-dum in our day.

—We played our instruments, said Outspan.

Jimmy looked at Outspan. He was right – Outspan had played rhythm guitar.

Les passed more cans around.

—Cheers.

—Yep.

—It should have been Des!

—I am the Des!

At last, life – a reaction came from across the field.

—Shut fuckin' up!

—I am the Des!

—Shut up!

—I'm the Des!

—You're the cunt!

—I am the cunt!

They were pissed but clear-headed – Jimmy was. Outspan was standing, away a bit, pissing on someone else's tent. Les was sitting cross-legged, straight-backed. Des was lying back, leaning on an elbow. The elbow was off the jacket, very slowly sinking into the ground. Des didn't notice or care.

Outspan was back.

—Alrigh'?

—Grand.

He took his time – a long time – bending his legs, dropping to the ground. There was one point, one second, when Jimmy saw how skinny he'd become. His legs didn't widen; his thighs seemed as thick as his ankles.

He landed.

—Where's me can?

—Any regrets? said Jimmy.

—I can't find me fuckin' can.

—Yeh brought it with you.

—Fuck, I'm not goin' back for it —

—Here, said Les.

He handed Outspan a fresh one.

—Cheers – thanks.

—Give us one there as well, Les, said Jimmy.

—And me, said Des.

Jimmy couldn't remember drinking as much, or for as long. He was breaking some kind of record. But he wasn't tired. He wasn't anything.

—So, he said – he remembered what he'd said a minute before.
—Any regrets?

—Wha'? said Outspan.—Me in particular?

—Yeah, said Jimmy.—But no. All of us.

—Well, said Outspan.

—Wha'?

—Chinese cock, said Outspan.

The air was full of Excelsior. It was the funniest fuckin' thing they'd ever —

—I've done all the rest, said Outspan.

They were on to the next cans before they'd stopped laughing and started and stopped again.

—I wish I'd had a few quid, said Outspan.

—Yeah, said Des.

—But, like, I did, said Outspan.—For a bit. I had a bit of a bundle. An' I spent it. So – no.

—More women, said Les.

—Yep.

—Yeah.

—But it's obvious, isn't it? said Jimmy.—Nothin' to do with health or gettin' older. We've probably felt tha' way since we were five.

—More women!

—More women!

—Shut up!

—I am the Des!

—Real regrets, said Outspan.—They're fuckin' pointless.

—I'm with yeh.

—Women, money, things tha' went wrong.

—What about you, Les? said Jimmy.

Les didn't answer.

—I wish I was you, Rabbitte, said Outspan.

—Fuck off.

—Serious.

—Fuck off.

—You're perfect.

—Fuck off.

—Sex but, said Outspan.

—Wha'?

—I read a thing, said Outspan.—A website, like. When I was – fuckin', yeh know – diagnosed. Kind of a list of all the things tha' were goin' to happen durin' the chemo an' after.

—I read that shite as well, said Jimmy.

—An' it is shite, said Outspan.—Isn't it?

—Some of it, said Les.

—Fuckin' all of it, said Outspan.—I never stopped – except when I was really sick – now, really fuckin' sick. I never stopped wantin' to ride nearly every woman I saw. It was business as usual. Still is. Even though —

—Wha'?

—It would fuckin' kill me.

—Good way to go.

—Not fair on the bird.

He coughed – or it sounded like a cough.

—But at least, he said,—there's the chemo porn.

—The what?

—Chemo porn.

—What the fuck is that?

—It needs fuckin' explainin'? said Outspan.

—Yeah, said Jimmy.—I think so – maybe. Just to be on the safe side.

—Ah, look it, said Outspan.—I thought yis'd know about it.

—No.

—Well, it's – like. It's people with cancer.

—Ridin'?

290

—Some, said Outspan.—Mostly just pictures. Good-lookin' women who still look good even though they're goin' through chemo. Men as well – some.

—Jesus.

—It's kind o' reassurin', said Outspan.—Yeh can see for yourself, if yeh have a smartphone there.

The dum-dum dum-dum was still going but something must have ended because they could see bodies now, long shadows, moving through the tents.

Les had his phone out.

—What's the web address?

—Which one?

—There's more than one?

—'Course there is, said Outspan.—Jesus. Chemo-porn.com. There's a dash.

—Between chemo and porn?

—No, between fuckin' an' eejit.

—Don't, Les.

—What?

—Why not? said Outspan.—What's your problem?

The shadows were huge but the kids that came after them weren't particularly big. They stopped dead at the lads.

—Old people! said a girl in shorts and wellies.—Old people!

—Oh my God!

Jimmy laughed. They all did.

—Put the phone away, Les, for fuck sake.

There were five of them – maybe six. Two girls and three lads – maybe four.

—Want a drink, kids? said Les.

—Cool.

—It's a bit gross, like.

—What is?

—It's like drinking with our dads, like.

—Could be worse, said Outspan.—We could be your fuckin' mas.

—Here, said Les.

He passed each of them a can.

—You don't have to stay, he said.

—Savage – thanks.

They tripped over guy ropes as they escaped to their own tents somewhere behind the lads.

—But look it, said Outspan – he'd lowered his voice.—There's a link. To an Irish site.

—Porn?

Not really. More online datin'.

—People with cancer?

—Yeah – 'course.

—And?

—I met up with one.

—A woman?

—A fuckin' chimp. Yeah, a woman.

—How was tha'?

—Grand, said Outspan.—Not too bad.

—You met her?

—Yeah.

—Where?

—First time?

—Yeah.

—Pub near hers.

—An' yeh went back?

—Yeah.

—And?

—An' wha'? It was great. I don't know – neither of us had to feel bad.

Jimmy wanted to cry. He wanted to hug Outspan.

—D'yeh still see her?

—No.

—Ah. How come?

—She's dead. Yeh fuckin' eejit.

There was silence – total. The whole of the Picnic and Laois had gone missing. Then there was a rattling noise – Outspan laughing.

—Yeh cunt, said Jimmy.—You were havin' us on.

He still wanted to cry. But laughing was easier and Outspan looked happier there than Jimmy had ever seen him.

—But, like, said Outspan.—I did go for a coffee with a woman in chemo. Once. We said we wouldn't talk about it but we talked abou' nothin' else. It was a bit borin'.

—I'd say so.

—Nice bird, though.

Les was looking at his phone.

—There is actually a site, he said.

—I wasn't jokin' abou' tha', said Outspan.—That's on the level.

There was a kid beside them, one of the boys they'd given a can to.

—D'you want some of these? he said.

The kid's hand was out but Jimmy couldn't see anything. Then he did. It was a plastic bag – a Spar bag.

—What have you got for us there? said Les.

Des was on his knees now, looking into the bag. He put his hand in.

—Lads – don't, said Jimmy – too late.

There was something sticking out of Des's mouth, like a tail. He was eating a mouse.

—Wha' the fuck are yeh doin'?

—Mushrooms, said Les.

That was what was sticking from Des's mouth, the mushroom's tail – or stalk.

Les held up a fistful and put his head back.

—Magic mushrooms? said Jimmy.

—Hope so, said Les.

He shoved the crop into his mouth. The kid was shaking the bag at Jimmy and Outspan.

—Want some?

—Fuck off, said Jimmy.

A good night out with the lads – actually, more a night in with the lads – was heading out of control.

But Outspan was relaxed.

—Fuckin' eejits, he said.

Des had spat his share back onto the grass.

—I can't swallow them, he said.—They're not even washed.

—Snob, said Outspan.

—They're too dry, said Des.

Les was chewing away. The kid was gone.

—Jesus, said Jimmy.

—Relax, said Les.

He drank long from his can.

—Wha' happens? said Jimmy.

He knew nothing about drugs. He was a white middle-aged man in the music business; he should have had a new nose from all the cocaine use. But he'd never seen cocaine.

—I'll start hallucinating in a while, said Les.—Any minute now.

Des was rooting through the mushrooms he'd spat out.

—One at a time, he said – he mumbled.—That's the trick.

He put a tiny mushroom into his mouth, then took a swig.

—You an' me in one tent, Liam, okay? said Jimmy.

He was calmer now. He wasn't going to look after this pair. Anyway, with Les's military training, he'd be able to find the antidote – whatever the fuck – in under the trees over there. He'd boil the bark or lick a lizard or something. Jimmy would be asleep – he didn't care.

—Definitely, said Outspan.—These cunts'll be off chattin' to the fairies in a minute.

—I am the Des!

—Ah, for fuck sake.

—One for the road, said Jimmy.

He leaned past Les and got hold of a can, and another one. He half expected to have his arm broken, or his eyes gouged. More of Les's training. Protecting the supplies. Act first, ask later. But nothing happened.

—Here yeh go.

—Thanks, said Outspan.

—Wha' were we talkin' about?

—Ridin' women with cancer.

—That's right, said Jimmy.—Time to move on maybe.

—Suit yourself.

—Nothing yet, said Des.—You?

He was staring at the ground.

—Nope, said Les.—Give it half an hour or so.

—Jesus, said Outspan.—This is borin'.

He got up on his knees.

—I'm not hangin' around to listen to this shite, he said.

He crawled across to the nearer tent.

—Where's the fuckin' zip?

Jimmy heard it, and saw Outspan slide into the tent, and heard him too now, inside. And he was right. Waiting for Leslie and Dezlie to turn into hobbits was boring.

—Seeyis, he said.

—'Night, Jim, said Les.

Des said nothing. He was still staring at the ground.

Jimmy followed Outspan into the tent. But it was hard to tell when out became in. The tent was so thin, it was as dark, as bright, as fuckin' cold, inside as it was out. The slight push of the nylon against the top of his head was the only real proof that he

294

was in the fuckin' thing. Outspan was already buried in a sleeping bag.

Jimmy took his boots off. It was hard – he didn't want to knee Outspan or put his head through the tent. He got one of the boots off. He was sweating, even though he was cold. All the sleeping bags were in here with him. He grabbed two of them and opened the flap of the tent. Des was sitting up now, cross-legged like Les, but staring at the ground. Jimmy threw a sleeping bag across to Les.

—Here yeh go.

And the other.

—Thanks.

—Is he alright? said Jimmy.

—Don't worry, said Les.

—'Night. Les.

—'Night, Jim.

—See you in the mornin'.

—You will.

—Big grass, said Des.

—Oh Christ. Goodnight.

Jimmy zipped up the tent.

—The grass is huge, said Des, outside.

—Fuckin' eejit, said Outspan.

He was tucked under the wall of the tent. Jimmy couldn't see any of him. He unrolled his bag. He could already feel the cold in the ground under him. He was tired, though – fucked. Darfur had filled up. It was like sharing a bedroom with thousands of brothers and cousins and more fuckin' cousins, all yapping. He'd never sleep. He would, though. He was bollixed. Les could mind Des; it'd be fine. He'd kill a deer and have it skinned and ready for their breakfast.

He left his socks on. They were a bit wet – but fuck it, they'd do. He left his jeans on too and waited till he'd got well into the bag before he started to take off his hoodie. But it was too complicated, too much bother. He left it on.

—Huuuge, said Des.—Look.

Jesus, Jimmy was freezing. He was lying down in his own fuckin' grave.

—Huuge.

—For fuck sake, said Outspan – his voice came through several layers.—If it was even tits he was talkin' about.

—It's miles away now, said Des.

Jimmy got his head into the bag. He held the top shut with his fist. He was so fuckin' cold.

—It's big again, said Des —Right over my head.

He was awake.

It wasn't dark. The spotlight outside lit the walls of the tent.

Something had woken him. There was noise outside – laughter, singing – but it wasn't that. It was the silence in the tent – it was so loud. No breath, no movement.

Oh Jesus —

Outspan's face stared up at him. It was locked – the expression. As if he'd turned solid.

Jimmy was out of the sleeping bag.

—Liam?

Outspan wasn't dead. The eyes were looking at Jimmy.

—D'yeh want your oxygen?

Outspan nodded – it was definitely a nod.

—Grand.

Thank fuck Jimmy hadn't undressed. He just needed to get his boots on. God, he was stiff – his fuckin' shoulder was falling off.

The boots were on.

—Nearly there, he said.

Outspan was staring at him. A gulp or a gasp – something – came out of him. Jimmy got the zip open.

—Back in a bit.

He was out. He could stand properly now. It was cold. Ten minutes to the car, he reckoned, and he wouldn't be carrying anything.

An idea – a good one. He'd get Les to keep an eye on Outspan. He'd be able to thump life back into the lungs or heart.

He unzipped the other tent.

—Les?

There was no one in it. The sleeping bags hadn't been opened. A new problem – but it could wait. He was worried though, about leaving Outspan alone.

He had to go – he had to go. He wanted to run but there wasn't room between the tents. The guy ropes were waiting to trip him.

The car, the fuckin' car key. He'd forgotten the fuckin' thing. It was okay – it was fuckin' disastrous – he hadn't gone too far.

He got back into the tent.

—Sorry – Liam —

Outspan stared at him.

—The car key, said Jimmy.

Outspan lifted his head slightly, just a tiny bit. His jacket was his pillow and Jimmy pulled it from under his head.

—Sorry about this.

The key was in one of the pockets, under a pile of tissues. He pushed the jacket back under Outspan.

—I'm gone again.

He was out and moving. He felt surer now. He had a clearer idea of the route in his head. He was through the tents, around them. Fuckin' ropes. There was dum-dum dum-dum still coming from somewhere. He was going past the tower with the spotlight now. He looked at his watch. It was just after five. There were zombies wandering – to the jacks, from the jacks. There was a big lad sleeping sideways on a half-inflated chair. Jimmy looked out for Les or Des. He couldn't see them. He heard a baby crying from not far off. Jesus – the thought of a waking baby in a fuckin' tent.

He was out of the tents, away. This was the path. Down to the gate and the road to the car park. He could trot now. He could go a bit faster. The gate ahead was open. Grand. He stopped running, kept walking fast. The trees met above him. It was darker, he was stepping into space he couldn't see. He tripped – he stayed up. Water went over his boot. Not much, though – he was fine. He'd walk the sock dry.

He was at the gate and puffing a bit. It was the tension, the worry – he couldn't manage deep breaths. Two guys, security, stepped out from behind the pillar.

—Can I see your wristband there?

Jimmy pulled back the sleeve of his hoodie.

—That's great, thanks.

Why did they give a shite if he had a wristband? He was leaving. It didn't matter. He didn't care.

—I'll be back in a sec, he told them.

—Fine.

—I'm gettin' an oxygen canister from the car, said Jimmy.

He saw that news change both faces.

—For a friend, said Jimmy.—Asthma.

—Okay, said the talker.

—Thanks.

He was running again. On the road. It was much quieter out here, as if the festival noise stopped at the gate. He wasn't sure how far he had to go before the gap in the wall for the field. He didn't think it was far. There was another spotlight ahead, at the edge of a field. The car park.

Jimmy got his mobile out of his pocket. He kept moving. He got Les's number. He was jogging again, sweating. Les didn't answer. He tried Des. No answer. The pair of fuckin' arses. Fuck knew where they were – and *how* they fuckin' were.

He'd found the gap in the wall. The going was bad here. Thousands of boots, months of rain. The muck, the water went over his boots. He had to pull them free. He went down on a knee. His leg was soaked.

But he was through. He'd another pair of jeans back at the tent. And socks – two spare pairs.

He couldn't find the car. He couldn't remember the car. It wasn't his; it was Outspan's ex's. He thought it might be a Saab – he couldn't remember.

He was near it, somewhere. He looked back at the gap in the wall. The angle was familiar. They'd come this way the day before.

He got the key out – the zapper. He pressed it and listened. He couldn't hear the locks pop open.

Shite.

He stood at the next row of cars. He pressed again and looked for a light, and listened. He went through two cars to the next row. He pressed again.

He heard it – the little whop. He locked the car he couldn't see, then pressed again.

He saw it and heard it. He'd found the car.

There were people asleep in some of the cars he passed, a family in one of them, and a gang of heads in another.

He got the boot open. He pulled back the blanket and pulled out the cylinder. It was aluminium, he thought, and smallish; it wasn't heavy. There was a face mask or something as well – there had to be. He found it.

He got the phone out. *On way bak – 5 min*. He sent it to Outspan.

He locked the car.

* * *

It was more than five minutes. Not much more, though – it couldn't have been.

—I'm back. Liam?

He'd run with the cylinder on his shoulder, where the beer had been the day before. It had been much easier to carry but right against his head; he'd half expected it to explode.

Outspan hadn't changed. He could've been dead or alive – but he moved a hand and helped Jimmy with the mask. The same hand went on to the cylinder and a finger pointed at the valve or whatever it was.

—I turn this?

The hand tapped the cylinder.

Jimmy turned the thing – it went easily – and he heard the hiss and watched as Outspan sank back into his jacket. He shut his eyes and lifted his thumb to Jimmy.

Jimmy put his hand to his own forehead, back into his hair. He could feel the sweat parting with his hand. He was dripping, fuckin' melting – and cold as well.

—Alright?

Outspan grunted a single syllable. It was fuckin' music.

—Great, said Jimmy.

The muck was drying on his jeans, although they were still wet – freezing – against his leg. He didn't care. He pulled the boots off, but it wasn't easy. The laces were slimy and thick. He couldn't get a proper grip on the heel. But he got them off and threw them in a corner – he didn't care. He got his feet, his legs into the sleeping bag. He could hear Outspan exhaling. He'd left the flap open. He leaned forward as far as he could and grabbed the zipper, missed it, got a proper hold of it – and saw Les climbing into his tent.

He shut the flap – he hated the noise zips made. He lay back, wriggled himself into the bag.

He was going to warm up. He might even doze. He'd a working day ahead of him. He nearly laughed.

—Come here, he said.

He sat up.

—Remember we were talkin' about Imelda Quirk?

Outspan kind of nodded.

—Well, I rode her, said Jimmy.

He looked across at Outspan, tried to see his face.

—Recently, like.

He heard a small grunt.

—Just thought yeh might like to know, he said.

He saw Outspan's hand. He lifted the mask a small bit.

—Thanks.

—No problem.

He woke again. He'd slept – he couldn't believe it. There was daylight bleeding easily through the tent walls. He took his arm out of the bag and looked at his watch. Quarter to eight. That wasn't too bad. He'd survive on that.

He looked across at Outspan.

Outspan was looking at him. He lifted the mask.

—Alrigh'?

—Grand.

—Okay.

—Stiff, said Jimmy.

—Comes with the room.

—How about you?

The mask was back on but the thumb, up, gave Jimmy his answer.

—D'yeh want to go home?

Outspan lifted the mask again.

—No way, he whispered.—Fuck off.

Jimmy lay there for a while. He was bursting. Earlier, when he'd got back with the oxygen, he'd have pissed in the sleeping bag, no problem; he'd have enjoyed it. Now though, he sat up – God, his back. He found the boots. He unzipped the tent and dropped them outside. There was blue in the sky. It wasn't too cold. He sat with his arse in the tent and put the boots back on. They weren't too bad, not as wet as he'd thought they'd be. Standing up wasn't easy. It was fuckin' agony, until he was upright and human again.

He wasn't the only one up. There were plenty of heads – hundreds of them – wandering, chatting. Cooking.

The jacks was no worse than it had been the day before. He stood at the urinal. There was no way he was going into one of those boxes. He could park the shite till he got home, then he'd wait till the house was empty.

—High point so far?

It was a young fella beside Jimmy.

—Wha'? said Jimmy.

—High point, said the kid.—Last night.

Jimmy couldn't remember last night; it took a while to bring it back. The kid was waiting for Jimmy's answer. He had some sort of a mohawk/mohican haircut.

—Christy, said Jimmy.

—Yeah, said the kid.—He was savage.

Jimmy's answer had loosened his head; he knew where he was again. There was a whole big day ahead of him. The kid walked with him out of the jacks area. A nice lad – he reminded Jimmy of his own.

—What about today? said Jimmy.

He'd just spotted a good-looking coffee van across the field. He checked his pockets. He had money.

—The Arab Spring, said the kid.

—Good?

—Savage.

—Annythin' else?

—Moanin' At Midnight, said the kid.—Have you heard them?

—No, said Jimmy.—Don't think so.

—They're Bulgarian, said the kid.—They're amazing.

—I might give them a go, said Jimmy.

He resisted the urge to buy the kid a coffee and a bun.

—Seeyeh, he said.

—Later, said the kid.

Jimmy wondered where his own were. Marvin was somewhere near; he'd come down with his buddies the day before, in the back of some cousin's van, with the instruments and gear. It was way too early to text him. Aoife would be coming down later with Mahalia and Brian, and maybe young Jimmy. He looked at his watch. They'd all be in bed too. Except Brian. He'd be at the Xbox.

He put milk in Outspan's coffee and pocketed four or five sachets of sugar. He watched out for guy ropes as he made his way back. There was another Darfur away to the right behind more trees, and a field of wooden huts and the fuckin' yurts on the other side of the lane, in behind the big house – the mansion.

He'd no hangover. He felt grand, fine – good.

He had to be a bit careful here with the coffee, getting back into the tent. He put down a cardboard cup and unzipped the flap. He put the other cup down beside it. He turned, back to the flap, and lowered himself.

—Fuck it.

His arse had missed the tent floor by a foot. He was sitting on the wet ground. It was grass; it wasn't too bad. He was soaked, though.

—Fuck.

It was only water – dew. He'd be grand, and he hadn't knocked the coffee. He got the boots off again – he was fuckin' sick of this. He left them outside. He leaned out – grunted – and grabbed the coffees.

—You awake?

—Yeah.

—Here.

Outspan groaned and started to sit up. Jimmy didn't know if he should help him or not. But Outspan didn't seem any more crippled than Jimmy. The oxygen mask was parked on top of his head, like a gobshite's sunglasses.

He was sitting up.

—Fuckin' hell.

He took the cup from Jimmy.

—D'yeh want sugar?

—Sound.

Jimmy got the sugar out of his pocket.

—How many? he asked.

—All o' them, said Outspan.

—I got yeh a croissant as well.

—Thanks – sound.

—Yeh like them, yeah?

—I do, yeah. Are they warm?

—No.

—Ah well.

Jimmy waited till Outspan had ripped open the sachets and poured the sugar into his coffee. There was nothing shaky or desperate about the way he operated. He stirred it a bit with a finger.

Jimmy opened the paper bag and held it out to Outspan. He looked in the bag.

—Two o' them.

—One's for me – fuck off, said Jimmy.

Outspan held the croissant in front of his mouth. He looked around.

—We won't worry too much abou' the crumbs.

He bit a good lump off the croissant. So did Jimmy. It was great, soft – he was starving.

—How're yeh feelin'? he asked.

—Shite, said Outspan.—Not the best.

—Are you okay?

—I'm okay, said Outspan.—Not too bad.

—How's your coffee?

—Grand.

—Croissants are nice, aren't they?

—Better than nothin'.

—You're sure you're okay?

—Yeah, said Outspan.—One thing but.

—Wha'?

—Why didn't yeh call an ambulance?

—Fuck, said Jimmy.

—Well?

—It never occurred to me – sorry.

—Fuckin' eejit.

Outspan looked terrible. He had the cylinder beside him, lying on the grass. Jimmy had watched him earlier, heading off to the jacks, bent over, slow. It had been horrible to watch. He hadn't known what to do – or say.

—D'yeh need a hand?

He'd half got up, ready to go after Outspan. Outspan didn't look back.

—Prob'bly, he'd said.

He'd looked livelier coming back, a bit easier in his movements. He sat down beside the oxygen.

—What's the plan?

Jimmy had put on his clean jeans. He leaned back into the tent –

—Fuck —

– and got the remains of the programme out of the pocket of the old ones. It was soggy but legible. He had to bring it right up to his eyes.

—There's one o' my bands on at a quarter past twelve.

—Who?

—The Halfbreds, said Jimmy.—Mad pair o' cunts. Husband an' wife.

—Fuck sake.

—They might break up onstage.

—Sounds good.

—They usually do, said Jimmy.—Tha' reminds me.

He got his phone out.

—Textin' the missis?

—The boss.

—I thought you were your own boss.

—The partner, said Jimmy.

Noeleen had the backstage passes for Marvin and the lads; he'd forgotten to bring them.

There was a text in that he hadn't noticed – *Leaving now X* – from Aoife. He texted back. *Great. X.* He'd phone Marvin. It would save him the bother of a half-dozen texts. And he wanted to hear Marvin's voice. He texted young Jimmy. *Alrite? Xx.*

—Hungry? he said.

—Starvin,' said Outspan.

—Rasher sandwich?

—Fuckin' great.

—There's a place over there sells them, said Jimmy.

He stood up. The night on the ground was out of his bones.

—I'll have a look in at this waster.

He unzipped the tent.

Les was awake.

—Mornin', said Jimmy.

—Alright?

—Grand. Yourself?

—Fine, yeah. I think.

—Does a rasher sandwich sound good?

—Sounds great.

—Grand.

There was a queue at the rashers. He phoned Noeleen. He didn't want to. He wanted to stay with Outspan. It had been so easy, slipping out of the life. But fuck it; it was his job, his income – his son, for fuck sake. And he loved it. He just needed to think properly.

—Jimbo!

—Howyeh, Noeleen.

—The big day.

—Yeah, he said.—Did yeh camp?

—There is no fucking way I'd camp.

She was on her way, still on the motorway. They'd meet at the gate. She'd text him when she was parking.

The queue had moved. He could smell the rashers. He was starving – fuckin' weak.

He'd call Marvin now.

He saw Des. With a woman. A good-looking woman. A bit long in the tooth for her shorts and mucky Uggs. But a woman – in shorts and mucky Uggs.

Marvin answered like he'd been waiting.

—Hi.

—Marv?

—Hi.

—How are things?

—Good, yeah. Grand.

—All set?

—Yeah – nearly. Yeah. We need – do you have backstage passes or something?

He arranged to phone Marvin after Noeleen had texted him. It was getting messy. He should have had the passes and everything sorted before the weekend. What if Noeleen had a puncture or went into a ditch?

But it was fine. Everything would be grand. He was next in the queue.

—Des!

Des, even at a distance, was still a bit stoned. He had to peer over his huge grass before he spotted Jimmy.

—D'yeh want a rasher sandwich, Des?

Jimmy watched as Des translated the question from English into Des, and back.

—Yeah!

Jimmy hoped Des would bring the woman over with him so he could get a good look at her. But he didn't. He kissed her on the mouth – fair enough – and they swapped phone numbers. They looked like they both needed help; she was in huge grass of her own.

The sandwiches were ready for him on the counter, a block of flats in tinfoil. He handed over twenty-four euro and got nothing back. He texted Aoife. *Bring sum money. X*

Des was beside him.

—You had a fuckin' adventure, said Jimmy.

Des thought about this.

—Yeah.

Les was sitting with Outspan, and Outspan was sucking on the oxygen. Jimmy was worried again. But he handed out the sandwiches and sat down.

—You didn't think of water, did you? said Les.

—No.

Les leaned into his tent and took out four cans.

—Oh Christ.

—Too much salt in the bacon, said Les.

They ate.

—Where were you? Outspan asked Des when he'd parked the mask on his head.

Des looked around.

—Somewhere over there, he said, although he didn't point or nod.

—With a woman, said Jimmy.

—Good man, Dezlie.

—What was her name, by the way? Jimmy asked.

—Em – .

Des took out his phone, but remembered before he looked at it.

—Yvonne.

—Sure?

—Yeah – Yvonne.

The rashers were working the magic on Outspan.

—Did yeh get into her?

Des was still searching for the bread inside the tinfoil.

—It was – , he started.—I —

He'd found the bread.

—Great.

He bit. They waited.

—It was unusual, said Des.—I woke – I kind of woke up with her.

—Nice.

—Together, said Des.

—That's the way.

—And, well – she definitely knew me but I wasn't sure about her. She – eh – she held me like we'd been —

—Intimate.

—Yes.

—Do yeh not remember but? said Outspan.—What's the fuckin' point?

306

He dragged the mask down to his face and gave himself a blast.

—Some of it – , said Des.—I remember – kind of flashes.

—That's not too bad.

Des smiled. There was a quick shift; he was one of the lads again.

—There was another man, he said.

—In the tent?

—In the bird?

—This morning, said Des.—Just there.

—Who was he?

—Her brother, said Des.

—Ah well —

—Or her husband.

That was great. They were back in last night's swing, stretched back and laughing.

—Are yeh serious?

—Yes, said Des.—I'm not sure.

—It could be important.

I know.

Outspan tapped Les's elbow with his foot.

—Wha' about you?

Les stared at Outspan's foot.

—I was off with the fairies, he said.

Jimmy was happy enough with the answer. He didn't want to know more.

—I've to work, he told them.

His phone rang just as he was getting it from his pocket.

—Where the fuck are you?

It was Barry, the Halfbred.

—Howyeh, Barry.

—Where?

—I'm on my way, Barry, said Jimmy.—I've been smoothin' the path for yeh. I'll be there in a few minutes. Are they lookin' after yeh?

He hung up before he had to hear the answer. He stood and wiped the crumbs off his hoodie.

—Yis right? he said.

—We'll follow you.

—No, said Jimmy.

He looked at Outspan.

—Are you up for all o' this, Liam?

Outspan shrugged.

—I'm not goin' in without you, said Jimmy.

—We'll all go.

—All for fuckin' one.

—We can always come back out, said Les.—If we need to.

They gathered up the things they'd be needing.

—Will it rain?

—No.

Les put the cylinder up on his shoulder and they started to make their way slowly to the entrance.

—Jacks first, lads?

—They should put you in charge of the fuckin' country.

Outspan took the cylinder with him into the phone box.

They waited.

Noeleen texted. *Gate 8.* Jimmy texted Marvin. *Gate 8. Remember your bulgarian X.*

Outspan kind of fell out of the box. But he was okay.

—Success?

—We used to ask tha' after a night ou', remember?

—Yeah.

—Now it's if I can go for a shite withou' passin' out or dyin', said Outspan.—For fuck sake.

Les took a babywipe from his bag and started to wipe the cylinder.

—No offence.

—Don't blame yeh, said Outspan.

Then they were moving again.

—I'll have to charge when we get through, said Jimmy.

—No problem.

—I'll be back but.

—Who gives a fuck, said Outspan.

The thought hit them all, even Des, just as they reached the security barrier.

—Oh Christ.

They'd never get through with the oxygen.

The security guy actually looked frightened when he saw the cylinder and followed the tube to the mask and he saw the state of Outspan.

—Can't let you through with that, he said.—Sorry.

—He needs it, said Jimmy.—It's medical.

—Sorry. It's too heavy – if someone threw it. There's no way.

Jimmy half expected Les to take over; this should have been something he'd trained for. Negotiating, mediating. But Jimmy was still in charge.

—Listen, he said.—Have you anny idea how many laws you'll be breakin' if you stop him from bringin' his oxygen in?

Jimmy had no idea if they'd be breaking any laws at all.

But it worked.

—Okay.

—Sound – thanks.

—Hold on to it though, said the security guy.

—Don't worry – thanks.

—Do they think I'm goin' to sell it?

—Shut up, for fuck sake.

They were in.

—Righ', said Jimmy.—I'll see yis outside the Crawdaddy tent in half an hour.

—Okay.

—Good luck.

He saw the sign for Gate 8, and he was on his way, charging across the field. It was early for the crowds so the going was straight. The next four hours would be mad. All his acts – his job, his fuckin' career – were compressed into the afternoon.

That was shite, too dramatic, but it was still going to be mad.

Noeleen was at the gate, and she was with someone – a man.

—Jimbo!

—Howyeh.

—This is Christian.

—Howyeh, Christian.

She had wristbands, passes, bits of important laminated paper.

—Great, grand, great – thanks. I've to run. The Halfbreds are waitin' on me.

—Poor you, she said.

—I know. Nice meetin' yeh, Christian.

—And you, Jimbo, said Christian.—Nice to be able to put a face on a name.

—Exactly.

The fuckin' eejit.

They both laughed.

Then Jimmy saw Marvin and the Bulgarians coming out of the trees.

—Here's Moanin' At Midnight, he said.

—They're gorgeous, said Noeleen.—So sweet.

—They haven't a word of English, said Jimmy.

He hoped she'd forgotten that Boris the drummer was also the manager, and that his English was fuckin' excellent.

—The education system must be shite over there, he said.

—Like here, said Christian.

—Spot on.

A thing in Jimmy's guts – his stomach – burst and charged through him; it nearly doubled him up.

Joy.

This was fuckin' great.

Fuckin' madness.

—Where – is – stage? said Marvin.

—Come, said Jimmy.—Come.

The lads followed Jimmy.

—See yis later, he shouted back to Noeleen and Christian. —Great job, he whispered to Marvin.

—Thanks.

The other two lads were laughing.

—All set? said Jimmy.

—For – sure.

They were a good bit ahead of Noeleen now. Jimmy handed them new wristbands and passes.

—Backstage passes.

—Cool.

—VIP area.

—Cool.

—Remain in character.

—This – no – worries.

—I've to look after another band for a bit, said Jimmy.—You know where to go?

—Yeah.

—Here.

He gave Marvin his last twenty.

—Do you need this?

—Not really, said Marvin.

—Grand.

He took it back.

—I'll look after you later.

He was gone, back across to the Crawdaddy.

The field was starting to fill. The first gigs of the day would be starting soon. Jimmy passed two drunk heads. Left over from the night before, or fresh? It didn't matter. Connie and Barry would be going spare, backstage. But fuck them, they'd be loving it.

There was a fence that blocked the backs of all the gig tents. Jimmy followed it, left. He was walking, trotting a good while before he saw the sign, Artists and Crew. He showed the girl at the narrow entrance his pass – and he was through. Backstage. The holy of fuckin' holies. He was in his natural habitat.

He heard Connie before he saw her.

That wasn't true. He saw her but he didn't realise it was Connie. She was wearing the dress she must have worn to her young one's graduation. She'd done something to her hair as well. She'd become a middle-aged woman, happy in her years. She was laughing – with her kids.

For fuck sake.

A text. From Aoife. *We're here. X*

—Hi, Jimmy, said Connie.

—Brenda.

—Lovely day.

—Yeah.

—I'm so excited.

—Great.

—We're trying out some new songs, she told Jimmy.

Oh fuck.

—Great. Where's Barry?

—Around somewhere, said Connie.

The kids looked nice. Like his own.

—Well done on the Leaving results, he told the girl.

—Thanks, she smiled.

—Did the soundcheck go okay? he asked Connie.

—Great, she said.—They couldn't be nicer.

There was something wrong. Something very wrong. He smiled again at the kids. Is your mammy on tablets? he wanted to ask – he nearly did ask. He checked his watch. They'd be on in a few minutes.

—So, he said.—New songs.

—You'll love them, she said.

—Grand.

—I'm worried about the polar bears.

—Yeah.

311

She'd become Cat Stevens, pre-Islam. Or Joan Baez.

—Will you still be playin' the drums? he asked her.

—God, yes.

He wanted to hug her.

—And the old songs?

—We'll lead with them, said Connie.

—Good.

—Don't worry, Jimmy, she said.—We know our fucking fans.

That sounded like Connie. She was in there somewhere.

—Here's Barry, she said.

Barry looked like Barry. He was pushed into his leathers.

—The Minister's son is here, he said.—Fuck.

—Howyeh, Barry.

—Yeah, said Barry.

—Good luck with the new songs.

—She told you?

—She did, yeah, said Jimmy.—There's one – is there? – about polar bears?

—It's a whopper, said Barry.

Barry smiled. And Jimmy smiled.

—Can't wait, said Jimmy.—Great, listen. I'm goin' to go round to the front. So I can see the show like a fan.

He legged it, and texted Aoife as he went. *Great. X.* There was one in from Des. *Tent is nearly empty.* That was fine. It would start to fill once the punters outside heard the opening bars of 'Erectile Dysfunction'. They'd charge in, hoping for a look at the young one in the video. Another from Aoife. *Where u? X.* He had to stop, so he could spell out *Halfbreds Crawdaddy don't miss x.* Then he was off again. The backstage area was actually backstages; it was like the back garden of four or five circus tents. It was huge. He'd been moving now for minutes and he still wasn't out. He heard the Halfbreds kick off. He knew the song immediately – 'Your Happiness Makes Me Puke'. Connie would look great, standing behind the drums in her party frock. If they gave 'Erectile Dysfunction' a good lash and the polar bear delivered, Jimmy's phone would soon be hopping – gigs, sales, telly.

He was back out with the public, charging across the field to the Crawdaddy. He thought he could hear 'Erectile Dysfunction'. Guitar chords drifted, stopped, then all he could hear was cheering. And all he could see as he came up to the tent was people pouring out.

He spotted the lads. He got through the crowd to them.

—That was fuckin' short.

—They broke up, said Des.

—It was brilliant, said Outspan.

—They were great.

—Wha' happened?

—The song about the erectile wha'-d'yeh-call-it, said Outspan.

—Yeah.

—Oh yes she does.

—It's great.

—Annyway, said Outspan.—She hit him across the head with one of her sticks.

—And he kicked her bass drum.

—She hopped on him.

—It was hilarious.

—Fuck, said Jimmy.—An' I missed it. It sounds better than usual.

—Have they broken up before?

—Fuck, yeah. Every time. They're married. Would yeh go see them again?

—Fuckin' sure, said Outspan.

—If they stayed together a bit longer. If you were buying a ticket.

—She was gorgeous, said Les.

—Connie?

—Gorgeous.

—Really?

The three lads were nodding.

They heard the noise. Music. Drums.

—They're back.

They charged into the tent. It was empty, then full and dangerous in ten seconds. And they were right: Connie was gorgeous. A middle-aged ma, just in from the hairdresser, standing behind the drums and beating the living fuck out of them.

—THE ICE CAP IS MELTING—AH —

IT'S MELTING IN THE SUN —

THE POLAR BEAR —

THE POLAR BEAR —

THE POLAR BEAR —

THE POLAR BEAR —

Jimmy could hear it now, the crowd shouting with Connie.

THE POLAR BEAR —
THE POLAR BEAR —
They'd never heard the song before but they'd a good idea of where it was going.
—THE POLAR BEAR'S AN ENDANGERED LITTLE CUNT—TAH —
The cheer ripped a hole in the roof of the tent.
And a brilliant thing happened. The crowd grabbed the song. Five hundred people shouted at the same time.
—OH YES HE IS —
And five hundred cheerfully disagreed.
—OH NO HE ISN'T —
It was a national debate, the country's response to climate change.
—OH YES HE IS —
OH NO HE ISN'T —
The thing – the joy – went off in Jimmy again. He nearly pissed.
—THE POLAR BEAR —
THE POLAR BEAR —
HE'S A—HE'S A —
HE'S A—HE'S A —
THE FURRY LITTLE POLAH BEAR-AH —
HE'S A—HE'S A—HE'S A —
The crowd took over.
—ENDANGERED LITTLE CUNT —
ENDANGERED —
LITTLE CUNT —
Outspan had the mask to his face between shouts.
—ENDANGERED LITTLE —
CUNT—TAH —
Connie pushed the drums out of her way. She threw her sticks into the crowd. She didn't lob them. She aimed and threw. The St John's Ambulance would be needed at the front. And she walked off. Barry lifted his guitar, ready to smash it on the stage. He held it high and stepped up to the mic.
—You're not fuckin' worth it!
And he followed his wife offstage.
They were done.
And Jimmy finally knew it: they were geniuses. This wasn't a middle-aged couple reliving the glory days in front of a few friends. This was the Sex Pistols in Manchester. Jimmy had another

sensation on his hands. He'd seen at least ten people filming it. The gig and both break-ups would be up on YouTube. They were probably up already.

They went back outside.

—Fuckin' hell.

—Amazin'.

Jimmy looked at his watch. It wasn't even one o'clock. The phone hopped. It was Aoife. *Cudnt get in, packed.* He sent one back. *We're outside.*

He saw it now. The inflatable chair. A big purple armchair. They'd parked it in against the side of the Crawdaddy canvas, at the backstage fence. Outspan dropped into it and tucked the cylinder in beside him.

—Where did tha' come from? said Jimmy.

—They're on sale over there, said Les.

—Les bought it for me, said Outspan.

He loved it.

Another text from Aoife. *Any toilet paper? X.* She could wait a while for the answer, after the slagging she'd given him yesterday, before he'd left the house.

—Where now?

—Grub?

—Great.

—I've to go to Body and Soul, said Jimmy.

—What's that?

—It's the fuckin' hippy place, said Outspan.

—There's a stage there, said Jimmy.—I've another band on.

—Who?

—The Bastards of Lir.

—Good as that lot?

—No way, said Jimmy.—Celtic Rock.

—Great.

—Christy on fuckin' acid, said Outspan.

—We'll follow you over, Jim, said Les.

Jimmy didn't want to leave them, especially when he saw Les and Des take a side each of Outspan's chair and hoist it and Outspan up onto their shoulders.

—I'm your man from *The Jungle Book*, said Outspan.—King Louie.

They marched away –

—See you in a bit.

– across to the food stalls. Jimmy wanted his shoulder under the chair but they were getting on fine without him. But then, he thought, he'd just given them the gig of their lives. He was at work and the elderly Bastards of Lir were waiting for him.

He texted Connie. *Brilliant.* He texted Barry. *Fuckin brilliant.* He texted Aoife and told her where he was headed. She'd appreciate the jacks paper better in a place called Body and Soul.

He texted young Jimmy. *Enjoyin yrslf?*

He texted Marvin. *Excited?*

He texted Noeleen. *Halfbreds brilliant. We'll make a few €.*

He texted Ned the Celtic wanker, the Bastard of Lir himself. *On way. Looking forward to it.*

He was dreading it.

The only reason Ned was on the ticket was because Jimmy still felt guilty for calling the da's attention to the daughter's arse at the Christmas do. It still made him weak – the guilt, not the arse. And there was the awful fact that the Bastards of Lir sold. No one went to see them live, but middle-aged men and women who didn't venture out after dark still craved the sound.

The Body and Soul stage, when he found it, was like something from *Lord of the Rings*. It was in among the trees, in a hollow, a tiny natural amphitheatre.

The Bastards of Lir were waiting there.

—Ned.

—Jimmy.

Five men, four ponytails. Three leather waistcoats.

—You're being looked after?

—We expected a tent, said Ned.

—This is your venue, Ned.

—It's an afterthought.

—It fuckin' isn't, said Jimmy.

He wasn't taking this.

—Some of the best gigs happen here, said Jimmy.—Look at it.

Now that he was down in the hollow, it was great, and a bit magic. The place would fill.

—The whole festival is built around Body and Soul, said Jimmy.

Ned wasn't looking at him.

—What if it was raining? he said.

—It isn't rainin,' said Jimmy.—How many times have you played the Picnic before?

Ned didn't answer.

316

—Do you think they actually wanted you? said Jimmy.

He got to an answer before Ned could.

—Yes, they fuckin' did, said Jimmy.—And they wanted you *here*. In Body and Soul. That was the ask.

He was saving the day, lying through his arse, and impressing himself again.

—Okay, said Ned.—I hear you.

—Read the email I sent you, said Jimmy.—You knew what you were gettin'.

The tin whistle player spat on the ground.

—You'll be brilliant, said Jimmy.

He looked at his watch. The stage manager was waving at them.

—You're on, said Jimmy.

The hollow was filling. There were no bald patches. Ned looked a bit happier.

The fiddle player sawed the strings with his bow.

—Whooo, said Ned, into the mic.—He's raring to go. No introductions, you know who we are. Here's one you might recognise.

Jimmy got off the stage.

—ON TARA'S HILL THERE STANDS A MAN —

For fuck sake.

—IN THE MISTY EARLY MORNING —

Jimmy climbed out of the hollow. He had to get away.

—HE LOOKS ACROSS HIS SACRED LANDS —

In the fuckin' mist – fair play to him.

—HE'S THE LAST OF IRELAND'S HIGH KINGS —

Jimmy didn't look back but he knew the hollow was a mass of diddley-eye-Provos, clapping and whooping.

—Toilet paper.

It was Aoife. Mahalia and Brian were behind her.

—Howyeh, love.

—Toilet paper.

He got the bag from his back and pulled out the roll.

—You're lookin' lovely, by the way.

It was true, but she grabbed the roll and Jimmy watched her go.

—HE HOLDS HIS SWORD UP TO THE SKIES —

—Wha' d'yeh think of tha' shite? he asked Brian.

—Class, said Brian.

—AND CALLS TO HIS LOYAL CLAN —

317

And here came the last of the High Kings, Outspan Foster, on his purple Celtic plastic fuckin' armchair. Les and Des parked him on the lip of the hollow.

—LET BLOOD FLOW RED FROM SAXON VEINS —

—Now we're fuckin' talkin'.

—AND ENRICH THIS SACRED LAND —

It was *Riverdance* for Nazis and the hollow was full of them.

—Here, Les, said Jimmy.—This is Mahalia. And Brian.

—Hi.

—This is your Uncle Les, said Jimmy.

He wasn't sure why, but he felt like a bollix. He was getting at Les.

Les shook hands with both of the kids.

—Great to meet you.

—I've to go, said Jimmy.—Tell your mam I'll see her at the Cosby.

—What's the Cosby? said Mahalia.

—A tent, said Jimmy.—Where Marvin's playin'.

—We'll follow you there, said Les.

—Grand.

—These guys are great.

Jimmy escaped. He felt like a cunt, abandoning the kids, his brother, his dying buddy and his wife. But he was working. He was genuinely working.

He texted Ned as he went. *Superb*. Ned would find it when he came offstage.

He was out of Body and Soul, running, back through Artists and Crew, into the vastness of backstage. He found the Bulgarians stuffing their faces at a table covered in sandwiches held down by little plastic swords.

—Everything okay?

—For – sure, said Marvin

—Nervous?

—Fock – narvus, said Marvin.

Then he whispered.

—Shittin'.

—You'll be great.

The other two, Docksy and Mush, seemed calm enough. He could see they had a plan. They stood at a platter till it was empty, then moved on to the next one. They were hoovering up the food for twenty bands.

318

The Halfbreds' daughter stood beside Marvin.

—Hi.

—Yes, said Marvin.

—I saw you, like, on YouTube.

—What – is – Oo-toob?

Marvin was overdoing it but Jimmy left him at it. He was safe enough there with the Halfbred daughter. The possibility of Barry and Connie joining the family scared him a bit – already – but she seemed like a nice, normal kid and she'd keep Marv occupied till they went onstage – Jimmy looked at his watch – in ten minutes.

The Halfbred daughter laughed. Marvin's English was improving all the time. She was a lovely-looking kid. Just like her ma.

Now Jimmy saw a guy he knew he had to stop from getting to Moanin' At Midnight. He moved, to get between the lads and Nathan Early. Jimmy had been in a room once – at a music e-zine Christmas do, a few years back – when he'd had to listen to Early list all the gigs he'd reviewed but had never attended. The man was a slug.

—Howyeh, Nathan.

Early hadn't a clue who was talking to him.

—Hey.

—Enjoyin' yourself?

—Well, said Early.—It's work, you know.

—You have to actually listen to the bands, do yeh? said Jimmy. —That's rough.

Early looked at Jimmy, then past him.

—They're not available, said Jimmy.

—They?

—Moanin' At Midnight, said Jimmy.—They've no English.

Early nodded at Marvin with the young one, and Jimmy wanted to kill him.

—He seems to be managing okay, said Early.

—Sorry, Nathan.

—Have a heart, man. I just want a sense of how they feel about being in Ireland.

—Make it up, said Jimmy.

Early looked at him properly.

—Who are you?

—Jimmy Rabbitte, he said.

—Gotcha, said Early.—You work for Noeleen.

It was quiet in the Cosby tent.

—That's righ', said Jimmy.

He realised now, there'd been no music coming from there for a good while. Marvin and the lads were on next.

—And she thinks you're a cunt as well, he said.

He turned and went across to Marvin.

—You're on.

—What?

—You play music now, the Halfbreds' daughter told him.

—For sure.

Early homed in on the daughter.

—When did you two meet?

—Like, a minute ago.

—You're into him, yeah?

The daughter looked at Early.

—Fuck off, like.

She followed Jimmy and Marvin and the other two lads. One of them – Jimmy thought it was Docksy – leaned over, puked, and kept going.

—Alrigh'?

—Alright.

There were steps to climb, more security to get past. Jimmy felt like puking himself. He could tell before he saw: the tent was packed.

—Fuck – , said Marvin, quietly.

—You alrigh', Marv?

—Yep.

The puker puked again.

—Irish – meat – bad – meat, he said.

That got them giggling.

Jimmy put his arm on Marvin's shoulder.

—I'm proud of you.

—Thanks.

Marvin didn't try to escape.

—It'll be brilliant.

—Yeah.

They were well back, but Jimmy went a few steps nearer the stage. The place was heaving. The crowd stretched to well outside the tent, as far as he could see. He got the phone out, texted Aoife. *R u in?*

He didn't know the capacity of the tent but there were more in it than there should have been. He was sure of that. The stage people, the men and women in the know, clicked into action. It was the time. Someone held back the black drape and Marvin and his pals walked through, and on, and the place went mad.

The band moved like everything they had to do was rehearsed and timed. The guitar and bass were up and on, the drummer had his sticks ready before he sat. He hit the snare as his arse hit the seat.

It was noise. A big cloud of the stuff – screech and thump. Then words came out – Marvin's mouth was right up to the mic – and they were playing the blues. How was it possible? How was his eighteen-year-old son able to sing like Howlin' Wolf? Fuckin' better than Howlin' Wolf.

—OH OHH TELL ME BAB-EH —

It was 'Smokestack Lightnin'' and it was perfect. Marvin's howl at the end of each verse was spot on. Only a man who'd actually heard a wolf, who'd stood and faced one in a forest clearing in Bulgaria, could have made that howl. Marvin howled and women screamed.

For fuck sake.

The phone buzzed in Jimmy's hand. It was Aoife. *On wheelchair access platform. Cant believe it.*

Jimmy couldn't see her. He was well to the side and he wasn't going to move any nearer to the stage. The lads got into the second song while the crowd was still roaring its approval of the first one. Again, it came out of the noise and it became 'Mannish Boy'.

—EVERYTHING —

EVERYTHING —

Marvin pronounced the Gs. He was still a Bulgarian, aping the black man's English.

—EVERYTHING GO'NE TO BE ALRIGHT THIS MORNING —

Jimmy could feel the bass in his chest, pushing him back. It was rougher than Muddy Waters, and way better. The crowd was spelling MAN with Marvin and there wasn't a dyslectic in the house.

—M —

—A —

—N —

Marvin didn't move from the mic. He stood at a slight angle. The bass roamed the stage. He never looked at the audience.

They fell back into the noise and feedback, let the cheers and roars roll across them. Then, again, the song took form – a chord, a beat.

Everyone knew it.

—I WANT HER ARMS —

I'M GOIN' TO HELL —

The tent was moving.

—I WANT HER LEGS —

I'M GOIN' TO HELL —

Were there a thousand in the tent? Two thousand? More? And a lot more outside. They were all going to hell, singing as they went.

—I PROWL THE STREETS —

I'M GOING TO HELL —

I LICK HER FEET —

A woman on top of her boyfriend's shoulders offered up her own feet.

—I WANT HER NOW —

I'M GOIN' TO HELL —

WON'T SAVE MY SOUL —

I'M GOIN' TO HELL —

DON'T HAVE A SOUL —

I'M GOIN' TO HELL —

It couldn't get louder – the crowd was the band.

DON'T WANT MY SOUL —

I'M GOIN' TO HELL —

I'LL GET MY HOLE —

I'M GOIN' TO HELL —

Jimmy left. He wanted to get around to the front of the tent. He wanted to move. His son was singing a song that Jimmy had written. He didn't know how he felt. Robbed and elated.

He texted Noeleen. *Theyre irish.*

He'd waited all his life for something like this.

He sent her another one. *Hes my son.*

He needed the walk, to detach himself. He wasn't onstage. Marvin was.

He was out of the backstage area now, walking back over to the Cosby.

He got the phone out. *Theyre playing our song. Love you. X.* He sent it to young Jimmy.

He was outside now, in the crowd, one of the audience. His son was in there, being screamed at, and Jimmy had nothing to

322

do with it. He could grin. He was the very proud father. That was all.

—Your working day over, Jim? said Les.
  —Yeah, said Jimmy.—That's me.
  —Best gigs of the weekend, I think.
  —Thanks, Les.
  —Seriously.
  —Thanks.
  —You always liked your music.
  —Yeah.
  —I think that's great.
  —Thanks.
He was numb, a bit. Happily numb. Aoife was off wandering with the kids. She was leaving him alone. He was here now, with these men, because of her. They were back under their tree, sitting around Outspan's purple chair.
  —How are we for readies? he asked Outspan.
  —Laughin', said Outspan.
  —How are yeh for gas?
  —Loads left.
  —Grand.
He'd texted Marvin. *You don't have to pretend. X.* Young Jimmy had texted him back. *Great gig.* Ned had texted as well. *Thanks, a chara.*
  —What about you, Les? said Jimmy.
  —What about me?
  —What do you do?
Les looked amused.
  —I'm a plumber, he said.—I thought you knew.
  —I did, said Jimmy.
But he didn't – he sort of did. He remembered it now. Les had always been a plumber. Did they have plumbers in the British Army? He could have texted his da. *Was Les in the British Army?* But he was sick of texting.
  —I just wondered if you still were, said Jimmy.
  —Yep, said Les.
  —Jesus, men, said Des.—It feels like a long day already.
  —Think of it as two days, said Les.
Jimmy liked that.

323

—That's a good idea, he said.

—And the second one's just starting, said Les.

—I like your style, Les.

—I want to see Dexys Midnight Runners, said Outspan.

—Good idea.

They were up and running again. This time Jimmy got to carry Outspan.

It was a good show, but a bit weird. Kevin Rowland and another chap, a singer, strode around the stage. There was a good-looking woman too, about half Rowland's age. It was like a musical for oul' lads.

—What did yeh think of tha'? Jimmy asked Outspan.

—Shite.

—I'm with yeh, said Jimmy.—How're yeh feelin'?

—There's a few more gigs in me, said Outspan.—What's next?

They were back across to the Crawdaddy, via the jacks, for the last ten minutes of Patti Smith.

—What did yeh think o' tha'?

—Brilliant.

—Fuckin' brilliant.

—Fuckin' amazin'.

—Would yeh give her one?

—Oh yeah.

—Food, gents?

—Bring it fuckin' on.

Jimmy was back in the night before; that was how he felt. Almost. But he was still rattled. His phone was hopping in his pocket. He was sick of the thing. He could hardly look at the screen.

But he did. Aoife was heading home after the Cure. Did he need the toilet paper? No, he answered. Had she seen young Jimmy? He was with Marvin. *Having time of their lives.*

Jimmy loved that. He could feel himself flattening out, really relaxing now.

See u 2moro. Love u. X

There was one from Noeleen. *Great story.* And another. *He's amazing.* Jimmy sent one back. *I wrote the song.* Then he turned off the phone.

Des had said something to him.

—Sorry, Des. What?

—Well, said Des.—I was thinking. After seeing the Halfbreds and your lad. Even Patti —

—Brilliant.

—Amazin', said Outspan.

—So I was thinking, said Des.—There's no reason why we couldn't – . Put a band together.

—The Irregulars?

—I could use the name, said Des.—If it made sense. We could look for a singer. Our age.

—Right.

—So, said Des.—Would you be up for it?

—Manage yis?

—Play, said Des.—Be in the band.

—Doin' wha'?

—Your trumpet, said Des.

—For fuck sake, said Outspan.

Jimmy had forgotten about the trumpet. He hadn't touched it in weeks.

—Okay, he said.

—Great, said Des.

I'm in a band.

—We'll pretend we're Romanian.

Les stood up.

—One more beer, then the Cure.

I'm in a fuckin' band.

Outspan was back on the oxygen.

—Are you okay?

He nodded.

—We can leave, said Jimmy.—We've seen plenty.

Outspan shook his head.

The Cure were playing in the main arena. It was getting dark, and cold. They carried the chair to the back of the crowd, then worked their way nearer the stage.

—Closer, said Outspan.

They kept going. The crowd was tighter.

The Cure were on and playing 'The Lovecats'. Maybe it was just the weekend, but Jimmy had begun to notice how much he liked old songs that he'd always thought were shite. Decades of solid opinion were turning to mush.

They weren't going to get any nearer and the chair was starting to slide off his shoulders. They'd have to put Outspan down.

—Ready, Les?

—Yep.

They made sure their arms were deep under the chair. Jimmy held Les's sleeves as they lowered it. Jimmy couldn't help it – it was like a coffin.

Ah Jesus.

Something happened. The weight wasn't there and the side of the chair scraped his face. It was out of their grip, and gone, over heads. The kids in front of them had grabbed the chair and sent it off. Outspan was hanging on and, propelled along by hundreds of outstretched hands, he was heading for the stage.

—For fuck sake!

They went after him – they tried to. But it was pointless.

—If he falls off —

They could only watch.

The chair was way ahead of them now. Outspan was still on it. Jimmy could see his head. The chair seemed to be flying along, quite smoothly from this distance, like it was on ice.

—He's right at the front.

—He'll fall into the fuckin' pit.

The chair seemed to jump. Jimmy could see it – there was a break in the heads in front of him. He saw – what he thought he saw was a clump of people jumping, hands up, and they sent the chair and Outspan up onto the stage.

—He made it.

—Fuckin' brilliant.

They watched Outspan struggle out of the chair. He brought the oxygen with him and it looked like he was going to skull Robert Smith with it.

—He isn't, is he?

Smith was a fair-sized target.

Security lads ran on from the wings. Outspan hitched up his jeans, dropped onto the chair with the cylinder, managed to turn it, back to the audience, and scoot – push – himself off the stage.

He was gone.

—Oh fuck —

But then he was up again, a fuckin' whale. They laughed as they watched the chair fly over the sea of heads and hands, away from them.

—We'd better get him.

The chair was being sent off to the right. They got out of the pack and tried to follow it. Jimmy tripped over passed-out kids, went around sleeping babies in buggies.

He looked. Outspan was still there.

Then he was gone. The crowd had thinned. There weren't enough hands to keep him up.

It wasn't far but it was dark, and there wasn't a landmark to help them.

But they found him.

The chair was on its side and Outspan was sprawled beside it.

—Is he alright?

—Oh fuck.

—Put him on the chair. We can carry him away from here.

The poor cunt was close to weightless. The cylinder was nearly as heavy as him. They carried him over towards an empty patch of the field. They lowered the chair to the grass.

—Are you alrigh'? Liam?

—Fuckin' amazin', said Outspan.

—Wha'?

—Tha' was fuckin' amazin'.

He was laughing. He looked a bit mad.

—The best ever, he said.

He'd stopped laughing.

—I was fuckin' terrified, he said.—It was great.

He took a blast of the gas.

—I gave a fuck, he said.

—D'you want to go now?

—I do in me hole, said Outspan.—Who's next?

They'd enough money left for hotdogs, autographed by the fuckin' pig, and another round. Outspan looked wretched but his eyes were lit. Like a kid's eyes.

—Jimmy told me you play rhythm guitar, said Des.

—Who? said Outspan.—Me?

—Yeah.

—Used to. Years back.

—D'you fancy being in the band? said Des.

It was the most amazing thing Jimmy had ever heard.

—I might, said Outspan.

—Great.

The most amazing, generous, fuckin' brilliant thing he'd ever heard.

—Plant the legend, said Outspan.—Wha'.

—Absolutely.

—Every half-decent band should have a dead guitarist, said Outspan.

It took a while, but they laughed.

—What about you, Les? said Des.—Fancy moving back to Ireland?

—No, said Les.

—No?

—No, said Les.—I'm happy over there.

—Grand.

They headed back to Darfur. The day was in Jimmy's feet and legs. They were heavy, sore. But Christ, Jesus. What a fuckin' day.

Outspan was asleep in the chair. The other three had one last can. Outspan woke and crawled into the tent. Jimmy stood –

—My fuckin' back.

– and followed him.

—Seeyis, lads.

—'Night, Jim.

He got the boots off, and kneed himself in the face while he was doing it. He burrowed into the bag. Lay back. Waited. For sleep. He was still buzzing. His ears. Everything.